A Drop of Magic

Ashuan Greed 1

Janna Ruth

First published in New Zealand in 2022

Copyright © 2022 by Janna Ruth

www.janna-ruth.com

ISBN-13: 978-0-473-63649-4

also available as ebook 978-0-473-63650-0

ASHUAN GREED BOOK 1

A DROP OF MAGIC

JANNA RUTH

For Brienchen
Without whom Ashuan never would have seen the light of day.
Thanks for 20 years of friendship!

A note about sensitive topics

There are a lot of magic and fantastical creatures in this book, but the teenagers at the core of this story are just that: they are teenagers. And as such they deal with a number of very real issues on top of the magical ones.

If you don't like spoilers and you're cool with anything, skip this note and start the book. If you like to be prepared, keep reading. I'm writing this because reading should be fun, not a bad surprise.

While this series starts out as a YA fantasy, there are mentions of sex, drugs and sadly no rock'n'roll. There will be no actual sex scenes until the characters are all of age, and even then I much prefer fade-to-black. In the first book, there is mention of drug abuse, but you won't see a character actually use drugs. You will, however, encounter teenagers and adults drinking alcohol, including an alcoholic mother who is neglectful to her children. As for the underage characters: the age of drinking beer and wine without adult supervision in Germany is 16. For drinking spirits and cocktails, it is 18.

I have tried my best to keep all swear words out of the text. If one has slipped through, I'm sorry.

As fun as it sounds, hunting monsters and wielding magic is dangerous. People will be hurt in this series and some will die. That includes characters who you got to know well. Their deaths will not be meaningless, though it might feel like that to the surviving characters. Because

I'm a big fan of consequences, that means you will see depictions of grief in various stages.

In this book in particular, you will encounter a demon that controls scores of insects, spiders and other invertebrates. If those descriptions make you squirmish, consider skipping the chapters Lucille-1, Lucille-2, and Fabian-3 in Part 2: Dreams & Nightmares.

Last but not least, there are instances of bullying, mostly verbal, by other teenagers. These scenes are few in between and our affected characters will rise above that.

The characters live in a dangerous world, but it's also beautiful. For every dark spot, there will be light and humour. And of course magic. Lots and lots of magic.

Enjoy!

Love, Janna

Part 1
Shadow & Light

Lucille

The sounds of the nightclub faded away as Lucille walked down the street. Her heels clanked alone in the darkness. It had been a good crowd in the club, although the music had left much to be desired. Out here, everybody was asleep. Soon, she regretted insisting on going out by herself. But after years of being closely watched in a prestigious boarding school, she was enjoying the freedom that moving back to her charming little hometown offered her. At seventeen, she was certainly old enough to go out at night without one of her father's employees hovering behind her. Speaking of hovering, though, was someone following her?

In the quiet of the night, Lucille could hear a slow shuffle behind her. Whoever it was, they weren't trying to stay quiet. It was probably nothing, except that the shuffle was coming closer.

Lucille decided to duck around a corner and pretend she lived in one of the houses downtown instead of in a villa on the hills. Sure enough, the person followed her. Her heart jumped into her throat, and her skin turned cold. There was no doubt they were after her. Now, she cursed herself for not calling the chauffeur. In a town as small as Greenvalley, she hadn't thought she needed the protection, but obviously, she'd been wrong.

She slipped her hand into her handbag and found the comforting round shape of her pepper spray. Her fingers shook as she slowly pulled it out and adjusted her grip. Over the sound of her own heartbeat, the shuffle was barely audible.

Well, whoever it was would get a good dose of pepper spray now. "One step more and I'll call the police!" Lucille whirled around and pushed down on her spray.

The irritating cloud hit the person behind her straight in the face. He'd been that close. Lucille could feel her own eyes itch, but the guy in front of her didn't even twitch. Probably because he didn't have much skin left to irritate. In fact, the skin he had—if it even was a man—was falling off his face in stringy, grey patches, and Lucille was convinced she saw something crawling through his equally patchy hair.

The creature raised its arms towards her, and Lucille screamed. She spun around and ran.

Running fast wasn't exactly her forte. While she didn't mind school sports, track and field days had often got the period excuse from her. Now, as she tried to sprint in heels, those lies were catching up with her.

The shuffling sped up behind her, the heavy footfall making Lucille think of bones hitting stone. Bitterness spread in her mouth, and she almost stopped to throw up. But she had to pull herself together, or that creature would get her.

Lucille turned into another alley and cursed when her heels got caught between cobblestones. Damn these charming little streets in this not-so-charming little town! She lost valuable seconds trying to get out of her shoes. Already, the creature had found her again. Lucille threw her best pair of stilettos into its chest and continued barefoot. Unfortunately, the cobbled street was a dead end.

"No, no, no!" She refused to believe this. The short run had already left her puffing. Her side was burning, and now there was no way out of here?

Barely slowed down by her shoe assault, the creature was approaching again. Lucille dashed to one of the doors and hammered her fists against it. "Open, please! Help! I need help!" When that didn't work, she turned and attacked the one on the other side. Nothing. The rooms behind the walls were either empty or the occupants were sound asleep. It wasn't even midnight yet!

Lucille suppressed a whimper when she realised that none of these doors would open for her. She retreated all the way to the back of the alley, pressing her body against the stones. The coldness of them stung her bare back.

Perhaps she could climb the wall? Lucille threw a glance above her head and shuddered in despair. It was at least four metres high. An experienced boulderer would have had no problem with the irregular stones, but even though she found fingerholds, her hands slipped the moment she tried to pull herself up. Her elbow scratched over an edge and started to burn. Lucille hissed through her teeth and held her elbow as she turned back around.

The creature was now only a metre away from her. There was enough space for her to dart around it, but the cold fear that gripped her melted the thought away. There was no escape from this monster. She stood no chance. None at all. Instead of fighting, Lucille sank to the ground and covered her head with her arms, as if making herself as small as possible would somehow save her from this creature.

"Please don't kill me!" she whimpered. She had so much planned for tomorrow, the start of her new self-determined life near her father.

Something soft fell on her arms and hair. Confused, Lucille lowered her arms and found a layer of dust covering them. It also matted her hair and plastered her forehead. There was even more dust in front of her and another set of feet than before.

Slowly, Lucille looked up, following the dark jeans to a low belt and a snug black shirt that held on tight to a muscular chest. Finally, her eyes came to rest on the strikingly handsome face of a young man with tousled blond hair—and a huge-ass sword raised in his hands.

The creature that had chased her was nowhere in sight.

Lucille swallowed. "Uhm... hi."

"Hi there." He flashed her a smile, and something in Lucille's stomach flipped. Her heart raced again, but it was no longer fear that was pumping all that blood.

Flustered, Lucille got to her feet, using the wall behind her to pull herself up until she was almost as tall as he was. "What just happened?"

The stranger lowered his sword and shrugged, as if it wasn't a big deal. "Just an errant revenant. It's dust now, so you should be safe. Have a good night."

A revenant? Dust now? Lucille rubbed the fine powder on her arm between her fingers. She shuddered when she realised it was someone's remains that were sticking to her. "Eww!" Then she noticed that the stranger was already at the end of the alley. "Hey, wait!"

He halted. In the light of the lantern ahead, he was even more beautiful, like one of the models her stepmother worked with. "What is it?"

Lucille's mind went blank. She only knew she didn't want him to leave like this. "I just... I just wanted to say thanks."

"That was nothing. I was on the hunt for it, anyway."

She swallowed heavily. He'd been *on the hunt?* "You were?"

He flashed her another smile and appeared to walk away again.

"Wait!" Once more, he turned, an eyebrow arched to perfection. "Will I see you again?" Internally, Lucille could have slapped herself for even thinking about flirting in such a situation. No, she only wanted to thank him properly, that was all.

His smile widened, and her stomach responded with a plethora of flutters. "Probably." And then he left.

Lucille ran after him, but when she looked down the street, she couldn't see her saviour anywhere. Disappointment flooded her, quickly followed by a pang of fear. What if he was wrong and there were more creatures like that around?

This time, she didn't hesitate to call the chauffeur. While she felt bad for getting Tobias out of bed, she experienced immeasurable relief when the glowing lights of his car came around the corner a couple of minutes later.

Welcome to Greenvalley! Come and experience our evergreen vale, healing springs, and rich history in witchcraft. Let your stay here be magical.

Witchcraft. Magical stays.

In her mind, Lucille saw the revenant before her, with his face falling apart. That kind of witchcraft?

She shook her head but caught herself before she snorted. Such behaviour wouldn't be proper for a young lady. It was something her stepmother never tired of pointing out, no matter how outdated it was.

They were sitting in the parlour in the eastern wing, watching the sun rise over the mountains. Though autumn had arrived, only a few trees were turning yellow. The rest were as evergreen as the brochure in her hands promised.

Watching the beautiful mountains, it was difficult to believe what had happened to her the previous night. As soon as Lucille had arrived home, she'd showered and scrubbed her skin and hair clean. Now that she was clean and safe, it all felt like a hallucination. If it weren't for the bruise on her elbow, she would've thought it a simple nightmare.

As it was, she stared wearily at the brochure that had come with her enrolment pack. The leaflet claimed that the warmer micro-climate in Greenvalley was the result of a magical spring. And the town had even gone so far as to build a fancy fountain for it on the town square. Lucille had seen the throngs of tourists gathering there, believing all sorts of magic coming from it.

She sighed. Rather, the magic of branding than any real magic.

The obsession with magic, witches, and devil stories in the Harz region had always annoyed Lucille. She was well aware that tourism in the area thrived on it, but she'd found it rather tacky. As if the town was taking part in an all-year-round carnival. Until she was attacked by a monster at night.

No, that handsome guy had said she was safe now. It was a one-off anomaly. Nothing to worry about. It probably hadn't even been a monster. And even if it was, Lucille would take fairy tales and the occasional monster over another year at Rosemary College, the all-girl boarding school down in Switzerland. She had two years left at school, and she intended to spend them in her tacky little hometown amongst normal teenagers—not monsters—and, most importantly, at home.

"Is Father not joining us?" Lucille asked when her coffee started to get cold. She had waited to eat her breakfast for a while now.

Her stepmother Linda was lounging next to the tall window in a silken robe, sipping from her cup and watching the sun rise. She turned around, wearing a slight frown, as if she hadn't quite heard Lucille. "Your father? Oh, he's taking a call. He'll probably have his breakfast in his office." It sounded as if that was a regular occurrence. "With luck, we might see him at dinner. But don't worry, I'll be there."

Lucille glanced at the untouched set on the table. The whole point of moving to Greenvalley full time was so she could spend more time with her father. Instead, she got breakfast with Linda, the woman who'd proposed sending her to boarding school in the first place.

After Lucille's mother had died fifteen years ago, Bastien de Cerque had remarried for the sole purpose of providing her with a mother. Why he hadn't picked one with actual maternal instinct was beyond Lucille.

She ignored her glazed waffles and grabbed the enrolment papers instead. The motion caught Linda's attention. "I still don't understand why you would give up an excellent education for such a..." She looked at the brochure in search of a proper word. "Common school. The teachers can't be any good."

"I'm sure the teachers are perfectly capable!" Lucille snapped. In truth, she wasn't quite as convinced, holding similar prejudices as Linda, though she would never admit as much.

Linda took a deep breath and rubbed at an imaginary smudge on her diamond ring. "Well, if you're so intent on ruining your prospects, be my guest."

A guest was what Lucille felt like in her own home. "Thank you. I will go then and ruin my prospects now," Lucille said with all the fake cheer she could muster and got to her feet.

"You haven't eaten anything."

Lucille glanced at the food. It was an exquisite spread, even better than the breakfast at Rosemary, but her appetite had completely waned. "I'll have my breakfast in my office." Not that she had a proper office. Just a study with a desk, a mini library, and a comfy seating area.

Linda huffed and clicked her tongue in distaste. Then she bent forward, tucking her silk robe tighter, and put some food on a plate. "I will ask Martha to pack you something extra for lunch."

"Very well." The cook would probably lap up the opportunity and pack her box so full Lucille would have to find someone to share with. It wasn't the worst strategy to make friends.

Once she was back in her bedroom, Lucille let out a deep breath. If going to school in Greenvalley meant having breakfast with her stepmother every day, she might have to reconsider her decision to leave Rosemary and her life there. Then again, it would be bearable if her father joined them. Surely, he couldn't have a phone call every morning.

A knock on the door made Lucille whip her head around. "What do you want now?" Instantly, she clapped her hands over her mouth, silently cursing herself for the slip in demeanour. It would get her another tsk.

"Excuse me, Miss Lucille." The voice didn't belong to Linda, but to her father's butler, Albert. "Do you have a minute to spare for me?"

Flustered, Lucille nodded. She liked the old man like a grandfather, though he would never allow her to call him that. Albert kept his professional distance at all times, even if he had a twinkle in his eyes whenever she came to him. Now he was entering her room, carrying an antique-looking box in his hands.

"Your grandmother left you this." Albert handed her the box.

Lucille carefully took it from him. With her fingers, she ran over the intricate carvings and the bronze metal clasp. "It's beautiful."

"Open it." Albert nudged her gently.

A flutter of excitement went through her as she undid the clasp. She had only fond memories of her paternal grandmother, and though Cecille de Cerque had died only a few years after Lucille's mother, Lucille still missed her terribly. Sometimes, it felt like her grandmother had been her only friend in this big, cold house.

The box opened with a soft sigh as the wood eased into motion. It must not have been opened for a very long time. Inside, on top of a velvet pillow, lay the most beautiful necklace Lucille had ever seen—which was saying a lot considering Linda's large jewellery collection. The threads were made of silver, though the metal had a peculiar red tinge to it. The centrepiece was made up of eight tear-shaped, fingertip-sized rubies. They were intricately laced in a net of silver in such a way that Lucille had a hard time figuring out how they were attached.

Gingerly, Lucille took the necklace from the box and marvelled at the craftsmanship. "This was my grandmother's?"

"Indeed. It was her most prized possession." Then he pointed to the picture frame above the bed.

It contained photos of happier times—of her mum and dad in love, and with her in their arms. And there was a photo of her grandmother reading to her. Lucille had never paid much attention to it, but her grandmother was indeed wearing the red jewels around her neck, and now that she'd noticed it, Lucille remembered never having seen her without it.

It wasn't until a tear rolled down her cheek that Lucille realised how touched she was by her grandmother's gesture. "She wanted me to have this?"

"Once you were old enough to appreciate it," Albert affirmed. "Let me fasten it for you."

Lucille handed the box back and turned around, holding up her blond locks. Albert's gentle hands draped the necklace around her neck and fastened the clasp.

Engrossed by its beauty, Lucille stepped in front of the mirror. The rubies nestled right on her collarbones. In the sunlight, they appeared as if they contained liquid fire. They even felt warm against her skin.

Behind her, Albert discreetly cleared his throat, reminding Lucille that she should be on her way soon. With one last look at her reflection, Lucille turned around. "Thank you, Albert. You have made my day."

"It has only just started," the butler said with a little bow. "I will get Tobias to bring up the car in about five minutes."

Lucille barely heard him. She had already turned back to the mirror, marvelling a little more at her late grandmother's gift.

Arriving at public school in an expensive BMW was a surefire way to get attention when Lucille didn't want any. While some students were driven to school by their parents, most of them walked or biked. Thus, when her car rolled to a stop right in front of the school gate, blocking everyone else, all eyes were on her.

Lucille leaned forward to speak to Tobias. "Would you mind parking around the corner when you pick me up?"

"Not at all, Miss."

"Lovely. Thank you so much." She grabbed her bag and stepped out of the car.

"Good luck on your first day!" the chauffeur called before resolving the traffic jam he had caused.

Lucille wouldn't be a true de Cerque if she didn't know how to handle herself in the face of unwanted attention. The students here probably didn't see many new faces, so she forgave their curiosity with a well-practised smile before approaching the first person she encountered to ask for directions.

"Hey, I'm new to this school. Can you point me towards the school administration? I'm Lucille, by the way." It was never too early to start making new friends.

She extended her hand, and the boy took it instantly. "I'm Robert! Welcome to Greenvalley High. The admin is just over there. Do you want me to tag along? I can show you around."

Taken aback by his over-the-top enthusiasm, Lucille smiled and shook her head. "No, thanks. I'm fine." There must be someone here who was a little more refined.

He pointed to a two-story building just behind the school gate. Greenvalley High was on the southern side of the little mountain river that ran through the town. It consisted of a sprawling arrangement of low-rise buildings with one larger complex in the middle. After months in the sun, the grass had turned yellow, but the trees were still green. It was a pretty, almost village-like school that was bustling with students aged from twelve to nineteen.

Lucille approached the administration building and found a notice board outside. A little witch puppet hung in one of the corners, and Lucille sighed. Hopefully, any witchcraft would be kept out of the curriculum.

Upstairs, she patiently waited for another student to finish chatting with the administrator. The girl was her age, with a head full of tight, black curls she had tried to tame with a high ponytail. Her clothes were a bit on the plain side, considering that there was no school uniform. While Lucille had embraced her newfound freedom with a cute skirt and a shoulder-free top, the other girl wore plain jeans and a nondescript T-shirt.

When the girl finally noticed her waiting, she took a flustered step aside. "Sorry. You can go."

But as she turned to hurry away, the administrator, a tall woman with short hair, called her back. "Samantha, please wait a second." Then she smiled at Lucille. "You must be Lucille de Cerque, our newest addition."

"I am." Lucille stepped forward to hand in the rest of her enrolment papers. "Here you go."

"Welcome to Greenvalley High. We're very pleased to have you, Miss de Cerque." The woman patted the transcripts before looking at the other girl. "This is Samantha Kollmer, our Deputy Head Girl. I believe you two are in the same class group."

The girl checked the stack of papers in her hand and nodded with a cautious smile. "It looks like it. Hi."

Lucille gave her a quick wave. "Hello."

"Samantha, be a dear, and show Lucille to the classroom, would you?" the administrator asked.

"Of course, Mrs. Schneider." She nodded towards the door. "Shall we? Class is starting in seven minutes."

She made it sound as if they would have to hurry to get there in time, and Lucille wondered how far away their classroom would was. "Sure."

As they walked down the stairs, Samantha pulled a paper from her stack and handed it to her. "This is your schedule. We're with Mr Zobel. I've never had him before, but he works with the student reps and is fairly decent."

"Fairly decent sounds good," Lucille replied, quickly checking her schedule. She had chosen her coursework upon enrolment and was happy to see that it was evenly spread with some additional perks. Her Tuesdays didn't start until the second period, and there were even some free periods for her to enjoy and relax. The teacher Samantha mentioned was listed as her tutor at the top of the page and appeared to be teaching her Politics and German classes.

"What are your majors?" Lucille asked as they crossed the school grounds.

For a student rep, Samantha seemed surprisingly shy, but now she perked up and replied, "Physics and Chemistry."

Lucille gulped. "Oh, dear." If she could, she would have got rid of all three natural sciences. As it was, she had chosen Biology as her main science and would suffer through Chemistry for two semesters.

Samantha shrugged, her smile quickly fading. "Yeah, I know it's uncommon. What did you choose?"

"History and Latin," Lucille said, eager to chat about it. "I love languages and picked as many as I could." She'd been pleasantly surprised to find out that Greenvalley High offered Latin as a major. On top of that, she was also going to study English, French, and Spanish.

"You could help me in Spanish then," Samantha said, peering at Lucille's schedule. "We share that class."

Lucille grinned. "Exchanging Spanish vocabulary for chemical formulas. That sounds like a deal to me."

She was rewarded with a small smile from Samantha. It lasted barely a second before the girl cast her eyes to the ground again. Lucille noticed that they were passing a group of students their age. In a sea of rather ordinary students, they were certainly the most fashionable and stylish.

"Who are they?"

Samantha took a deep breath. "The Elite Clique."

"Elite? Is that a self-picked name or does everyone else call them that?" There had been more than enough cliques at the boarding school—more than Lucille could stomach—and she'd hoped it wouldn't be as bad at a public school.

"Both. Cheryl came up with it. That's the one with the corkscrew locks. The rest adopted it quickly." Samantha glanced over her shoulder with a little sigh.

Lucille spotted the girl she referred to instantly. She was pretty and definitely came from money, but the way she carried herself was so tacky she would've barely lasted a day at the boarding school.

There were seven of them in total, and Lucille had to admit that the boys were rather good-looking. Just then, the tall one with the dark hair glanced at her. As their eyes met, he smirked appreciatively.

Lucille chuckled and turned back to Samantha. "Who's the black-haired one?"

"Alan Aster. He's the Police Chief's son and Cheryl's on-and-off boyfriend." Samantha sounded as if she was already tired of talking about them.

But Lucille couldn't let it rest. She glanced at the boy once more, who was now joking with the sunburnt blonde next to him. "So, are they on, or are they off right now?"

Samantha sighed. "I have no idea." She took another look. "Probably off. When they're on, she's clinging to his arm all the time."

Lucille stored the information away. Coming from an all-girls school, the prospect of cute guys at Greenvalley High was exciting to her.

They arrived at the main building. "Most of our classes apart from the sciences and PE will be in here," Samantha explained, as if eager to talk about something other than the Elite Clique. "Over there is the hall with its cafeteria and the stage. Next to it is the atrium, which is only accessible to Year 12 and 13 students."

"Oh, great," Lucille said. With so many younger children running around, it would be nice to have a place just for the older students.

Samantha nodded. "Yeah, it's definitely a perk this year." She pointed to a staircase. "Our room is on the second floor. Number 203."

Soon, they arrived in what looked like a standard classroom. The individual tables were pushed together into a U-shape with two short extra rows of tables across the middle. At the other end of the room was a whiteboard, not one of the high-tech boards they had at her old school.

Most of their classmates had already arrived and taken seats. Samantha handed her stack of papers over to the teacher in the front, a smart-looking man in his mid-forties with thinning hair and a slender pair of glasses. "Mr Zobel, this is Lucille. She's new to Greenvalley." She glanced at Lucille. "I'll leave you to it." Then she took her place next to a black girl with two long braids in the first row.

"Well, welcome to our school, Lucille. Go and find a seat, if you please. We'll be starting in a minute," Mr Zobel said with a kind smile.

Lucille surveyed the room and its exits before choosing a seat on the U-shape near the window, not too far from Samantha. As she unpacked her belongings, she listened to the other students catching up after their summer holidays. A smile slipped onto her lips in response to the vibrant chatter. At the boarding school, they'd all been quiet the moment a teacher entered in the room.

A bell rang a few moments later, and the excited chatter died down without Mr Zobel having to raise his voice. When the room was quiet, he began. "Welcome to Year 12! It's good to see you all. As you know, you're now entering the final stages of your school education, which comes with a few changes. The most important one being that every grade will count towards your Abitur diploma, so no slacking off." It sounded more ominous than it was. Lucille preferred this arrangement over a single exam at the end of the year. "Apart from Politics, there will be no shared classes for the entire group, which means we'll have to make a little time for housekeeping at the start of each lesson."

"What a shame," a tall and lanky ginger boy behind Samantha in the middle rows said, eliciting a few chuckles from the rest of the class.

At first, Lucille was taken aback, but when she noticed that even Mr Zobel smiled thinly, she allowed herself the leniency of a giggle.

"Yes, don't you worry, Fabian. We'll manage to keep ahead of our curriculum somehow," he said, then turned back to his introduction. "Apart from these few hours, you'll all be off to the courses you chose at the end of last year. I'll pass around your schedule. Take a good look at it." He passed the larger part of the pile he had received from Samantha to the boy at the beginning of the U-shape. It was Robert, the enthusiastic one from the school gate. "If you need to make any changes, there's a two-week deadline. For anyone interested in how your marks will add up with exams, I have some handouts here." He handed the smaller part of the pile to the girl sitting next to Lucille.

"One more thing. As you will be turning eighteen or have already done so, you will be able to excuse your absences yourselves. Please do so responsibly." Mr Zobel looked sternly at a buff guy in the back row who had the audacity to wear a black tank top to school, showing off a crooked tattoo.

The boy shrugged as if he had no idea what his teacher was talking about. "Sounds good to me," she heard him mumble.

Done with the general housekeeping, Mr Zobel continued with an overview of how their politics class would be structured and assessed, explaining the details for the better part of the first hour.

Lucille took some notes, but mostly, she let her eyes roam the room. Samantha stayed true to her first impression and hung onto the teacher's every word, scribbling down what he said without a pause. The girl next to her didn't take any notes but stared at Mr Zobel, never blinking once. Most of the others paid mediocre attention. Some, like the ginger boy Mr Zobel had called Fabian, had taken to doodling on their schedule or leafing through the handouts by themselves. But then her eyes caught sight of *him.*

The guy who'd potentially saved her life last night.

In the daylight, he was drop-dead gorgeous. There was no other way to describe him. Brown eyes the colour of milk chocolate and blond hair just long enough for a fashionably wind-swept style. His physique was flawless, with chiselled cheekbones and a chin to cut herself on. His deltoid muscles bulged under the simple black shirt when he crossed his arms. He certainly knew the effect he had on her and answered Lucille's prolonged stare with a cocky little grin.

Flustered, she looked back down and up to Mr Zobel, but her gaze kept returning to her handsome saviour, who somehow turned out to be a classmate. That must've been what he meant when he responded affirmatively when she asked if she was going to see him again.

Unable to fight her attraction, Lucille leaned into it and began flirting herself. She knew she wasn't bad looking either, and despite the all-girls school she went to, she'd had more than enough flirtations over the last few years. She knew this game of coy looks and 'accidental' fingertip touches to her bottom lip that sent a boy's heart racing.

When the bell suddenly rang, she startled. She had completely zoned out of the lesson.

Mr Zobel left the room, but as it was a double period, not everybody followed him. Like some of the others, Lucille chose to stay. One, because she didn't want to risk getting lost, and second, because the handsome boy was staying as well.

But before she could talk to him, the ginger boy who'd spoken up earlier turned around to her. "I don't remember seeing you before. Which class were you in?"

"I just transferred here from a boarding school in Switzerland," Lucille said, feeling a little tense because it wasn't the chat she'd been hoping for. The only thing special about this boy was how tall he was and how many freckles fit on his nose.

"How come?" the boy next to him asked. He had the same dark skin as the girl in front of him, a close-cropped afro, and a ready smile.

Lucille sighed. "Let's say I wasn't particularly fond of the rules. It was a girls-only school." Then she got over herself. After all, she wasn't here to find a new boyfriend but to make a fresh start. "I am Lucille de Cerque."

"Fabian," the ginger replied. Then he began to introduce the guy next to him. "This is Nico. That's his sister Rachel"—the girl who'd never blinked turned around to her and gave a shy wave— "and the one busy with whatever is Samantha."

"I'm not busy with whatever, and we've already met," Samantha protested, though she was still scribbling down something. Nevertheless, she sounded a lot more confident replying to Fabian than she had when she'd talked to Lucille.

"Well, what are you doing, then?" Fabian asked, rolling his eyes in a show for Lucille.

Samantha straightened her back. "I'm preparing for the first meeting of the school council. Adrian wants us to get started right away."

"I'm pretty sure Adrian hasn't even thought about it at this stage," Fabian replied promptly.

Feeling a little left out of their spat, Lucille asked, "Is Adrian your boyfriend?"

"No!" Samantha seemed aghast she had suggested it. "He's just the Head Boy, and I'm his Deputy. And yes, Fabian, he has thought about it. Not everyone puts school out of their mind over the entire summer holidays."

"Well, they should. That's what holidays are for." Fabian smiled at Lucille again. "She's practically busy all the time."

Samantha rolled her eyes and pulled a book from her bag. "See?"

Unwilling to take sides, Lucille turned around to the blonde guy she'd been ogling in class. "Since we're doing introductions... what's your name?" She hadn't been able to ask him last night.

His responding smile made her stomach weak. "Matt."

"I haven't seen you at school either," Nico said, jumping in without an invitation. "Are you also a boarding school student, or an exchange student, or...?"

"I just moved in with my father. My parents are separated," Matt said casually.

Judging by his reaction, Lucille surmised it wasn't a recent split, but she still offered her sympathies. "Oh, I'm sorry about that. It must be tough."

"Not really. I'm just... curious," Matt said.

And mysterious, Lucille added. Like how he ran around at night with a sword.

Fabian was still nagging Samantha. "What are you reading, anyway?"

"Something that you detest very strongly."

Instantly, Fabian groaned, once more drawing Lucille's full attention. Her curiosity piqued, she asked, "And what might that be?"

Fabian wasted no second to clue her in. "Magic. Sam's obsessed with it. I think it's ridiculous. I know our entire tourism sector is built on it, but that's all just pretend."

This time, Lucille found herself agreeing with him. "It gets a bit annoying, doesn't it?"

To her surprise, Matt got up and leisurely walked around the class to tip Samantha's book back just enough to read the title. "Magical Herbs: Growth and Use. And what are you planning to do with your new herbal knowledge?"

Samantha regarded him with trepidation, as if she were awaiting his mockery. Lucille saw her nervously lick her lips, unable to hold his gaze. "Nothing. I just really like plants."

It was such a boring answer, Matt immediately lost interest. He glanced over Samantha's head at Lucille and gave her a little nod towards the door at the opposite side of the classroom.

Lucille took the hint with delight and met him there, ready to reel this guy in. He was obviously as interested in her as she was in him. "Hey," she said with a coquettish smile as she leaned against the wall.

Matt came closer. It was a distance that was too close to ignore but far enough away as to not seem like overstepping. "Hey."

"I, uhm... wanted to say thanks for last night."

"Don't worry about it." It didn't seem to be a topic he wanted to elaborate on.

That was fine with Lucille. She didn't want to dwell on it either and rather wanted to forget about the whole thing. Contrary to the guy she got out of that. "So, how are you liking Greenvalley so far?"

His eyes roamed her body, and he smirked. "It seems to have got better than expected just now."

Lucille laughed and cast her eyes down for a second, displaying her thick eyelashes. From the corner of her eyes, she saw the other four glancing at them and talking. Feeling a bit more apprehensive about her flirting, she played with the rubies of her necklace. "I agree. My stepmother thinks it's a bit backwater-ish, but I like it." She allowed herself to check out his upper body. The black shirt was like a second skin to his muscles. "A lot."

"Excuse me?" Suddenly, Samantha was at their side. "May I have a look at that necklace of yours? It's a witch charm, isn't it?"

Behind her, Fabian groaned. Meanwhile, Lucille's mood took a serious dive. It had taken less than an hour for this town to drag her into its magic craze. "It's an heirloom, not some New Age garbage."

She regretted her harsh words a little as Samantha's eyelids fluttered. "I didn't mean it like that. I—"

"Leave it be, Sam." Fabian had rounded the tables as well, putting his hands on Samantha's shoulders and trying to steer her back to her seat. "No one actually believes in witchcraft."

"I certainly don't," Lucille said, wanting to make sure she wouldn't be bothered with it again. "This belonged to my grandmother whom, I can assure you, was certainly not a witch." The very thought made her scoff.

Matt had taken a step back, leaning against the table instead, but not daring to interrupt.

"I was only asking a question." Samantha lowered her face.

"And I apologise if I hurt your feelings." Though why anyone would believe in witchcraft at their age was beyond Lucille. "The thing is that I'm not particularly a fan of this whole witchcraft business. It comes off a bit juvenile."

"Sure," Samantha said hastily, finally responding to Fabian's nudging and returning to her seat. She dropped herself down and opened her book so rapidly, a piece of paper came flying out of its pages.

Lucille had hoped she could return to her flirting with Matt, but Samantha's body language was clear enough. She had upset the girl with her words, and it wasn't how she wanted to begin her new school year. Especially because Samantha had actually seemed really nice.

With a sigh, she left Matt and walked over to Samantha, bending to pick up the piece of paper. The words on it caught her eyes. Some of them were short phrases, some were single words. At first, Lucille thought it was a vocabulary list, as most of the words were in Latin, but then she started translating them. "Globus igneus?"

Fireball.

Sure enough, a ball of green fire appeared in her free hand. The heat of it blasted her face as the light flickered in front of her eyes. Lucille started screaming.

In an instant, Matt was there and closed his hand around her fingers, extinguishing the fire.

Her knees went weak, and she stumbled into Matt's arms. "Oh god, oh god, oh god."

Everyone was staring at her. Just then, the door opened, and the buff guy from the last row returned. He sniffed the air. "Did somebody smoke in here?"

While the others denied the question, Lucille's head was still spinning. There had been a fire. In her hand. A green fire.

"What did you do to me?" she hissed at Samantha, pushing the implausible out of her mind.

Samantha glanced at the other students who were now returning one by one as the break neared its end. She lowered her voice. "Me? I didn't do anything. You're the one who read the spell out loud and bound magic to the words."

"That is out of the question," Lucille replied. The heat was still burning in her cheeks. It couldn't be. "There's no such thing as magic."

Annoyed, Samantha closed her book and tugged the list from Lucille's hand. "Fine! You keep telling yourself that. Just be careful not to set the school on fire the next time you read something aloud."

Lucille felt heady, her knees weakening again.

"Sam, I don't think—" Fabian started.

"You shouldn't mess around with magic if you don't know what you're doing." To the surprise of all of them, Matt had finally joined the conversation.

Lucille stared at him, feeling as if she'd run face-first into a wall. "You believe in magic?" He was suddenly a lot less appealing to her. Or at least a little less.

"I believe in what I know," Matt said simply.

"Why didn't you say so earlier?" Samantha asked, holding up her book.

Matt snorted. "You said you loved plants. Besides, nobody asked me."

Lucille stumbled away from the group. First a monster, and now magic? "I think you are all completely out of your minds. I will apply for a change of class straight away, or even better, go back to boarding school." Everything was going wrong. The whole move was one big disaster.

"I thought you hated boarding school." For the first time, Samantha's friend Rachel had opened her mouth. "As soon as something exciting happens, you run away?"

As Lucille stared at her, Mr Zobel entered the class, carrying a big pile of books. Robert was helping him with a second pile.

The whole situation quickly overwhelmed Lucille. She wanted to quit and run away, but Rachel's words had struck a nerve. Besides, she only had to think of Linda's smug face if she decided to return to Rosemary College, to change her mind yet again.

"Fine," she hissed. "I'm staying, but you better stay away from me with that nonsense."

Samantha glared but didn't say a thing. Instead, she gave all her attention to Mr Zobel, who was handing out the books.

Lucille straightened her shoulders and returned to her seat. Only when she was seated, a shiver ran down her spine, and the fear returned. Had she really performed magic? Completely out of the blue? The heat still lingered on her face.

She shook her head. No, that couldn't be true. It just made absolutely no sense. Just like the revenant hadn't made any sense. Grateful for the distraction, she received one of the books from her neighbour. *Political Sciences.* Now, that made sense. That was something she could deal with. Not this magic nonsense.

Samantha

Magic. The new girl had done magic!

Samantha had barely followed Mr Zobel's second hour of Politics. Instead, she'd tried to get a grasp on what had happened. She herself had never doubted that magic existed, even if everyone ridiculed her for it. But she'd never managed to make a spell work. And then Lucille had simply read them off the paper and done what Samantha had been trying to do for years.

And now she wouldn't even look at her.

After the bell had rung, Lucille had left the room as fast as possible. When they'd met again for Spanish, Lucille had taken care to sit as far away as possible from her, and slowly, Samantha's excitement had been replaced by dread.

Lucille would ignore her gift, and if Samantha pushed, she'd probably turn to humiliation. Once Cheryl and her cronies got wind of it, they'd have a field day. Samantha knew it was only a matter of time until the Elite Clique would become interested in Lucille. The de Cerques had money, a lot of it. Lucille's father owned half the town, and her mother was a renowned fashion designer. Samantha hadn't even known they had a daughter, but she'd seen the beautiful villa with its fairy-tale turrets nestled in the mountainside that Lucille called home.

Yes, Cheryl would certainly dig her claws in her, and once she did, there was no hope for Samantha to ever broach the topic again. Not without enduring another round of cruel taunts this year. It wasn't fair. The one time magic was within her reach, it was immediately snatched away.

"Do you really think she did magic?" Fabian asked when he picked her up after their last period.

Samantha raised an eyebrow. Usually, Fabian gave that particular topic a very wide berth. Right now, she was bursting with the need to discuss the morning's events. The fact that he'd brought it up on his own was a chance she couldn't ignore. "What else would it be?"

"Well, some sort of trick, I suppose. A lighter, for example."

Samantha groaned. That was so typical of him. "Sure, we arranged the whole thing beforehand. I actually wrote the insults and handed them to her this morning so she could throw them at me in class." Her voice faltered a little at the end. Insults were something she was more accustomed to than most people.

Fabian looked uncomfortable. "I didn't mean it that way. I'm sorry that I..." For a moment, he seemed lost for words.

She was more than happy to help him out. "Made me seem like some lunatic?" He was her best friend. He should have backed her up, not thrust a dagger into her back to impress some girl he'd only just met.

"Oh, I don't think anyone needs to make you seem like that, sweetie."

Bracing herself, Samantha turned towards the speaker. Cheryl and her posse were blocking the way. Samantha cursed herself for not watching where they were going and running into the group. The only saving grace was that there were only four of them rather than the usual seven. In her opinion, these were the worst four, though: Cheryl and her fangirl Ani, and the tied-to-the-hip couple Jennifer and Boyd.

"Yeah, yeah, I'm a lunatic. We all know." If she took Cheryl's words out of her mouth, maybe this would be over fast. Walking past them wasn't an option since Boyd had blocked the path, legs spread, and arms crossed. The guy spent every afternoon at the fitness centre and was practically one square block of muscle.

"Indeed," Cheryl said, with a devilish smile. "I'm so glad you've finally figured that out. It means there's hope for you yet." She paused. "Or not!"

She and Ani burst into giggles.

Samantha kept her mouth shut. Anything she said now would be horribly twisted and used against her. Her mere existence was enough to amuse the Elite Clique for hours.

"So, how was your summer?" Cheryl asked with faked interest. "Did you curse anyone? Come up with some more spells?"

Instantly, Samantha thought back to the morning's class. She had found the spells on her list in the plant book. The fireball was to be used as a magical heat source for the more tender plants. But when she had tried it, nothing had happened.

"We went camping," Fabian said, as if Cheryl were really interested in their summer activities.

"I didn't ask you, Bendtfeld," she said in a voice that could cut through ice. But then her lips started to curl up again. "Camping. Have you two finally realised that the other is the best you can hope for?"

Fabian turned bright red. His skin flushed way too quickly, something the Elite Clique had always picked on. "I didn't say that."

"Aww, look at that. He's turning bright as a tomato," Ani said in a singsong voice. "He still loves you, Sammy. You should take him back. It's not like there's someone else who'll accept your crazies."

Fabian was turning even redder, much to the delight of their tormentors. Jennifer was pointing at him, giggling. "Watch out! He's gonna pop if you're not careful. You know how hard it is to get ketchup out of fabric." She flicked her butt-long, straight hair over her shoulder and laughed.

"Come on." Samantha grabbed Fabian's arm and turned him around. The Elite Clique might've blocked off one exit, but there was another at the back of the building. It'd take them longer, but not as long as it would take waiting for these bullies to tire of their game. The others didn't bother following them, but their taunts and jeers did until they reached the staircase.

"I hate them," Fabian said through pressed lips. "I wish they'd all get sick of this town and leave us alone."

Samantha sighed. "That would be amazing." But with seven of them, the scenario was highly unlikely. "You'd think they would grow out of it eventually, but no." Taking the route behind the central building, they made their way over to the bike stand. "Don't take their words to heart."

"What? That I still love you?"

Samantha winced. It had been her who had ended their relationship five months ago. They'd been best friends since birth. Three years ago, a deep love for each other, teenage curiosity, and raging hormones had led to a different type of relationship. But they hadn't truly been in love. At least, Samantha hadn't been, and once she had realised that her feelings weren't what they should be, she had been unable to lead Fabian on. He deserved better than that.

"Sorry," he said, pushing his hands into his pocket. "Guess they hit a little too close to home."

"They always do that." If it weren't for their friendship, Fabian wouldn't even be a target. He only got his measure of bullying because of her. "Do you think I am a lunatic?"

Fabian was about to unlock his bike when he stopped and screwed up his face. "What the hell? No!"

Samantha stared at her own bike. "Well, the new girl certainly thinks that way. But it was real." She looked up at him. "It was magic."

In response, Fabian rubbed the back of his neck, still not a fan of the topic. "Why don't we ask my mum about it? Just to make sure."

Instantly, Samantha's mood brightened. Fabian's mother owned a shop dedicated to witchcraft. Samantha loved it there as much as Fabian was embarrassed by his ties to the store. "Yes!" It was rare enough for him to offer on his own.

Fabian yanked his bike off the rack. "Then let's get it over with."

From the outside, the Magic Circle was a typical souvenir shop with witch puppets, charms, and mythical books on display. Inside, it was filled with all things related to witchcraft: herbs and potions; candles and tarot cards; athame knives and jewellery; and books, most of which Samantha had already devoured.

A wind charm announced their entrance, calling Caroline to the front. Fabian's mother had the same ginger hair as her son, but hers was long and braided, with several charms and strings tied into the strands.

Her eyes widened when she saw them. "Fabian? Did something happen? Did you get lost?" Her eyes sparkled with amusement.

"Hello to you, too," Fabian said in a flat voice, while Samantha giggled.

Caroline leaned on her counter and grinned. "What brings me the honour? You usually take great efforts not to pass by my shop." Then she looked at Samantha and her smile warmed. "Hello, dear."

She was one of Caroline's best customers. Though Caroline rarely fully charged her and let her read all the books if she promised to be careful with them. In return, Samantha supplied her with herbal potions she experimented with, and which were a hit with a couple of regular customers in the shop.

Fabian dropped his backpack near one of the display tables and picked up a candle, as if he were interested in buying it. "Something weird happened at school. We have a new student. She said a couple of strange words, and suddenly, poof, there was a ball of fire in her hand, just like that. Green fire, by the way."

"What kind of strange words were they?" Caroline asked.

"It was a spell," Samantha answered, annoyed that Fabian had made such a mess of telling the story. "A spell to conjure up a fireball."

Caroline chuckled. "Well, that explains it, doesn't it?"

Fabian put the candle down, looking as if he was about to be sick. "So, you think it's magic, too?"

"Fabian. What am I doing here?" Caroline pushed herself up, spreading her hands.

"You're at work?"

"In a magic shop."

Fabian whimpered softly. "I know that. But I always thought you were just piggybacking on the whole tourism business and earned your money from other people believing in magic."

Caroline sighed. "If only you knew."

"Knew what?"

Samantha could no longer keep it in. "She's a real witch!"

Her belief in magic didn't come from nothing. Her grandmother was a witch, and she'd watched her weave magic into spells hundreds of times. Caroline wasn't that gifted, but she'd been her grandmother's student. She also ran a second, smaller store in the back, where she sold potent ingredients and potions to the Harzer witch population. Samantha had hoped she, too, would become a student of witchcraft someday, but so far all she could do was mix potions, which was practically chemistry with magical ingredients.

Fabian seemed stunned. It took him a minute to find the ability to speak again. When he did, it was a half-assed joke. "Well, you certainly look like one with the red hair. Lucky we no longer live in the Dark Ages."

Samantha couldn't help but correct him. "Witch burnings happened at the onset of the Modern Age. It's not really a medieval thing." A glare from him shut her up.

Caroline was more serious now. "Magic is real, Fabian, and this friend of yours better knows what she's doing."

"She doesn't," Samantha said, then sighed. "It must've been the first time she cast a spell. It scared her, and now she doesn't want to talk with us about it."

Caroline's brow creased with worry. "That isn't good. Magic can be very dangerous in the untrained hand. What's her name? I'll see if I can get in touch to her and help her out."

"Lucille de Cerque," Samantha answered readily. At the same time, she wished Caroline would drop it. If Lucille took offence at the intrusion, Samantha would be the one to bear the consequences at school.

But Caroline paused, her mouth hanging slightly open. "De Cerque? Don't tell me this is Cecille's granddaughter."

"Cecille?" Samantha was reminded of how touchy Lucille had reacted when she had asked about the necklace. It had been her grandmother's. The one who had most certainly not been a witch.

"Cecille de Cerque was Elda's oldest friend," Caroline affirmed. "She came from a long line of witches based here in Greenvalley. A demon killed her about ten years ago."

"A demon?" Fabian hadn't spoken since the terrible joke he'd made. Now, his fingers were clawing at the table as if it was the only thing holding him upright. His face had gone white as a sheet. "Witches. Magic. Demons... You must be joking! Come on, Sam, let's go and... and do homework." Another rare suggestion from him.

He grabbed her arm with more force than necessary and yanked her around towards the door. "What? But..." She wanted to know more about Cecille de Cerque who definitely had been a witch and whose magical necklace was now adorning her granddaughter's neck.

"I'll let your grandmother handle it," Caroline said with a sigh. Then she looked at her son. "And we'll talk about this tonight."

His fingers dug even deeper into Samantha's skin. "No, we're not. Absolutely not." Then he dragged her out of the door. He only let go once they'd reached their bicycles, taking several deep breaths.

Samantha rubbed her aching arm. "Why did you have to do that?"

"You don't believe her, do you?" Fabian said, his eyes wide. He was still incredibly pale. "This nonsense about Lucille's grandmother. Lucille would know whether her grandmother was a witch, wouldn't she?"

"Maybe she lied." Samantha hoped as much, though she couldn't figure out why she would do such a thing. "Or her parents kept it from her. If Cecille died ten years ago, Lucille was still too young to understand that magic was real. And if her parents were somehow against it...?" She certainly wasn't allowed to mention magic in front of her father, and he'd grown up with it.

"Sam, stop!" Fabian shook his head. "I don't want to hear it. I don't want to speculate, and I certainly don't want you or my mum or your grandmother to go up to Lucille and confront her about her dead grandmother. That's just wrong! Can we..." He gasped for air. "Can't we forget about it?"

Samantha lowered her head. "Consider it forgotten." Her friendship was worth more than magic. Or being right.

Fabian huffed, slowly calming. "Okay. Shall we do some homework, then?" He offered homework almost as little as visiting the Magic Circle.

But Samantha shook her head. She wouldn't bother him with it, but she wouldn't turn her back on the first real magic lead in years either. "I want to hear what your mum has to say."

She almost wished she could take the words back. Fabian stared at her in disbelief. Then he yanked his bike around and pedalled off without another word. He didn't even glance over his shoulder one last time.

Samantha knew he would expect her to follow him and give in. Part of her was tempted to, but she was always the one giving in, the one taking care of his sensibilities. And magic was real! Fabian might choose to close his eyes to it, but she wanted more of it.

Fabian

A ball of green fire. Brought to life by some random words uttered by a teenage girl.

Fabian looked down at the picture he'd sketched, then ripped it off the block and crumpled it into a tiny ball. Like a basketball player, he aimed for the bin and missed by an elbow's width. Now the stupid picture was lying just in front of the door. Fabian left it there and returned his focus to his sketchpad.

He should've been doing his homework. This year, he'd planned that he wouldn't stress at the last minute as he did so often and do them nice and early. But now that he actually had some homework to do—and on the first day at that—he didn't feel like it. Fabian had been looking forward to his Physics major, but by some cruel twist of fate, school had set him up with a teacher who hated his very existence. Just thinking of two years under Mr Herbert's tutelage made his stomach turn.

Instead, his thoughts kept returning to the fire incident at school and to Samantha. Until this morning, he'd thought her obsession with magic to be a loveable quirk, which sometimes bordered on annoying. Now magic was supposed to be real?

Once more, the green fire popped up in his mind. It had been hot, and yet it hadn't burnt Lucille's hand. That made absolutely no sense at all. Magic was made-up, a fairy tale, a lack of scientific explanation. Real magic...

Well, real magic was scary.

Fabian looked at the giant ball of fire he'd drawn without thinking yet again. Groaning, he ripped off another piece of paper. This time, the ball hit the rim of the bin and bounced off, landing further away than the first one.

To avoid the same thing from happening thrice, he purposefully started to draw water features. A pretty spring. Not like the one in the town centre claiming to be the source of all magic, but a waterfall, a mountain run. Soothing pictures. Cool pictures. Then he added heavy rain clouds, intent on drowning all thoughts of fire, once and for all, and stopped.

He liked the rain. The patter on the roof, the shimmering puddles on the road, Samantha's dark curls pasted against her wet skin. The sight of her had been too much for fourteen-year-old Fabian to resist. They'd found cover from the downpour under a bus stop. After laughing and giggling for minutes, Fabian had leaned in and kissed her for the very first time. It had only been a quick peck, but he'd followed it up with a longer one. Even now, he could still feel the intensity of that first kiss if he closed his eyes.

Fabian sighed. While he had, of course, accepted Samantha's reasons for breaking up with him, he still didn't get it. How could she not be in love with him after three years of bliss? Sure, they fought sometimes, and there were things that were annoying about both of them, but those things didn't matter. Just as it didn't matter that his mum owned a magic shop. He still loved her despite that embarrassing business, and he still loved Samantha even if she dreamt of being a witch or was an annoying know-it-all at school.

She was simply family. And as silly as it was for a boy his age, Fabian had thought that she would stay that way until they were much older and he would marry her.

He turned over the page and began mindlessly drawing the two of them in the rain. Unfortunately, Cheryl had been right. He *had* hoped something would happen on that camping trip. But they'd just had fun as friends: swimming in the lake, roasting marshmallows, night walks, and a lot of hikes. It had been a great week with just the two of them, but Samantha had kept her distance and her stupid reasons.

And now, magic was going to tear them apart. She'd chosen *his mum*—and magic—over him. And if magic was real... His pen faltered. If magic was real, he wanted to be as far away from this place as possible.

A demon killed her about ten years ago.

If magic was real, so were demons and witches and other monsters. Hell, his own mother claimed to be a witch, though Fabian doubted she was one of the mean kind. And what would one of the mean kind be able to do with magic?

He shuddered at the thought of Cheryl and her cronies discovering magic. Sure, they might make fun of it now, but if they had real power at their disposal, a true reign of terror would begin at Greenvalley High. At least for Samantha, it would.

His thoughts returned to Lucille and her green fireball. She'd seemed nice at first, but she'd immediately flirted with that other newbie, and the things she'd said to Samantha... Fabian could easily imagine her as a mean girl of Cheryl's calibre. And this one had access to magic. The way she'd attacked Samantha as if it had been her fault she'd cast a spell didn't bode well.

No, nothing boded well for the new year.

Not the new girl.

Not school with mandatory politics and a teacher who hated him.

Not his strained relationship with Samantha.

And certainly not the occurrence of actual magic.

If a demon appeared on top of all this, Fabian was ready to hand in his resignation.

Frustrated, he crumpled up yet another picture of the fireball and the one of his first kiss and attempted the shot again. Now four balls of paper were strewn across his bedroom floor.

Yeah, this didn't bode well at all.

During the night, Fabian had dreamed of green fireballs, magic, and lots of water. He had tried to fight the fire with buckets of water, and when the buckets wouldn't suffice, he'd cut his hands open to use his blood instead. Only, instead of blood, there had been water spouting from his hands.

He woke up way before his alarm clock, but couldn't go back to sleep without seeing the fire in his dreams. At last, he gave up on it and went to take a shower. The water reminded Fabian of his dream, but it didn't scare him nearly as much as the fire, magic, or mention of evil demons had. Water was good. Water was soothing.

The drops shimmered around his hands in a fascinating pattern that held his tired gaze for a solid minute. Then Fabian closed his eyes and sank back against the shower wall, letting the patter fill his ears and drown out all the fears and worries.

When he finally left the shower, he felt ready to take on the day. Tomorrow, he would face his hated teacher, but today would be a good day. He would make up with Samantha, and she wouldn't mention magic at all. It would also be a short day for him, with only six classes on his schedule instead of the usual seven or eight.

Sufficiently convinced that he'd be fine today, Fabian went outside to feed the chickens that roamed around the garden. At the door to their little barn, he halted. One of his mother's artworks hung around the handle as usual. She was into this nature art, binding branches, feathers, or a bunch of dried berries together with a piece of straw or similar material. He'd seen so many around the house over the years that he'd never paid her hobby much mind. After all, Fabian considered himself an artist as well, though he much preferred the smooth surface of paper over actual crafting.

Today, he paid the inconspicuous bundle a little more attention. It was surprisingly heavy in his hand for a bunch of herbs and twigs—and a rabbit foot.

Shrieking, Fabian let go of it and stumbled backwards. The rabbit foot bundle fell onto the ground with a thump. How in all that was good in the world had his mother got her hand on a rabbit foot and what for?

"Fabian?" His mother must've heard his cry. Wrapped in a bathrobe, she was running out of the house and strode towards him. "What are you doing?"

"I-I..." He pointed towards the bundle. "What is that?"

His mother bent down and picked up the disgusting artwork. She didn't seem to mind the rabbit foot at all. "This? It's a charm to ward off predators. What are you doing up this early?"

"A..." No! There would be no magic today. His mother was *not* a witch. Just an eccentric woman who did artwork with animal body parts. "Must've been sleepwalking. I'd better go back to bed."

"Darling!" she called after him, but Fabian ignored her and hurried back into the house.

He met his father inside as he poked his head out of the bedroom and rubbed his tired face. "What happened?"

"Nothing. A... a spider." As if he was afraid of spiders all of a sudden. His father frowned. "A spider?"

"Never mind. It's gone now. Go back to sleep." Before his father could ask any more questions, Fabian slipped into his room.

Breathing heavily, he leaned against the wall. Only then did he notice the chicken food still in his arms. For a moment, Fabian considered bringing the food back, but he didn't want to risk running into his mother again. Instead, he set it down on his desk and shooed off the white and grey cat who lay curled-up on his bed. "Move over, Merle. I'm tired."

But by the time he found himself drifting away, his alarm clock shook him awake again.

Samantha didn't mention a single word of magic on their way to school. In fact, they hardly said anything to each other until they picked up the Hadden twins from their house and split into two groups. While the girls walked ahead of them, holding a quiet conversation, Nico and Fabian were discussing perfectly normal video games.

But in front of the school, the girls stopped so suddenly Fabian stumbled into Rachel.

A big crowd had gathered in front of the gate, blocking the entry. Everybody's eyes were fixed on the wall that surrounded the school, whispering. For a quick moment, Fabian hoped it meant that school was closed, but slowly, some kids made their way to the gate and entered the school grounds, still whispering in confusion.

"Come on, big one, make us a pathway," Nico said with a flourished bow.

Fabian rolled his eyes but complied. With his height, he managed to plough through the crowd of younger students until they arrived in front of the wall. Someone had sprayed graffiti onto the school property.

WHO'S AFRAID OF THE BOGEYMAN?

"No one?" The line of the children's game came to his lips immediately. *And when he comes? Let him come!* It was one of those warm-up games used in PE in primary schools. One student started as the bogeyman and infected the other players by tagging them until, eventually, all children had been caught. It was a weird choice for a graffiti artist to spray across the school's wall.

Confused, Fabian turned to Samantha, but she'd already been approached by Adrian, a Year 13 student, who was the Head Boy of Greenvalley High.

"Hey, Sam. Just a heads up that Renner wants to speak with us right away." The headmistress was very peculiar about how she wanted her school run.

Samantha groaned. "Great."

The boy responded likewise. "I know. Great fun. I'll wait for you over at admin." He was about to head off when Fabian held him back.

"Any idea who did this?"

"Nope." Adrian's gaze fell on the bus that had just arrived and the disembarking students from the northern part of town. "Why don't you ask them?" He nodded towards a group of friends that were messing around with each other. One of them, Jan, was a casual friend of Fabian, but the rest of the gang was annoying at best and a little frightening at worst. "I bet this is right up their alley."

"Jan wouldn't..." Fabian started, but Adrian had already left.

Samantha followed him towards the admin building, while Nico and Rachel made their way inside with the rest of the students who had lost interest in the weird scripture. Fabian watched Jan as he sauntered over. He was the school's troublemaker, missing more classes than he attended, always on the lower end of the grade scale, and known to spend his weekends drinking, smoking, and probably taking drugs. But Fabian had experienced a different side of him, and when Jan wasn't causing trouble, he was quite chill and refreshingly unbothered by trends and people's opinions. A couple of years back, when Fabian had still been regularly bullied by Alan Aster, Jan had taken his side. With a green belt in karate at that time, he'd taught Alan a lesson or two about picking on other people. They'd been sort-of-friends ever since.

"What's going on?" Jan said with a sharp nod before clasping hands with Fabian. As usual, his grip was a bit too strong. Before Fabian could answer, he read the words for himself. "Who's afraid of the bogeyman?" He shrugged. "No one is. What a joke."

Fabian glanced at him, Adrian's words still running through his head. "So, did you have anything to do with it?" He wouldn't exactly put it past Jan.

Jan snorted. "As if I didn't have better things to do than spraying nursery rhymes across Greenvalley." He clapped Fabian's shoulder. "Sorry, you need to look for another scapegoat this time." Then he checked his watch. "Time to go. The bell's ringing soon."

"Since when do you care about being on time?"

"Since my day starts with PE. See you later. Perhaps." Jan gave a crooked grin and strode away.

Fabian sighed, his eyes returning to the sprayed words. Something about the scraggly red letters made his skin crawl. After all, if magic was real, the bogeyman might be real as well.

Lucille

It was Lucille's first free period, and while everyone else hurried to their classes, she found herself a sunny spot in the atrium and opened her lunch box. Martha had outdone herself, preparing little mini burgers, strawberry-filled crepes, celery sticks with yogurt dip, and freshly baked granola.

Lucille was about to dip one of the celery sticks into the homemade yogurt dressing when a shadow fell upon her. To her dismay, it was Samantha. She'd managed to avoid the girl for twenty-four hours, but now it seemed like her time was up. Struggling to put on a friendly smile, she asked, "How can I help you?"

Samantha bit her lip. "Can we talk about yesterday?"

Not if Lucille could avoid it. "I am currently enjoying my lunch."

"Sorry. I just wanted to apologise for coming on too strong."

Lucille struggled to maintain her smile. "Please forget about it."

"You must have a ton of questions." Samantha continued to press the issue.

"No, I don't." The smile slipped off Lucille's face. How many hints did this girl need?

Samantha wouldn't give in. She almost looked as if she was about to take a seat next to her. "What you did was magic. You can do magic." She sounded excited. "How can you not have any questions?"

Lucille tightened her grip around her lunch box. "As I told you yesterday, I am not interested." The whole episode with the strange fire was something she would rather like to forget. It had been some freak accident, nothing more.

"It could be dangerous if you don't know what you're doing."

Lucille's eyes narrowed. Was Samantha trying to scare her into magic now? "I will take my chances. Thank you very much." Her voice was sharp enough to drive even the most oblivious student away.

But not Samantha. "You are a witch!"

"I am not!" How dare she? Before Lucille could find some very choice words to send Samantha on her way, they were interrupted by the girl with the corkscrew locks Samantha had introduced as some sort of self-proclaimed Queen Bee.

"Let it be, Sammy. No one's interested in your childish fantasies." She smirked.

Samantha paled instantly. Her gaze fell on Lucille, but Lucille lowered her head. She was too bothered to stand up for the other girl. Samantha's witch fantasies *were* childish. When Samantha found no support from her, she mumbled an excuse and rushed away.

The blonde girl laughed cruelly. As she turned to Lucille, her smile became more genuine. "I'm sorry she bothered you. Every village needs a village idiot, right?"

The words rubbed Lucille the wrong way. She was annoyed by Samantha's persistence on a topic she wanted nothing to do with, but she had no interest in talking negatively about her. "And who are you?" Samantha had mentioned her name, but Lucille had already forgotten it.

"I'm Cheryl," the girl offered all too readily. "I don't have to ask who you are, of course. I love your mum's fashion."

The word 'mum' made Lucille bristle even more. "Is that so?"

"Oh, yes. I've got half my closet filled with *Linda*." She wasn't wearing any *Linda* clothes today. Having apparently decided that they were friends now, Cheryl sat down. "So, listen. I know you're new to this school and still adjusting. If you want, you could hang out with us." She leaned forward with a conspiratorial twinkle in her eyes. "Everyone wants to be part of our clique, but make no mistake, we don't make this offer lightly. Only to special people." And by special, she likely meant the wealthy and beautiful.

Lucille closed her lunch box. It didn't look like she was going to get to eat anytime soon. She knew she was standing at a crossroads here. She could take Cheryl's offer and join the popular crowd. It would be easy to fit in with them. She liked fashion and make-up and would probably get along brilliantly with those girls, and even better with the cute boys. But she couldn't ignore the mean girl vibe coming from of Cheryl. Sure, she was nice enough to her, but the way she had treated Samantha spoke volumes. To buy herself some time, she asked. "Who is 'us'?"

Cheryl grinned. "Well, there's me." Of course, she would name herself first. "Ani is my bestie. I mean, we're all friends, really. Over there are Shayna and Cian." She pointed towards a corner of the atrium where the blond guy with the sunburnt tan kicked a ball with a short-haired girl who somehow managed to make sportswear look cute. "Cian and his best friend Alan are the cutest guys in school. Alan's father is the Chief of Police."

Lucille remembered the good-looking, dark-haired guy from the previous day and was disappointed not to find him in the atrium.

"And last, but not least, are this school's favourite couple, Boyd and Jennifer. Jennifer's mum owns a boutique in town where we all get a forty percent discount." Cheryl's eyes gleamed with delight. "We throw the best parties, know the coolest guys, and are on the VIP list of the hottest club in the area."

And probably the only club. Lucille doubted that the hottest club in such a rural area even bothered with a VIP list. Most likely, the owner knew everyone by their first name and had done so since they were children. Lucille sighed. It would be so easy to say yes. She wouldn't even have to stick with them long-term, but she certainly didn't mind an introduction to Alan or a guaranteed invitation to parties.

Her gaze drifted through the large windows into the school hall. Inside, she could see Samantha diligently working on her schoolwork.

"What are you looking at?" Cheryl glanced over her shoulder. "Oh, her. Don't worry. When you're with us, Sammy won't bother you. She's so annoying with her childish act and how she sucks up to every teacher in sight. Have you seen her best friend slash ex? He's such an idiot. Always stumbling over his own feet. One time, he hit his head on a doorframe." Cheryl giggled. "So stupid. And he's just as bad. His mother runs a magic shop. How pathetic is that?"

Lucille's stomach tightened. She was no stranger to bullying. In Rosemary, she had occasionally been the target of attacks from jealous classmates. There had been one or two weeks where everybody had pelted her with petty insults just because of an unfortunate outbreak of pimples. And there had been one girl who always brought up her deceased mother when they argued. Lucille had learned how to stand up to such bullies, and she wasn't going to become one now. "Actually, I like them. They're really nice."

Cheryl's smile faltered. Suddenly, she didn't seem as amiable. "Piece of advice, you don't want to be caught dead with them. It'd be social suicide."

"Is that a threat?" Lucille asked sweetly.

Cheryl's eyes narrowed. "You don't want to mess with us."

"Relax." Lucille rolled her eyes, still smiling. "This is high school. It's not that serious. Nobody in the real world cares about who was in or not in school. I bet Samantha's going to be quite successful later in life. Someone with her intelligence will fly up any career ladder."

Cheryl snorted derisively and stood up abruptly. "As if! Well, it's your loss. If you want to hang out with the losers, I won't stop you."

"Bye!" Lucille wriggled her fingers in a mock-wave and watched Cheryl stalk off in her high-heels.

Her smile faded as soon as Cheryl was out of sight. She would probably come to regret her decision. Not that Lucille wanted to be a part of the Elite Clique, but it seemed that she made enemies wherever she went. Cheryl wouldn't let her live this humiliation down, that much was certain. And as for Samantha...

Lucille gazed through the window, once again noticing how lonely the Deputy Head Girl appeared. If only the magic issue didn't stand between them. She doubted Samantha would ever talk to her again, not after how she'd pushed her away.

Frustrated, Lucille reopened her lunch box. If she continued like this, she'd be left with no friends at all.

After school, Lucille asked Tobias to drop her off in the city centre so she could do some shopping. Retail therapy always helped improve her mood. But not so much today.

The area around the city council was only accessible to pedestrians. Beautiful timber-framed houses with baskets of colourful flowers lined the historical centre. Small shops and cafés were nestled into the lower storeys. On this glorious day, people sat outside in the sun, enjoying a piece of cake and a cup of coffee.

Lucille had found a small boutique, but the clothes were nothing to write home about. Drab, uniformly coloured shirts and skirts. For a town that was home to renowned fashion designer Linda de Cerque, the quality of these clothes was extremely poor.

A helpful saleswoman approached once she had finished the payment process for another client. "Ms de Cerque," she said with delight. "May I be of assistance?"

"There's not a single piece in here that doesn't have some sort of flaw. Loose threads... there is even a small hole in this one." Lucille stretched the fabric of a shirt, showing the hole that would expand with wear.

Flustered, the saleswoman didn't know where to look. At last, she snatched the shirt off the railing. "Oh dear, someone must've put out the donation items. I will return these to the back immediately."

"I'm still going to buy it," Lucille said hastily.

"Seriously?"

Lucille had no idea why she'd suddenly changed her mind or why she wanted to buy such a boring piece of fabric. Perhaps she felt sorry for her dismissive comments. They had been rather nasty, not at all like her usual self. "I might be able to use this as an accessory piece. The price is very reasonable." The clothes were a lot cheaper than what she was used to.

The saleswoman beamed. "I'll put it in a bag for you."

With a sigh, Lucille returned her attention to the rack. Some of those tops weren't half bad. She was just in a foul mood.

The decision to attend school in Greenvalley had excited her for most of the summer. Greenvalley was her hometown. Her grandmother's family had lived here for a long time, maybe even since its founding, and she'd been looking for a connection. A home.

But her actual home was empty and lonely, with her father constantly hiding in his office, and at school, she'd made nothing but enemies. Add to that the strange ball of green fire that had appeared in her hand. In her mind, Lucille whispered the words. *Globus igneus. Fireball.*

Was she imagining things, or did her hand feel warm even now? The fire had been hot against her face but not on her hand.

What if magic was real?

"Excuse me?" She went to the till, ready to pay for the faulty top. "Do you believe in magic?"

The saleswoman stifled a bubbling laugh. "Me? No, not really. But if you are interested in more than just the standard souvenirs, you should check out the Magic Circle."

"The Magic Circle?" There was a magic shop in this town that sold more than souvenirs.

"It's in the eastern part of the town, down Uferweg, I believe. They sell the typical souvenirs you can find anywhere around here, but also some... real magic. Or at least, you know, wicca stuff and the like."

Disappointed, Lucille took out her credit card. "Yeah, I'm not into that." Some of the girls at the boarding school had dabbled in tarot readings, and she had even sat down with a Ouija board, but all of that was fake magic, make-believe. The green fire had been real.

She put her smile back on to complete her purchase. "Thank you."

As she walked back to where Tobias had parked the car, she noticed a group of children playing that weird children's game someone had scribbled on the school wall.

"Who's afraid of the bogeyman?" rang out in a singsong voice across the square.

Strangely enough, there was nobody to answer the group. Lucille had expected some surviving children, but the street behind her was empty. The bogeyman children had the entire line to themselves. Then they started running, and instead of tagging other children, they tagged the adults in their way.

Lucille only escaped being tagged because her shopping bag was in the way. Confused and slightly freaked out by such a blatant disregard for her personal space, she quickened her pace until she reached the car.

"Home, please," she said, slightly out of breath.

As the car started rolling down the street, Lucille saw that adults had now joined the game with the same enthusiasm and endurance as the children. "What a weird little town."

On the ride home, Lucille saw several more groups of children and adults playing the silly game she had last played during her elementary school years. She figured it must be some sort of local festival or event because nothing else made sense.

It filled her with an unease that she couldn't shake. Moreover, it made her reconsider Linda's assessment. This town wasn't just behind the rest of the world; it was odd, and not in a quirky, charming sense of odd. A town where people actually believed in magic, while others indulged in a town-wide children's game? Coming here seemed like the worst decision of her life.

Maybe, if she hurried, Lucille could still go back to Rosemary College. The year had only just started. If she called the office today, she might be able to return. They wouldn't be pleased after she had turned them down, but money had a way of changing minds.

They arrived at the villa, which was thankfully empty of bogeyman players. While Tobias parked the car, Lucille gathered her courage to find Albert and tell him about her decision. However, when she entered the foyer, it was her father who looked down at her from the balustrade.

Lucille's heart skipped a beat. He'd been waiting for her. Her father was making time for her. All thoughts of returning to Rosemary College vanished from her mind, and she gave waved at him. "I'm home!"

"Who's afraid of the bogeyman?" her father's voice echoed.

Lucille froze.

"No one, no one," a voice answered from the side. Albert.

"And when he comes?" Linda's soft voice joined the others.

"Let him come," all three of them sang together.

Lucille turned on her heels and fled through the door, rushing right back into the car.

The chauffeur looked at her in confusion through the rear-view mirror. "Is everything all right, Miss?"

"Yes, yes. I just... I need to buy shoes. Please take me to the nearest shoe shop."

Lucille leaned back into the seat, her heart racing. As they drove away, she kept glancing back at the house. She no longer believed that this was some innocent game or quirky festival. No, her father would never tolerate such childishness. This was something more sinister; like dark magic.

Samantha

"Who's afraid of the bogeyman?"

Samantha stood outside her little sister's door. As usual, Meg was singing in her room, but for the past ten minutes since she'd returned from tennis practice, Meg had been repeating the same four lines over and over.

"No one, no one. And when he comes? Let him come. Who's afraid of the bogeyman? No..."

There was an eerie cadence to her singing. Initially, it had been annoying, but the repetitive singing quickly become more aggravating.

Samantha braced herself for the impending confrontation. At sixteen years old, Meg was in the midst of puberty, always looking for a fight and reacting dramatically to the smallest issues. Samantha had never been like that, but even the slightest criticism, such as asking her to stop singing that irritating song, could unleash the teenage monster.

Gathering her resolve, Samantha opened the door. She expected to find her sister to be playing on her phone or doing her homework. Instead, she discovered Meg sitting cross-legged on her bed, staring blankly at the opposite wall. And singing.

"And when he comes? Let him come. Who's afraid...?" Her head turned a quarter of the way, and her eyes locked onto Samantha.

In a panic, Samantha quickly shut the door. Moments later, there was a loud bang against the door, causing it to shake in its frame. Reflexively, Samantha gripped the door handle. Seconds later, it jerked violently, forcefully yanked from the other side.

Expecting Meg to start screaming any minute, Samantha found herself in disbelief when all that came out of her sister's mouth was a slightly more aggressive version of "Who's afraid of the bogeyman?"

Frantically, Samantha searched for something to block the door with but found nothing. Meg's relentless assault on the door handle was starting to hurt Samantha's hand. Unable to endure it any longer, she let go and fled to her own room. Within a split second, she had traversed the length of the corridor. Meg's door flew open just as she opened her own. Without hesitation, Samantha dashed into her room and locked the door behind her.

From outside, she could still hear Meg singing the verse, now in a melody that seemed designed to lure her in. Samantha stared at the back of her door, her nerves on edge, waiting for the handle to tremble under a touch. The seconds felt interminable.

Then... silence.

With her heart pounding in her chest, Samantha approached the door cautiously. She half-expected it to jolt suddenly, but it remained still, just like the corridor outside. As she pressed her ear against the door, she could still hear Meg's singing, though it was becoming fainter. Her sister was descending the stairs, moving away from Samantha.

Samantha let out a deep breath and slid down the door until her backside touched the floor. Her heart was still racing, but her mind began catching up, raising questions. Had she really just run away from her little sister? What was so terrifying about a nursery rhyme on repeat? Why was Meg behaving so strangely?

She had pondered the latter question many times before, but this felt different. It was unsettling, as if Meg had been possessed.

A tingle of excitement coursed through Samantha's spine. Not that she wished for her sister to be possessed, but if she was, then *something* was possessing her. Something magical.

In spite of herself, Samantha found herself grinning. As terrifying as it was, it was also tantalising. Magic had entered her life, along with a mystery. She *needed* to uncover the truth.

Samantha pulled out her phone and quickly composed a group message: *Let's meet up for some ice cream.* She knew Fabian would never agree if she suggested meeting at his mother's shop. They would start at the ice cream parlour and proceed to the Magic Circle from there.

Half an hour later, Samantha met with Rachel and Fabian at the ice cream parlour in the city centre. On her way there, she had observed other people singing the nursery rhyme, ruling out the possibility of a single ghost causing the possession.

"Maybe it's an army of ghosts," Samantha mused.

"Huh?" Fabian asked, then turned to the sever. "A triple-scoop cone, please, with chocolate, marzipan, and... cookies'n'cream. What do you want?"

Distracted, Samantha shook her head. "Nothing. Why don't you ask Rachel?" Her attention was caught by a commotion outside. People were running towards each other, seemingly playing tag.

It was surreal to watch adults in suits and fancy dresses playing on the streets like children. Even an elderly woman using a walking frame was participating.

"Everyone is obsessed with the bogeyman," Rachel said softly, savouring a single scoop of pistachio ice cream. "It was all over the news."

"Well, that's Greenvalley for you," Fabian chimed in. "Nothing interesting ever happens here." Samantha detected a hint of tension in his voice that he tried to mask.

Just then, Samantha spotted a familiar blonde figure. "There's Lucille!" The whole ordeal had started with the arrival of the new girl, and Samantha had a strong feeling that it would end with her.

"You haven't even bought ice cream!" Fabian called after her as Samantha pushed through the door and ran onto the square.

It was indeed Lucille, although she appeared lost. Samantha came to a halt, slightly out of breath. "Lucille! Hi!"

Lucille spun around, her eyes wide. "You... I mean, hello. What are you doing here?"

"Getting some ice cream," Fabian interjected, raising his towering cone as he and Rachel joined them. "You can share mine if you want."

"Ugh." Samantha waved him off. "No, we... what are you looking for?"

Lucille bit her bottom lip, constantly glancing over her shoulder. "Have you noticed something strange with people?"

"What's wrong with people?" Fabian asked, his voice growing more intense.

"They're creepy."

Samantha knew exactly what she meant. "It's that bogeyman game, right? My sister has been singing that nursery rhyme non-stop since she got home."

"Yes!" Lucille's eyes lit up. "Everyone at my place was coming at me with those lines. I think they were trying to catch me."

"No offence, but your family sounds weird," Fabian remarked without thinking.

Samantha jabbed her elbow into his side and shot him a glare. He always managed to say the wrong thing.

Lucille frowned. "Well, they're not usually like this. And it's not just my family; everyone else seems to have lost their minds too, except for you three."

"That's new," Rachel commented softly.

Samantha couldn't contain herself any longer. "I know you don't want to hear it, but I think something magical is going on."

"You're calling this creepy ass stuff magical?" Fabian stared at her, ice cream dripping down the cone and onto his fingers. He shook his head. "No! No more magic. I thought we were done with that."

But Lucille took a deep breath. "I think you are right. About everything. Although, I'm not sure I signed up for this."

"They're coming for us," Rachel said, her gaze fixed on the approaching people playing tag.

She was right. People were closing in on them, arms outstretched.

"Let's get moving," Samantha said, leading the way.

They hastened away from the crowd. A woman walking her dog wasn't as fortunate. As soon as she was touched by the bogeyman players, she let go of the leash and joined the others in their eerie chorus, while her dog barked fearfully.

"What do you think is happening here?" Lucille asked, suddenly fully engaged.

Samantha's heart pounded as they hurried away. There was a mix of fear and excitement coursing through her. The existence of magic could no longer be denied. "I'm not exactly sure, but I think it's some kind of contagious disease, only... more magical."

"You can't be serious," Fabian muttered. However, when he saw a whole line of bogeyman players following them, he quickly changed his mind. "Or maybe you're right."

The line blocked off the entire length of the square. There was no escape that way. Fabian dropped his ice cream as they started running, but soon, another line of bogeyman players approached from the other side of the square.

"Here! This way!" someone called. It was the new guy from school, Matt Traidous.

Samantha had no idea what he was doing here, but he stood at the entrance of a small alleyway—an escape route—so they ran towards him.

He ushered them through a narrow gap in the shops that led away from the pedestrian area. They crossed several streets, frequently changing directions until they reached the deserted river promenade. "That's better."

"What are you doing here?" Lucille asked him.

"I was out on a date when I came across this manifestation of magic," Matt explained.

Samantha could see Lucille swallowing and remembered how interested she seemed in the new guy during class.

"A date?" Lucille asked, her voice faltering slightly.

Matt kept looking over his shoulder. "Yeah, but he got infected before we got anywhere."

"He?"

Samantha had no patience for her relationship woes. There were more important things in Matt's explanation. "A manifestation of magic? Are you sure?" She had read about it but never seen it.

"What does that mean?" Fabian asked.

"Long story or short?" When Fabian huffed, Samantha chided herself for not being more considerate. "Sorry, the short version is this: Magic is all around us, but we can't see it. Some people, like Lucille, can access it. A manifestation of magic means that magic has somehow taken shape, like a story come alive."

Lucille was gnawing on her bottom lip again. "So, what do we do?"

"We need to find the source and eliminate it. That will stop the whole thing," Matt said, and Samantha nodded. That was exactly what she'd read in the books.

"Eliminating?" Lucille's pitch rose suddenly. "I am not going to do any eliminating. In fact, I think I'll leave this town on the next train and never look back."

"Great idea," Fabian said, taking a step to her side. "I'm coming with you!"

Samantha stared at them in horror. "Guys! We can't just leave Greenvalley like this. What about everyone else? Our families?"

"I can do without mine," Rachel muttered.

Samantha ignored her. "We need to do something about this."

"How?" Lucille shook her head, aghast. "What can a couple of teenagers do against dark magic that brings the bogeyman to life?"

It was a valid question. Samantha had no powers, only knowledge. She didn't know if Matt had any powers or if he was like her. The only one she knew for sure could perform actual magic was Lucille, and she had already freaked out over one small fireball, which might have been a fluke. Still...

"Look at it this way. We're probably the only ones who have any idea of what's happening. We can't turn our backs on this."

Apart from Matt, Rachel was the only one who didn't seem freaked out. "It started at school, didn't it?"

Fabian stared at her, then at Matt, and finally at Samantha. "You're nuts. You're all completely nuts." His face had turned pale.

"Did you hear the rhyme?" Matt asked. "They keep singing *who's afraid of the bogeyman* and then *no one*. So, if we aren't afraid—"

"BUT I AM AFRAID!" Fabian shouted, shocking everyone into silence.

Samantha's heart went out to him. She could see how scared he was. Yesterday had been the same, experiencing magic in the classroom and then receiving all the information from Caroline that blew his mind. Fabian wasn't the bravest guy on a normal day, and these new monstrous events were downright terrifying him.

Tenderly, Samantha took a step forward and put a hand on his arm. "But that's just it. You know the verse. And when he comes? Let him come."

"Sure, sure. Let's get run down by a mob. Nothing's gonna happen as long as we aren't afraid."

He had a point there, Samantha thought. She doubted anyone had been afraid of a few children, and yet they had been turned.

Before she could think of a different solution, Lucille asked, "Aren't there any adults who can deal with this? I can't be the first one who does magic in this town, right?" She looked at Fabian. "Cheryl said your mum had a magic shop?"

"Cheryl—"

"Yes!" Samantha took a step towards the others again. "Caroline is a witch, just like my grandmother and—" She almost mentioned Lucille's grandmother again but caught herself. "Never mind. I was actually planning to go see Fabian's mum about this. I'm sure she can help. Let's go and see her together."

"Do I get any say in this?" Fabian asked, still sounding so terribly scared.

Samantha threw him a pitiful look. Under normal circumstances, she would've given in, but that would only get him hurt today. Instead, she linked her arm with his and dragged him along. "Not really, no." One way or another, they would have to face the bogeyman. She wouldn't rest until she found a way.

Fabian

The entire world had gone mad. Not only was there a monster made of pure magic roaming the streets of Fabian's beloved hometown, but now his friends were talking about facing said monster with literally nothing in their hands.

"If it's a manifestation of magic, don't you think it came alive in the town square?" Lucille asked as she walked along the bookshelves in his mother's store, her finger tracing the spines of spellbooks. "That's where the source of all magic is, isn't it?"

The store was deserted, which was not like his mother at all. There hadn't even been a sign at the door. Anyone could walk in and rob the store blind. Fabian leaned nervously against the till, while Samantha and Lucille searched the shelves and Matt checked out the athames. Only Rachel had stayed with him, but she was quiet as always. Her calm and patience were slowly rubbing off on him, and his heart rate slowed again.

Meanwhile, Samantha was blossoming before his eyes with every explanation she gave Lucille. "The fountain in the city centre is only for show. Somehow, the rumour of a spring of magic got out and whoever was mayor back then decided to capitalise on it. There is a real spring, but it's in the middle of the forest. My grandmother knows where. Now that you're a witch I'm sure she can take you there someday."

Lucille still seemed a bit anxious about the whole deal, but she was warming up quickly to Samantha. "Maybe someday. How come a magic spell is nothing more than a bit of Latin? I mean, I've studied Latin for five years now, and while it may be a dead language no one really speaks anymore, I have certainly read it out loud without some Roman senator appearing in class."

Samantha giggled. "That would've been awesome. Talk about living history." More seriously, she added, "No, it's not just Latin. You did something when you read those words. My grandmother describes it as binding magic to the words. That's why spells fall under verbal magic. But she was never able to explain how it works exactly since it's not her speciality, and no matter how much I try, it doesn't work for me."

Fabian watched them move through the shop. Of course, he knew Samantha's grandmother Elda, who had a little hut in the woods. She had taught him and Samantha all about the different herbs in her garden, but he had always assumed their effects were purely pharmaceutical, not spell ingredients. Same with Samantha's interest in magic. It had always been there, but he hadn't known how deep the desire to actually do magic had been rooted. It made him wonder if he truly knew everything about his best friend.

"But I didn't do anything different from any other time I read Latin," Lucille protested, playing once more with her pretty necklace.

Samantha noticed the gesture as well. "First off, I assume that you didn't exactly work with spells in class. And second, when did you start wearing your grandmother's necklace?"

Lucille clutched the rubies with her hand, reminding them all how touchy she'd been about it in class. "I... oh no. Albert... That's our butler," she explained. Of course, she would have a butler. "He gave it to me two days ago, just before school. He said my grandmother wanted me to have it once I was old enough to appreciate it. He gave me a magical necklace, didn't he?" She turned a little pale around the nose and lowered her hand.

Samantha took a closer look and nodded. "That's what I thought when I first saw it. Uhm... I know you said your grandma wasn't a witch, but..."

"She was one, right?" Lucille sighed.

"Yeah. Apparently, her family has been in Greenvalley for a long time, and she was friends with my grandma. She..." Samantha paused, and Fabian was glad she did. The last thing Lucille needed to learn right now was that a demon had killed her precious grandmother. "If you want, I can take you along when I visit her again. I'm sure she has lots of stories about your grandmother."

Lucille smiled warmly. "I would love that. Now, about—"

The wind chime across the door rang, announcing his mother's return. Fabian pushed himself off the counter. "There you are. We were—"

"Who's afraid of the bogeyman?" his mother said in a loving voice, as if she were asking what she should cook for dinner.

Fabian felt as if someone had emptied a bucket of ice over his head. This couldn't possibly be real.

"Your mum's one of them, too," Rachel whispered.

"Nonsense. Mum?" He walked towards her, each step falling more heavily than the one before.

She smiled and stretched her arms out. "No one, no one."

"Mum!" Fabian bellowed. "Snap out of it! Don't you recognise me?"

She cocked her head. "And when he comes?" Her hand reached for him as if she was going to caress his cheek, a gesture familiar and welcome.

Just before her fingers touched his skin, Matt yanked him backwards. "Do you want to get turned?"

"Turned?" Fabian shuddered. His mind was a mess. Nothing made sense anymore. This was his mother, goddammit.

But her smile was turning ghastly now. "Let him come!" Then she lunged at him.

A book hit her on the shoulder, drawing her attention towards the girls. Samantha stood with widened eyes, as if in disbelief that she'd just thrown a holy book across the room. As his mother repeated her rhyme, Lucille tugged at Samantha's sleeve. "We need to get out!"

Samantha still stared, but when his mother lunged for them, she jumped away and hid behind the bookshelf with Lucille. Next to Fabian, Matt grabbed one of the athames from the table.

"Are you out of your mind? That's my mum!" Fabian still didn't understand what was going on.

For a moment, it seemed as if Matt was considering charging her anyway, but at last he let the knife fall. As it clattered to the ground, he grabbed a broomstick instead. Swinging it around, he pushed the bristles against Caroline's chest. "Go! I'll hold her off!"

Fabian stumbled away from him. His mother was focused solely on Matt right now. She tried to reach him over the bristles of the broomstick instead of going around it, but he mercilessly pushed her out of the way. Lucille and Samantha darted towards the door.

Rachel tried to follow them, but she was passing dangerously close to Caroline. His mother threw herself at her, screeching the lines from the rhyme. Matt was faster. The moment the tension let off, he swung the broomstick around, hitting her with the long handle across the stomach. Fabian saw his mother fold under the impact and winced.

"Come on," Matt barked.

His feet wouldn't work. The girls were at the door. His mother was groaning, but she was already righting herself and starting the rhyme anew.

"Fabian!" Samantha called.

Her voice finally did the trick. But instead of going towards the door, he dashed to the counter, leaned over it, and grabbed the keys from the corner. Then he ran for the door. He had to navigate around his mum, but Matt had her well under control—as horrible as it was.

A moment later, Fabian was out on the street, fumbling with the keys. Matt followed him and held the door shut. His mother was scratching and banging against the door like a madwoman. She was still shouting the bogeyman rhymes. Fabian's hands were shaking. The keys fell. He picked them back up and found the right one again. Meanwhile, his throat tightened. At last, he managed to put it in the keyhole and turn it twice.

The door was locked. His mother was trapped in her own shop.

"Is there a back door?" Matt asked, letting go of the door handle.

Fabian shook his head. He was still grappling with the fact that he'd locked his mum in. She was going to ground him for life. "What happened?"

"She got tagged by the others. They infected her as well," Samantha answered. "So much for Caroline taking care of this for us."

"Can we go to the school now?" asked Matt. He sounded impatient, as if they were all just wasting his time.

Thankfully, Lucille had a more reasonable reaction to the whole situation this time around. "And do what? Take care of the bogeyman? No!" She hugged herself. "I can't. I don't know what to do, and... I can't."

Fabian took a few steps away from the shop, unable to face his screaming mother. "She's right, you know? We're no match for... this." They'd only managed to escape because Matt had assaulted his mother with a broomstick.

And he didn't even seem upset about it. "It doesn't matter whether we're a match. We're all Greenvalley has left. I'm gonna go to the school. Alone, if I must."

"I'm coming," Samantha said. "But I need to get a couple of things from home."

"I'm coming, too," Rachel said without even the slightest hesitation. She sounded uncharacteristically determined. "I'll get Nico's bat. Just in case." Somehow, Fabian couldn't even imagine little Rachel beating up people with a baseball bat.

The three of them looked at Fabian and Lucille. To his horror, Lucille took a deep breath and nodded. "Very well. It's either facing the bogeyman or becoming one of his puppets, right? If that's the case, I'd rather go down with a fight."

Fabian's stomach was still twisting and turning. Fight people? Fight manifested magic? This wasn't his Greenvalley. This wasn't him. But what choice did he have? Join his mum and get infected as well? And besides, what if something happened to Samantha? She was his best friend, the girl he loved more than anyone. He'd never forgive himself if he let something happen to her. "Okay, I... what do we need?"

Samantha smiled. "A few extra spells for Lucille, for example."

"Well then," Matt said with a nod. "I'll see you at school in an hour."

One hour. It felt to Fabian as if it would be the last hour of his life as he knew it.

Rachel

With one ear against the door, Rachel listened for sounds inside the house. There was none. Most likely, her mother wasn't even home. It might have been a Tuesday night, but that wouldn't stop her from finding a party and getting drunk.

Carefully, she opened the door, trying to make as little sound as possible. If her brother or her mother were infected by the bogeyman, she didn't want to alert them to her presence. She was only here to grab Nico's baseball bat before leaving again to meet the others at school.

It turned out, her mother hadn't found a party. The party had found her. Or at least, the living room looked as if it belonged in a club. Rachel found at least three empty wine bottles and a broken glass. A spill of red wine had ruined yet another throw carpet, while her mother was lying on her stomach on the couch, snoring.

Rachel watched her for at least a minute, bottles forgotten in her hand. She tried to search for any pity inside of her, but there was none. Just disgust.

She startled at the creaking of the stairs. A few seconds later, Nico and his girlfriend came down. He was only wearing some jogging pants, while Svenja was sporting a yellow sunflower dress. She was cute, and Rachel asked herself not for the first time, how her brother had managed to find someone like her.

But now she waited, subtly changing her grip on the bottles. If they were controlled by the bogeyman, she'd use them, though she really didn't want to.

However, Nico only sighed. "Oh man. She's such a mess."

Svenja gave their mother a pitiful look. "You should call the authorities."

"Nah." Nico shook his head. "She's a mess, but she's our mess."

Relief flooded Rachel, and she relaxed again. "Tell me about it." She turned around to deposit the bottles in the kitchen.

Nico said goodbye to his girlfriend and got the dustpan and brush out to pick up the glass. "I thought parents were supposed to take care of their children, not the other way around."

"After all these years?" Rachel asked doubtfully. What had started with an occasional glass of wine had devolved into a bottle a night years ago.

Nico threw the glass pieces away and returned with a blanket. He draped it over their mother with way more care than she deserved in Rachel's opinion. Then he looked at her. "So, you all went for ice cream without me." He obviously had been busy with his girlfriend.

It reminded her that the others would be waiting. And of something else. "Forget the ice cream. Do you remember the dream I told you about four days ago?"

"The weird one where our schoolmates were hunting you while chanting a children's song or something?" He sat down on the backrest of the couch, facing her.

Rachel nodded. "Not a children's song. A rhyme—the same one we saw on the wall this morning."

Nico scrunched up his nose, then rolled his eyes. "Coincidence!"

Rachel groaned. "You always say that!"

"Because it's true." Nico pushed himself off the couch and put his hands on her shoulder. "You are a brilliant observer, and though you might be a little too quiet during the day, your brain keeps analysing people and their behaviour. That doesn't stop when you dream. So, occasionally, you dream something that comes true in some fashion. It's not a premonition, but excellent knowledge of human nature."

"Except that's not it." Her heart was beating faster with possibility, and she started walking to let some of that energy out. "Because, today, it happened."

"What happened?"

"The entire city has gone mad. People are running around chanting the lines of that silly game, and they catch each other. Once you're tagged, you're one of them. It's infecting everyone." Nico was frowning deeply. She was probably speaking gibberish for all he knew. "Samantha thinks it's a manifestation of magic."

"Samantha sees magic in everything."

"But this is real. The new guy said the same thing."

Nico wasn't convinced. "So, he's a little weird, too. That's oddly charming, makes him a little less perfect, I guess."

Rachel groaned. Nico had an answer for everything. Or believed as much. "Fabian's mother attacked us in her shop!"

His eyes grew big. "What? Why? Caroline wouldn't hurt a fly. She's the best!"

She agreed with him. Compared to their own mother, Caroline was the epitome of motherhood. Fabian might complain about her, but Rachel only knew her as a caring and involved parent. Not so much today. This version of Caroline had been outright frightening. "She was chanting the same lines as everyone else. Exactly like they all did in my dream."

"Well, did your dream tell you how to return her to normal?"

Rachel paused. In her dream, the puppets had chased her through endless school corridors. There had been no light, just shadows in the darkness. If she closed her eyes now, she could still hear them shuffling and chanting.

At some point, she had simply woken in terror. "No, only... that it took place at school. Which is where we're meeting the others at seven thirty to get to the bottom of it." But that wasn't what had got Rachel all excited. "Anyway, my dream—"

"We're doing what?" Nico frowned. "I feel like I'm missing half the conversation here. The bottom of what?"

"Of the bogeyman's appearance in Greenvalley and his infection of its citizens. The others want to stop him. I mean, I want that, too. I just..." The conversation was slipping away from her as it did so often.

"They want to take this monster on?" Nico huffed. "Woah, this is wild!" His gaze fell onto their mother, who was still snoring between them. "You know, a real parent would never allow this."

Impatiently, Rachel shook her head. "Yeah, well, she's out of it."

Her brother's face hardened. "I'm gonna come. Do we need to bring something? How do you fight the bogeyman? Or magic?"

"That's not important!" Instantly, Rachel clapped her hands over her mouth. She hated raising her voice, but it had slipped out just now.

Nico paused. "What is it?"

She took a couple of deep breaths to calm herself and keep the nervous excitement down that kept trying to bubble up. "The important thing is that what I saw in my dream cannot be explained by good observation skills. It's too random, too specific. But it is happening right now, which means..." A smile crept onto her face, impossible to hold back. "My dreams show the future."

There had been no time to discuss Rachel's vision-heavy dreams. They both had to hurry to meet the others at school. While Nico wasn't fully convinced that what she'd told him was true, her brother trusted her enough to come along and bring the baseball bat. That meant she had nothing to defend herself with, but that wouldn't stop her from seeing the end of her vision.

Lucille had gone with Samantha and Fabian to retrieve the spellbook. Now, she was constantly looking over her shoulder and clenching her fingers. "Where is Matt?"

"Here." He stepped out of the shadows, a weapon strapped to his back. But not just any weapon. A sword, and by the looks of it, a pretty fancy sword. Rachel couldn't see much of it, but the handle ended in a black sphere of glass, and she was pretty sure it had runes etched into the metal.

"You own a sword?" Fabian asked, his voice ending in a high pitch. "Don't you need a license for that? Or something? Why do you even have one lying around?"

"To cut off heads if nothing useful comes out of their mouths." Matt shook his head. Rachel remembered how readily he had leaped into action when Caroline had attacked them, and she guessed this wasn't his first rodeo. He didn't seem like a weapon-crazy lunatic, just someone who was ready for anything. "We don't know what exactly we're facing here."

Samantha cleared her throat. "Hopefully, nothing that needs killing with a sword."

Nico swung his baseball bat. "Well, I may not have a sword, but I'm ready... I think." Matt snorted.

While the others kept discussing the sword, Rachel peered into the darkness. There was a soft noise, as if something was dragged over the ground. Shoes! Someone was dragging their feet. And not just some*one*, but many. "Guys?"

Nobody heard her. Fabian was having another panic attack over the sword and why they would even come here in the darkness when they could stay at home or leave town.

Rachel cleared her throat. "Guys!"

This time, Samantha and Nico looked towards her, and slowly the discussion between the other three died down as well.

"We're not alone."

The first few people came into view when they crossed the light cone of a lantern. As in the city centre before, they walked towards them in a closed line, leaving no gap. Others were approaching from the opposite side.

Fabian was whining softly. "What do we do now?"

"We go in," Matt said promptly. He grabbed the upper railing of the school gate, and in one swift motion swung himself over.

Everybody stared. At last, Lucille said, "There's no way I can do this."

"We're all gonna die," Fabian cried.

"We will not die!" Samantha said in a harsh tone. "And we can go through here. It's open."

When she simply opened the school gate, Matt grinned sheepishly at her. "Should've tried that first."

Around them, the chant of the bogeyman rose. Rachel's arms were covered in goosebumps, and by the looks of everybody else, they felt similarly crept out. Suddenly, they were all on board, hurrying through the gate.

They had barely made it inside when yet another group came at them from the inside. Matt's hand was inching towards the handle of his sword, but Samantha pointed towards the main building. "The doors are open there, too!" Apparently, they'd never been locked today.

Once again, they rushed forwards. Behind them, the song began to swell until Rachel didn't even hear her own pulse rushing through her ears. Samantha had taken the lead, while Matt seemed to purposefully stay at the back. Nico was constantly checking whether Rachel was keeping up, but it was Lucille he needed to worry about. She didn't seem used to sprinting across the concrete floor, especially not in heels.

Rachel passed her, following Fabian's steps, when she heard Lucille squeal. Startled, Rachel glanced backwards, only to see that Matt had thrown her over his shoulders. How he was able to keep up with the extra weight was beyond Rachel, but at least Lucille hadn't been caught by the bogeyman puppets as she'd feared.

Then, they were through the door, and Nico slammed it shut, quickly ramming the lock bar in. A second later, people ran into the door, making it shudder and creak on its hinges. But the door held, and no amount of kicking and scratching from the outside could make it budge.

Lucille was returned to the floor, and slowly, they backed away from the door, deeper into the corridors. Rachel's breath hitched in her throat, suddenly reminded of her dream. This was it. The location of her dream.

A sudden shuffle behind her alerted her, followed by something heavy hitting the floor. Rachel spun around, to catch the glint of a blade in the moonlight.

Matt had drawn his sword and used it against a boy who now lay crumpled at his feet.

"You killed him!" Lucille shrieked before frantically crouching down to check on the boy. There was no blood as far as Rachel could see.

Matt said with an annoyed shake of his head, "Don't be ridiculous. I didn't kill him. I knocked him out before he could touch you."

The boy was about thirteen and lying as still as if he were dead.

"Knockouts can do harm," Samantha said. With a few quick movements, she had checked the pulse Lucille hadn't found. "He's alive, but... oh, he's coming to."

"Then I'd recommend we leave," Matt said, still annoyingly impatient.

Lucille glared at him. "We cannot just leave him here. He needs medical attention."

Meanwhile, Rachel noticed how pale Fabian had become. He looked as if he was going to pass out as well. Knowing how sensitive he really was, her hand itched to reach out to him. But that was something she'd never dare.

"Sure!" Matt snapped. "I guess we could wait until he wakes up, attacks us, and I knock him out again, doing harm eventually. This way, we'll pass the entire night, while in the meantime, the bogeyman turns Greenvalley into his soulless army."

Nobody said anything as the boy groaned on the floor. Straining her ears, Rachel picked up the rhythm of the bogeyman rhyme in his groans.

"Let's go," Nico decided, quickly walking towards the staircase. Not that they had any idea what to look for. Right now, getting away from the puppets was all they could think of.

The rest followed Nico to the second floor. Somehow, Rachel found herself next to Fabian. He was mumbling to himself. "This isn't right. This isn't right at all."

Her fingers were twitching. He was so close she could've easily touched his arm or his hand. Just thinking about it made her cheeks burn, though, and she left her fingers where they were.

In front of them, Samantha was talking to Matt. "You seem to be awfully comfortable with all this." It was the understatement of the year. He had clearly done this before.

To Rachel's surprise, he didn't claim otherwise but admitted to it. "It's nothing out of the ordinary where I come from."

"And where's that?" Samantha asked.

But before Matt could answer her, someone jumped out of the connecting corridor, the lines of the nursery rhyme on her lips. Matt kicked the girl in the stomach, narrowly avoiding the outstretched hands. Meanwhile, Samantha ducked under the arms of a second attacker.

"Come on, do something!" Lucille crouched behind Fabian, clutching his shoulders as if she'd known him for ages and not since yesterday. "Fight them off!"

"What?" Fabian's voice broke. "You're the witch!"

"What am I supposed to do? Burn them to ashes?"

"Watch out!" Rachel shouted.

A teacher was lunging at Fabian, but Nico jumped in to push the arms away with his baseball bat. He winced the moment the wood made contact with flesh. "I can't..."

Instead, someone else stepped in. Two kicks and a quick hit later, the teacher crumpled to the ground. Matt must've dealt with the two kids because he swung around, sword at the ready, and pointed the weapon at their unexpected ally. The tip of the sword halted only a finger's width in front of his throat, prompting the guy to raise his hands in defence.

"Woah there! Steady!"

Rachel recognised the voice, but it was Fabian who asked, "Jan? What are you doing here?"

"You know him?" Matt asked.

Meanwhile, Lucille pulled out her phone and used the flashlight to shine a light on Jan, causing him to wince.

"Put that down," he begged.

Matt sheathed his sword, and Lucille turned her light to the ground.

"What are you doing here?" Fabian asked again. His voice had regained a little strength.

Jan looked past their shoulders. "There's no time for that. We've got visitors."

Behind them, the puppets of the bogeyman were approaching en masse. They must've found another entry into the school. Jan lunged to the side and opened a window, leading to the fire escape. "Through here."

Rachel looked down. More children and adults were gathering below. "They're waiting for us."

"That, my darling, is why we go up!" And with that, Jan swung out onto the fire escape and ran up the stairs.

Rachel followed him up to the fourth floor while the rest scrambled after them. Once again, Matt was the last one to leave the battlefield. Meanwhile, Jan broke the window upstairs with a quick jolt from his elbow, grabbed inside, and opened it for Rachel.

She swallowed a groan. Jan was nothing but trouble. Breaking into school was probably one of his hobbies. But she saw the necessity of it in this situation and climbed inside without commenting on it.

When they had all gathered, Jan ushered them through a door, which they managed to bar from the inside. In the darkness, they paused, each of them catching their breath.

"Now, we can talk," Jan announced.

"What the hell are you doing here?" Fabian shouted.

Jan grinned sheepishly. "Same thing as you, I guess."

"You're trying to defeat the bogeyman?" Lucille asked.

Jan burst into laughter. "What? No, I haven't been afraid of the bogeyman since I was five."

"So, you just broke into the school for fun?" Samantha's voice was flat. She had crossed her arms and sighed.

"What if I did? You're not gonna tell, are you, Kollmer?"

"I'm not a snitch." Samantha lowered her arms and rolled her eyes. Rachel knew full well how much it grated on her to find someone breaking the rules, but technically, they all were.

Jan grinned again. "Just checking. Now, you don't happen to have seen my friends anywhere?" He looked around the dark corridors. "Ah... never mind. Let's go this way."

He put his hands on Rachel's shoulder and turned her around to push her towards the empty corridor. Behind her, someone banged against the door. A second later, it flew open with a loud crack.

Once again, they were running. Rachel took the stairs down, almost stumbling over her feet. Next to her, Jan opened another window and jumped onto the lower roof of the school's hall. Rachel wanted to turn and follow him, but Fabian grabbed her arm and dragged her down another flight. Behind him, Samantha and Nico followed. There was no sight of Matt and Lucille.

Her vision was coming true. She was being chased by strange singing people through the dark and empty corridors of her school. At every corner, a new group awaited them. Rachel lost count of the turns they made and the stairs they took. Up and down. Left and right. It all lost meaning. Just like it had in her dream.

And now Rachel realised how foolish she'd been. She'd seen this in her dreams, felt its truth, and yet, she had still come. To find the end of her dream, not realising that this might be the end. That this was it. She was being hunted across the school. Until she got caught.

"Where are the others?" Fabian asked, panting. He was no longer touching her. Instead, he was holding his side as if he had a stitch.

Behind them, there was the shuffle and off-key singing of the bogeyman puppets, but there was no sight of her brother or Samantha—or any of the others.

"Doesn't matter right now. Keep moving. The exit is that way." The short break had given Rachel the opportunity to gather her bearings. They only had to take one staircase down, run through the doors at the bottom, and then down the corridor until they reached one of the back entrances. Which would be doable if there wasn't a horde of bogeyman puppets on their heels.

It went well until the door. Rachel ran through, but the backswing of the door caught Fabian, and in that moment, one of the puppets touched him. He managed to lock the door behind him, then paused.

A terrible thought crept down Rachel's spine. "Are you okay, Fabian?"

"I..." He turned around. "Who's afraid of the bogeyman?"

They got him. They got Fabian. And now he would get her.

"Oh no." Slowly, she backed away. There was no singing behind her. Only Fabian, who stretched out his arms, his eyes lacking their usual warmth. "Don't do this. I..."

"No one. No one."

"I'm not afraid of you. I..." *Love you,* would have been the correct continuation, but that didn't matter anymore. He'd never know because they wouldn't escape the bogeyman. At least, not both of them.

"And when he comes?"

She ran away.

Lucille

"This is insane!" Lucille whispered.

She and Matt were hiding behind the curtain of the stage. They'd lost the others early on, but somehow, Matt had managed to carve a path down the stairs and finally lose their pursuers in the assembly hall.

"What were we thinking?" Her brain was on fire. She couldn't think, couldn't even remember what stroke of madness had told her that going after a magical entity would be a good idea. "This isn't normal. Magic isn't real. This isn't real."

"It's real enough at home. And here as well, it seems," Matt answered in a calm voice. He had been so cool and collected throughout this adventure. Lucille didn't know how he did it.

Meanwhile, she felt like she was losing her mind. "I came to Greenvalley to reconnect with my roots. To find a place where I belonged and not feel like a stranger in my own hometown. Like I had only spent a few weekends or the odd week in Greenvalley before being shipped off again to some fancy language school or on a holiday abroad."

Her breaths came faster and faster. "Everyone told me I was mad to leave such a refined institute as Rosemary College. I wanted to show them they were wrong. That I could thrive just as well at a public school. And now I'm stuck at night in my school, running from my classmates, and probably going to die within the next hour."

"You won't die," Matt said. He suddenly seemed as overwhelmed as she was, but he kept his voice firm. "You'll just become one of them."

"And spend the rest of my life roaming the streets, assaulting unassuming passersby with a nursery rhyme." While Matt chuckled, Lucille gasped for air.

Her face hurt from the effort of holding it together. "I should've stayed at Rosemary. I should've... I don't want to die or lose my soul or—"

Suddenly, his lips were on hers, and for a few precious seconds, there were no thoughts at all in her mind. His soft lips were like melting chocolate on hers, leaving her with the same warm feeling that spread through every nerve of her body. She folded into his embrace, eager to have more of him, and Matt complied, parting her lips. The touch of his tongue was electrifying. Her knees grew weak. It wasn't Lucille's first kiss, but it was the first she never wanted to end.

When Matt let go of her, her breathing had calmed, but the blood was rushing even faster to her cheeks. He looked at her nervously. "Better?" Lucille nodded, still caught up in the sensation of his kiss. "You're not going to die, and you're not becoming one of them, either. We will defeat this thing."

"How?" They didn't even know what to look for.

"I don't know," he admitted. "But I can promise you this much." He looked deep into her eyes. "I will get you out of here. If everything else fails, I will get you out of here."

The words set her stomach aflutter. Only now, her brain registered that he'd kissed her. Lucille touched her lips. "The kiss."

"You want me to do that again?" he asked, a trace of his flirty smile returning to his lips.

She blushed. "No. I... I mean, I thought you weren't interested in girls." She wanted those lips on hers again as soon as they got out of here. And for that, she needed to clarify some things.

"Why wouldn't I be?" Matt frowned. "Boy, girl, non-binary... they're all great."

"Oh." A smile spread across her face. So, she hadn't imagined his flirting yesterday. "That's good. That... doesn't actually matter right now." Finally, her brain's synapses snapped back to where they belonged. But it had helped. She was regaining her composure. "I'm sorry I'm such a mess."

"You're doing fine," Matt assured her. "It's your first time going up against something like this, right?"

Lucille snorted. "Yes, I didn't even know things like this existed."

His smile made her knees go soft again. "Ready to soldier on? We need to find the others."

Was she ready? Probably not. But she had committed to this hunt, and she also felt responsible for the others. Sure, they'd all come of their own will, but *she* was the one with the supposed magic powers. "Let's do this."

When Matt held out his hand, Lucille swooned a little. If they survived this night, Lucille was going to ask him out. But first, the bogeyman.

The school was scarily quiet as they crossed the hall. They passed the entrance they'd originally entered through. Lucille felt a strong longing to just cross the foyer and leave while they had the chance, but then she heard the singing. It came from the side and then from behind.

Matt started running, pulling her along. Since he'd carried her outside, she had taken her shoes off. The next time she'd be hunting monsters, it certainly wouldn't be in heels. Next time. What was she even thinking? There wouldn't be a next time if they didn't hurry.

They kept running, frequently changing directions as more and more people chased after them. It was as if they could smell the fear. There was no more hiding, just running and avoiding. Someone lunged at her, and she hit them in the face with her heels. Matt knocked people away with the hilt of his sword, taking great care not to actually hurt anyone.

Lucille kept looking over her shoulder, to the side, everywhere but the front, when she suddenly ran into someone. Both of them went down with a yelp, and Lucille threw her shoes, eliciting a second yelp from underneath her. Something hard pressed against her ribs.

"Lucille!" That was Samantha's voice, but it sounded further away. The person she had collided with was Rachel's brother. While she'd heard his name before, she couldn't recall it in that moment.

Moaning, he held his forehead. "Sorry." Then he pulled on the baseball bat he'd been carrying. That was what had been pressed against her ribs.

"We didn't know where you were!" Samantha's eyes were wide, and she was out of breath. "I thought you had been caught, too."

"Run!" Matt told her, while he helped Lucille back to her feet and reached for the hand of Rachel's brother.

"We can't!" Samantha cried. "There's nowhere to go."

Lucille saw that she was right. People were coming at them from all directions. "The classrooms! There!" She pointed at the nearest door.

Samantha made a dash for it, only to find it locked. "It's locked!"

"Who's afraid of the bogeyman?" echoed through the corridors.

"Let me!" Matt stepped forward, while Samantha made space for him.

With an impressive kick, the door flew open. The four of them rushed into a standard classroom. Matt held the broken door closed, shuddering under the first onslaught of the bogeyman puppets.

"Get some tables here!" he shouted.

Rachel's brother was already on it. He pushed two small tables against the door. "That won't hold. Wait... the cupboard."

The three of them worked together to push the cupboard, which must have been full of schoolbooks, far enough to block part of the door. Matt gave them a hand, and as a team, they moved the cupboard in front of the door.

It held—for the moment.

"What do we do now?" Lucille asked.

"Regroup and figure this thing out." Matt guarded the door nervously.

Lucille felt faint and flopped down on the nearest chair. "Figure what out?"

Outside the windows, she heard the chorus of the bogeyman. In the corridor, something slammed into the door again and again. There was no escape. They were trapped.

"Has anyone seen my sister?" Nico asked. That was it. His name was Nico.

Everyone shook their heads. At last, Samantha answered, "She was with Fabian."

A flash of a grin crossed Nico's face. "Well, there's always a silver lining, right?"

"What?" Lucille asked in confusion, but Nico waved the question off.

Meanwhile, Samantha had sat down next to Lucille and was scouring her spellbook under the light of her flashlight. Lucille couldn't help but be drawn to her. "What are we looking for?"

"A spell. Something helpful. Anything, really." There was a hint of desperation in Samantha's voice.

Lucille watched the shadows slither around the small cone of light. The book was full of illustrations and lists of spells. Some words Lucille knew, but most rushed by too fast for her to grasp. Then the light on Samantha's phone died.

"Here," Lucille said, pulling out her own phone. She tried to turn on the light, but the phone didn't react to her touch. "It must've broken when I fell." The screen wasn't cracked, though. It just didn't work.

Samantha put a hand on her arm. "I don't think that's it. Nico?" Her breath caught in her throat. "Can you turn on the light, please?"

Of course. They were in a classroom. They didn't have to sit in darkness.

Nico reached over and pressed the switch. The light flickered on. For a moment, Lucille saw each of their frightened faces clearly. Then, the lightbulb burst.

Lucille screamed and covered her head. The banging on the door became more intense.

"That's it!" Samantha sounded exalted. "The bogeyman hides in the shadows. He hates light."

Lucille stared at her in disbelief. The words made sense, but she didn't understand why that would make Samantha happy. "Well, I don't want to burst your bubble, but whatever is in this room—bogeyman or shadowman—has just destroyed our only source of light." It was now clear that he was also blocking their cell phone lights.

Samantha's mood didn't even take a small dive. "And that's where magic comes into play."

"Girls?" Matt's voice was strained. "Could you please hurry? They're breaking through." Though he and Nico pushed against the cupboard, it moved a few centimetres forward with each assault.

Lucille's mind swam. There was the chanting, the loud banging, and a shadow entity in this very room. And magic. Samantha wanted magic from her. "I only know that fireball one."

"Let's start with that."

"O-okay." Lucille had to take several deep breaths to calm her nerves enough to speak the words. "Glo-Globus igneus."

She hadn't tried the spell since that first occurrence, but it manifested in her hand as easily as before. Green fire spilled over her fingers, warm to her touch but not hot.

Immediately, Samantha returned to her book. Meanwhile, Lucille held the fire and looked around anxiously. Something was drawing closer. The shadows around them deepened. They reached for her, crawling over her body. Goosebumps spread over her arms, and she held her breath.

"There!" Samantha pointed at a page. "A light spell. Erit lux. Say, erit lux!"

Lucille didn't know if she still had a voice. "What i-if it d-doesn't work?"

Through the ghastly green fire, Samantha looked like a ghost. "Then we probably die, or—"

"All right. I-I'll do it!" She swallowed. The shadow was smothering her. The fire flickered dangerously. She could no longer hold it. As Matt had done for her before, she closed her fingers.

Darkness enveloped them so heavily, Lucille gasped. A terrible crashing sound came from the left. The cupboard had burst, and haunting rhymes filled the air.

"Everyone, close your eyes!" Samantha shouted, her clear voice like a lifeline to Lucille.

Erit lux. "Erit lux," she whispered. Something flickered. It wasn't enough. The words needed to be stronger. Filled with magic.

"Erit lux!"

Warmth spread from her necklace, and light flooded the room so completely that not a single shadow remained. They fled from her hands under the tables and into the corners, but the light reached them everywhere. It was brighter than daylight, so bright that it hurt

Lucille blinked, her eyes watering. Samantha had her head covered in her arms. Standing in a heap of schoolbooks and splintered wood, Matt had his eyes firmly closed. Nico was precariously balanced against a table, an unknown teenager grabbing his arm. Lucille noticed that they weren't the only bogeyman puppet who had entered the room. Three more were in the process of climbing through, though they stopped now and rubbed their eyes, groaning in pain. None of them were reciting the lines of the children's game.

"It worked," Samantha whispered, now carefully opening her eyes. "It's over."

"At least these ones seem to be all right again," Matt said, squinting against the light.

The teenagers also started to move, raising their arms to shield themselves from the brightness. "Where are we? Is this the school? What the hell is going on?" Their voices reflected panic and confusion.

One boy looked down at the spilled schoolbooks and broken pieces of wood. "Whatever this is, we'd better get out of here. If Renner sees this, we're done for." The group hurriedly left, eager to return to their normal lives.

Nico rubbed his wrist. "They're right. The headmistress will be livid."

"We didn't do this," Matt said, slightly irritated.

"Yeah, but somebody did," Nico stressed. "I don't think the headmistress will accept that the bogeyman destroyed school property. You'd better make sure you have an explanation for her, Sam. I'm sure she'll want to speak to you and Adrian first thing tomorrow morning."

"Who cares about Renner?" Samantha giggled giddily. "Guys, we did it! We defeated the bogeyman! I mean, Lucille did."

"No way!" Slowly, the excitement took hold of Lucille as well. "This was your brilliant idea! We all did it." They would've been lost without the boys holding the door for as long as they did. "We're like... heroes or something."

It had been frightening, but the exhilaration after the fight was worth every minute of her fear. Lucille felt like she could do anything right now. Fight shadow creatures, save the world, stand up to her dad...

Samantha grinned. "Well, there's no doubt about it now that you are a witch."

For a moment, Lucille paused, letting the words sink in and testing their value. She decided she liked them. "Yes. I guess I *am* a witch." What had scared her yesterday was now a world of possibilities.

"While we're at it," Matt said in a low drawl. "Can we please turn off the light again? My eyes really hurt."

"My apologies." Lucille closed her hands, and the light flickered off.

"Thank you," Matt muttered.

While the darkness was almost as blinding after the brightness had gone, Lucille was relieved. It was a normal darkness, no creeping shadows around her, and slowly, their eyes readjusted to it.

Samantha moved to put her book away, then paused. "Would you like to borrow this?" A sliver of uncertainty had slipped back into her voice.

"Yes, please." The words were out before Lucille could stop them. Here she was, barefoot, sweaty, and more exhausted than she had ever been before, and yet, she could've kept going for days, trying to explore her gift. She wanted more of this. The excitement, the thrill, the relief. She hadn't felt this alive in a very long time.

"Let's leave before the police come or something," Nico said. He and Matt had placed the majority of books on nearby tables and moved the remnants of the cupboard and door out of the way.

The four of them left the room and followed the corridor towards the stairs. Lucille picked up her shoes, faintly noting that one of the heels looked in dire need of repair. A worthy sacrifice in her opinion.

At the bottom of the stairs, they ran into Fabian and Rachel. The moment they recognised each other, Fabian gathered Samantha in an enormous hug. "Are you okay?"

"Yes, I am. Are you?"

"Rachel said I was caught," he said and shivered at the memory. "I almost got her as well, but it's all good now. What happened?"

Samantha freed herself from his embrace and hugged Rachel. "A lot. It truly was manifested magic. The bogeyman of the game manifested as some kind of shadow creature. It almost got us, but Lucille defeated him with a light spell." She let go of Rachel and grinned at Lucille. "It was amazing."

Lucille found herself grinning back, adrenaline still rushing through her. "I don't know about you, but I can't wait to do this again. This isn't the only monster Greenvalley has hiding in its shadows, is it?"

Instantly, Fabian paled. "Not the only one? Why would you hope for that?"

"Well, I'm not *hoping* there is another one. Just thought it would be cool to fight more monsters with my magic and Samantha's knowledge and—"

"No, no, no!" Fabian shook his head and backed away. "You know what? I am exhausted. I might sleep forever or so. I better go to bed right away. Wake me when the monsters are gone." He started briskly walking away but then checked with Samantha.

Samantha rolled her eyes and turned to Lucille. "Give him some time. He doesn't respond well to change."

"I don't respond well to life-threatening situations." Fabian put his hands in his pockets, drew up his shoulders, and stalked off.

"Wait!" Samantha ran after him and looped her arm into his. "We need to let your mum out first."

"See? I'll be grounded for life, anyway."

Samantha groaned loud enough for everyone to hear. Then she looked over her shoulder, straight at Lucille, and mouthed a very clear, 'Yes, please.'

Lucille giggled. Oh, yes, Samantha was totally on board.

Next to her, Rachel sighed a little. Lucille couldn't figure out the cause, but her brother picked up on it. He put an arm around his sister and nudged her gently. "Tough luck that he got turned."

"Yeah."

"Well, we better get home and... I honestly don't know. Shower. Recover..." Nico sighed, then tried a wonky smile. "See you guys at school tomorrow."

Rachel waved before taking her brother's arm. The siblings followed Samantha and Fabian out of the school.

Lucille felt a little deflated. They all couldn't get away fast enough. Only Matt remained. "Are you up for another monster hunt?"

He chuckled. "Not tonight." The mirth fled his eyes far too quickly. "But it doesn't look like we'll have a choice."

"What do you mean?" She cocked her head, a tinge of worry creeping through her adrenaline-addled brain.

"Magic rarely manifests itself," he said. "There's more behind this. This was only the beginning."

A shiver ran down Lucille's spine. "You think so?"

He smiled again. "Yeah, but as I said, not tonight. What do you think about a drink or something more?"

Her cheeks filled with heat. She was suddenly reminded of the kiss they'd shared behind the curtain. *Something more.* He couldn't be much clearer, and to her surprise, she wanted it. Wanted to kiss him some more and find out what could grow from this.

Just then, her phone vibrated. It wasn't broken after all. Instead, a message appeared on her screen. A message from her father. *Where are you? I've tried calling you several times.*

A smile crept onto her lips. "Not tonight. I have to check on my family."

"Of course." Matt bowed his head. "Shall I bring you home? To make sure you get there safely."

Once again, her stomach fluttered. "Yes. Yes, I would love that."

Lucille took his arm and started calling her father. Magic, a potential boyfriend, and her father actually caring for her. It looked like her decision to move back to Greenvalley was the best she'd ever made.

Part 2
Bugs & Water

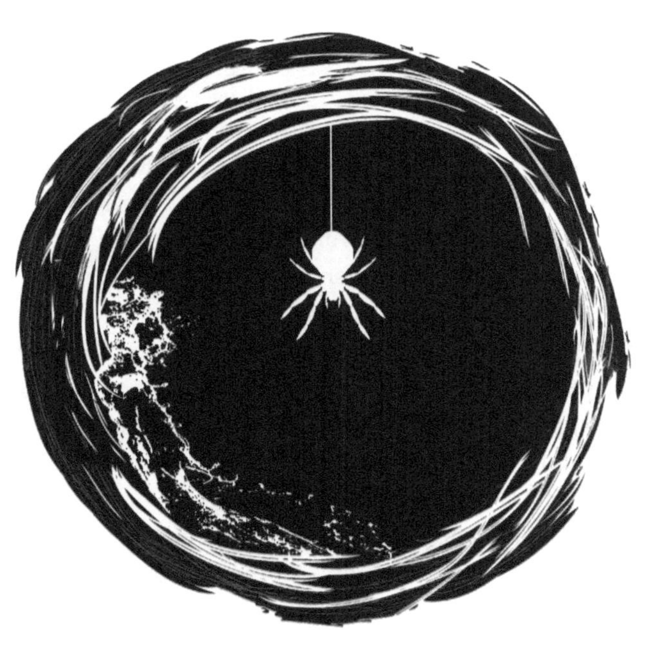

Fabian

After their late-night adventure, the six of them had become fast friends. Matt didn't even seem aware of the fact that a good-looking guy like him was hanging around with the social outcasts, while Samantha and Lucille had become practically inseparable, talking about magic all day long.

Fabian was not a fan.

Since the bogeyman, no other monster had reared its head, but he couldn't shake the memories of it. Magic was real. Real and dangerous, and as much as he tried, he couldn't go back to believing otherwise. It was either 'get with the program' or 'get out'.

And getting out wasn't an option when your best friend had nothing else to talk about.

"Morning! Did your mum's new shipment arrive?" Samantha greeted him when they met at the bridge as usual. "I'm waiting on a new book. It's supposed to be a really good overview of healing potions."

"How would I know? I don't work for my mum." Fabian kicked his pedals and rolled down the bridge on his bike.

Samantha followed, not even complaining. Together, they rode along the river promenade towards school. "Sorry I asked." She kept quiet for almost a minute, then started again. "I've done a little bit of research on the manifested magic thing. You know, because Matt said something must've been behind it."

"Did Matt say that?" Fabian asked and cursed himself for how jealous it sounded. Matt seemed cool enough, but that was exactly the problem. He was perfect in every way Fabian was not. Charming, good-looking, and effortlessly cool. And to top it all off, he was really into magic. Or monsters. Or both.

Samantha didn't remark on his tone, probably because she was too engrossed in the supernatural. "Yes, we had a chat yesterday in our free period, and he's a bit of an expert. But it turns out, he's not really an expert on magic itself, just the magic users."

Fabian sighed. She didn't have to sound so damn excited about it. "Magic users? You mean monsters?"

"Is Lucille a monster?" Samantha asked and laughed when he looked a little sheepish. "Yeah, sure, some magic users are monsters, but there are lots of different kinds of witches, mages, wizards, and specialists."

"And what kind of specialist is Matt?" Fabian grumbled.

This time, Samantha picked up on his mood. "Are you okay?"

"Yeah, I just wish we could talk about something other than magic. Like... have you finished that analysis for German?" Fabian tried to lighten his tone. It wasn't that he liked school. Before the whole magic thing, he would've hated to talk about school, but anything was better than magic right now. "I just don't get these poems. They're all about love."

"But a different kind of love: courtly love." Samantha made the switch effortlessly. "They were more in love with love itself than... well, the actual fulfilment of love."

"Well, that's boring," Fabian grumbled. "I can't really see knights running around, writing odes to love, anyway. Or how that matters to us now."

"It's... whatever." Samantha rode a little faster, leaving him behind. Apparently, his topic change hadn't improved things between them.

Next to him, the Reese was full of choppy waves, fitting his mood perfectly. Fabian didn't try to catch up to Samantha, staying three bike-lengths behind her. Everything that came to his mind was yet another complaint, sure to antagonise Samantha further. At least this way, he didn't have to hear any more about magic for the five minutes it took them to reach school.

As soon as they'd left their bicycles at the bike stands, they met up with the others, and Samantha shared her findings with Matt and Lucille instead, while Fabian and Rachel stood next to them in silence.

Sick of listening to the other's favourite topic, Fabian turned to Rachel. "Where's Nico?"

"Snogging his girlfriend behind the gym," Rachel said in a flat voice. Then she was silent again.

Fabian sighed. Nico had been his only hope of getting out of this magic talk. He tugged on Samantha's arm. "Can we go to Physics? If we're late, Herbert will give me a zero for oral participation."

"We have ten more minutes," Samantha said, slightly annoyed.

"You're not the one that's getting picked on by Herbert." At least not as much as he was.

Samantha rolled her eyes, but she turned around and started walking towards the science building. "You know you could tell Mr Zobel about it…"

"And get bad grades all year around?"

She groaned. "He can't actually do that. Not if you ace the exams and everything."

"Yeah, I'm not perfect like that," Fabian answered snidely. Acing exams was not exactly his speciality.

"I didn't say you need to be perfect. I'm saying that if your performance is good, it doesn't matter whether he holds a grudge against you or not. So, just ignore him and focus on the curriculum."

"Which I can't really do if I ignore him."

While Fabian kept arguing, the little dispute helped to lift his mood. This was his Samantha, berating him for not taking school seriously enough, being all reason to his ridiculous whining. Bickering was their love language, not this magic thing.

Physics turned out even worse than Fabian had expected. As soon as Mr Herbert entered the room, his eyes were fixed on Fabian.

"I want your report, Bendtfeld!" Mr Herbert bellowed. "Now."

Fabian sighed. There were only eight people in this course, and despite it being only week three, it was the second time he'd been asked to hand in the reports they had to write for each class experiment.

"And yours too, Kollmer, so I can see how much he copied from you."

Fabian ground his teeth as he got to his feet, collecting both his and Samantha's reports. She shot him an apologetic look. Last time they'd done their reports together, which must've shown. This time, the difference couldn't be more obvious. Three pages of neat description and a schematic drawing from Samantha, and half a page of scribbles with a drawing that almost jumped off the page in its realism from him. Not very scientific.

Mr Herbert, who was more than a head shorter than Fabian, clicked his tongue. "That's all?"

"That's all." Fabian turned around, focusing on his breathing. Deep breath in. Deep breath out.

"Well, that makes my job easier."

As Fabian took his seat, Mr Herbert took out a red pen and scribbled down a short note. Fabian stared at him. Sure, he may not have filled five pages, but he'd taken notes and wrote down the results and conclusion. He deserved more than zero points for that.

Under the table, he clenched his fists while Mr Herbert continued to use his report as a negative example of how they should write up their experiments. He closed by addressing him directly. "I have no idea why I expected more from you. All you want to learn is how to take a car apart. You don't need to major in Physics for that."

"Just because my dad is a mechanic doesn't mean I want to be one!" Fabian spoke up, unable to suffer this much injustice. "I want—"

"What are we doing today?" Samantha asked, while kicking him under the table.

The rest of the class looked up hopefully. No one enjoyed watching the two of them go head-to-head. But Mr Herbert only changed his target. "Kollmer, in this class, we raise our hands before we speak."

"Uhm..." Samantha raised her hand meekly. "I'm sorry."

"Now keep your mouth shut unless you have something valuable to add to our lesson."

It was one thing for Mr Herbert to come down hard on Fabian; that he took out his frustrations on Samantha was too much to bear. He jumped up and slammed his hands on the table. "She didn't do anything wrong! You're the one who's keeping us from learning anything."

"Fabian..." Samantha sounded as if she was about to throw up.

Mr Herbert's face darkened. "Looks like you're going to visit the director."

Fabian was so angry he couldn't even grasp the threat. "Would love to. I'm sure she would like to be made aware of any teachers who abuse their power and—"

Out of the blue, the ceiling above Mr Herbert cracked, and a surge of water drenched the teacher from head to toe. Shivering and in shock, he cursed the handymen, then pointed at Fabian. "See? This is what happens when you think school is nothing but a joke!"

A second pipe burst. Some of the other students couldn't help laughing. Others, like Rachel, were staring at their wet teacher in shock. Fabian sat down, crossed his arms, and glared at the window, clenching his jaw.

Samantha jumped up to grab a towel from the equipment cupboard. "Here's a towel. I'll see if I can find—"

"You are staying right where you are!" Mr Herbert was so enraged, spittle was flying.

A third surge of water washed over him, splashing Samantha as well. The whole room stood under water now. Amusement had changed to panic as people scrambled to save their bags.

"Everyone out! Out!" Mr Herbert screamed.

The students left only too gladly. Outside, they gathered in small groups to chat about the weird mishap. Fabian was still fuming.

"This is so weird," Rachel said. "How can three pipes burst at once?"

"Because the builders did a shitty job or something," Fabian snapped. "Probably because they had to take Physics with Herbert."

Rachel lowered her head, but Samantha was only just starting. "The pipes were only done two or three years ago." Her wet T-shirt clung to her skin, but she didn't even seem to notice.

"So?" Fabian asked, not interested in discussing a burst pipe after everything else that had gone down.

"Well, I'm just thinking that if it was a construction issue, we would have seen the leak? The ceiling boards are just a little thicker than cardboard. A leaking pipe would've left a wet spot. And besides, once the first broke, the pressure would've been released. There's no way all three can burst like that."

Fabian groaned. "Fine, Little Miss Know-It-All, what's your explanation then?" Samantha swallowed. He'd gone beyond bickering now, but he truly wasn't interested in why the stupid pipes had burst.

"Well," she said extremely carefully. "You were pretty angry with Mr Herbert, and the pipes burst every time he said something that pushed you over the edge. Or you pushed yourself."

Snorting, Fabian took up walking back and forth. "Right, these are magical pipes, who are holding a grudge against Herby as well. I bet he tightens their outlets too much or—"

"No, you're the one that's magical!" Samantha snapped at him.

Fabian stared at her, mouth hanging open. Then the words sank under his skin and fed into his rage. "You're blaming me for a burst pipe? Okay, listen up, Sam! The pipes were a perfectly normal accident in a perfectly normal world." He raised his hands because words weren't enough to stress this point. "I certainly didn't establish some magic link with the pipes or mumble a spell while I stood up for you to Mr Herbert. Magic is real. Awesome! Doesn't mean the whole world revolves around it. Enough is enough! Just because you're obsessed with it doesn't mean everyone else is!"

Samantha blinked, then turned away to brush a strand of hair out of her face. Fabian had seen this gesture enough to know she was fighting back tears. Rachel was looking back and forth between the two of them. She seemed to have something to say, but her mouth stayed shut.

Before Fabian could even attempt to fix this, Mr Herbert came out of the room, still drenching wet. "I spoke with the school office. We'll continue our lesson in U142. I'll meet you all there in five minutes."

Samantha was the first to set off walking.

Samantha didn't speak with him for the rest of the day, leaving Fabian to stew in his own thoughts. The anger wouldn't subside, though there were no more burst pipes. By the end of the day, he was even more convinced he'd been right. Samantha *was* obsessed now that her wildest dreams had partially come true, but that didn't mean magic was everywhere. And certainly not in him.

When they all met up at the school gate, Samantha gave him one glaring eyeroll before hooking her arm with Lucille's. "Hey, what do you think about visiting my grandma today? She can tell you about magic and maybe some stories about your grandmother."

"Sounds good to me," Lucille said, while Fabian took a deep breath through his nose.

Not to be outdone, he turned to the only other guy present, Matt. "Do you have plans, or can I hang out at your place for a bit?"

Matt frowned as if he'd asked him whether they should go on a date. As Fabian thought about it, that would've probably been less confusing to Matt, since he seemed to flirt with pretty much anyone. "Uhm... sure."

With a smug smile, Fabian turned to Samantha, but she and Lucille were already walking away, chatting excitedly about magic. Belatedly, he noted that he'd completely forgotten about Rachel. "If you want..."

She sighed. "It's alright. I probably have to go grocery shopping anyway if I want to eat anything other than wine."

Unsure of what to say to that, Fabian shrugged. "Okay. See you Monday then." He turned to Matt. "Where do you live?"

"Right next to the zoo." Matt shuddered slightly. "I usually take the bus, but we can walk if you want to get your bike."

"No, that's fine. I can leave the bike here and pick it up later, or tomorrow." Fabian would probably regret the decision, but the whole thing was awkward enough without them going for a stroll. And besides, Samantha was at the bike stand.

Even so, the trip on the bus was hard to endure. Matt didn't say a word, and Fabian couldn't think of anything to talk about either. He knew nothing about Matt apart from the fact he fought monsters on a regular basis. With a sword. The only thing that wasn't dangerous territory to venture into was commenting on the looks Matt got from the other passengers—mostly younger girls, who giggled and whispered excitedly. But that was yet another area Fabian had little expertise in. And so they stayed silent until it was time to get off.

Fabian's neighbours were all living in little houses with gardens, some larger, some smaller. In this part of town, the buildings were higher and housed several families, couples, or singles. Matt's flat was up on the fourth floor. He hadn't lied when he mentioned the proximity to Greenvalley's small forest zoo. From the windows, one could look straight down into the deer enclosure.

The flat Matt shared with his father was tiny. The bathroom was right next to the corridor, which led straight into a living room with a small balcony. The kitchen was through one door. Two other doors must've led to the bedrooms, but Matt never brought Fabian there.

Instead, he pointed to the dining table. "Make yourself comfortable. Do you want something to drink?" The words came out awkwardly, as if he wasn't used to hosting visitors. At least none he didn't plan to sleep with.

Fabian nodded, overwhelmed by curiosity. "Some water would be nice."

"Okay." Matt dropped his bag near one of the doors, then vanished into the kitchen.

Meanwhile, Fabian took a seat and looked around to see if he could spot the sword or other obscure things. Everything seemed surprisingly normal. Two paintings adorned the wall, the TV was on the small side, and the table was covered in a pile of papers, a forgotten cup of coffee, and a few letters addressed to Matt's father.

"Your dad is René Traidous?" Fabian asked when Matt set down two cups of water in front of them.

Matt took a seat opposite him. "Yes, why?"

Fabian chuckled inadvertently. The two images in his head didn't fit together at all. "He was our first to third-grade teacher in elementary school." René Traidous had been a kind and gentle, nurturing man. They had all loved him. Matt, on the other hand, was all cool and tough, and the only thing he nurtured seemed to be a healthy sex life. Fabian had to tell Samantha about this... but then he remembered that she wasn't talking to him at the moment.

"Do you want to help him out?" Matt asked.

"Help him out with what?"

With a shrug, Matt explained, "Apparently, he's taking his class to the zoo next week and doesn't have enough parent helpers. He asked me whether I could help and offered to clear it with the school. Would be next Tuesday."

Tuesday was when they'd be having their next Physics class. But herding first-graders? Then again, Fabian liked going to the zoo. He knew most of the animals by name and had worked there for two summers. "Can I think about it?"

"Sure. Maybe Sam..."

"I said *I'll* think about it!" Fabian snapped. Immediately, heat rose to his cheeks. He grabbed the glass in front of him with both hands but didn't drink it. Instead, he stared at the resettling surface, suddenly reminded of the Physics lecture. How had those water pipes burst?

After a while, Matt began drumming against the table, seemingly bored out of his mind.

"Can you stop that?"

Matt put his hands flat on the table and puffed out some air. When another minute of silence had passed, he asked, "Is this some kind of ritual, or..."

Fabian raised his gaze. He'd been mesmerised by the way the water caught the light. "A ritual?"

"This whole sitting together in silence, staring at our drinks?" It almost sounded as if he wanted an honest answer to that.

Annoyed, Fabian pushed his chair back to get up. This had been a terrible mistake. "Just forget it."

"Can't you just tell me what you want from me?" Matt seemed desperate now.

"I don't want—" Fabian sat back down again. It was time to bite the bullet. Matt was a supposed expert in this, after all. "Today, in Physics, three water pipes burst in quick succession. I was pretty angry at the time. Mr Herbert, our teacher, hates me. It's completely out of line. Apparently, my dad..." His rambling led Matt to empty his glass of water in one gulp. "Sorry. It's... the thing is, Sam said the burst pipes were my fault, and I'm pretty sure she's lost her mind."

"And what exactly do you want from me now?"

Fabian sighed. This bad idea was getting worse and worse. He was obviously keeping Matt from something important—or anything really. "Well, I thought, since you know your way around magic... because Sam thinks it was magic. That's nonsense, right?"

"I wasn't there," Matt said, snorting a little. "If Sam thinks it was magic, she's probably right. She's big on the theory, isn't she?"

Annoyed, Fabian took a sip of water. "Just because she swallows books whole doesn't mean she's always right. If she had her way, she would declare the entire world magical."

"Well, technically, it is."

Fabian ignored him. "But this time, she's gone too far. I'm not a witch or a mage or whatever!"

"Okay."

"Okay!" Fabian imitated his voice. "Okay doesn't help me!"

Matt didn't react to his outburst. Instead, he took his empty glass and held it up in the air. Only, the glass was no longer empty. It was filling with water, almost spilling over the top in the process. "Thanks for that."

"Thanks? I didn't do that!" Fabian was beginning to feel faint.

A raised eyebrow was Matt's answer. "Sure, the glass just decided to fill itself."

Fabian slid down the chair, making himself as small as possible. Dread was filling his stomach. This couldn't possibly be happening. "Well... at least, you can't say you haven't been there now."

Amusement flickered across Matt's face. "I think Sam is right. There are some people who cause magical eruptions if they're agitated."

"And you think I could be someone like that?" Bile was rising in Fabian's throat, and he felt like he'd throw up any moment.

Matt regarded the mysteriously refilled glass. "I'd say chances are good you are."

Samantha

"Sometimes, I don't even know why I'm friends with him. He's so stubborn and childish." Samantha groaned.

They'd reached the beginning of the forest path that led up to her grandmother's house. Lucille was struggling a bit with the soft ground and her heels, but commiserated in fashion. "I guess he just has to come to terms with it on his own. Men are like that."

"If you say so." Samantha enjoyed this one-on-one time with her. While she loved Rachel to bits, talking about boys wasn't easy. Or rather, talking about Fabian had been the problem. It had taken Samantha years to find out why, and knowing that Rachel was secretly in love with Fabian hadn't made those talks any easier. "You seem to have some experience with relationships?" she asked carefully.

Lucille laughed. "A little bird... well, a pretty annoying bird, sang about you having some experience as well. Cheryl said Fabian is your ex-boyfriend or something?"

"Ugh." Samantha groaned. "Piece of advice. Don't listen to anything Cheryl says. I mean, yeah, she's right this time, but she's nothing but a nasty piece of work."

"I got as much," Lucille assured her. "Believe me, I know these types of girls. They're a dime a dozen at Rosemary. That school breeds them. Cheryl would fit right in." Then her eyes gleamed. "But back to you and Fabian. You are best friends and exes. What's the deal there?"

Samantha sighed. 'It's complicated,' would have been the most fitting answer. "Always best friends. Our fathers were best friends in high school. They now run a workshop together. We're like the second-generation friends, and of course, because we are of the opposite gender, we need to get married." She rolled her eyes hard. Sometimes, she thought the break-up had hit her dad harder than it had her.

"It was mostly curiosity," she admitted. "And a sense of, if everyone is saying you two belong together, why not give this a go?" It hadn't all been bad. In fact, they wouldn't have stayed together for almost three years if there hadn't also been some very fond memories. "It was sweet, but..." She fixed a curl behind her ear. "But then I found out about Rachel's feelings for him."

"Rachel?" Lucille sounded surprised, as if she had only just remembered the other girl's existence. "Is this a juicy sort of love triangle?"

Samantha burst into giggles. "No, sadly not. You must have noticed already that Rachel keeps her feelings very close to her heart. I wouldn't have known if Nico hadn't had a slip-up. Anyway, Fabian and I were still together, but when I found out about Rachel's feelings, I started questioning everything. She's really in love with him, and I... I felt comfortable. Like being with a friend." And that had been the end of everything.

"More like friends with benefits," Lucille joked, and Samantha chuckled again.

"No, I couldn't do that after I'd already broken his heart." Samantha had assumed that he had come to the same realisation that they worked far better as friends than lovers. But Fabian's feelings for her had been real, and she had hurt him with her rejection. He hadn't talked to her for over a month then, just like he wasn't talking to her now.

She shook her head. "Enough of that. What is with you and Matt?" They were almost at her grandmother's place, so there wasn't much time.

Lucille waved the question off. "I have no idea. After our fight with the bogeyman, I thought there would be something, but he hasn't made any advances. Instead, I constantly see him flirting with other people. I guess he only kissed me to stop me from panicking."

"He kissed you?" The very notion excited Samantha. "How was it?"

Now, Lucille grinned wildly. "Really, really good. I wish I could kiss him again."

Samantha nudged her side. "Then do it. Don't wait around for him! Ask him out on a date."

Giggling, Lucille nodded. "Maybe I will." Then she gasped in delight. "I've got an idea. What about I invite the lot of you over to my villa? We can label it fighting training. You know, just in case there are more monsters around, and then I offer Matt the private tour."

"Be careful that it doesn't get too private." Samantha had to giggle as well.

"I wouldn't exactly mind," Lucille said with a coquettish grin. But her eyes widened, all thoughts of boys forgotten. "Is that it?"

Between the trees, a little house had appeared. It was a simple cottage build. There was only one level with a few rooms, an attic, and a cellar to explore. Half the house was covered in climbing vines, some of which were blooming even this late in September. An equally flourishing garden full of herbs and vegetables surrounded the house. In Samantha's opinion, it was the prettiest house in Greenvalley.

"This is it!" she declared proudly, then leaned her bike against the wall. "Come, I think I can see Granny in the garden."

They found her between the elderflower bushes and the small but sweet grape-bearing vines she was harvesting. Samantha's grandmother might have had a hair full of grey, but she was fitter than many half her age. When she heard the two of them approaching, she turned and smiled warmly. "Hello dear, this is a nice surprise."

Samantha went to her and gave her a hug. "It's only been a week or so. Do you remember me telling you about Lucille? This is her. Lucille, this is my granny, Elda."

"My gosh." Elda straightened her back and passed the bowl of grapes to Samantha, who continued the work without being asked to. "You look just like your grandmother."

Lucille swallowed. "So, you were really friends with her? Is it true that she was a witch?"

"One of the best," Elda said, and Samantha knew she couldn't have found much better words. Lucille was already tearing up. "Come on, let's leave the grapes. I've baked some cookies and cut some fresh mint. Let's have some tea and talk."

The inside was even better than the outside, in Samantha's opinion. There was no television, not even a radio in the living room. Instead, bookshelves stretched up to the ceiling, filled from left to right with books, old and new, small and large. It was practically Samantha's dream house.

"Are these all spellbooks?" Lucille asked, her eyes wide in wonder.

"Most of them. Some are monster manuals, and a few are diaries and essays from other mages. Eric, Cecille, Albert, and I gathered a lot of them," Elda explained.

Lucille stared at her in surprise. "Albert? Our butler is part of this, too?"

Elda chuckled. "He's no longer active, but he's been a friend of Cecille's for a long time. He stopped when... when she died."

At the mention of Cecille's death, Samantha began gnashing her teeth. She hadn't yet found a way to tell Lucille how her beloved grandmother had died. "Lucille has no idea what happened," she said softly.

"Oh dear. Well, that's a story best told with tea and cookies. Make yourself comfortable. I'll be back in a minute." She left the room to go into the kitchen.

Lucille raised her eyebrows at Samantha, but when Samantha avoided her gaze, she was quickly distracted by the books again. "This is unbelievable. So many spellbooks, monster manuals... You must've read them all."

"I wish, but... not enough time!" Samantha moved her finger across the familiar backs. "I like the theoretical ones best, the ones that explain magic or the world. Did you know, for example, that magic flows around the world in rivers?"

Lucille laughed. "I know nothing. Rivers of magic?"

Slightly embarrassed, Samantha nodded. Fabian had never wanted to talk about these kinds of things. And while Rachel listened to her, she rarely added her opinion. The only person she had shared her passion with was her grandmother, whom she loved to bits. It was weird to let someone else in. Weird and exciting. "Yes. But they're invisible, that's what makes it so hard to prove. My grandmother can see them. She says they spring from the forest and then flow through the town."

"You mean the very spring of magic they celebrate in the town square?" Lucille guessed.

"Yes, exactly. And apparently, it occasionally attracts monsters."

"Like the bogeyman?"

Samantha wasn't sure. There were still so many questions about that. "I don't know. My grandmother said there was a protective barrier around town, so it should've been safe, but somehow..."

"Somehow, it wasn't." Lucille seemed to readily accept the lack of explanation. She was drawn again towards the shelves and picked a book at random. "*The Circle of Magic.* What's that?"

"Huh?" Samantha couldn't remember seeing that book before, but then again, there were a lot of books she hadn't read.

The book was quite thick and bound in leather, with the title imprinted with gold leaf. Lucille set it down carefully on the table, and Samantha moved closer to study it.

"It's interesting you've picked this particular book from the lot of them." Elda was back, carrying a tray with cups and biscuits.

Samantha jumped up to help her grandmother set the table. The smell of fresh peppermint filled the air. When she sat down again, she noticed something white between the pages of the book. "What is this?"

Lucille flicked the book open to the page and found a handkerchief. 'C.C.' was stitched into the corner. When she picked it up, a gasp escaped her. Hidden by the handkerchief was a sketch of the very necklace Lucille was wearing.

"Cecille was incredibly proud to have owned an Emblem of Power," Elda said in a soft voice.

The phrase was entirely unfamiliar to Samantha. "What is it?"

"A powerful and ancient artefact. Some say that the fate of the world will forever be changed when the Circle of Magic is closed. The Circle consists of six emblems."

Lucille touched the necklace. Her back was straight as a board. Samantha recognised the body language from school. This was a boundary Lucille wasn't quite ready to cross yet. "This necklace is an ancient artefact? Are you sure?"

Elda nodded and put a comforting hand on Lucille's arm. "It is called the Nadellyan's Tears, and it has been in the hands of your grandmother's family for centuries, always handed down from witch to witch. Once we found this book, Cecille was obsessed with the emblems. But we never found a trace of the others."

Meanwhile, Samantha was drawn to the text. Aloud, she read, "From the hottest flames and the most precious mountain jewels, the Nadellyan crafted a necklace to gift to King Morrigan, so he could save his people. It was the Nadellyan's last gift to the world, holding inside it the red flame of creation. As the Emblem of Trust, it lends power to its bearer when it is most needed."

"What does that mean?" Lucille whispered, as if she was too afraid to raise her voice in the presence of such powerful words.

Samantha's grandmother didn't show the same reverence. In a chatty tone, she explained, "A lot of what's inside this book are fragments. Oral histories and wisdoms from all kinds of cultures. To bring them all together must have taken decades, if not centuries."

Out of curiosity, Samantha checked the title page. "The Seer. Who's that? Did you ever meet them?"

Her grandmother hesitated. "I'm not sure. There are a lot of stories and rumours."

"Well, I doubt they're still alive. This must've been their life's work." Though Lucille was still in awe, she seemed overwhelmed by all this extra information. She pushed the book aside, leaving it to Samantha's curious hands. "You wanted to tell me about my grandmother."

A sad smile slipped onto Elda's lips. "Yes, of course, my dear. First, you must know that your family—not the de Cerques, but Cecille's ancestors—were one of the first families who settled in Greenvalley. Cecille was taught by her mother, as her mother was taught by hers. Not like me, who was an absolute wild child when it came to magic." She chuckled lowly. "We met when we were about the same age as you two are now. My parents were seasonal workers, newcomers in this town. I had all this wild magic, while she came from a long line of witches and had to deal with all the expectations that it entailed.

"We became friends in an instant. She taught me about the theory of magic, and I taught her my ways. Together, we hunted monsters of all kinds. And yes, Albert came along, though he was more of the stock taker, librarian type. And he was the one who got a job at the de Cerques before your grandmother met your grandfather."

As her grandmother told her story, Samantha sifted through the book. It was really a collection of fragments and interpretations, all handwritten and not all by the same writer. Pages and pages were filled with legends and stories from countries and people Samantha had never heard of.

"And I met Eric, a demon hunter. He was so cocky." Elda laughed. "Determined to show us girls how it was really done. Of course, I ended up saving him that night. Sadly, he died when Ben—that's Samantha's father—was only fifteen. And as for your grandmother, she wanted to put an end to the frequent attacks. Twelve years ago, she summoned a demon from Hell, one of the Seven, to suggest a truce, but he wouldn't even hear her out."

Samantha could hear Lucille sniffle a little and handed her the handkerchief. Her own eyes were currently stuck on the sketches and descriptions of the six Emblems of Power. Lucille's necklace was a 1:1 replica, but some of the other sketches as much a guess as the text. The Flowers from Freya's Gardens didn't even have a depiction. Then she turned the page.

"Oh my gosh, Lucille!" She tugged at her friend's sleeve. "Check this out! Doesn't that look exactly like the sword Matt carried at school?"

'The Sword of Amain' was as detailed as the necklace. She hadn't got a good look at Matt's sword since it had been dark, but it was very much like this one. There was a crystal ball at the top of the handle, and the parry bar wasn't flat but looked like stylised wings. Both handle and blade were engraved with runes. It looked magnificent on the page.

"It does look a lot like his," Lucille admitted.

Meanwhile, Elda had paled. "You've seen the Sword of the Gods?"

"The Sword of the Gods?" Samantha checked the page, and sure enough, there was a plethora of names for the sword. Its history was surprisingly well-tracked through time.

"The sword that split the world," her grandmother mumbled.

Lucille burst out laughing, but it was a nervous sound. "I'm sure it's not that, just a cheap replica. I don't even really think it looked that similar. Wasn't the handle grey instead of blue? How would Matt get his hands on a divine sword, anyway?"

How would Matt get his hands on any kind of sword? Samantha bit her lip. This couldn't be an accident. The whole thing with Lucille, and now Matt as well. And then the bogeyman appearance. She had a sudden urge to check who else was new at school this year.

Her grandmother was still mumbling. "Two Emblems of Power at the same time, at the same place..."

"Can I take a picture of these pages?" Samantha asked, pulling out her smartphone. "Then we can show them to Matt." She was convinced that this was one of the books her grandmother wouldn't let out of her sight.

The question seemed to have broken the spell. Elda shook her head. "No, of course not. Go ahead. This Matt... he's a friend of yours?"

Lucille blushed instantly. "Hopefully a little more. This tea is really good, by the way." Then she nudged Samantha with her elbow. "How long did you want to stay?"

It was clear that she'd heard enough for one day and was looking for a way out, but there was something else Samantha wanted to investigate. If only she were brave enough to suggest it. She turned the pages back to the necklace. "It says here that the necklace strengthens the bearer's powers. I assume that's why you've suddenly discovered your magical powers. They must've been there all along, but the necklace gave you a jump start."

"I'll clean up the dishes," Elda said, swiftly getting to her feet.

Samantha was grateful for the privacy. This might go very wrong or end up embarrassing. "Anyway, I thought that maybe... I don't want it permanently, but I thought if it could kick-start my powers..." Samantha bit her lip. She didn't even know whether she had some. As immersed as she'd been in magic and visiting her grandmother countless times, they surely would've shown by now. "It probably doesn't work, anyway."

"You don't know if you haven't tried it," Lucille said. Graciously, she took the necklace off and handed it to her.

The silver was warm in Samantha's hand, and she immediately thought of the fires it had been forged in. Not that she had any idea who the Nadellyan or even King Morrigan was.

"Do you have a spell in mind?"

She *did*. Holding the necklace in one hand, she looked at the pot plant near the window. Her heart beat at double speed, and her breath caught in her throat. The hand around the necklace was turning sweaty. At last, she managed to force the word from her lips. "Incresco."

Nothing happened.

Samantha swallowed down the tears that sprung to her eyes and forced herself to breathe in and out. She was probably too nervous. Calmer now, she said, "Incresco."

Again, nothing.

"Perhaps you need to actually wear it. Come on, I'll help you put it on." Lucille took the necklace from Samantha's fingers and gently draped it around her neck. "Gosh, you've got so much hair!"

Blinking furiously, Samantha held up her locks. Perhaps Lucille was right, and magic was like electric circuits. The necklace was a piece of the *Circle* of Magic after all.

The rubies lay heavy against her collarbone. They were still warm. It took Samantha a while to calm her breathing enough to try again. "Incresco," she whispered.

And still, nothing happened.

"Incresco. Incresco. Erit lux. In..." Her pulse raced again. Suddenly, the necklace felt constricting. She couldn't get enough air. Fumbling, she reached for the latch, but couldn't find it. "Take it off! Take it off!"

Lucille set to work quickly, pulling the stones away from her. Samantha gasped for air. Her eyes burned, and even though she pressed them shut as tight as she could, a few tears squeezed out and rolled down her cheek. Samantha shuddered. She couldn't do magic. Not even with a mythical, ancient, powerful artifact.

"Are you okay?" Lucille asked.

Their friendship was too new for them to be comfortable with each other's darkness. Breaking down was not an option. Samantha wiped her cheeks, took a deep breath, and put on a smile. "Yes, don't worry about it. It would have been too easy."

Lucille looked at her with pity. She hadn't even known about magic until three weeks ago but already had everything Samantha had ever dreamed of. "I'm sorry."

"Don't be! It was nonsense anyway. The necklace obviously belongs to you and you alone. And eventually, your daughter, or..." Just the thought of all the future witches was enough to call back the tears. She jumped up. "Let me show you something else."

Before Lucille could even put the necklace back on, Samantha rushed out of the room. In the corridor, she took a few shaky breaths, then Lucille was there, her forehead still creased.

"It's over here. My grandma's witch room." Her favourite room in the house.

Inside was a big, black, cast-iron cauldron. The walls were full of dried herbs, and there was a working bench with several knives and a pestle and mortar. Above it, a shelf was bent under jars and potion bottles. On the left, an array of weapons hung behind locked doors: her grandfather's tools.

"Woah!" Lucille's eyes widened, her mouth hanging open. "This is what a witch's lair really looks like, huh?"

"It's not a lair," Samantha said, "just the workshop. I work a lot here." She pointed at the cauldron. "Potions. See, I don't need to learn spells. I can brew potions." That had to be worth something, didn't it? If only she could convince herself of it. "All you need are some magical ingredients—and you have no idea how many everyday plants have magical attributes. Anyway, follow the recipes and voilà!" She picked up one of the fragile bottles. "Magic in a bottle."

Lucille's eyes were fixed on the slightly purplish liquid inside the bottle. "What does this one do?"

"It's like a fertiliser, but on speed. One drop is enough to sustain plants. A few more and they explode! I mean, they grow enormous and then die because they can't sustain that size for more than a few days."

Bright laughter rang through the room. "Why do you want to learn spells if you can do that?"

Samantha had intended this whole excursion into the witch room to distract herself from her failed attempt at doing real magic, but the innocent question tore the wound open once more. In a flat voice, she answered, "Because this isn't really magic. It's just like chemistry or cooking, only with magical recipes and ingredients. Anyone could do that. Even someone who doesn't believe in magic."

The pity returned to Lucille's eyes. "I think this is fabulous. And I seriously doubt that just anyone can do this."

Samantha forced herself to smile. "Maybe not. Thanks. You know, I make some of these for Caroline's shop. Nothing really potent, just drops that make you feel a little better on a bad day or stave off colds. Small things like that."

"Sounds amazingly helpful to me," Lucille stressed. Then she checked her watch. "I have to go, unfortunately—my father invited us to dinner—but I'll call you tomorrow, and your grandma will have to let me visit again someday. I have so many—"

She'd been on her way out when she almost bumped into Elda. "There you are." Elda gave Lucille three small books. "I found these. They were Cecille's notes from her training. They might help you understand your magic a little better."

Samantha's stomach twisted. Jealousy wasn't pretty, but she couldn't help herself. The gnawing pain inside her remained. She would never receive witch training, would never learn what real magic felt like.

Nevertheless, she waved at Lucille and smiled until her new friend was swallowed by the forest. Only then did she let out a huge sigh.

"I know, darling," her grandmother said, putting an arm around her. "What works for the de Cerques doesn't always work for us."

"Nothing works for me." Samantha wiped her cheeks once again, annoyed at how much it still affected her. She thought she'd come to terms with her inability to do magic, but then Lucille had appeared, and everything was coming so easily to her friend. "It isn't fair."

"Magic rarely is." Elda turned her away from the door and led her back into the living room. "But that doesn't mean you can't do your part in protecting this city. And right now, I could use a little help."

Confused, Samantha sat down. "What do you mean?"

Elda looked at the shelves and picked out a few books. "Your encounter with the bogeyman. It's been on my mind ever since."

"Matt said magic wouldn't do that without someone shaping it. Or at least giving it a little push." The mystery around the bogeyman was helping a little to bury the nasty feelings of envy.

"He seems to be an odd one, this Matt," Elda said, her brow wrinkling. "Perhaps you could convince him to visit me as well?"

"Maybe." Samantha doubted Matt would be interested in spending an afternoon with her grandmother when he could go on dates instead.

Her grandmother sighed. "But yes, I agree with him. There's something you need to be aware of." The ominous tone settled like a weighted blanket on Samantha's shoulders. "Before Cecille died, we erected a magical barrier around our town. One that would protect us from monsters and demons. It's held all this time."

Samantha could taste the following words on the tip of her tongue.

"Someone or something tore it down the night before the bogeyman appeared."

Fabian

It was Saturday morning, and Fabian was already awake. Usually, there would've been a text from Samantha last night or in the morning to make plans for the weekend. Instead, there was silence. And all because of the accident with the water.

He hated fighting with her. Squabbling, yes. But outright fighting with nasty words and tears and prolonged silences? Those things made his stomach ache and his sleep a mess.

Because of it, he was awake early on a Saturday morning instead of sleeping in. In fact, he felt as if he'd only slept in small bursts, if at all. Now, the sun shone brightly, promising a perfect day to spend outside. A perfect day he would have to spend on his own, fretting about what had happened yesterday.

"You look like you need to go back to bed," his mother greeted him when he shuffled into the kitchen. Since his father worked at the garage on Saturday mornings, there was no big breakfast. His mum was sitting alone at the kitchen table with a cup of coffee in her hand and Merle on her lap. "There's coffee over there."

Fabian poured himself a cup, thankful it was coffee and not water. Then he sat down next to her. Promptly, Merle decided to switch laps and jump onto his. "Didn't you get enough attention over there?"

"Your fingers are fresh," his mum joked, to which Fabian snorted. "Everything okay?"

Despite his words, he sank his fingers into the cat's fur and scratched her behind the ears. The soft purr that resulted improved Fabian's mood a little. "Yeah..."

"Let me guess. You're fighting with Sam?" His mother chuckled. She knew him that well.

Fabian sighed. "She said some things... I said some things. It's really stupid." The magic was at fault. His magic. "So, Mum..."

"Yes?"

"You're really a witch?" The whole idea still seemed foreign to him.

"Not a very strong one, but yes." She smiled again. "What do you want me to tell you?"

There was only one thing he really needed to learn more about, but he had no idea whether his mother could help him. Considering she was the only one talking to him right now, he thought he'd better give it a shot. "Mum, is it true that there are some people who do magic when they have a lot of feelings? Like, for example, by bursting water pipes?"

Her cup fell and coffee spilled over the table. His mother took a quick breath before she stood up and got a cloth to wipe the spill away.

Fabian began regretting he'd asked her. "That bad?" Of course, it would be bad. Entirely uncontrollable magic outbursts were bad.

His mother paused. "I thought you'd lost all that."

Now he was confused. "Lost it?"

"Don't you remember? You loved playing with water as a child."

Fabian began to feel heady again. He didn't want to remember that, but images from his childhood came to him, no matter how much he pushed them away. "I played with water pistols and bowls or in the pool." Most of the memories were exactly that. He could easily find an explanation for the water. Nothing unusual there.

"Hmm." His mum sat back down. "Well, I remember you giving your water pistol away to Sammy because you didn't need it." Lost in memory, she smiled inwardly. Then she sighed again. "But you *do* remember the fever you had when you were about ten or so?"

"Was that the one where I had to spend three weeks in hospital?" Fabian couldn't remember much of that time. But he still had the 'Get well' card Samantha had made for him.

His mum nodded, her face still sombre. "Yes, it was quite worrying. The doctors had no idea what caused it, and magic didn't help. We almost lost you, but you pulled through. Afterwards, the water was gone. I thought the fever had burnt it out of you, or something like that." She shook her head as if to dispel the memories. "Anyway. So, it's back now?"

"Apparently?" Fabian still had no idea how to feel about it. As fun as those childhood memories sounded, he'd rather not have magic erupting around him every time he was upset. "But only when I'm angry."

That made his mother frown. "It is true that elemental magic is tied to emotions to some extent. Other mothers struggle when their children throw a tantrum in the supermarket. I always had to take a change of clothes for both of us when we went for a walk along the river." She chuckled. "But it didn't happen every time, and soon you were pretty much in control of it. Most of the time, you were quite relaxed when you played with water." She shrugged her shoulders. "Maybe you're out of shape. It'll come back."

Fabian groaned. He didn't want it to come back. He wanted it to go away. "I don't want to be a witch or witcher or whatever."

"It's called an elemental mage," his mother said with a smile. "The ones I read about couldn't do any other kind of magic, only control their element. That's why I can't teach you."

"That's okay." Magic lessons were the last thing he wanted. Then he groaned. "So, of course, Sam was right." She usually was.

"You want to go over and make up?" His mum nodded towards the door.

Fabian sighed heavily. "I probably should." If he really was some weird water mage, he wanted his best friend at his side. Especially his magic-obsessed best friend.

Samantha wasn't at home, but her little sister Meg told him that she was helping at the garage, so Fabian took his bike there. The garage was a little further downriver at a reasonably busy intersection. As usual, the parking lot was full of cars, waiting to be inspected or repaired. While they couldn't compete with the big franchise workshop north of the river, they had their loyal clients, doing reasonably well.

Fabian leaned his bike against the side of the building and entered through the workshop area instead of the office. Of his father, he could only see a pair of legs sticking out from under a red car that had seen better days. Samantha's father, Ben, however, was currently wiping his hands on an oil-stained towel and smiled at him.

"Hey, Long John. Come to help out a bit?" he greeted him.

"Not really." While his father paid him a little pocket money if he did, it was rarely worth the trouble. "I heard Sam's around."

Ben jerked his head in the direction of the office. "Cleaning up our files and grumbling about it as usual."

"Well, you guys should keep them in better order," Fabian admitted. It wasn't a particularly rare occasion that they got someone in to help with the paperwork. Usually, their respective wives. "Or hire someone."

"Look who's made out of money now." Ben started walking towards the office and held the door open for him.

Fabian had to physically push himself to take the steps. While he wanted to make up with Samantha, he dreaded the actual act.

"Do you have Mrs Orten's file?" Ben asked and promptly received the corresponding clipboard. "Ah, thanks. If you want to head off, that's fine. I can finish up later."

Samantha shot a quick glance at Fabian, then turned her attention back to the piles of paper she had amassed around her, ignoring him. "I'm fine."

Fabian had half a mind to turn around and leave, while Ben picked up on the tension between them. "You two are fighting?" When he didn't receive an answer, he raised his hands, signalling that he wouldn't get involved. On the way out, though, he whispered to Fabian, "Good luck."

As the door shut behind him, silence returned to the office, only broken by Samantha sifting through the papers. Fabian watched her, the muscles around his mouth tightening. If he didn't make up with her soon, he'd become angry again, and who knew what consequences that would have.

"Do you know who Matt's father is?" No reaction. "Mr Traidous. I mean... our first-grade teacher. René."

Samantha halted, but then she continued her work, as if she was forcefully stomping out her curiosity.

Fabian rolled his eyes. He knew her better than anyone. She *wanted* to talk about it. But not with him. Not yet anyway. It seemed like deflection wouldn't get him out of this hole. "Turns out..." He bit down hard on his tongue. It still infuriated him how she'd immediately thrown herself at his powers. He bet if it were her that developed scary abilities of not-controlling water, she'd be elated, excited even. Instead, it had to be him. "You were right," Fabian murmured, then louder. "You guessed right."

Silence. Samantha had gone completely still. Then she said quietly but pointedly, "I didn't *guess*."

"Oh, come on! You couldn't have known this from one burst pipe!" Why did she always have to be such an insufferable know-it-all?

Samantha glared at him. "Three burst pipes. Which isn't physically possible. And they were water pipes. You always had a connection with water."

So, Samantha remembered more than he did. "You knew I was a water mage all this time?"

Her nose paled a little. "No, I didn't," she admitted at last. "You're right. It was a guess. An *educated* guess."

"Of course," Fabian said as seriously as he could muster. Still, he couldn't prevent the corners of his mouth from twitching afterwards.

Her face softened a little, then the tension moved out of her shoulders. But instead of smiling, she sighed. "Congratulations. That's a pretty cool power."

"Are you kidding me?" Fabian pushed himself off the wall and walked over to her. "There's nothing cool about it! It's scary. I can't even control the water. I don't want this power."

He stumbled over the hurt flashing in her eyes. Hastily, Samantha turned away. "Well, you could learn to control it," she said in a flat voice.

"I don't want to learn it. I want it gone!"

Samantha whipped her head back around. Tears were shimmering in her eyes. She had been in the process of berating him, but when she opened her mouth, only a meek "Why?" came out.

Fabian plonked himself down on the small sliver of table she had already cleared. "Well, what do you think? Do you really believe what happened in Physics was cool? I've destroyed the Physics room. And Herbert will blame me, whether he believes in magic or not." Even if it had been a normal burst pipe, the association would be there.

Instead of answering, Samantha rested her head on her hands. "I talked to my dad about it. He says Herby—that's what he and Jo call him—were in a class together. And, well, Dad said that he'd always been a weirdo, and that's why they made fun of him. He also said Herby had a thing for my mum."

"Ew."

"Tell me about it!" She raised her head again. "So gross. Anyway, it sounds to me like they bullied him..."

"...so now, he bullies me. Great!" Fabian groaned, then he regarded Samantha from the side. "Do you think he still has a thing for your mum?" Mr Herbert wasn't quite as harsh on Samantha, after all.

"Ew!" Samantha grimaced and leaned back from him. "No! And if he does, I want to order another dozen burst pipes."

Despite himself, Fabian burst out laughing. Seeing his most-hated teacher drenched from head to toe had been rather cool now that he thought back on it. But the mirth was gone quickly. "Would love to fulfil the order, but for that, I would need to be in actual control of it."

Samantha looked at him hungrily. "Then let me help you. I can research material, find out about training methods, be there..."

"Can you find a spell that would make it go away?" he asked instead. "Maybe block my chi or something."

Her face fell, and she looked away again, pretending to pick up some files. "Sure, I can see if I find something."

The gratitude Fabian had been expecting didn't fill him. Samantha was visibly upset instead. And then it hit him. He was afraid of this new ability, but she would've given an arm and a leg to do magic. "If I could give this to you, I would," he whispered.

She raised a hand as if to defend herself from his words. "It's fine, I..." She paused, and a strangled sob rang out. "It's... it's..."

"I get it." Fabian put a hand on her shoulder and squeezed. It wasn't fair. He was desperate to lock these powers away again, and she wanted them more than anything. "You know, having magic would make you seriously overpowered? You're already smarter than the rest of the class."

Samantha laughed, wiping away her tears. "Nice try, Fabi. Nice try."

"I mean it, though. You know more about magic than any of us. You're brave and smart. You went on a monster hunt armed with a book and won. I got eaten by the monster." Fabian didn't remember any of his time as a bogeyman puppet, but just thinking about it made him break out in hives.

"You can do more than you think," she said, reciprocating the kindness. When Fabian only shrugged, she pressed the point. "You came along, though you were scared out of your mind."

"It's not like I could let you go alone!"

Samantha smiled at him. "And that makes you just as brave."

As Fabian soaked in her smile, his chest hurt with longing. He would go through fire for Samantha. Or take it up with the bogeyman.

"Is Matt's dad really our first-grade teacher?" she asked, apparently eager to change the topic.

Fabian readily took the opportunity. "Yeah. I saw letters. They were addressed to René Traidous, and Matt confirmed it."

"I wasn't aware he had a son our age."

"Can't remember him ever mentioning it, but I can't remember being a little water mage either, so that's not saying much."

Samantha nodded thoughtfully. "Well, and Matt said his parents were separated. He must've been living with his mum back then."

"Yeah." Then he suddenly remembered something else. "Hey, how fond are you of Mr Traidous?"

"Weird question." Samantha said and pulled a funny face. "Why are you asking?"

Fabian grinned. "Matt said he was looking for a couple of people to accompany his first-graders to the zoo on Tuesday. Mr Traidous would get us out of school." Missing Physics was still the biggest draw.

"We'd miss school?" Samantha asked, but curiosity won her over. "Well, I guess it's only for one day." Her eyes shone. "Let's do it!"

Excitement made her eyes gleam, and Fabian found himself mimicking her grin. It was good to have his best friend back.

Lucille

When Matt had invited her to the zoo, Lucille had hoped it would be a date between the two of them. Instead, they were accompanied by ten screaming six-year-olds.

Matt's father, René, was the opposite of his son. Sure, he wasn't bad-looking for a forty-year-old. He had the same blonde hair—though his was already thinning at the sides—but not Matt's milk chocolate eyes or fine features. Beyond his looks, he was kindness personified, the softness to Matt's cool edges.

Samantha and Fabian had been beside themselves when they'd met him. Apparently, René was a former teacher of theirs, and he'd been equally happy to see the two of them. Then they had split into three groups, and now they were dragging the children around the tiny forest zoo. Lucille had visited many zoos, but never one this small. The most exotic animals on display were a bunch of sika deer.

Nevertheless, the kids loved it. They spread out along the fences, making their job to keep them together near impossible. Matt already looked as if he deeply regretted his decision to help his father.

Sensing her chance, Lucille hooked her arm into his while they followed the children to the raven enclosure. "So, Matt."

He gave her a side-eye. "Yes?"

"You know what I was thinking of?" She bit her lip and batted her eyelashes at him. "A certain kiss behind curtains."

A quick smile flashed across Matt's face. "You want to sneak away and make out?"

Her cheeks flushed with heat. "Uhm, we can't... I mean, your father would kill us." Nevertheless, the idea appealed to Lucille. There was something exciting about sneaking around.

"He wouldn't." It was as if Matt missed the point on purpose.

"He'd be disappointed, though," Lucille said, while telling herself that they were with children. Children who were currently fighting with each other. "Later."

She let go of Matt and walked towards the two boys who were pushing each other. "Hey, hey, what's going on here?"

"Tommy says ravens are stupid!" one of the boys wailed.

"No, you are stupid!" the other responded, equally upset.

"As far as I know, ravens are pretty intelligent," Lucille said, wondering at the same time whether that was actually true. "However, that's no reason to push or hit each other. And we don't say 'you're stupid' either. Okay?"

The two boys glared at her, but the rest of the group had noticed that the lynxes were out in their enclosure, and all the children ran off.

Lucille sighed. "They're worse than a bag of fleas."

Matt fell in step next to her. "So, you want to have sex once we get out of here?"

"What?" Lucille caught her breath. "I... uhm..." Sure, she had a crush on him and fantasised about doing more than kissing. But sex on the first date? "I usually take things a bit slower."

"Why?" Matt asked with such honesty, it took her breath away. "You want me. I want you. Why should we wait?"

The heat burned in her cheeks. He wanted her. He... "Wait! If we are both interested in each other, does that mean that you and I are... well, could be together?"

"Together?"

"You know, officially dating. Boyfriend, girlfriend. A couple." Each of her suggestions were met by a blank face. "In a relationship."

Matt was frowning, as if he had to figure out what a relationship even meant.

Which was more than enough of an answer for Lucille. "You only want sex. And I happen to fulfil your requirements. No feelings attached," she surmised. "You sleep with me and tomorrow you'll make out with someone else."

He had the audacity to shrug. "If I'm in the mood."

"Ugh!" So, the kiss had meant absolutely nothing. Just as a second kiss or even sex would mean absolutely nothing. "What's wrong with you?"

But Matt's attention was already elsewhere. "Where are the kids?"

"The..." Startled, Lucille looked around. A part of her was glad that none of the children had heard their inappropriate discussion; the other was starting to panic. She kept looking around until she saw a short person with a red jacket slip into a building. "There!"

They hurried after them, when suddenly, Matt stopped, staring wide-eyed at something above the doors.

"What are you doing? We need to catch up with them." Lucille had half a mind to simply grab his hand and drag him along.

"You go inside. I'll check whether they're somewhere else," Matt said without taking his eyes off the signage.

Irritated, Lucille checked the name of the building as well. *Terraria — World of Snakes, Spiders & Insects.* There was nothing unusual about it. "I saw Jule, or whatever her name is, go inside. I bet the rest are there as well."

"You don't know that."

This time, she grabbed his hand and pulled. "Stop being silly! Just because we have different ideas of what a proper relationship entails doesn't mean you have to shun me now. We promised your father we would take care of his children. You can manage to be around me for a little longer, can't you?"

He looked at her as if she'd asked him to marry her. "Lucille..."

"Let's go." Lucille pulled on his hand, and despite himself, Matt followed her.

He still looked as if he'd rather throw himself into the wolf enclosure. "What's terraria?"

"A terrarium?" She frowned at the odd question. "You mean the glass box they use for reptiles, amphibians, and invertebrates? Like an aquarium just without the water."

"The animals are in glass boxes?" Matt asked, his voice shaking slightly.

Confusion spread through Lucille. This day was getting odder and odder. Then a thought came to her mind. "Matt, are you afraid of spiders? Or snakes?"

His face hardened immediately. "Don't be silly." He strode off and opened the door for her.

Lucille raised her eyebrows at him. Talk about a non-reaction.

Once inside, Matt kept his eyes firmly on the ground, not giving the terraria on either side the slightest glance.

"Unbelievable." The coolest guy in the entire school, the guy with the sword, Mr I-Don't-Do-Feelings, was afraid of creatures many times smaller than him. "Look, there are the children. They're all together."

"That's nice of them."

"So, which one is it? The snakes?" Behind the glass, they were fascinating, but she wouldn't have liked to meet one outside of its terrarium. "Spiders?"

"I don't know what you're talking about."

"Your phobia. Your hands are shaking. So—"

"Ew, look at these worms! There are so many of them," one of the children shouted.

Promptly, Matt's face became ghostly white. He swallowed heavily.

"Worms? You've got a worm phobia?" Lucille couldn't help it. A giggle burst from her lips.

Matt glared at her. "I don't! I—"

Screams rose in the air. Many terrified screams, and not just from the children. Startled, Lucille looked around until her eyes found a dark, fast-moving cloud. Then she heard it. A low, heavy hum. The sound of hundreds or thousands of insects.

"What on earth is that?" Lucille stared at the impossibly large swarm, which was definitely not behind the glass walls. "The kids!"

Lucille darted towards the kids. And towards the swarm. Some of the children were running in her direction, and she quickly hurried them on. "Go outside and wait there!" She dived under the insects to grab two children who were cowering on the floor.

She couldn't tell whether the swarm were bees or wasps or something else entirely. All she knew was that they were aggressive.

One of the children was holding her arm, crying over a sting. The other cried because the first one was crying. Lucille ushered both out when she felt an impact on her neck. It was worse than any wasp sting she'd ever experienced. Pain shot through her body, as if this insect had a ten-centimetre-long stinger. The burning sensation brought tears to her eyes.

"Go!" she shouted at the children, and they finally started moving. One of them, however, was getting caught behind the swarm. Lucille quickly took off her light autumn jacket, ducked under the insects, and threw it over the child. "Come on. Let's go."

While the air was buzzing, the floor was covered with worms and spiders of all kinds. Bile rose in her throat, and she had to force herself to move forward, squashing insects under her heels. Finally, she grabbed the child and ran back to the entrance. Only then did she notice Matt still standing where she'd left him. Sweat was running down the sides of his face, and his breath came out choppy. The whites of his eyes were visible as he stared at the ground where worms were crawling over his shoes.

"Matt!" Lucille didn't want to stay in this insect-infested hall a second longer. But he wasn't moving. At all.

Cursing in a way her stepmother would have been horrified to hear, she ran back to him, grabbed his arm, and yanked him.

The movement seemed to bring him out of his shock. Matt suddenly turned and ran so fast that Lucille could barely keep up. The insects followed them, but just as they reached the door, they turned back around. Not a single animal was left in *Terraria*.

Outside, the other groups had found them. Samantha was going around, drying tears and blowing on itchy stings, while Matt's father rummaged through his first-aid kit for some cooling salve. When he noticed them, his brow furrowed. "What happened in there?"

"Insects," was all Matt had to offer.

Lucille rolled her eyes. Now that they were outside, she was annoyed with him again. He hadn't even tried to help the children. Meanwhile, she had been stung. The spot still hurt, the skin burning with a vengeance. But *she* wasn't going to complain. "Some of the creatures must've broken out of their terrariums."

"Some? All of them," Matt mumbled, still shaken.

"No..." Suddenly, she realised that there had been far more insects than could ever be displayed. And who would display bees and wasps in their zoo, anyway?

Lucille glanced at Samantha, and her friend understood immediately. "Mr Traidous, should we take the children to a doctor, or at least back to school?"

"Let's head to the exit. The zoo wants everyone to evacuate and then we'll figure out the rest." Matt's father quickly counted the children and nodded. With an enviable calm, he called the children to gather. "Okay, 1B, find your partner and let's go that way!"

Samantha helped him herd the children. Meanwhile, Fabian joined them, frowning deeply. "What was that?"

"Honestly? Something out of a horror film," Lucille answered, rubbing her neck. "A huge cloud of insects, worms on the ground." Next to her, Matt shuddered. "You really are afraid of worms."

"What?" Fabian turned around in confusion.

Matt snapped in response. "So, what? It's not like I choose to fear them."

Fabian looked back and forth between them. "What? For real now?"

"I'm leaving!" With one last glare, Matt turned around and stomped off.

"It's a pretty severe phobia," Lucille said. Slowly, her panic and annoyance towards him was replaced by pity. "He couldn't even move."

Fabian struggled to contain his laughter. "Poor... sorry, but this is... forget about it."

Lucille smiled as well. "Yeah, well, I guess that makes him a little more human."

"True!"

Together, they turned towards the exit. Lucille threw one last glance over her shoulder. She couldn't help it, but her ears still picked up the low hum. As if the entire building was filled with insects, and the ceiling would explode any minute.

Samantha

The Villa de Cerque resembled a small mountain castle that throned over the town at its feet. It came with cute little turrets, romantic corner windows, and a balcony to make every Shakespeare couple jealous. It wasn't the only mansion in Greenvalley, but it was certainly the grandest. The driveway alone felt royal enough with its bright gravel surface. On the sides, a gardener had maintained an almost tropical array of plants that had no business of growing in the Harz mountains.

And then there was the door. First off, it was so large, even Fabian had a metre to spare above him. And second, there was no doorbell, only a presumptuous doorknocker in the shape of a lion.

"Are we allowed to touch it?" Fabian asked, voicing Samantha's doubts.

Now that he said it, she felt the urge to be more reasonable. "It's a normal house with a normal door, so I suppose—"

"Nothing about this house is normal!"

Before she could fight with him about it, Nico stepped forward and rapped on the door three times. Samantha noticed how Fabian straightened his shirt as if he was expected for dinner. Then the door was opened by an older gentleman in a suit.

"Welcome to the Villa de Cerque," he said with a nasal voice and a flourished bow. "May I take your jackets?"

Nico, who wasn't even wearing one, looked for his sister's help.

"Uhm... I guess." Fabian shrugged off his jacket, then held it awkwardly in front of his chest, unsure of how to actually hand it over.

Rachel had no such qualms. She was a fan of period dramas and was probably enjoying herself. "That is very kind of you. Thank you very much."

"I'd rather keep mine," Samantha said, amused by how much of a fuss these three made, just because there was an actual butler in this house. A butler she had seen laughing over tea and getting way too excited about a round of rummy at her grandmother's place. "So, this is where you work, Al. I should have guessed." She hadn't made the connection between Granny's butler friend and the de Cerques until Elda had mentioned it to Lucille.

Rachel's eyes widened, as if scandalised by the casual manner of Samantha's address, but Albert chuckled. "This is it, indeed. Now, if you please, follow me. Miss Lucille has prepared the Yellow Room for your meeting."

"There is a yellow room?" Fabian whisper-asked Nico as they followed Albert. "So, does every room have a colour?"

Naturally, Albert heard him and answered before Nico could give his opinion. "Not every room, no, but most of our exhibition rooms have been designed with a colour scheme in mind. One of Mrs de Cerque's ideas."

The room was indeed yellow. Not a garish kind of yellow, but rather a bunch of yellow accents. The walls were painted in a pastel colour, but the curtains were a bright, sunny yellow, and light enough to flutter in the soft breeze of an open window. The gigantic couch, on the other hand, was more of a subtle cream. On it, Lucille and Matt were sitting about half a metre apart, neither close enough nor far enough for comfort.

As soon as they entered, Lucille jumped up and took Samantha's hands. "There you are!" She sounded overjoyed to see them, and Samantha noticed that the air between her and Matt was thick enough to be cut by a knife.

"Is there anything else I can do?" Albert asked, his head slightly bowed.

"No, that will be all for now. Thank you, Albert," Lucille said with all the grace of a princess.

Once the door was closed, Nico walked around with wide eyes. He ran his fingers over a fancy art installation that resembled a tree made up of metallic toilet rolls. "Is this a museum or something?"

He wasn't too far off. The walls were hung with impressionist paintings, and there were a number of small sculptures which had been pushed to the side. Now all that remained in the room was the large couch and a lot of space.

"Well, it certainly feels like living in one, half of the time." Lucille sighed softly, but before anyone could commiserate, she clapped her hands. "Let's hope I don't burn it all down during training."

"If you do, we've got Fabian at the ready. He'll extinguish it," Samantha said with as much confidence as she could muster. She knew Fabian wouldn't have any, so she would have to make up for his.

Fabian laughed hoarsely. "Great idea. I wouldn't even know how to start calling the water to me."

Samantha gave him a bright smile and took a heavy book out of her bag. "Leave that to me." She went over to the couch and opened the book on her lap. "Granny suggested starting with this book. It's not directly for elemental mages, but the magic works in a similar manner." She opened the book to a pre-marked page. "Okay... so, we're beginning with a simple meditation exercise."

"Meditation exercise? Are you kidding me?"

She saw Rachel swallow a giggle. To avoid upsetting Fabian, Rachel quickly took out her laptop and muttered something about 'homework'.

Samantha took a deep breath, bracing herself against Fabian's undue panic. "You need to focus on the magic within yourself. So, listen!" She looked down to read. "This exercise can be done standing or sitting. First, you need to close your eyes."

When Fabian didn't respond, she gave him the stare of death. How was she supposed to help him if he didn't even try? At last, Fabian sighed and rolled his eyes, then closed them.

"Now you extend your arms, palms turned upwards, and breathe in and out in a deep, controlled measure."

For a few seconds, Fabian did exactly that, while the rest of them watched on. Nothing was happening. And sure enough, Lucille and

Nico could no longer contain their giggles. Rachel had to lower her head, and even Matt smirked.

"Sam!" Fabian bellowed.

"Yes!" Samantha clicked her tongue. "Remember, you're supposed to relax. According to the book, you need to focus on the magic... I mean the water in this room."

Fabian opened his eyes in confusion. "There is no water here."

"Ever heard of humidity?"

"Of course! Humidity. How stupid of me to forget about water in a *gaseous state*!" The last words were shouted.

Matt got up from the couch and crossed his arms. "Try it again."

"Oh, now he can talk," Lucille muttered just loud enough for everyone to hear.

As Matt snorted, Rachel and Samantha exchanged a confused look. Something was going on between the two, and Samantha had a pretty good guess at what it was. But that didn't mean she would get involved.

"Can't we get a bowl of water or something?" Fabian asked. He was starting to sound a little whiny.

"Or we could try to make you angry," Samantha suggested. "That helped last time."

Fabian's face darkened. "Well, keep going and it might happen yet!"

Samantha took several deep breaths, doing her best to acknowledge that he was scared and didn't actually want this power.

In the meantime, Nico jumped in. "It wouldn't hurt in the beginning, would it? We're here for training purposes, so..."

"I'll go," Lucille offered.

"Can I come?" Nico asked, already following her to the door. "I want to see more of this amazing place."

"Only if you promise not to repeat these words in front of my stepmother." Lucille glared at Matt for good measure, as if he had made that mistake when he'd arrived. "In the meantime, Matt can start with his self-defence lessons." It sounded more like a challenge than a suggestion.

Matt massaged the bridge of his nose and took a deep breath. He regarded the two girls on the couch. "What are you two capable of?"

Rachel hid her face quickly behind the laptop screen, leaving Samantha to respond. "Pretty much nothing?" She'd never fought with anyone.

Upon that answer, Fabian crossed his arms with a smug grin on his lips. "Now, this is going to be interesting."

"Well," Matt started, "judging by how reliable your water magic is, you should probably think about self-defence as well."

Samantha couldn't fight the grin claiming her face. She'd been about to say something similar.

But Fabian didn't take the bait. "No, thank you. Jan already tried that one on me. Most embarrassing lesson of my life." He shook his head vehemently. "Besides, isn't it ladies first?"

Before she could roll her eyes at him, Matt took a flourished bow as if he was asking her for a dance at the ball instead of a fight. "Let's show him how it's done, then."

If she was totally honest with herself, Samantha wasn't particularly keen to learn actual fighting. But with no powers to herself, she didn't have a choice if she still wanted to be involved. Besides, someone had to be proactive in this room. "Can't wait."

Matt led her to the middle of the room, where he let go of her hand and turned to face her. "Okay, try hitting me."

Her heart rate accelerated. She'd never hit anyone in her life, not even the bogey man puppets. Watching Matt, he seemed to be ready for anything, no amusement in his eyes, muscles slightly tensed. Samantha assumed she wouldn't actually manage to get a hit in, and that was the push she needed to just try it.

She pushed out her hand without fully clenching her fingers into a fist. Before she even got close to him, Matt caught her by the wrist. At the same time, something hit her knees from behind. Her legs folded immediately. In her panic, Samantha grabbed for something to hold on. Her fingers dug into Matt's shirt just before she fell backwards, dragging him down with her.

Somehow, Matt managed to avoid landing his full weight on her, but his leg got stuck under her in the process. He caught himself with his free hand, pinning her down by her hair, his hot breath against her cheekbones. They were both breathing heavily from the sudden movement.

Loud laughter rang through the room and a soft giggle. The whole interaction must have looked pretty ridiculous.

"Interesting move," she said with a chuckle.

Matt's face lit up and he, too, started laughing. "Not what I had planned."

"Wow! You really *do* jump on anyone who's even remotely available." Lucille had returned, a bowl of water in her hand. Nico grimaced and quickly ducked in to plunk himself down next to his sister.

Samantha felt as if Lucille had dumped the water on her head. She was aware of how this must look to her friend. Not very favourable. Matt moved enough for her to get up to her feet, and Samantha wasted no time in doing so, avoiding his helping hand as she did so. "We didn't—"

"I was teaching her how to defend herself. As you asked me to," Matt said, not a hint of compassion in his voice.

Lucille snorted, while Fabian chimed in obliviously, "Which looked more like one mishap following the next."

Matt turned his back on Lucille and faced Samantha instead. "That wasn't quite what I had in mind, but at least you would've surprised your opponent."

"Sure, but who will recover quicker from that? Me or my opponent?" Samantha glanced at Lucille, who was handing the bowl of water to Fabian.

"Probably the opponent," Matt admitted, not paying Lucille any attention. "But did you see what I did there?"

Samantha forced herself to concentrate on the task ahead: learning how to defend herself. That was the only thing she wanted from Matt, nothing more. "Not exactly, but I felt it." She rubbed her backside. "That wasn't fair." Before Matt could say anything, she rolled her eyes. "I know monsters aren't fair, either."

He smiled at that. "No, they aren't. Shall we go again?" When Samantha nodded, he put his hands on her hips to readjust her stance. In front of Lucille, the fingers burnt like fire. "You need to be balanced, so you can't be knocked down that easily."

Her eyes met Lucille's, but her friend only clicked her tongue and whispered something to Rachel. It was obvious that she was purposefully ignoring them—and making sure that they knew that. Or at least, that Samantha knew that.

Matt, on the other hand, was completely engrossed in his tutor role. "If your stance is balanced, I can't knock you down that easily. It also helps you keep your balance when you attack. So, let's give this a few tries, so you can—"

"I think you should do this with Lucille," Samantha interrupted him. The last thing she wanted was to ruin her new friendship over a boy. Sure, Matt was a very handsome guy, but he was just a guy, and a flirt on top of that. The kind of boy she could find attractive without actually being drawn to him. She hadn't broken up with Fabian to become a number on some other guy's list of conquests. And she certainly wouldn't get between him and a friend of hers.

Before he could protest, Samantha walked away and sat down next to Nico, pretending to be interested in whatever Rachel was doing. It wasn't homework at all, but news articles about the insect attack.

Meanwhile, Lucille got up, her chin slightly raised, as if she was truly going to battle. "Well, show me what you've got."

Samantha watched them face off. The tension was rising again, though she had no idea whether they were about to come to blows or start making out. Matt was slowly raising his hands. Samantha watched his leg closely and saw it shift slightly, ready to repeat the trick. Lucille had no idea what was coming for her. Matt was just too fast. In a swift movement, he knocked her legs out from under her, but then moved in close enough to catch her, as if she'd only slipped and he'd been there to save her. He flashed his teeth in a mischievous grin.

Lucille seemed completely unaffected by it. She raised a hand and spoke in a cool, collected manner, "Erit lux."

Bright light filled the room. A loud splash followed by a thump could be heard, and then the light was gone again.

Blinking rapidly, Samantha tried to recover from the glaring light. Matt had his arms raised to cover his eyes, while Lucille had fallen to the ground, after all, grimacing in pain. Meanwhile, a puddle of water was soaking into the carpet.

"So much for my water," Fabian said.

"Magic wasn't part of the plan!" Matt snapped. His patience must've reached its final straw.

Lucille got to her feet with a snort. "Why wouldn't it be? Do you think it's not fair to the monsters?"

Matt threw his arms into the air. "This is ridiculous."

"You know, if you start crying, Fabian might get his water back," Nico chimed in.

While Matt glared at him, Samantha chuckled. It *was* ridiculous. They had absolutely no idea what they were doing.

As if Rachel had missed the entire afternoon's actions, she turned her laptop around. "Hey Fabian, check this out. Do you have any idea what these are?"

Samantha bent forward to look for herself. There was a gallery of close-ups from the insects, all of them slightly pixelated.

"Someone grabbed these from a video and now everyone is guessing what kind of insects they are," Rachel explained.

Fabian shrugged. "Sorry, we don't really spend much time on insects in Biology, but I'm sure there's a useful app." He took out his phone and started searching. "I'll see if I can find something."

"Shouldn't there be a list from the zoo?" Samantha suggested. "They should have a record of what they've got, shouldn't they?" She looked up at Matt and Lucille, who had been in the invertebrate house when it happened, but Lucille's eyes just widened a little, while Matt had found a new interest in the sculptures on the other side of the room.

Instead, Rachel answered, "But that's part of the mystery. They can't reach anyone at the zoo, and the few patrons who know their way around Terraria have never seen anything like this."

Upon hearing that, Matt came closer, though he still held a wary distance to both Lucille and the laptop. Meanwhile, Fabian announced that he'd found an app and was using it now to search for one of them.

Samantha was starting to get a bit nervous. The insects *had* been acting rather strange. None of them had left the building, as if there had been an invisible wall keeping them in.

"I can't find anything in this app," Fabian said, scrunching his nose in frustration. "It's probably useless."

"Or the insects aren't from this world," Matt said.

Lucille forgot her animosity for a moment to deal with the strangeness of his answer. "What do you mean, not from this world?"

"I mean they're not natural. They're monsters."

Lucille groaned. "Of course. They would all be monsters to you."

Samantha looked back and forth between them, trying to make sense of their spat. For the millionth time, she asked herself *what* exactly had happened at the zoo.

"I mean real monsters. From Hell," Matt clarified.

Instantly, Fabian paled and began to stutter, "F-f-from w-where?"

"From Hell. It exists. Deal with it." All of Matt's patience seemed to have been burnt away by the light spell. Instead, he bent forward to look closely at the images. "That one, for example, is a whipping executioner's locust."

"A what?" Fabian's voice was starting to shake.

Matt ignored his growing anxiety and started to point at the others. "Devil's bee, grey-black corpsemoth, clean-off beetle."

"That one sounds harmless." Nico was obviously trying to find the silver lining here.

"It's named that because it cleans off the flesh from the bone incredibly quickly," Matt said dryly. "I know now what's happening there. There's a konnurar in the zoo." He spun around and left.

The rest of them stared at the closed door. Fabian was the first to break the silence. "Sam? What is a konnurar?"

She shrugged. The word was completely unfamiliar to her, but her fingers itched for a book to see if she could find out more.

"I suppose we'll find out when we go back to the zoo," Lucille suggested.

"Did you hear the names of these creatures?" Fabian protested. His face was still devoid of any blood. "Devil's bee? Corpsemoth?"

Lucille rolled her eyes. "Matt has an insect phobia, so he probably makes them sound worse than they are." But then her face softened. "He can't face them alone. Last time, he froze on the spot. We need to help him."

Slowly, the pieces were slipping into place. "Matt has an insect phobia?" Samantha massaged her temple. Everything was moving too fast. "We need to stop him. He's probably trying to prove something to you, but if you're right, he can't do this alone." Not if he had a real phobia. "We shouldn't just run in there in any case. Not unprepared as we are. For example, we need to find out what a konnurar is and how to keep those hellish insects away from us."

"Would a wave of water help?" Nico asked.

"Probably, but I only have the gift of not controlling water," Fabian muttered.

With a sigh, Lucille pulled out her phone. "I'm gonna call him and try to stop him before he gets stung to death because he can't move past the doorstep."

"You do that. How about we reconvene at my grandmother's house?" That was their best chance to find out more about these monsters and pick up things that could help them. "We'll go over everything and make a proper plan." After all, the horror insects were stuck in the zoo for now. "Does that sound like a plan?"

"I'll grab some snacks," Nico replied, as if they had just arranged a sleepover.

"Corpsemoth..." Fabian muttered, but no one truly protested.

Rachel

"Looks like we've got another adventure ahead of us." Nico was positively buzzing once they'd separated from the others to do a quick detour. "Crazy insects from Hell. This town really upped its game this year, don't you think?"

"There's a man behind it," Rachel said, deeply lost in her own thoughts.

Nico regarded her thoughtfully from the side. "Another dream vision?"

She smiled at him. After the dream with the bogeyman had come true, her brother was no longer questioning her ability. "Last night. I was at the zoo, in the Terraria building, and there were insects all around me. They'd transformed the building into their own little world, and when I looked at them, they all came together until they took the shape of a man. And I believe that's what a konnurar is."

"Why didn't you tell Sam and the others?"

Rachel bit her lip. She'd thought about that, especially after learning of Fabian's powers, which hadn't truly surprised her. Whenever Fabian appeared in her dreams—and that was a lot—he'd been surrounded by water. In her dreams, he never seemed to mind, but in reality, he was scared. And so was she.

"What good would that be? They're only dreams."

"Dreams that are coming true. They might help us defeat these things." Nico walked a little faster so he could step into her path and look her in the eye.

Rachel turned her head away. "The bogeyman dream didn't help at all. And in trying to follow it, I almost got turned." No matter how she tried, she couldn't see how her ability would be of any use to anyone. "The future can't be changed. I see a glimpse of it, but that's like reading a spoiler. It'll still happen whether I like or not."

"You don't know that," Nico insisted. "Come on, tell me more about that konnurar dream. We'll pick a detail and change it."

"How are we going to change insects coming together to form a creature? A living, crawling creature?" She shuddered. While she was completely aware of when she was dreaming or not, the dreams had the same intensity as the real thing. And the konnurar was absolutely disgusting.

"Did you wake up afterwards?" Nico returned to his spot by her side and they continued their walk.

Rachel shook her head. "No, but..." For a moment, she recalled the dream. The konnurar had looked at her, and then the insects had come for her, until she was like him. Nothing more than a creature with a crawling, living skin. *That* was when she had woken up. "I didn't see how—or *if*—we defeated him."

"There must've been something. What did he do once he was transformed?"

"I don't know." Rachel sighed. "Let's try this another time." There was a detail she could change quite easily, but if she told Nico, he would order her to stay home. If Rachel didn't go, the konnurar couldn't swallow her.

She wasn't suicidal or stubborn. Under normal circumstances, she would avoid facing off with the konnurar any day. But there was this feeling. It was hard to describe in the daylight, something she was only sure of in her dreams. She had to be there. If she wasn't, it wouldn't work. Though *what* exactly wouldn't work was just out of her reach.

"I still think you should tell the others. It might be useful, you know." Nico got his keys out and unlocked the door.

"Where have you been?" Their mother stood in the doorless frame that led from the entrance to the living room, a glass of wine in her hand.

"What do you care?" Nico said, pushing past her.

Their mother gasped, then went after him. Rachel noticed how her steps were slightly unsteady. She didn't follow, opting to wait in the entranceway.

Most of the time, they ignored each other, but lately, Nico wouldn't stop fighting back. With their eighteenth birthday only a month away, he'd decided he no longer cared about what their mother wanted. After all, she'd never cared about what they wanted, either.

"You didn't even leave a message," their mother complained. "The fridge is empty. You were supposed to go shopping."

"You mean the wine is empty," Nico said. He was opening the pantry, which was filled well enough, and grabbed two bags of potato chips. Then he faced their mother. "You drink too much."

Rachel bit her lower lip. While the statement was undoubtedly true, the reason they were fresh out of wine had nothing to do with her mother's drinking habit and all to do with the fact Rachel had secretly emptied the bottles late last night. Well, not *all*, because their mother had obviously found one she'd missed.

"Excuse me," their mother said in an increasingly shrill voice. "Are you the parent now? I can drink as much as I want, and I don't need my teenage son to tell me what to do."

Nico slammed the pantry doors shut again. "Well, then my grown-up mum can do her own wine shopping. Oh right, you're already too drunk to drive. And it's what? Not even six yet. Great example. As always." He grabbed a Coke from the corner and walked towards Rachel. "Let's go."

"Where are you going?" their mother screeched.

"Out!" Nico bellowed back. He pushed the bottle into Rachel's arms and stuffed the crisps into his backpack.

As he ripped the door open, Rachel looked back at their mother. The alcohol had done her no favours. Her face looked much older than the fifty-three years she'd lived through, and no amount of garish make-up could hide the damage the drinking had done. She looked exhausted and at the end of her wits; there would never be enough to drink in the house to cover all the pain.

"I poured out six bottles of wine," Rachel found herself saying as she stepped outside.

She was answered by a swear word that made her ears burn, accompanied by the sound of shattering glass against the fast-closing door.

Rachel gulped. For a moment, her head was spinning as if she was the one who'd drunk too much.

Nico took her hand, roughly rubbing his thumb over it while he regarded her with concern. "What did you do that for?" He sounded more puzzled than accusing.

"I don't know." Rachel shrugged him off and started walking away. "You realise she never even noticed she *hadn't* drunk all of them, don't you?"

An hour later, Rachel was still replaying the moment her mother had thrown a glass at her. She sat in the corner of the witch room while Samantha brewed some kind of potent anti-insect spray in the huge cast-iron cauldron. Lucille was helping her, or rather complaining about Matt, who'd been asked by Elda to assist her with something in the kitchen. To avoid the room being too crowded, Nico had taken Fabian outside to help him train his water powers.

Normally, Rachel wouldn't have passed up the chance to watch Fabian, but today her mind was elsewhere. Not with Fabian's fickle powers or whatever task Matt was helping Elda with, and certainly not with Lucille and her ongoing complaints about Matt. She seemed to have missed the memo that he wasn't interested in a relationship. Instead, her mother's face replayed in her head in a constant loop. How it had transformed into an outraged snarl just before she hurled the insult and the glass at her. If Nico hadn't closed the door at that moment, it would've hit her in the face. Too bad doors couldn't stop nasty words.

One month until she turned eighteen. It should have been something to look forward to, but Rachel knew it was only an arbitrary date. Yes, she would be a legal adult and well within her rights to move out. But with what money? Sometimes she dreamed of using the child support her father paid to get a small flat, but technically she'd still be in school for two more years, and until then, she wouldn't really be able to move out, especially if she stayed in Greenvalley.

"He looked at me as if it was an entirely novel concept that people don't jump into bed with each other on the first date," Lucille complained loudly. "As if I was already asking too much of him by taking it slow. And when I said he only wanted sex, he never refuted it."

"So, what's the problem?" Rachel asked, tired of listening to her whining. "He's making it clear what he wants. Nobody's forcing you to have sex on your first date with him." She normally kept quiet, but her patience had reached an all-time low.

Both Lucille and Samantha looked at her, startled. A blush slowly settled on Lucille's cheeks. Any minute now, she would say something nasty back. How it wasn't Rachel's business or how she wouldn't understand.

But before that happened, Samantha jumped in. "Rachel's right. At least he's honest about what he's looking for."

"Look, it's not like I'm looking for a long-term relationship either," Lucille said, turning away from Rachel and continuing as if she hadn't been interrupted. "But it's just so... callous? I mean, there must be something wrong with him. I get fooling around, but sleeping with a new person every other day? At seventeen! It's a bit much, don't you think?"

Samantha was trying her hardest to concentrate on the anti-insect potion while also attempting to be compassionate towards both Lucille and Matt. "Well, maybe there is. Obviously, his parents are separated, have been for a long time. He probably doesn't believe in love."

"My parents are separated," Rachel said drily. "And I'm a virgin. And Nico has been going strong with his girlfriend for four months."

"I didn't mean... I'm sorry, Rachel." Samantha grimaced at her. Rachel knew she hadn't meant it that way.

She was well aware some children of broken homes were very much like Matt, but there was something different about him. He didn't seem unable to have a long-term relationship. He just really enjoyed the flirting and sleeping with other people, as if it was second nature to him. And unlike her, Rachel didn't get the feeling that he was in any way damaged by his parents' separation. Perhaps because it'd happened so early in his life that he'd never known any different.

"It's fine." Rachel took a deep breath, only to see how Lucille was regarding her as if it was the first time she'd noticed her existence.

"Yes, I'm sorry as well," Lucille said. "I... I think I'm just disappointed that..." She shrugged, seeming suddenly very lost. "It's just another guy who doesn't really have any interest in me."

Samantha frowned and then said exactly what Rachel was thinking. "I don't believe Matt is in any way representative of other guys. You may not have noticed it, but the boys at school are definitely interested in you. I even saw Alan checking you out. You liked him, didn't you?"

Lucille snorted but couldn't quite hide the smile. "But he's one of the Elite Idiots." At the same moment, she clapped her hand over her mouth. "Oh, shit..."

"I..." Samantha grinned. "I love it. Elite Idiots. That's gonna stick."

And suddenly, all three of them were laughing. Rachel even forgot about her mother for a bit. But she didn't forget about what Lucille had said. So, when they calmed down again, she asked, "So who was—or *is*—the other guy that's not interested in you?"

Lucille sighed heavily before taking a seat next to Rachel. "Well... there was actually another reason I quit boarding school. And no, it was not the gardener's boy or any boy at all. I came home because..." She stared at the soot-stained floor. "Because this is my home, and I've never been here. I'm a stranger in my own hometown—and in my home." Her voice became quieter and quieter. "I thought if I lived in Greenvalley, I would be able to spend more time with my dad, but he's always in his office, always working. I'm now in the same place as him, but it's exactly the same as before."

For the first time since they'd met, Rachel felt a connection to the pretty girl who seemed to have it all: looks, brains, and money. She put her hand on Lucille's. "I know how you feel. My mum spends more time with her wine bottles than with me."

At the cauldron, Samantha kept quiet. She knew all about Rachel's broken relationship with her mother and had often offered support in the past. But as empathetic as she was, she couldn't truly understand how it felt. She and her father had an incredibly close relationship, and while she was often annoyed with her mother because they seemed to be such polar opposites, they weren't on bad terms or anything. All in all, Samantha—just like Fabian—had a pretty normal family. It was everything that Rachel wanted. And apparently, Lucille did as well.

"She threw a wine glass at me before I came here," Rachel admitted, and suddenly it felt a little more ridiculous than sad.

"She did *not!*" Samantha exclaimed.

Lucille gasped in shock. "That sounds horrible. Why didn't you say something? Why did you let me blab on about stupid *non*-relationship drama when you had that going on in your mind?"

While the two of them were appalled, Rachel found herself smiling. "I'm probably so used to it by now."

Immediately, Lucille grabbed her hand. "No! You do not get to keep those heavy emotions to yourself. I'm sorry I was so focused on such a ridiculous thing. It won't happen again. We are friends now." She smiled to herself. "Because the way I see it, I might not have found the home I was expecting, but I found a home." She looked at Samantha. "One where I can truly be myself, where it doesn't matter whether I act like a lady or have proper aspirations, but I can explore who I truly am and who I could be. And the same goes for you two. And those silly boys!"

Rachel thought back on what Nico had said. Lucille was right. Their dynamic had changed. Where, if not here, could she honestly be herself? "I need to tell you something."

"Anything," Lucille declared, and Rachel's heart warmed slightly. Lucille was so different from her, wearing her heart on her sleeve, while Rachel bottled up all her emotions. It would be good to be a little more like her.

"Don't laugh. But I am pretty much convinced that I have magical dreams."

"Really?" Samantha asked. For a moment, she stared at her, a million unspoken thoughts behind her eyes. Then she turned to the bench and started pouring her potion into spray bottles. "What do you mean?"

Rachel shrugged sheepishly. "It's hard to explain, but I'm aware of when I'm dreaming, and there's a difference between my normal dreams and the special dreams. In some of them, I can see a glimpse of the future."

"No way," Lucille said, her eyes gleaming with excitement.

Rachel wasn't sure if she was quite as excited about it. "Well, I did see a little bit of the bogeyman puppets. I didn't know what it meant until it happened, but the dream was spot on. And I dreamed of Fabian's powers long before he developed them. His dreams are always surrounded by water. Mostly mountain creeks, which checks out because he loves hiking and nature." It was like a dam had broken. She never spoke that much without interruption unless on a sleepover with Samantha.

"You dream of Fabian?" Lucille asked.

Naturally, she would latch onto that, and Rachel blushed. "Well, yes and no. It's more than that. I think I actually visit his dreams. Like his actual dreams." The visions were rare and something she couldn't control, the wandering, however... "That's what I mean with magical dreams." That part had been too embarrassing to confess to Nico. She neither wanted him to know about how many dreams she spent with Fabian nor who else she visited at night.

Lucille's eyes were big. "Did you know about this, Samantha?"

Samantha finished screwing the tops onto her bottles. She shook her head. "No, but colour me intrigued! Dream wandering sounds pretty cool. So do dream visions."

Rachel smiled. She'd been afraid they wouldn't believe her, but Lucille had been right. There was no judgement between them.

Just then, there was a knock on the door. They all watched as it opened, and Matt put his head in. He was rubbing his neck and grimacing as if in pain. He also seemed to be in a particularly bad mood. "Are you ready to take on this konnurar? Because I could use some insect squashing right now."

"We'll see about that once you're in a room with them," Lucille teased him, but it no longer sounded as malicious as it had at her home.

Samantha grabbed her bottles. "I'm done."

"Great. Let's go then."

Lucille

Lucille couldn't remember when she'd last used public transport. The stuffy bus crossed town and would eventually bring them to the zoo's gates. She was sitting at the window, Samantha next to her, and felt every bump in the road. Her chauffeur would've got them there in fifteen minutes, but the bus kept on rolling through the residential streets like a snake.

"You could've warned me about your grandmother," Matt muttered. He was standing in the aisle, one hand above his head holding onto the rail as he leaned down.

Both Lucille and Samantha leaned in curiously. "Warned you about her?"

"Yeah, that was not helping her. It was an interrogation." Matt scowled and rubbed his neck.

"Well, maybe she recognised you immediately for what you were," Lucille chimed in. When Matt's eyes widened, she giggled. "An irresistible flirt." She nudged Samantha in the side. "I'm sure she would want to protect her innocent granddaughter from you."

Matt stood up straight again. "Yeah, something like that."

In front of them, Fabian turned around. "Samantha isn't innocent. I... I mean she's... You and Matt?" he asked Samantha, who was staring daggers at him.

"Well, thank you for declaring the loss of my innocence to the entire bus," Samantha hissed. "And no, there's no Matt and I. And there never will be."

Lucille looked up at Matt in time to catch him mentally filing that information away. He truly would've considered it. She'd just been too blind to see it. Or listen to him. "Oh well, at least we're all being honest with each other."

At that, Rachel flushed. Her eyes shot to Fabian next to her and back down again. Immediately, Lucille's gossip-hungry side awakened. Sure, there was no future for her and Matt, but she could cheer Rachel on to find her love match.

"Did she talk to you about the sword, though?" Samantha asked Matt.

"A little," he said almost tentatively.

"What about the sword?" Nico asked, leaning in from the back.

"We found a sketch of it in an old book," Samantha explained only too readily. "Apparently, the sword and Lucille's necklace belong together. They are both Emblems of Power. There are six of them in total, and together they form the Circle of Magic, which it's claimed has the power to change the world. Whatever that means."

Nico got to his feet and did a quick count. "What are the other four? Because we happen to be six people."

"Oh no. I like the world the way it is," Fabian declared immediately.

"A feather of a legendary bird, magical flowers, a dreamweb—" Samantha paused, her eyes fixed on Rachel. "One of the Emblems of Power is a dreamweb. If Nico is right, that one might belong to you."

Visibly overwhelmed by the sudden attention, Rachel looked around. "I... don't know. I don't have one."

"Why would it belong to Rachel?" Fabian asked, seemingly the only one out of the loop.

Sensing her chance for meddling, Lucille leaned forward, putting her arms on the backrest. "Because Rachel might be the most talented of us all. She can walk through dreams and see the future in them."

Instead of marvelling, Fabian turned pale. "The future?"

"Only small visions, things that happen the next day, like facing a konnurar," Rachel said in that quiet voice of hers.

Lucille was annoyed by her mousiness. It made sense Fabian hadn't noticed her yet if she clammed up the moment he showed any interest in her. And to top it all off, Fabian paled when he'd heard that. Frustrated,

Lucille leaned back in her seat. "Stop being such a coward, Fabian. I think Rachel's dream powers are fascinating."

"What did you see of the konnurar?" Matt asked, with considerably more interest.

"Just the konnurar taking care of his insects," Rachel answered meekly. Then she added, "I believe he cares more for insects than humans and... well, wouldn't mind if his insects got rid of the human plague."

"Great, a demonic ambassador for Greenpeace," Fabian muttered.

The rest of them broke out into laughter. The idea of some demon advocating for insect rights was too ridiculous to behold.

In the middle of their laughter, Samantha pushed the stop button. "We have to get off."

"Here we go," Lucille muttered.

They all shuffled into the aisle and got off the bus when it stopped in front of the forest zoo. It was already dark, but the zoo was open, not a soul in sight.

"Does anyone else find this creepy, or is it just me?" Fabian asked, tentatively putting his hand on the gate.

"Wait until we're in that house of horrors." Matt went through the gate and drew his sword out of thin air.

Lucille rubbed her eyes. He definitely hadn't hidden it in his backpack on the bus. He wasn't even wearing a belt. "How did you do that?" When Matt stared at her in confusion, she pointed at the sword. "Where were you hiding that before now?"

"Well, didn't you listen to Sam? It's an Emblem of Power. It comes to me when I need it," Matt said, as if it was the most normal thing in the world. "I think school might have a problem if I was running around carrying it openly, like you do with yours."

"You think?" Lucille waved him off. They had more important issues to face.

Next to her, Nico chuckled. "So, are you gonna kill the bees with a sword?"

Lucille could've sworn Matt was blushing and muttering something like, "If I have to."

Armed with a bunch of flashlights, they made their way over to Terraria. Once there, Samantha provided each of them with a bottle of her special anti-insect spray. "I have two spares. That's all we got."

"And this will work?" Matt asked full of doubt. "We're talking about hellish insects."

"Yes, there are a few components in there which are poisonous to demons or demonic insects only," Samantha explained. "And I brewed them in a way that made them more potent."

Matt regarded the bottle with newfound respect. "Well, let's give it a try." He approached the door and kicked it open. The wood splintered, and the door hung askew on its hinges.

"Was that necessary?" Samantha asked.

"Yeah," Fabian chimed in. "Now we're not only getting stung to death and rapidly cleaned of our flesh, but they'll also report us to the police tomorrow."

"Our dead bodies?" Nico asked and followed Matt inside. "Oh well, I'd say let's hope they do. My mum wouldn't report our absences, that's for sure."

Lucille had to take a deep breath before stepping inside. Suddenly, the idea of taking on swarms of insects didn't seem so great anymore. The sting from this morning was still itching, even now.

Apart from their flashlights, it was pitch black inside. And it was quiet. A little too quiet. Slowly, they went in deeper until their light fell on an elongated, solid shape hanging from the ceiling.

"What is that?" Lucille asked.

Matt hushed her, and they all listened in. From inside, a low hum rose. Sweat trickled down Lucille's neck, and she took a step back. Then another one. And another—

The structure exploded. Countless red, glowing bees swarmed out in all directions. The humming was so loud Lucille's ears hurt.

Fabian jumped back, stumbling over his feet. Matt threw his arms in the air, trying to protect himself from the insects. Samantha let out a shriek, but then she took her bottle and pushed the button down on it. Purplish fog enveloped the bees in front of her. A second later, they dropped.

Encouraged by the prompt result, the others followed suit.

"Globus igneus," Lucille whispered instead. The fire seemed a much safer way to deal with these critters.

For a few minutes, there was nothing but green flickering flames, purple fog, and incessant humming. When the latter died off, all they could hear was their own panting and huffing. Thousands of bees covered the floor.

"I'd feel really bad about this if these weren't more aggressive than African honey bees," Fabian muttered. His fingers were cramped around the spray bottle while he caught his breath.

"Definitely not feeling bad," Matt said while scratching his arms and neck. He'd been so close to the nest he must've been stung at least twenty times. His swollen and blotchy skin looked painful, but Matt seemed more annoyed than in agony. "I hate insects."

"Well then, the next critters shouldn't be a problem for you," Nico said from further ahead.

Lucille followed his voice, both spell and spray ready at hand. But when she saw what Nico's light had caught in, she let out a scream.

"What the hell is *that*?" Fabian asked, stepping next to her.

In front of them, overlapping curtains of grey covered the path from ceiling to floor. Spiderwebs. Layers and layers of spiderwebs, and on the edges, waiting patiently for their prey, sat fist-sized black spiders with glinting, dagger-like thorns on their legs.

"Oh no," Matt muttered, his voice pitching slightly. "Those are poisonous hellspiders."

"Do you even feel the poison once they slice you open with these legs?" Fabian quipped in a shaky voice.

As if it had been a serious question, Matt nodded. "Yes. Yes, you do." He swallowed. "I think I know what's going on here. This is a... present."

"A present?" Lucille asked. Who in their right mind would gift poisonous hellspiders to a zoo?

"From my brother, yes." Matt must've been so caught up in his thoughts that he didn't realise what he was saying. Only when five pairs of eyes looked at him in disbelief, he explained, "Sorry, one of my half-brothers is a psychopath. I mean, they all are, but this one hates me."

"He hates you enough to send you an entire zoo full of demonic insects?" Samantha asked, a hint of sarcasm in her voice.

Matt shrugged. "Let's just say I wouldn't put it past him."

Lucille had a million questions at once. How many siblings did he have? Why would one of them hate Matt? Was that why he had moved towns? Or why he was emotionally unavailable? And how would his brother have even get his hands on a bunch of demonic insects or a konnurar?

But before she could pose any of them, Rachel asked, "What are we gonna do about the spiders?"

"Let's see if this works on them, too." Matt held up his spray bottle and gave the three fat spiders a good dose.

At first, they crawled away from the spot, but soon they hung still, legs curled beneath their bodies. Encouraged by the result, they all started to spray the webs. Matt used his sword to slice through the spiderwebs, and Lucille followed a little more reluctantly with her fireballs. Overall, the spiders weren't quite as bad as they'd seemed.

Or at least, they weren't until she heard Samantha call out behind her, "Shit, shi— help, please!"

The spiders were so much faster than Lucille could've ever believed. Three of them practically raced around Samantha's body, spinning their webs so firmly she'd gotten stuck on the spot. After several attempts, she managed to spray one of them, but the other two crawled up her arm and tied it firmly in place. Samantha cried out in pain. Through the grey around her arm, red bloomed where the legs had ripped open her exposed skin.

A purple cloud enveloped her, emanating from three spray bottles at once. One spider curled up almost immediately. The other stretched its legs towards Samantha's neck, leaving a thin trace of blood as gravity dragged it down again. Nothing else moved.

"Shit!" Fabian exclaimed before moving forward to free Samantha.

"No, don't!" she shouted in near panic. "These are incredibly sticky. You'll get stuck." She was panting now. "Just go and get rid of the monster. I'll free myself."

Matt nodded with a grave expression. "Okay, we'll..."

"We can't leave you here alone!" Fabian protested. "What if there are more spiders? You can't even move your right arm."

"But you need to stop the konnurar!"

"I'll stay with her," Lucille said, taking her place next to Samantha. "I have my fire and the leftover potion, plus a manicure set in my handbag to cut through the webs." It meant staying in this spider-infested area, but Lucille thought that by now the spiders were more afraid of her than she was of them. If only she could convince herself of it.

Samantha smiled and nodded at her, a little too frantically. "The rest of you go!"

Fabian seemed of half a mind to stay, but then he growled, "You'd better be here when we come back."

"I'll be right here, in this spot." The words took her breath away, and she swallowed.

Fabian grimaced, but Rachel touched his hand, and with a deep breath, they followed Nico and Matt deeper into the building.

"And you'd better come back," Samantha whispered. She shook her head to face Lucille. "Alright. If you give me your phone, I can hold it while you get to work."

Lucille exchanged the spray bottle in Samantha's hand with her phone, then took out her scissors. Without the lights of the others, darkness had crept in a little too close for her liking, reminding her of the bogeyman and its shadows. Behind her, there was a scuttle near the walls, and something was crawling at the edge of their light. It was quiet. So quiet, she could hear each of her breaths.

Lucille's fingers were shaking as she moved her scissors closer. They were high-quality nail scissors, but Samantha had been right. The webs were incredibly sticky and surprisingly firm. Lucille got through them by jerking and tearing, rather than cutting. The progress was unbearably slow. Especially with the sound of scuttling feet all around.

Fabian

Fabian had never realised how big Terraria was. From the outside, it looked little bigger than their school hall, and yet time had stretched indefinitely since they'd entered. It felt like they'd been here for hours. The lights of their smartphones could hardly penetrate the thick darkness inside the house, but what he saw of the enclosures didn't fill him with much confidence.

Once, his light caught on the glass enclosure of one of the bigger snakes, but it was nowhere to be seen. Instead, a long line of vertebrae lay stretched out on the substrate, not a remnant of flesh remaining. Two beetles were crawling over the bones.

The clean-off beetle. Fabian swallowed. Part of him wanted to ask Matt more about their characteristics, but the larger part decided he rather didn't want to know how quickly these beetles went for another target.

His fear was nothing compared to Matt, though his friend tried to act cool. Fuelled by determination and anger, he led the group deeper and deeper, but his skin shimmered with sweat, and Fabian noticed him swallowing almost as frequently as he blinked. Whatever his breaking point was, he wasn't far off from it.

Nico and Rachel, on the other hand, seemed to be as relaxed as if they were going for a stroll. Fabian had done plenty of night hikes in the forests around town, but this was not like any of those. The most that could happen in the forest was a misstep that sent you rolling down a slope. Here, the ground was the only thing that probably wouldn't kill them.

A buzzing noise rose to the right of them. Nico shone his light there, but he couldn't make out anything in the penetrating darkness.

A slither behind them. What if not all the snakes had been eaten?

Fabian invoked Samantha's voice. She would be all rational, telling him that the snakes at this zoo were harmless. Probably a lot more harmless than the new inhabitants of Terraria.

The silence became unbearable. "So, if this is your bro—"

"There's something on me," Matt said in a voice so thin Fabian didn't even recognise it at first.

Rachel shone her light at him. "There's no—it's a worm. It's crawling across your sock."

Matt turned so pale Fabian thought he would pass out. In fact, he was swaying slightly back and forth. His lips moved, but no sound came out. Only on the second try, they heard "...'ay... 'em."

"Spray them?" Nico asked. "Sure." He moved forward and sprayed the potion against Matt's ankle.

Matt hissed in pain, and when Nico picked the dead worm off, the skin underneath was burned. Instantly, Nico let the worm fall and shook out his fingers. "What the..."

"There are a lot more coming," Rachel said.

His hand shaking, Fabian raised his phone and spray bottle at the same time. The light fell on a dark mass, but the mass began to move and wriggle, and Fabian swallowed his breath. Countless worms, maggots, and centipedes covered the ground, creeping forward like a tide of invertebrates.

"Spray!" Nico shouted, and he, Rachel, and Fabian leapt into action.

Purplish fog spread all around them, slowing down the wriggling tide. But slowly, the mist dissipated. The bottles were empty.

"Shit!" Fabian threw away his bottle, unsure of what to do now.

"Flush them away, Fabian!" Rachel called for him. "I know you can do it!"

Fabian dropped his phone into his pocket and raised his arms. *Concentrate on the water.* There was some water in the turtle enclosure. Or the fountain. There was a fountain at the front. Gosh. He didn't even know where the front was.

Instead, his eyes drifted to Matt, who hadn't moved a finger since the worms had appeared. His left hand holding the spray bottle was half raised. The other one with the sword had already sunk. His lips moved constantly without making a sound, and his eyes were dry from staring too long. There would be no help coming from Matt.

Apart from one thing. Fabian grabbed the spray bottle from Matt's limp fingers and advanced again. Contrary to his own, it was still half-full, and Fabian managed to get the flood of worms under control.

When the purple mist lifted, only a few still wriggled on the ground—but not all were dead. Instead, they had retreated, slithering back into the darkness, from which a figure emerged.

Not even Fabian's worst nightmares could've prepared him for this sight. The person who stepped into the light was as tall as an average human, but the only part remotely human about him were the green eyes in his face. Everything else was covered in—or *made of*—insects, worms, and spiders. And they moved. The shape of his nose, mouth, and ears stayed true, but the surface ebbed and flowed and wriggled until Fabian was overcome by motion sickness.

"What the hell is that?" Nico whispered.

"The konnurar," Matt replied, his voice sounding as if he had to drag his tongue out of mud.

The figure remained at the edge of the light, where the last worm joined him. "You're the intruders. The murderers." His voice had a low hum to it, like a swarm of bees discovering speech.

"Murderers?" Nico protested. "We're not the ones controlling bloodthirsty little monsters!"

"Instead, you're killing them," the konnurar said, sending a chill down Fabian's back.

He'd only made a stupid joke about the demon being an ambassador for his creatures, but now he realised he'd been right. And they had just killed thousands of his protégés.

The konnurar smiled, a terrible sight. As if the insects stretched with him, crawling in and out of his mouth. "And thus, you'll have to pay the price. You and all the other mindless humans."

"Yeah, I think not!" Matt suddenly launched himself forward, raising his sword.

Fabian watched in terror as the sword sliced through the konnurar as if nothing but air held the creatures together. The insects fell apart, once again becoming a flood. They washed over Matt, who screamed and ran.

Matt *actually* ran. Fabian was half a mind to follow him. What else were they supposed to do? What else *could* they do? But by then, the wave of creatures had reached the Hadden twins. Nico cried out, batting at the bees and spiders now crawling on him. Fabian stumbled backwards only to see the insects washing over Rachel. He heard her scream and then—

Nothing.

Rachel quieted down. She had been completely encased by the crawling mess. It made her look like the konnurar had before. A moment later, his face appeared on the back of her head, and Fabian's legs gave way.

He landed on his bum in a mess of worm entrails and maggot corpses, staring at the konnurar who'd taken over one of his best friends. Just like that.

"Rachel!" Nico screamed. He lunged at her, swiping his hands all over her body. It didn't do anything. The areas he cleared were repopulated by other creatures, and a moment later, Nico went to his knees, screaming in agony. His hands shone so red Fabian thought they were bleeding.

"Maybe if I…" Matt had stopped running. He was turning back, his sword raised in front of him.

"No!" Fabian shouted in horror. Slicing up the konnurar was one thing, but this time it wasn't just air under him but their friend. Rachel was under there. "She's alive."

The konnurar smirked. "Barely."

Anger rose in Fabian's chest. This demon, who hated humans so much he would kill them all for his precious insect friends, was holding Rachel hostage. And he found it amusing.

Suddenly, the water was there. He sensed the vast amount of it in the fountain, saw it in the enclosures, heard how it moved around the pipes. It was everywhere: on the sides, in the air, in all the bodies of the little critters enveloping Rachel. All Fabian had to do was seize it.

His index fingers and thumbs met in front of him in the shape of a capital delta. Fabian had barely blinked before the water shot through the delta and hit the konnurar in the face. More potent than a mass of creatures, the water washed over their enemy, ripped apart the blanket of worms and insects, and flushed them all down the corridor.

More and more water came from Fabian's hands, washing in front of him until the aisle was as clean as if it had been newly built. Not a nest or web in sight. And still, he could not stop.

A headache was building in his head, as if the water he drew on now came from his own brain. Pain flashed before his eyes. His arms grew heavy, yet they were stuck. Fabian had forgotten how to lower them.

Suddenly, there was a hand on his arm. It pressed down gently until his arms gave way. He fell back onto his knees as the pressure left him.

"You can stop now," a soft voice said to him. And there was Rachel, free from the critters that had taken over her and wet to the bone. But she was smiling as if she'd seen an angel. "You did it."

Steps sounded next to him. A sword was sheathed. "Yeah, there's no way he can reform himself after that," Matt said, now back to being all confident.

"It even soothed my hands," Nico said. He was still out of breath and as wet as his sister. His focus was entirely on his reddened hands. They weren't bloody as Fabian had initially thought, but they looked painful, nonetheless.

Slowly, the realisation hit him. The water and him. He'd done this. The water had followed his call when he'd most needed it. He had destroyed a monster—and half of the building. The pressure of the water hadn't just washed away all the creatures but broken glass and bent railways. A finger-width of water still shimmered on the floor.

Fabian looked at his hands. He should've felt elated, but instead, he was terrified. This sort of power, so uncontrollable and foreign. He couldn't allow himself to get angry anymore. Or feel any other strong emotion. Not unless he figured out how to wield this power safely.

Just as he was slipping into a panic attack, Rachel crouched down, put her hands on both sides of his face, and looked into his eyes. "You saved me... all of us. This is a good thing, Fabian."

"But I don't want to do this. This whole… monster-fighting thing. I never want to face another demon like this." Every word was true. Because that was the consequence. If he had this power, and Lucille had her spells, and Matt his sword, and Rachel her dreams… If Nico's theory was true and those Emblems of Power would eventually belong to the six of them, then that meant fighting monsters would become a regular part of their lives. And he couldn't imagine anything worse than that.

Rachel sighed and lowered both hands and face. "Not even if it means you can keep the people you love safe?"

"Sam!" In an instant, he was up on his feet and running back to where they'd come from, feet sloshing through the water.

There were still threads of spiderwebs in this part of the hall, but as far as Fabian could see, there were no spiders or any other creatures. It was still wet, though. Fabian slipped and slid, and barrelled right into Samantha and Lucille.

"Woah! Slow down!" Samantha said, steadying him. "Are you okay?"

He looked down at her, searching for the spiderwebs, and found Lucille tearing off the last bits. She was huffing from exhaustion. "Thanks for the water. It made them slightly less sticky." She wiped her hand on her cheek and grimaced at the same time. "Gosh, I'll probably have spiderwebs stuck in my hair for the rest of my life."

"We can pretend it's a new style," Samantha joked. There were more than enough spiderwebs left on her. But she beamed at Fabian and then at the others who appeared behind them. "Did you find the konnurar?"

"Oh yeah," Nico answered. "Found and defeated him. Or at least, Fabian did."

"He's a hero," Rachel claimed, barely audible.

And Matt added, "Cleaned the whole hall out."

"Yeah, and almost destroyed it in the process," Fabian grumbled. "Well, at least nobody will complain about the door anymore. Could we leave before someone asks us what happened here?"

All of them chuckled. Matt clapped his shoulder and was the first to leave the dreaded Terraria hall. "Hopefully, they'll demolish the whole thing with all the inhabitants gone or dead."

"Oh no, Greenvalley loves its zoo, and Terraria is its prized gem. The donations will flood in tomorrow morning, make no mistake." Nico gleefully put an arm around Matt's shoulders.

Lucille picked something up from the ground and dropped it on Matt's arm. "They might even start a worm farm."

Matt jumped, slapping at his arms until the piece of spiderweb had stuck to his hand. His eyes narrowed. "I hate you."

"Not as much as you hate worms," Lucille said in a delighted, singsong voice.

Despite his exhaustion and dread, Fabian found himself smiling. He could live without the life-threatening monster hunts, but he wasn't so sure the same could be said about the monster hunters.

Samantha slung an arm around his waist and grinned up at him. "So, you were a hero back there?"

Fabian felt himself blush. "An accidental one."

"Mmm, my favourite kind." She giggled and leaned against him.

Fabian put an arm around her, glad to see her safe and mostly unharmed. Yeah, he could definitely live with that part of the adventure.

Nico

It was close to midnight when Nico and Rachel returned home. The excitement of the fight against the konnurar had worn off, and exhaustion had befallen both. Nico's hands were itching worse than anything he'd ever experienced, while Rachel frequently scratched her head, as if insects were still crawling through her hair. She had a long detangling session ahead of her.

Washing wouldn't help his hands. As Nico checked them under the light of a streetlamp, he saw a number of pink traces and dark bulges where he'd been bitten, and when he bent his fingers, three of his knuckles hurt.

"Maybe we should go to the hospital," Rachel suggested.

"And what are we gonna tell them? Hello, I got bitten by hellbees while acid-secreting worms crawled over my hands?" He shook his head, then subtly checked on his sister.

She'd been encased from head to toe in the demonic critters. The konnurar himself had claimed she had only been barely alive under his presence. On first looks, her skin seemed to be unblemished, but in the light of a street lantern, there were bruises all over her body. "Do *you* want to go to the hospital?"

Rachel shrugged. "I feel okay. It hurts, but I don't think they can do anything about it."

Curiosity hit him suddenly. "How did it feel?"

"Weird. Like... like I was buried alive," she said, in such an eerie voice that Nico shuddered. "I couldn't move, couldn't see or hear... The only thing I could feel were the insects. They were crawling all over me and... in me." She shuddered. "It was, quite frankly, disgusting and frightening."

Nico put his arm around her shoulder and drew her close. "I'm so sorry."

"It's okay. Fabian saved me. It's all good now," she said, but Nico knew that tone. Rachel rarely complained, instead shutting all her worries and pains—and even love—inside.

"He did. I guess that means he's got my approval."

Rachel laughed. "As if your best friend didn't have that before."

Nico pretended to be doubtful and grimaced. "I wouldn't be so sure. You're still my sister, so even best friends need to prove themselves."

"By defeating demons?" Rachel asked, still amused.

"Minimum requirement."

She laughed again, and Nico's heart soared. He'd seen her unhappy way too often.

They reached their house, and Nico got out the keys. "Do you think she's still awake?" In his mind, he saw his mother fretting in the living room, startling at every sound as hope surged, only to be disappointed again. And when they entered, she'd hug them so tight their ribs might burst.

Instantly, Rachel's mirth evaporated. Instead of answering, she inspected her feet. Nico sighed and opened the door. Yeah, wishful thinking was just that: wishful thinking.

Affectionate laughter rang out from the living room. Their mother had company. She was sitting on the couch with an unknown man, running her hand through his hair while she balanced a wine glass in the other.

Nico's face flushed. He stomped on the floor and dropped his keys with an audible sound. The noise drew his mother's attention, and she looked over her shoulder, annoyed. Then she waved him off. "Go to bed, Nico."

"Rachel is hurt," he said instead.

Next to him, Rachel looked absolutely horrified that he would pull her into this. She shook her head and retreated to the stairs.

"Rachel is big enough to take care of herself," his mother said dismissively, then returned her attention to the stranger, smiling at him. "Kids these days."

"You didn't even look at her!" Inadvertently, Nico was getting louder. "I'm hurt, too." He raised his hands to show off his marks.

The man in the living room was getting agitated. "Perhaps I should..."

"Stay." Their mother clicked her tongue, pushed the wine glass into her lover's hand and got up. "I said go to bed, Nico."

"So, you never actually care about us. It's midnight. We were god-knows-where, didn't leave a message, and came home badly hurt," he listed, fishing for any kind of reaction.

"And you're here now and obviously well enough to start drama. Go to bed!" she said for the third time and pulled the door shut. Behind it, he heard her walk back to the couch.

Nico clenched his fists. The anger coursing through his veins was strong enough to make him want to smash the key bowl. Or something else. March into the living room and punch the stupid guy who was more important to their mother than her own children.

"Let's go upstairs," Rachel whispered. Her eyes were shimmering with tears.

Tears that were their mother's fault. And she didn't even care enough to see them. To go upstairs—to *bed*—was impossible for Nico. He needed to let off steam. Needed to vent. To... his gaze fell on the key bowl.

If his mother didn't care about them, why should he pretend to be a good boy? There was school tomorrow. Other parents would worry if their children weren't home by midnight. His mother hadn't even noticed her children had been out past bedtime without so much as a message. She'd never even bothered clearing away the splinters of broken glass she'd thrown at Rachel. The shards were in a heap to the side of the door.

"Nico..."

"Tell Mum I don't know when I'll be back." He grabbed his key and was out of the door before Rachel was able to stop him.

Outside, he grabbed his phone and pulled up Svenja's number. Without thinking, Nico pushed the button to call her. It took her almost ten seconds to answer. Ten seconds in which Nico prowled the lawn in front of his house.

"You can't call this late," Svenja complained.

"I need to come over," he said instead. "I just had a fight with my mum and—"

"You can't!" Svenja interrupted him. "Look, I'm sorry, but it's a school night, and my dad wouldn't allow it."

Nico stopped, growing more desperate. "You could sneak me in." He clenched his painful fingers to retain some of their mobility.

"No, I can't. Stop this, Nico. I'm tired and... I can't deal with your drama right now. Good night."

The call broke off. Nico stopped cold. His girlfriend had just hung up on him when he'd needed her most. Granted, it was almost 1 a.m., but he would've let her sneak in. Not that his mother would care. He could probably seduce Svenja right there in the living room, and she'd just get another glass of wine.

Nico tightened his grip around his phone, sneering at the grass. So, going to Svenja's was out, but going back inside was unbearable. Where did minors go when they should be off the streets?

Nico's anger brought him to the docks. It was a well-known place to avoid at night. But after facing a demon-insect hybrid, a few rowdy teenagers who met each night to drink, smoke, and potentially exchange drugs didn't seem like such a huge risk.

Still, his heart beat a little faster when he made out the dark shadows near the building. Rachel would freak out if she knew he was here. His sister would, but not the mother who was supposed to care for them. The thought gave him the final push Nico needed to walk onto the dock as if he owned the place.

Instantly, two shadowy figures moved away from the wall and stepped in his way. The guys weren't much older than Nico, though he couldn't remember seeing them at school. A cloud of beer reached his nose. Under normal circumstances these pasty white boys wouldn't seem like much of a threat, but give them the power of numbers and make them drunk enough to do something stupid, and Nico could feel his skin tingle.

"Who are you?" One of them asked. He had deep-seated eyes and a crooked nose. His feet were planted in a wide stance, and he had crossed his arms, trying to appear more imposing.

His friend, a taller blonde with acne on his face, staggered slightly, bumping into the other. "Got lost?"

"I'm right where I want to be," Nico said, trying to keep his voice smooth and confident. Inside, his heart was racing. The adrenaline shot to his head and made him feel far too awake for the time of day.

"I asked who the hell you are!" the first one spat.

Nico pretended to measure the two of them up. "Does it matter?"

Internally, he wanted to shake himself. Why was he provoking them? He wasn't looking for a fight. In fact, his hands still hurt too much to clench them into proper fists. But the pain also fuelled his anger, and right now, he didn't truly mind testing how far that would carry him.

"Guys, relax!" Someone came from behind him and put an arm around his shoulder. It was Jan. "This is Nico. Nico, meet my friends Felix and Leon. He's a good man. Right?"

Slightly flustered, Nico turned to him. "Uhm, yeah, sure."

Jan clapped his shoulder. "Alright. Let's get the man a beer and relax."

A few minutes later, Nico knew all their names, had downed his first beer, and had settled down at the water's edge with Jan, a six-pack between them. Jan was rolling a joint in his lap and lit it. "You want one?"

"Nah, I'm good," Nico said out of reflex. Rachel would be so disappointed if he tried drugs. But not his mum. The thought bubbled up unbidden, fuelling his anger once more. "Okay, fine."

Jan grinned. "Atta boy."

He handed him the joint, and Nico took a careful puff. Sickening sweetness filled his lungs. It scratched slightly in his throat, so he took another to get rid of it. Slowly, the scratching subsided, and he felt his muscles—and more importantly, his brain—relax.

"Not too bad, huh?" Jan took the joint back and inhaled with a smile on his lips. Then he took another swig from his beer and passed the joint back. "So, what brings you out tonight?"

"Nothing really. It's more..." Nico searched his brain for the right words. "I think it's more what keeps me from being in. Inside, I mean."

Jan chuckled. "And what's that?"

"My mum? She's... oh god, she's a mess. Worst mum of the year. The decade!" Nico raised his bottle high, as if to toast her.

It had been almost ten years since the divorce. Something had gone wrong between his parents. His mother had once told him when he was much younger that it had finally caught up to them that they'd only married because she'd gotten pregnant. And now she was stuck with two children, supporting herself as a mediocre hairdresser, while their father lived it up as a Maths professor in LA. Rachel adored their dad, but Nico didn't think any better of him. Obviously, he hadn't fought for them to stay with him, which made Nico assume his mother was right. Their father probably enjoyed having the freedom returned that their conception had cost him.

"Parents," Jan agreed. "Always meddling. Always trying to control everything."

"I wish," Nico laughed out loud. "My mother doesn't care what I do. If I get run over by a car or stung to death by a hellbee, she'd only notice when the police knocked on our door. And then probably wouldn't care."

Jan shook his head. "Oh, man. That's rough! If I got killed by a hellbee, my father would tell me to knock it off and stop that nonsense." He grinned again. "He's such a tool." For a while, he chuckled softly, then frowned. "What actually is a hellbee?"

Nico waved him off. "Aggressive bugger." He stared at his hands, examining the light traces and darker bumps on his skin. And suddenly, there was this urge to talk about it. "Do you believe in monsters?" Nico knew he should shut up, but his brain couldn't figure out why. It's not as if the monsters were his secret. Or needed to be kept secret from anyone. "Like real monsters. And magic."

"I believe in magic mushrooms," Jan joked. He started patting his jacket. "I might have some or something similar, if you want to."

Nico stared at the dark river under his feet, only half-hearing Jan's words. "My sister can walk through dreams. Samantha brews magic potions and Fabian can control water." In his mind, he saw Fabian taking the dark river water and flooding all of Greenvalley with it. Washing it all away: the negligence, the pain, the anger.

Shaking himself out of the vision, he looked at Jan. "And those new guys, Matt and Lucille. He's got a magic sword, and she can do actual magic, like spells and curses."

Jan stared at him, the bottle half-forgotten on his lips. "Maybe I'll try what you've got."

Nico found himself laughing. Louder and louder, until the laughter turned to sobs and tears ran down his cheeks. He rubbed them away with his arm. "My sister almost died today. I think. I mean, I don't know. A demon made up of worms and spiders and horrible hellbees took control of her at the zoo, encased her from head to toe, and then spoke through her. It was mega-creepy. If it weren't for Fabian washing them all away with his magic, who knows what would've happened?"

"That's dope!"

Anger flared in Nico. "I'm serious, man! Check these out!" He dropped the beer bottle and held out his hands for Jan to see.

In the pale light of the street lamp, the damage was hard to make out. Nevertheless, Jan bent over them and inspected them from the top, the side, and the bottom. "Woah. It *is* magic."

Nico's hands were itching as if a thousand ants were crawling under the skin. He hissed and clenched his fists in a desperate attempt to stop the sudden attack. *Poisonous* went through his mind. "I..." And then he saw what Jan was seeing.

A soft golden glow had surrounded his hands, dissolving the bites and stings. The swelling went back, and the pinkish traces were replaced by smooth, dark skin. When the itching subsided, his hands were entirely healed, spotless as before. Even more than they'd been before. Nico had always had a little scar on his left pinkie, but it was gone now. As was the gold.

He repeated Jan's expression. "Woah."

"That is pretty dope. Beer?" Jan offered him a replacement bottle.

Distracted by his hands, Nico took the bottle and chugged half of it before he realised what he was doing. His head was swimming. But the pain was gone. And so was the anger. It had all been replaced by endless wonder. His hands had healed themselves, just like that.

"You're right. That is pretty dope."

Rachel

From next door, soft moans rang through the wall. They were only soft because Rachel had plugged her ears and buried her head under two silk-covered pillows. She was tired and exhausted after washing and detangling her hair, and she still couldn't fall asleep. The problem was that her ears strained to listen for the door and steps on the stairs, while at the same time tried to shut out the sounds from her mother's room.

It was past two o'clock and Nico still hadn't come home. Rachel turned to her phone for the fiftieth time since he'd left. Their chat still looked the same. She'd asked him where he was. And when he was coming home. According to the app, he'd read the messages, but never bothered to reply.

Something was wrong with him. They'd always been close, often feeling like they were the only thing stable in a world hell-bent on breaking apart. She'd always shared everything with him, even her stupid crush on Fabian. Mostly because he read her like a book, anyway.

Rachel used to be able to do the same, but no longer. Since he'd got himself a girlfriend, he barely spent any time at home anymore. With his sister. She didn't know Svenja very well. She was one year above them and part of the school's volleyball team. A sport Nico also enjoyed. Last year, they'd entered as part of the mixed team at the Harz school tournament. The team had made it into the finals, winning third place, and the two of them had emerged as a couple.

They never hung out together with the rest of their friends, and he rarely brought her home. If he did, they were either up in his room or left again quickly. Rachel had met her, of course, but they'd never been together in the same room for more than five minutes. He must've been with her and too busy to check his phone.

But he'd *seen* the messages. The notifications didn't lie. And besides, as far as Rachel was aware of, Nico had never slept at Svenja's. Would she be a person who would sneak him in after midnight if he suddenly turned up at her door? Rachel had no idea, and it frustrated her. It was almost as if she didn't know her brother that well.

Steps on the stairs.

Rachel raised her head from her pillows, straining to listen. Someone came up the stairs. No, down. And it wasn't Nico.

The moaning had stopped. Her mother was done and sent her lover home in the middle of the night. Rachel heard them talking quietly at the door. Her mother laughed. Then the door shut, and she came up the stairs alone.

Her heart beating faster, Rachel focussed on the steps coming closer. She'd left the door to Nico's room wide open. Her mother must notice he wasn't home yet. Then she'd come to her and ask...

But that never happened. Her mother's feet never faltered. She entered the bathroom, took a shower, brushed her teeth, and went to bed without so much as stopping at Nico's door, much less knocking on Rachel's.

When the sound of soft snoring rang through the wall, Rachel swallowed down a bout of tears. She didn't get it. She simply failed to understand how her mother had just stopped caring. It hadn't always been that way. But over the years...

Where are you, Nico? she typed into her phone.

No reaction.

Rachel waited and waited, but no confirmation of the message being seen appeared. And slowly, her vision blurred, her eyelids grew heavy, and she fell asleep.

She opened her eyes to a green meadow, flowers all around her. A soft wind blew through the grass, bending it in her direction. And though Rachel saw the entire meadow in its beautiful colours, the sky above her was the night sky, full of stars and nebulas, as if the entire cosmos had drawn closer.

This was the place she always felt drawn to. Her happy place, in a way. It was always at peace. No nightmares, no disturbance. Nothing but the wind, which caressed her like a loving parent.

But it wasn't just Rachel's place. The meadow didn't belong to her, but the young woman with the long brown hair and doe-like eyes. Annette was her name, and she always sat in the middle of the meadow, picking her flowers, and braiding them into a wreath that never neared completion.

"There you are," she greeted Rachel with a loving smile that made her heart melt like butter. "Again."

"Yes, it's me again." She sat down next to Annette and picked one of her flowers.

The girl stopped and hugged her fiercely, her chin snuggling into the hollow between neck and shoulder. "I love you, Rachel." Her lips brushed her cheek in a quick kiss.

"I love you, too, Mum." But then she picked the arms off her. "I just wish you'd love me outside of the dreamworld, as well."

"I do." Honesty washed over Rachel, making her believe every word.

But how real was this? Her instincts said yes, yet her brain convinced her otherwise. What if she'd wandered into her mother's dream or what if it was her own, the dreamworld she'd built for herself, because reality didn't cut it. "You threw a glass at me and called me—" She couldn't speak that word out loud. Not here. Especially not here.

"I'm so sorry, honey. I didn't mean it." Annette sighed heavily, and the meadow darkened a little. Petals fell from her wreath. "I don't deserve you. Or your brother."

"He's so angry!" Rachel rubbed her cheeks. They were wet, though she hadn't shed a tear yet. "You're getting worse, and he's getting worse, and I don't know what to do."

The wind picked up, blowing more petals across the grass. "It scares me," Annette whispered. "All of it. This is the only place that's safe."

Rachel didn't know what to make of her words. What could possibly be scary about raising two children? Sure, it might be a struggle sometimes, but that didn't explain the depth of feeling that washed over the meadow. The words came from her mother's heart, but what scared her so much?

"You."

The word plunged like a dagger into Rachel's heart. The wind was a storm now, tugging at Annette's braid and drying Rachel's tears. No flower survived the onslaught.

Her mother sat there, crying, without making a sound. "All of it. You. You're all of it. It's all of you. And if you're not careful..."

Rachel refused to listen. Reality was bad enough. She wouldn't allow her dreamworld to suffer the same fate.

"Leave!" she said in a voice as cold as the hail that now fell on them—and as hurtful. "You don't want me in your life? Well, I don't want *you* here. Go!"

And with that, her mother vanished. The meadow was destroyed. It was no longer safe. Not safe from Rachel, at least.

She sighed, sadness returning with the breeze. Rachel rejected it as forcefully as she'd rejected her mother. This was her world, her dream. And it would be beautiful again, now that her mother no longer had a place here. After everything she'd done and said, Rachel hadn't had a choice but to cut her out. But it was better this way. The meadow bloomed again, more beautiful than ever before.

All she had to do was cut her mother out. It'd taken years for her to come to that realisation, but now she had. She didn't need her mother, not the shrill, colourful version of her, and not the innocent, vulnerable girl with her stolen dreams.

What had worked in the dreamworld would work outside of it as well. Rachel only had to find out how to do it without getting hurt herself. And when she finally did, she could bloom there, as well.

Jan

"So, magic is real?" Jan tipped the bottle to his lips and took another sip. "And monsters, too?"

Nico didn't even listen to him, completely enthralled with his newly healed hands. But Jan didn't need to hear his confirmation. He knew it. All these years, he'd known monsters were real. And nobody had believed him.

He emptied the bottle and leaned back to grab another. "You want one, too?"

"Yes. Yes, please." Nico finally stopped looking at his hands and grabbed the bottle from Jan's hand. But he didn't move to open it. Instead, his dark eyes focused on the glass.

Jan chuckled. "It's not going to open itself, you know." Watching other people drunk as heck was hilarious. And Nico was no different. "Here, let me help you."

"No." Nico's eyes gleamed with a sudden—and probably idiotic—idea. "Let's check this out."

Before Jan could stop him, Nico smashed the neck of the bottle against the edge of the dock. The splintering of glass cut through the night, making Jan wince. It was a horrible break. So low that half the beer sloshed out and dripped into the Reese. With its jagged edges, there was no way in hell Jan would drink from it. Not even in his drunken state.

But would Nico?

The thought flashed suddenly through Jan's addled brain. The boy was a mess. Parental trouble. The usual thing, but it had driven him to seek out their spot.

More alert than he cared to be, Jan watched Nico's every move. For a moment, it looked as if he considered drinking from the bottle, but then he tipped it over and emptied the entire contents in the river. "Oh, man, it's not like we've got an endless supply," Jan complained.

But Nico wasn't finished. He spun the bottle around, then quickly drew the edge over his thumb.

Jan wasn't quick enough. His hand caught the bottle after the fact, when blood was already spilling out of the thumb. "What do you think you're doing there?" he barked, tearing the object of danger out of Nico's hand and throwing it into the river.

"Relax! I'm testing my healing power."

"Your healing..." Jan shut up. Like Nico, he bent over the thumb and watched it intently. Blood was still flowing, dripping onto Nico's pants. There was no healing.

With a click of his tongue, Jan grabbed a tissue from his pants and took hold of Nico's thumb. A sharp pain flashed through his own thumb. "Ow." There must've been a glass splinter. But by the time he looked again, the golden glow had appeared and healed the cut.

"It really works!" Nico grinned. "Give me another bottle."

Jan's hand shot out to stop him. "No, no, no. You've had enough for today." Contrary to Nico, the incident had sobered him up. Healing powers were cool, but he could do without a bloodbath tonight. "Come on, I'll bring you home."

"I don't want to go home!" Nico protested. "It's not even a home. I mean a home should be warm, right?"

"You've got heater issues?"

"No! I mean human warmth. Like love. Motherly love."

Gosh, Nico was drunk. Jan hunkered down to hear the rest of what was sure to be an entertaining ramble.

"Like my mother needs to be warm... to care. That's it. She needs to care. And if a mother doesn't care, then it's not warm. I mean, it's not a home. So, I don't have a home. And I don't wanna go there." Nico nodded as he made that important point. Then he turned a little too much and almost keeled over into the river.

"Woah!" Jan held him back by his jacket. "Okay, okay, I got you. Then do you want to come to my place?" His mother cared. Quite annoyingly so, which meant it was a home, by Nico's definition.

Nico looked at him in confusion. "Your place?"

"Just come!" Jan got up to his feet and dragged Nico with him. The lightweight stumbled around until he sagged into Jan's shoulder. He put an arm around Nico to steady him, grabbed the remaining beer bottles, and handed them to Felix as they made their way across to the others. "I'm calling it a night. Getting him somewhere safe. I'll see you guys around."

The others just hooted and turned to their substance abuse again.

Jan readjusted his grip and pulled Nico along.

"Would you be quiet?" Jan hissed as he leaned Nico against the wall outside his family's flat. The stupid elevator was broken again, so they'd had to take the stairs to the fifth floor. And all the way, Nico had been either talking loudly or banging his hand on the railing, so that the sound reverberated through the entire building.

He pushed his key in and opened the door to a long corridor, then kicked his shoes off. "My parents are sleeping."

"Why?" Nico asked, not even trying to keep his voice down.

"Because it's like three in the morning, idiot." Jan didn't bother with Nico's shoes. He'd take them off once they got into his room.

But before they could, the door on the right opened and his little sister peeked into the corridor. "Jan?" she asked sleepily. "Who's that?"

"A friend. Go back to sleep, Anne."

Anne was fifteen, four years younger than him, and everything he was not: hard-working, kind, helpful, ambitious. The whole lot. And mostly, she was annoying, always butting in where she didn't belong.

"Is he okay?" she asked.

"Of course—" Jan broke off when he saw Nico almost bending in half in front of the mirror to look at himself upside down. "Yeah, all great. Now go to bed and leave us alone." He grabbed Nico and pulled him into the room next to Anne's.

His bedroom was narrow, almost tunnel-like, thanks to the furniture on the left and right. At the end of it, a cluttered desk sat under the window. His bed was on the right, snugly fit between two cupboards. On the left was a set of drawers and his crystal collection. A bunch of comics were piled up next to the drawers. Jan had meant to sort them, but then just left them where they were. Now Nico was sifting through them.

"Can I borrow these?" he asked.

Jan shrugged. "Sure." He sat down on his bed and rubbed his face. Then he grabbed the water bottle near his bed and drank a few sips. Feeling his head clear a little, he nudged Nico with his foot. "Hey, Nico. Tell me more about that monster you fought."

"My mum?" Nico asked before giggling over his own joke. He straightened his back only to plonk himself back down, making a terrible noise as he hit the drawers. "It was a konnu— konner— Demon-Greenpeace guy."

"Demon-Greenpeace guy?" Jan asked, wondering if he should believe anything Nico said tonight. But he had to. It had to be true.

"Yeah. He was an 'all-insects rule'-kind of guy. But all the insects were from Hell. Which is a real place. Not where my mum goes to. Or maybe she does. Gosh, I wish I could send her to Hell."

Jan snapped his fingers in front of Nico. "Focus, man. We're talking monsters and magic here, not your stupid mum. And you and the others fight monsters?"

Nico's hand wandered around the knob of the bottom drawer. As he talked, he kept pulling the drawer out and watching it roll back in with a thump. "Yeah, kind of. We're pretty new to it. Only this crawly-creatures guy and the shadow at school."

"There was a shadow at school?" That sounded like some drunken talk. But then Jan remembered that weird night when the rest of the world had gone mad. "Wait a minute. You mean the bogeyman?" He remembered meeting the guys in school. That had been odd, but with all the odd stuff happening that night, Jan hadn't questioned it.

"Yeah, that one. He hated light. So, Lucille light... lightified him." A particularly loud bump occurred as Nico let the drawer roll back from the maximum distance.

Jan winced. "Can you stop that?"

"Sorry." Nico folded his hands into his lap. "Anyway, we totally beat the shit out of those monsters."

"That is so cool." All his life, Jan had believed in monsters. He hadn't grown out of it like other children because he'd *seen* the monsters. He'd even been attacked by one when he was only three years old. But no one had believed him. They'd been too busy worrying about Anne, who had come into the world prematurely, to listen to a toddler's rambling. Jan had never forgiven them.

Every time he tried to talk to his parents about the monsters and magic he saw in Greenvalley, they'd told him off and tried to gaslight him. And here it was, the proof he'd been looking for all his life. No, he wasn't stupid enough to take a drunken boy's rambling for the plain truth, but even as smashed as Nico was, some things were too wild to be made up. Like *freaking Samantha Kollmer* going on monster hunts. Sure, everyone talked about Samantha believing in magic like a five-year-old, but she was smart. And she was a total goody-two-shoes who didn't run around in abandoned zoos on a school night.

Unless she really fought monsters.

"I'm gonna call Svenja and tell her about my healing powers," Nico announced.

Jan frowned at him. "Who's Svenja?"

"My girlfriend." Nico had his phone out already, letting it ring.

"Don't—" But the poor girl had already picked up. Jan massaged the bridge of his nose as he watched the disaster unfold. Calling girlfriends when you were drunk was a big no-no.

"Hi, beautiful," Nico slurred into the phone. "Guess what! I can do magic."

"Give me that!" Jan moved in and grabbed the phone from Nico's hands. "Hey, Sven. Jan here. Don't mind your boyfriend. He's gonna be fine. Have a good night." He didn't wait for Svenja to respond and ended the call.

Nico protested. "You can't do that!" He lunged forward to get his phone back, but Jan held him off with one arm. There was a bit of a scuffle, which ended with Nico crashing into the bedside table and sending Jan's bottle spinning onto the floor.

"Shit!" Jan hissed.

A moment later, there were steps in the corridor, then banging on the door. "What the heck is going on here?" his father barked. Jan shot to his feet as the door was opened and his father stepped in, his face in a familiar scowl. "Do you know how late it is?"

"No, tell me," Jan shot back, fully aware of the early morning hour.

"Your mother and I are trying to sleep. She has to get up for her shift in less than an hour."

"Well, I bet she's glad she's not going to sleep through the alarm then." Jan couldn't help snap. Riling him up had become second nature.

As did the darkening of his father's face whenever he had to deal with him. "I told you not to talk to me like that."

"I'm only talking to you the way you taught me." Jan bit his bottom lip, forcing himself to calm down. Every conversation with his father made his blood boil. He couldn't wait until he got his own place.

"You little—"

"Yes? Little what?" If his father wanted a fight, Jan was ready for him. He had a black belt in karate. His father only knew his way around a pickaxe. "Come on, say it."

But before his father could do so, his mother appeared in the doorway, pressing into her husband's side. "What is going on here? Jan, who's that?"

Jan didn't even look. "A friend."

"Is he okay?" his mother asked, concern creasing her forehead.

Nico hadn't said anything so far, and when Jan looked down, he found him passed out and slightly snoring. "He's fine. Just sleeping it off. He'll be quiet now."

His father shook his head in disappointment. "Drinking on a school night. It's no wonder your grades are taking a dive."

"Taking a dive? They've been solidly at the bottom for a while now," Jan quipped.

"That's not funny, Jan." The look on his mother's face was full of dismay. It pained her that he was scraping the bottom of the barrel, but Jan couldn't care less. If it had been up to him, he would've left school after tenth grade, but his parents had pressured him to seek higher education. As if he wanted to go to university one day and receive even more schooling.

"Dad said you need to be up for a shift. So maybe we should all go to sleep?" Jan offered, hoping they would leave him in peace for now.

His father's face darkened again, but his mother talked to him in hushed tones. "Let it go, Stefan. We can talk about it in the morning."

As if Jan would stick around for that.

"No more noise. There are other people in this house who want to sleep too," were the words his father left him with.

Jan had half a mind to turn on his stereo and listen to some music at the highest volume, but decided to let it go. There were monsters to think about. Dangerous, exciting monsters.

Part 3

Ghosts & Dragons

Samantha

As the only girl in the ten-person Chemistry major class, Samantha found herself once again in a working group with two guys: Robert, one of the clumsiest students she knew, and Cian, one of Cheryl's lackeys. It could've been the worst group, but it was surprisingly fun. Both were treating her like a normal classmate. Not that she had expected anything else from Robert, but Cian had defied all worrisome expectations.

She'd never shared a class with him until this year, and all she really knew about him was that he was Alan Aster's best friend, played and loved soccer, and was well-liked by the girls, but had only ever had a longer relationship with Shayna Richards, the only girl of the Elite Clique Samantha could remotely stand when she met her on her own.

"Did you watch that alchemy thing last night?" Robert said, revealing himself to be the only teenager still watching cable TV. "It was really interesting to learn about all the wild ideas they had, but also the techniques people used back then."

Samantha kept her head down, focusing on the acid-base experiment they were currently tasked with. The TV show sounded interesting, but with Cian there, she wouldn't as much as hint that she was interested in magic-related things like alchemy.

"Can we find it in the media library?" Cian asked, sounding quite intrigued. "If it is, maybe we could ask Richter to let us watch it during class." He cast around, searching. "Has anyone seen the uni ind?"

The little bottle was right next to Samantha's arm. She handed it to him and got ready to make a note on her experiment report. The tip of Cian's tongue appeared between his lips as he carefully put a few drops of universal indicator into a beaker. The liquid inside turned deep red. Acid.

Robert grinned on the other side of the experiment. "And then we'll do an alchemy project. Alchemy instead of chemistry. Imagine if we could turn something to gold."

Samantha chuckled quietly, but Cian's eyes widened with delight. "Yeah. And then we'll buy the school some proper equipment. Everything here is broken." Frustrated, he gave up on turning on the heating plate.

"May I?" Samantha moved in, grabbing the switch. Cian was right. The switch felt loose, as if it was going to break off any minute. But she knew exactly how to handle it. Instead of turning it around, she pushed it in until she was sure it had grabbed the ignition, and then turned it. "There you go."

Cian nodded appreciatively. "Not bad. Robert..."

"What are you doing there?" Samantha finished his sentence.

Their project partner was holding a funnel in place with his face while he tried to pour in base from a three-litre bottle. Any minute now, he would pour the base over his chin. Robert's eyes had narrowed in intense concentration. "I'm working on the experiment?"

"Would you like another funnel? You could balance it with your foot," Samantha suggested. Cian grinned widely.

Robert sighed. "No! But you could hold the funnel. It's falling off, I think."

"Oh, really?" Samantha shook her head in annoyance. "Guys! Give it to me." She took the bottle of base and the funnel from Robert, filled a wide-rimmed beaker with the base, and poured it into the burette. "And that's how we women do it."

Offended, Robert pressed his lips together, but Cian gave a mock round of applause. "Impressive work. But what would've happened if you'd got the base on your hands?"

He was referring to how she hadn't used a funnel to pour the base into the burette. Samantha felt her cheeks grow hot. She'd done so many potions, her hands never shook when she was pouring. "Well, I would've probably washed my hands as quickly as possible."

Cian laughed, and for a moment, Samantha tensed, but it was an honest laugh. Not ugly at all. "Makes sense. Sorry, carry on! Enlighten our inept male minds."

His friendly jokes were starting to get to Samantha. Irritated, she pushed an unruly lock behind her ear, which sprung back to its original position as soon as she lowered her hand. For years, she had filed Cian away as one more elite idiot—as Lucille had called them so aptly—but now that she'd worked with him for a few weeks, he seemed to be quite amiable. Not at all like Alan, or even Cheryl.

"Hey, Sam," said Robert, who was continuing the experiment. "Can't you do something like that?" When Samantha stared at him in confusion, Robert elaborated with, "I mean crafting gold. Because the presenter said alchemy is often lumped in with witchcraft."

Instantly, Samantha's stomach clenched. It had all been going too well. Instead of answering, she stared at the experiment with exceedingly painful eyes.

"Do you believe any nonsense they tell you, Robert?" Cian said at her side.

"It's not nonsense," Robert protested. "I thought you were into magic. Ani said you were pretending... I mean that you were a witch." He looked around nervously. "That's a thing nowadays, right? Women rediscover magic, their inner witch or..."

"You mean wicca?" Samantha asked before she could stop herself. Her cheeks were burning. This conversation had gone far off the deep end, and she needed to turn it around fast. "It's all nonsense. I'm not—"

"Ani's just talking shit, Robert," Cian said with far more confidence than she had. "Seriously."

Astounded, Samantha raised her head. He looked annoyed, but not with her.

"Nobody really believes in magic," he continued, "and alchemy wasn't magic either, just the predecessor of chemistry practised by a few megalomaniac dreamers. If you want to know more about it, look it up online or go to the library."

Samantha felt a bit sorry for Robert's smackdown. He pouted and continued their experiment, clearly disgruntled. But inside, her stomach relaxed. Sure, Cian didn't believe in magic, but that wasn't important.

He had defended her, not just against Robert, but against his friend as well.

She found herself smiling at him and quickly focused on the experiment before he got the wrong idea. The base was now dripping into the earlier beaker with the acid. Slowly but surely, the colour changed from red to green.

Later, when they tidied up, Cian stayed behind to help her. "Did you write down when it changed pH levels? I missed the four-to-five transition."

Asking for her notes. Now that was something she was familiar with. "Sure, you can check over there. I haven't put my stuff away yet."

Cian finished washing out the beaker before he went over and copied the base-acid ratio at the transition. "Thanks for that."

Instead of walking off, though, he waited until Samantha was done with putting away the rest of the equipment and packing her bag.

"Robert is such a tool," he joked as he fell in step beside her. "Of course, *he* would find a way to make gold. A year-twelve Chemistry student."

Samantha chuckled softly, still a little unsure what to make of this sudden familiarity. "Oh well, it would be something. I could use a little extra pocket money." There were quite a few spells and potions that all claimed to transform one material into another. But they were either so complicated Samantha wouldn't even know where to begin, or it was only a temporary transformation, an illusion really.

Cian shook his head. "He always has these wild ideas. You two know each other?"

"No. Not much, really. He used to be in your class, right? I've got like five courses with him this year, though." Robert had already made his mark on her, often speaking before thinking. He wasn't the smartest tool in the shed, but he meant well.

"Yeah, he was." Cian rolled his eyes, but he smiled almost fondly. "We're not friends, but he's okay. Like you. I mean... you're pretty fun to be around. Not at all crazy."

Samantha nodded, face turned to the ground, a swirl of emotion in her head. A part of her echoed the feelings, but the larger one was careful to trust. It could all be an elaborate joke. Cian would be nice to her until she let her guard down and then they'd all come down hard on her. "Well, you're not as arrogant as I thought, either," she muttered.

He surprised her with laughing. "Is that what you think of me?"

"You're Alan's best friend." Samantha tried to rack her brain about whether Cian had ever taken part in one of Alan's practical jokes, but she couldn't remember any instance. Alan, however, was truly an ass, and any friend of his was... well, a friend of Alan's.

Cian grimaced, looking a bit torn. Then he sighed. "Alan is... okay, to be quite honest, he still has a lot of growing up to do. But yeah, he's my brother. I mean, not really, we're only neighbours. Our backyards are right next to each other, and it's pretty much a mi casa es su casa situation. Like you and Fabian. He can be a bit of an idiot as well."

"Excuse me?" Samantha bristled for a moment, only to reconsider. If she was honest, Fabian *could* be an idiot. Still... "Only I can call him that."

Cian grinned. "Fair enough. I guess I'm just saying that we're not our friends even if we love them dearly."

It was impossible not to reciprocate Cian's grin. "Okay. I'll try not to call Alan an Elite Idiot, either." Oh, crap. Why had that slipped out of her mouth?

"Elite Idiot," Cian picked up on it, but he only chuckled. "Nah, sometimes he's exactly that. But nothing a good rap on his head or kick against his shin can't solve. Usually delivered via Shayna."

Samantha struggled with reconciling his words with the image she had of the Elite Clique. Cian made them all sound so normal. Perhaps they were just a different group of friends in the end.

Just then, Cheryl and Ani stepped into their way. Cheryl had her arms crossed and was pursing her lips as she looked up and down at Samantha's simple outfit. Self-conscious, she assessed herself. Years ago, she'd been into cute skirts and colourful tops, but the constant harassment had taught her that those styles were either childish or distinctly witchy. Nowadays, Samantha opted for a pair of jeans and a plain T-shirt, nothing that would accentuate her body the way Cheryl and Ani—or even Lucille—liked.

"What are you doing there?" Ani asked, her eyes flitting back and forth between Cian and Samantha.

"Walking from Sciences to Main because it's our break, and at least *I'm* pretty hungry?" Cian asked, his tone sounding the slightest bit aggressive. Then he looked at Samantha. "Aren't you?"

Oh no. Samantha knew better than to say yes to that one. It didn't matter that she hadn't eaten since breakfast. "I've got my lunchbox."

Her stomach was cramping again. The path was wide enough to walk around Cheryl and Ani, but her feet wouldn't move. She doubted they would let her get away this time.

Cheryl finally broke her weird stare, took a deep breath, and addressed Cian. "Are you in need of tutoring?"

Please say yes, Samantha begged of Cian. He didn't need it as far as she could determine, but that would get her out of this. Sure, she would still receive a few nasty barbs, but if it was just tutoring, Cheryl would probably not bother for more than a minute.

Cian, however, didn't get the memo. He bristled with indignation. "You know I took Chemistry because I'm good at it, not because I enjoy playing around with inflammable substances. I am walking with Samantha because we're on the same course and have to go to the same place afterwards. Do you have an issue with that?"

Unfazed by his little rebellion, Cheryl turned her face to Samantha. "What do you think, Sammy? Do I have an issue with that?"

Samantha felt her face burn up and her breath hitch. The cramps became more painful. She lowered her eyes and whispered, "Yes?"

Looking at the floor, she could hear Ani tell Cheryl, "I think she's got a crush on him."

"Do you?" Cheryl asked, her voice like ice.

"Cheryl—" Cian interjected, but he was cut off with a sharp flick of her hand.

"I asked Sammy, not you."

Samantha's mouth felt dry and the sickness in her stomach was climbing up her throat. "No." The word came out in a meek, toneless whisper.

"You better not have one, because Cian is so far out of your league, his eyes would hurt squinting at you in the distance," Ani said, taking a step closer until her chest almost touched Samantha. The Elite Clique rarely got physical—unless one crossed Boyd's path—but they loved physical intimidation.

"Could you please stop talking for me!" Cian protested. He pushed himself between her and Ani, causing Samantha to stumble back in surprise. "I make my own choices about who I spend my time with, even if it's just a simple walk between buildings."

Hidden by his frame, Samantha could hear Cheryl sigh. "Cian. This is all very chivalrous of you, but Ani's just concerned. You're so nice to Sammy. She'll only assume you're interested in her. And believe me, you don't want to be on the other end of her crush. It'd be so embarrassing."

Cian snorted and shook his head. "What if I'm the one with the crush?"

Everyone was holding their breath. Even the students passing them seemed to have stopped to watch. Samantha herself stared at Cian's back. He must've only said that in a theoretical way, pissed off at Cheryl's condescending tone. It couldn't possibly be real.

"There you are." Suddenly, Lucille was there. She hooked her arm into Samantha's and dragged her along, past Cian, Cheryl, and Ani. "Sorry, it took so long to get here from PE. Are you hungry?" she asked, completely ignoring the presence of the Elite Clique.

Samantha didn't dare to look back, letting Lucille take the lead. Then they were inside the building, leaving the Elite Clique behind, and Samantha could breathe again. The first breath made her feel heady, almost as if she was about to pass out. "Thanks."

"No worries," Lucille said, patting her arm. "You'd hope they'd mature enough to realise bullying is stupid, but I guess that's why they're Elite Idiots."

With a few simple words, Lucille had eased the cramps in her stomach. Samantha even found herself chuckling softly. "I keep hoping that each year." But the confrontation wasn't what had her brain all muddled. "You know... boys, right?"

Lucille made an appreciative sound. "Sure, if you're not counting my recent disaster with Matt. I've never encountered one like him before, but..." She stopped, apparently noticing that she'd gone off course. "Why are you asking?"

"Uhm..." Samantha wasn't sure if she should voice her thoughts. They seemed so ludicrous. "When a guy says that he might be the one to have a crush on you during a fight with his friends... that's just that, right? It's an argument in a fight. A theoretical construct that bears no importance in reality."

Lucille's eyes widened. She squeezed Samantha's arm and even let out a small squeal. "Did Cian say that? Does he have a crush on you?"

Panicked, Samantha turned around and hushed her. The last thing she needed was a rumour to spread. "He said 'what *if* he had one," she hissed, her eyes darting up and down the corridor.

But Lucille wouldn't stop grinning or squealing. "Oh, this is so exciting." Finally, she noticed Samantha's panicked expression. "Okay, calm down. He said 'what if'. BUT! He said it to Cheryl's face. He took your side in a fight with his friends. That means a lot!"

Samantha thought back to the confrontation. Cian had done that. He had taken her side, right from the start. "I guess so."

"This is perfect," Lucille declared with glee. They continued walking. "Do you like him?"

"I-I don't know. We've only had a couple of classes together." Samantha had never considered Cian in that way.

"He's quite handsome," Lucille cooed.

Samantha shook her head, trying to banish thoughts of Cian from her mind. But now that she didn't want to think of him, his image kept popping up. He was a good-looking guy, about Matt's height, with more sandy blonde hair compared to Matt's golden tresses. Cian's hair always stood up a bit around a whirl on his left side, giving him a cheeky look accentuated by the smattering of freckles on his nose that almost disappeared in winter but came out in full force during the summer. Why was she noticing these details? She enjoyed working with him, but that was it. There was nothing more.

"And into the same things as you."

"No, he's not," Samantha said, finding her confidence at last. "He doesn't believe in magic, for example."

Lucille rolled her eyes. "Because he doesn't know better. I didn't believe in magic either when you first told me about it."

"Oh, hey, Sam!" Her sister Meg and her best friend Anne were coming down the corridor on the other side. "Jan's looking for you."

"Jan?"

Anne nodded. "Yes, he asked me to tell you if I see you. I have no idea what he wants, though."

The two girls passed them, quickly returning to whatever they were chatting about before. Samantha looked at Lucille in confusion. "What is it with today?"

"I have no idea. Let's just enjoy it while it lasts." Lucille giggled. "But first, I need something from the cafeteria. PE always makes me hungry."

They turned a corner and walked into the large hall where the cafeteria was located. Last year, under the old management, the lines had always been long, but now only a handful of people were hungry enough to tolerate the higher prices. Of course, Lucille didn't mind. She probably would've paid five euros for a simple piece of bread with a single slice of cheese without batting an eye.

In front of them, Robert was trying to buy a pretzel, one of the cafeteria's favourites. "Three euros? They were only one-fifty before."

"Well, they're three euros this year," the new owner said with a growl. He was an imposing man, the kind Samantha would've expect to see working in a bank rather than a school cafeteria. He even wore a suit.

"But that's way too much!" Robert protested.

The cafeteria man put his hand on the pretzel as if he was afraid Robert would snatch it and run off with it. "Let me explain this to you. You pick something from my shop, I tell you what it costs, and then you pay the price and not a cent less."

Robert's eyes were fixed on the pretzel under the man's long fingers. "Uhm, I'm no longer hungry."

"I can't sell this to someone else now. You need to reimburse me for the loss."

Robert stared at him, not even blinking. Then he turned around and walked away quickly.

"I'll put it on your tab," the cafeteria owner called after him and put the pretzel back where it had been hanging on display. "Next."

"Uhm." Lucille seemed too startled to remember her order. "A coffee, please," she said at last.

The man sloppily poured her a cup from a pot that had probably been sitting around for quite some time and pushed it forward. "That'll be two euros."

"Two..." Lucille swallowed her words. "Sure. Here you go. Have a lovely day."

If she had hoped it would brighten his day, Lucille was sorely disappointed. The man shrugged at her, then glared at Samantha. "What do you want?"

"I-I'm just with her." There were only two more hours on her schedule. She would just grab something from the bakery on the way home.

"Next time, you wait over there." The man pointed towards the tables. "You're blocking the line for people who want to pay for their food."

Samantha imitated Robert and quickly backed away. Lucille followed her, and the two of them exchanged a look. "He won't be in business for long, right?"

"Not with that attitude," Lucille answered.

The others were occupying a table near the back of the hall. Samantha let herself fall into the empty seat next to Fabian and leaned her head against his shoulder. "I think I need a break from this break."

"What? Why?"

She waved him off, shaking her head and sitting up straight again. The last thing she wanted to discuss with him was Cian Funke and his unexpectedly amiable behaviour. "Looks like it's not over yet."

Through the mass of students, Jan was heading towards their table. "Hey guys." Lacking a chair to sit on, he hunkered down on the table. "Nico." He clapped hands with Rachel's brother, and Rachel and Samantha exchanged a quick look. Somehow, they'd both missed the memo that these two were now friends.

"Jan," Fabian said, sounding equally confused. "Everything okay?"

"Kind of you to ask." Jan waved his finger in front of Fabian's face. "Alas, it's not."

He seemed completely oblivious to the confusion around the table. Lucille was less than amused that he was sitting right in front of her, his pants dragging so low she could see the rim of his shorts. Nico kept looking down and fiddling with his hands, and Matt stared at him as if he was contemplating pushing Jan off the table.

"Did you smoke something?" Fabian asked.

"I wish. I wish." Jan yawned, not bothering to cover his mouth. He *did* look tired rather than high, as if he hadn't slept for days. "But you might be able to help with a problem."

Samantha remembered that Meg and Anne had mentioned Jan was specifically looking for her. "Do you need tutoring for the exam?"

"Which exam?"

"Politics next week?"

"I might need tutoring," Fabian interjected.

But Jan waved her off. "Nah, I'll wing that. Weimarer Republic, blah blah. No, my problem is a ghost problem."

Lucille's face suddenly lit up. "A ghost problem?"

"You should definitely stop smoking whatever it is you're smoking," Fabian muttered.

Jan clicked his tongue. "Well, it looks like a poltergeist got stuck in our flat."

"A real one?" Lucille asked, excited.

"Are there unreal ones?"

Samantha sighed. This was yet another practical joke. "It's not funny, Jan."

"I know!" He got up and pushed his hands on the table instead. "First, I thought it was one of Anne and Meg's stupid jokes. You know, whatever teenage girls find amusing these days, but we definitely have a poltergeist in our flat. First, there was a giant mess in the kitchen, ketchup everywhere. And, of course, *I* got in trouble for it, as if I suddenly became interested in ketchup art. And then it partied all night long. Banging, hissing, gurgling, all night..."

Fabian furrowed his brow. "Still sounds like you're tripping to me."

Jan didn't seem offended. "Well, drugs usually don't throw berg crystals around the room or cover the floor with your graphic novels while you sleep."

"You have berg crystals lying around?" Lucille asked in surprise.

"Oh yes, berg crystals are perfect for charging other crystals," Jan replied, completely distracted from his issue.

Fabian bowed over to Samantha. "It is drugs, right? Crystals charging crystals?"

Jan's behaviour was certainly erratic enough, but Samantha only shrugged. "They can do that. That's why your mum has a dozen or so in the shop."

Meanwhile, Lucille asked the more important question. "You believe in crystals and... let's say, magic?"

"Don't you?" Jan looked down at Nico, who was still doing his best to avoid eye contact. "Nico told me you're all running around fighting monsters and playing with magic, or something like that."

"You did?" Rachel asked her brother.

Nico looked as if he wanted to melt into his chair. "I was drunk."

"Well, are you or not?" Jan was once again oblivious to the change in mood around the table. "Anyway, I'm planning a séance at my flat this afternoon. I need a couple of people to help me get rid of this poltergeist, so are you in?"

"I'm in," Lucille said almost immediately.

Samantha wasn't so sure. "Séances can be dangerous."

Fabian turned to her, his eyes wide. "You've done one?"

"No, but I've read about it." She'd been tempted to try it one day but hadn't felt safe enough to do it on her own. The idea of doing one in a big group held a certain amount of appeal to her, though.

"It's not really that dangerous," Jan claimed. "You just need enough salt, and you can't be all scared when it starts getting creepy."

"And I'm out," Fabian announced.

Now Lucille took over. "I think we should do it. If poltergeists are real, then Jan came to the right place."

"We're not monster hunters," Fabian protested.

"But we are. Sure, we've only dealt with two so far, but I'd say we did pretty well." She smiled at Jan. "Don't worry about it. We'll take care of it."

Jan pushed himself off the table with a grin. "Perfect. I'll see you at three at my place. Fabian's got the address." And without further ado, he sauntered off.

"Are you mad?" Fabian asked Lucille. "I don't want anything to do with this poltergeist, if it even exists. And no, I'm not a monster hunter. I don't want to be a monster hunter. I want to go to school and fret about stupid Politics exams, not about all the things that could kill me."

Samantha put a hand on his arm. "Fabian's right. I mean, not about monster hunting. It is sort of our duty to protect this town, but I also don't want this to get out." She looked at Nico. "Why did you tell him? Soon the whole school will know about it, and then Cheryl will be on my case for the rest of my life."

"I told you. I was drunk." Nico looked away. There was more to it, but he seemed adamant about staying tight-lipped.

"Well, I don't have time for this idiot," Matt declared, getting up. "I've got a date."

"With whom?" Lucille asked.

Matt grinned sheepishly. "I still have to decide that."

"Aren't you curious about what a poltergeist wants from Jan?" Rachel asked. She'd kept quiet until now.

"Thank you, Rachel! At least someone's up for an adventure." Lucille made sure to look each one of them in the eye. "Matt, you can move your date to tomorrow. Maybe by then, you'll remember who it is you wanted to date." Matt snorted, but he sat down again. "And Nico, you told him. So, now you have to bear the consequences. And you two." She pointed at Fabian and Samantha. "One of our fellow students needs our help. I don't care whether you're afraid of a little ghost action or scared of a stupid school bully. If Cheryl causes trouble, I now know a spell or two to make her reconsider her stance on magic. Either way, Jan needs our help, and we should be happy to offer it."

Fabian sighed heavily. "Fine."

"We'll be there," Samantha promised. Lucille was right. If there truly was a poltergeist, Jan needed their help. And besides, a poltergeist wasn't the weirdest thing that had happened today.

Jan

Anne was out with her friend, and his parents were still at work, which meant Jan had the flat to himself. At least, if one discounted the malicious presence of the poltergeist. Glitter from Anne's crafting materials covered the entire corridor, and no amount of vacuuming got him anywhere. Nor would his mother appreciate the red wine stains on the carpet.

The doorbell rang, and Jan breathed a sigh of relief. In a little bit, this poltergeist would be history. It took the others a couple of minutes to come up the stairs. When they finally appeared, Jan was a bit disappointed to see that none of them had changed out of the clothes they wore for school or brought any exciting weapons. For a bunch of wannabe monster hunters, they looked quite ordinary.

Nevertheless, Jan was glad to have somebody else around. He clapped his hands and led them inside. "Welcome to the messy cave. Don't worry about your shoes or anything, really. As you can see, he found the glitter pot. After he covered the entire corridor with it, he went on to the bathroom to clog the toilet and cover the mirror with shaving cream." The shaving cream his father was very particular about.

Jan opened the bathroom door at the end of the corridor to check. From left to right, streamers of toilet paper hung under the ceiling.

"Yep, still in the bathroom."

"That is... impressive," the new girl said. She was trying her best to sidestep the glitter on the ground, probably worrying about her shoes or something. Well, that was a fight she'd already lost.

Fabian looked as if he wanted to back out again. "This is crazy. Absolutely crazy."

"Maybe it's confused," Rachel suggested.

"It's a poltergeist," the annoyingly handsome newbie said. "It isn't confused. It just likes making a mess."

"And how do you know that?" Jan asked, narrowing his eyes. He was well aware of his poltergeist's messiness; he just didn't like Matt. They were part of the same soccer team at school, and while Matt was an absolutely brilliant goalkeeper, Jan was of the opinion he was just a little too good. And he never trusted things—or people—that were a little too good.

Matt frowned. "Isn't that why you called us?"

Jan decided to give him a pass this time and turned left, leading them into the living room. On the carpet, he had already done his best to prepare by drawing a crooked pentagram with salt and putting five black candles at each point. He had also covered the smoke detector and turned out all the protective crystals he could find in his room.

"The poltergeist did that?" Fabian asked, turning pale.

Samantha pushed past him, taking in the setup. "Of course not. That's for the séance." She looked at Jan, impressed. "You thought of everything."

Satisfied, Jan took a bow. He knew he could count on Samantha's expert knowledge when it came to magic. "Thank you. But we should be done before my parents come home. Otherwise, they'll think we're all doing drugs." The boring bunch didn't even so much as smirk about it. "Let's get started."

Matt put his backpack down. "A séance rarely does much to improve a ghost's mood. This could be dangerous. Poltergeists are very... irritable."

Once again, he had this annoyingly superior tone, as if he regularly met poltergeists for brunch. "You seem to be quite familiar with what my poltergeist likes or not."

"What's that supposed to mean?"

"You're the one who sent him, right?"

Matt scrunched up his nose as if Jan was nothing but an unappetising cockroach. "Sure." He picked up his backpack again and turned to the corridor. "I'm out of here."

Jan didn't mind him leaving—they only needed five people any-way—but the new girl put a hand against Matt's chest and begged him to stay. She was probably screwing him. Girls!

"If you want my opinion—and I know you don't," Fabian started, "we should forget about the whole thing and have a nice movie date with pizza instead." At that moment, the TV turned on. "You see?" Fabian's voice had turned very thin. "The ghost likes that idea."

Shaking his head, Jan took the remote and turned the TV off. "How many times have I told you? We're not watching TV!" Noticing how the others stared at him, he explained, "He loves watching TV, but only at maximum volume, which doesn't go down very well with the neighbours."

The TV turned on again.

"I said NO!"

The moment Jan turned off the TV for the second time, a flowerpot flew through the room, narrowly missing Rachel's head. It slammed into the bookshelf and broke.

"Are you okay, Rachel?" Nico asked, his eyes wide with shock.

Jan didn't have time to check on her. He glared at the broken pot and said out loud, "Stop throwing a tantrum. We've got visitors, so get in line!"

To his surprise, the broken flowerpot shuffled into a corner where it was out of the way. The poltergeist had actually listened to him!

He decided to go with the flow. "That's better. Now leave the TV off—" A few books fell out of the shelf. "Fine. I'll give up."

"You two seem to get along well," the new girl, Lu-something, said. "Are you sure you want to get rid of it?"

"Oh yes!" There was no doubt about that. "Okay, so let's get started. I need five of you to stand at the points of the pentagram. I'll light up the candles. Does everyone know what to do?"

"Uh, no?" Fabian said.

Lu smiled prettily. "We have no idea."

"But you're the experts!" Jan exclaimed.

Nico rubbed the back of his neck apologetically. "We're still learning."

"I've read about it," Samantha declared, making Jan lose all hope.

"Once we start, nobody leaves their position until the ritual is completed," Matt stepped into one corner. "I assume you're doing the incantation and we repeat your words."

Jan stared at him, unsure of what to make of his expertise. Sure, he was disappointed that the other so-called monster hunters were clueless, but it irked him that this newbie knew exactly what he was doing. Another fight wouldn't get him anywhere today, though, so he just sighed. "Yeah, pretty much. Well, come on, everyone."

Fabian raised his hands, making it clear that he was going to be the one to sit this one out. The others took the candles and a point, looking around a bit nervously. Jan stepped into the middle and turned around slowly, lighting the candles. When the fifth candle was lit, the room darkened.

Ice crawled down Jan's back. This was *real*. Until now, he had held a small sliver of doubt that the séance would actually work, but now it had become a certainty. They were about to summon the poltergeist. "Spirit, we call to you. Spirit, listen to our pleas! By the heavens and the Earth, by fire and water, we command you. Step into our midst!"

None of the others were doing anything. Jan glared at them, and at last, Matt led the chorus. As they repeated the words, something was changing around them. The books on the shelf moved back and forth. The TV was edging closer. Fabian took a couch pillow and held it defensively in front of him when a cold wind rose. A book fell off the shelf.

"...our midst!" All the books fell, the light bulb above them exploded, and another flowerpot flew through the room and hit Lu's shoulder. As she cried out, something punched Jan in the stomach. He groaned, dropping to his knees.

There was something inside him! Something that had no care at all for the body it tried to possess.

Shivering, he bent forward. His body was cramping up, trying to get rid of the presence. But there were words. *Mine. Bloody axe—*

Suddenly, the presence was gone. Jan's vision cleared, an empty feeling left inside of him.

"Jan!" Samantha was kneeling in front of him, holding her candle to the side and placing a hand on his shoulder. "Are you alright?"

Still a little confused about what had happened, Jan looked around. The line of salt had been broken in Matt's corner, and anger rose within him. "I almost had it!"

"It almost had *you*. Idiot!" Matt spat.

"Oh dear, that's gonna be a bruise," Lu said, rubbing her shoulder. "I guess no more shoulder-free tops for a while."

There was something else. The sound of flowing water. Jan jumped up. "It turned on the taps!" He sprinted into the bathroom, getting caught in a whole lot of toilet paper, but managed to reach the sink in time to turn off the taps before they overflowed. "Seriously!" He thought back to the weird words the poltergeist had projected into his brain. "And 'bloody axe'? Could you be any more cliché?"

The answer was another tantrum in the corridor, where the ghost threw around old newspapers. Jan sighed and returned to the others.

"I was able to prevent the flooding, but now it's messed up the corridor even more," he announced.

"I don't think it's evil," Rachel said. "I think it's just angry because it can't figure out how to communicate with us."

Bloody axe. Mine. Jan wasn't quite so sure he wanted the poltergeist to communicate with him.

"If it wanted to communicate with us, it could do so more politely, instead of throwing flowerpots at us," Lu exclaimed, instantly endearing herself to Jan.

A soft wind blew through the curtains, and the TV turned on again.

Jan groaned, grabbing the remote, but Rachel put a hand on his arm. "Wait."

The poltergeist was zapping through the channels with sickening speed until it stopped on a news channel. The report showed a place Jan instantly recognised: the Greenvalley Coal Mine. Billows of dust were rising from the entrance. Emergency services were amassed, and the reporters said something about a collapse. People were being transported from the mine, blood running down their dust-covered faces.

Jan's face turned ashen. "That's my father."

His father was one of the shift supervisors at the coal mine. A man was assisting him as he limped out of the mine. His face was just as dirty and bloody as the rest of them. Then the screen turned black.

Not a bloody axe, but a bloody accident. At the mine.

A hand fell on his shoulder, and Fabian said, "I'm so sorry, Jan."

Jan blinked, only now realising that he had been staring at the black screen. Then his phone beeped. His mother.

Dad was in an accident. I'll meet you at the hospital.

Jan put the phone away, swallowing heavily. "I have to go."

He hated the hospital with its boring white walls and the smell of disinfectant with a passion. And the fretting people in the waiting room. One of whom was his little sister. Every time a door opened, Anne jumped out of her seat, her eyes wide, hands clutched to her chest.

"Do you think he'll make it?" Anne asked.

Jan, who'd been browsing on his phone to focus on anything but the hospital, nodded. "It wasn't that bad." His father had been walking out of the mine in the news.

"What if it is?"

Annoyed, Jan put the phone away. "Anne, we know absolutely nothing at this point. Could you please stop assuming the worst?" His sister slid back into her chair, and he was reminded that despite all her teenage attitudes, she was barely fifteen. "It's gonna be okay."

He was just about to put his arm around her when Anne jumped up again. "There's Mum!"

She wasn't the only one who looked up this time. Their mother was one of the nurses at the hospital and, thus, could carry news for any of the waiting family members. The Kerschers weren't the only family affected by the accident. The entire waiting room was filled with worried wives, husbands, sisters, parents, and children who all assumed the worst. Their mum had come to inform other families twice before, but this time she came for them.

Anne ran to her and wrapped her arms around her. "How's Dad?"

"Considering what happened, pretty good," their mum said, smiling comfortingly. "He's been very lucky. Just a few lacerations, a concussion, and a few bruises, but there are no broken bones. He'll stay overnight for observation, but I'm sure he's going to be absolutely fine."

"Can we see him?" Anne asked, still fretting.

"Yes, of course. Come along."

Jan pushed himself out of the chair and followed them. Once they were through the security doors of the intensive care unit, he asked, "So, what happened? The news is absolute rubbish. One of Dad's colleagues was talking about voices." He'd been scouring every tidbit of information about the accident while they'd been waiting.

His mother sighed. "One of the old tunnels collapsed while your father and his crew were securing it. A few of them got hit pretty badly, but it looks like there won't be any casualties."

"So, no mysterious voices?" One of the rescued men had definitely mentioned hearing a whisper in the tunnels during his interview on the way to the ambulance.

"Jan, what's this about?" His mother sounded exhausted. Once again, he was too much for her to deal with. "Many people were hurt, and you want to know whether they heard voices?"

"That's what they said on the news," Jan complained.

Anne took his hand, and he fell silent. Granted, there was something more important on everybody's mind. His mother sighed and opened the door to one of the patient rooms. Inside lay his father and two of his men. His father's head was bandaged, and someone had cleaned him up. Upon their entry, he smiled. Anne ran to him and hugged him as fiercely as she dared.

"I'm so happy to see you!" Anne cried.

His father pressed her to his chest and kissed her head, a gesture he hadn't done for Jan in more than a decade. "We were extremely lucky."

"Which we're all very glad about," his mother said, squeezing his father's hand. Then she looked at Jan, full of hope. "Jan is interested in the details."

"Oh really?"

Jan was quite aware that this was another attempt by his mother to bring father and son together, something he couldn't care less about. "I just wanted to see if you heard any voices." After what happened with the poltergeist, he needed to know more.

"If I what?" His father grew angry in an instant. "Have you lost your mind, boy?"

"Oh, come on!" Jan clicked his tongue in annoyance. "Can't you just answer a simple question?" It didn't matter what he or his father did. They were always at each other's throats, much to Anne's and his mother's chagrin.

His father tried to push himself upright, ignoring his wife's attempts to calm him down. Before he could start his tirade, one of his colleagues spoke up. "I heard them."

Jan recognised the man from the TV. "What did they say?"

The man massaged the bridge of his nose, thinking hard. "Run! And danger from below." He looked over at Jan's father. "You saw it too, didn't you, Stefan?"

"There was absolutely nothing," his father said a little too quickly. "You must've hit your head. We all did."

Leave it to his father to discard any supernatural sighting. But Jan was elated. "What did you see?"

"Jan!" his father bellowed.

The colleague seemed a bit unsure after the heavy dose of Kerscher-level gaslighting he'd just received from his boss. "Something... big, horrible."

"Something big and horrible?" Jan asked, impatiently. What was he supposed to make of that?

But now his mother had come over and was tugging his arm. "Come on, Jan. Leave Martin alone. He needs some rest."

"It was an accident, Jan," his father reiterated. "Nothing but an accident. So, stop this nonsense. God, it's always something with you."

"Something with me?" Jan protested. "Well, I'm not the one who endangered his crew because he always keeps his eyes and ears shut."

His father paled from the low blow, and his mother gasped. Anne's eyes widened as if he'd pushed his father out of the hospital bed. Jan answered their judgement with an eye roll. "I'll go and have a smoke."

He left the room before they could protest and found his way to a terrace where he could smoke. The cigarette helped him calm his nerves and focus on the important things. Not his stupid father who'd come up with any excuse to pretend there weren't any supernatural forces in this world. But the voices and the poltergeist.

The poltergeist had known what would happen. That's why he'd come to their flat, but no one had listened to him. And there was something in the mine. Something big and horrible that would frighten a grown man. A monster.

It was time to call in the monster hunters.

Nico

The swing creaked under Nico's weight as he swung slightly back and forth on his heels. His focus was on the knife in his hand, its tip balancing on the palm of his hand, and yet he didn't cut himself.

A week ago, when he'd been drunk, he'd cut his own thumb. Nothing remained of that cut because his body had healed itself. Though Nico didn't have memories from the night he'd woken up in Jan's room, way too late for school, he remembered the golden glow that preceded the wondrous healing process. It had even healed the little scar on his pinkie, the scar that had always reminded him of his mother's neglect. He'd got it when he'd attempted to cook dinner for himself and Rachel after they'd moved here and their mother had stayed out all night.

Now it was gone, and Nico felt a world of possibilities. There were no limits to what he could do, nothing and no one to hold him back.

He'd skipped school with Jan that day, coming up with a bullshit excuse for the teachers. And it had been freeing. He didn't need to be a good boy for his mum anymore. He never had to. She didn't care. Good or bad, he was invisible to her. Why hadn't he realised this earlier?

The tip of the knife pressed a little harder, almost nicking the skin. But hurting himself was much harder when he wasn't drunk. It was stupid. Wrong. Even if he healed easily.

"God, what is wrong with you? You're going all gangster on me now?" Svenja's voice interrupted his thoughts.

Nico looked up at Svenja walking up to him. Her eyes were fixed on the knife in his hand. Quickly, Nico folded it up again and slipped it into his pocket. "Of course not. And that's a terrible cliché."

"Sorry." Svenja smiled a little and put her hands on his shoulders. "So, what's with the creepy meeting place?"

Nico opened his legs so she could move a little closer and put his arms around her. "You find playgrounds creepy?"

"At night, yeah." She pointed to the chain above them. "Like this creaking. Like, I'm so not gonna sit on your lap in this swing."

"It's not gonna fall." Nico laughed, then pulled her in to kiss her.

Svenja came reluctantly, but once their lips met, she wrapped her arms around his head and sank into it. Nico slipped his tongue between her teeth and lured her out of her shell, enjoying the sweet sharpness of the mint gum she always chewed. His hands wandered over her back and under her shirt, but there Svenja stopped him. "Not here."

"Nobody's watching."

She pulled away again. "You don't know that. There are houses all around us and people walk their dogs."

The thought excited him more than it dampened his mood. He enjoyed being a little naughty. "So, let them watch."

Svenja's eyes widened, and she gasped. "What's wrong with you?"

It was the second time she'd asked him that today. "Nothing. Sorry if I'm feeling a bit adventurous tonight."

She poked his chest. "*Why* are you feeling a bit adventurous? Is it your mum again?" He couldn't help but hear the little sigh at the end of the sentence.

"No. My mum's fine. She's doing whatever." Nico pulled her close again. "I'm done with her. She's got nothing over me now. I'm my own person, and I don't need her anymore. Or anyone, really."

He realised it was the wrong thing to say the moment it slipped out of his mouth. Svenja pushed him against his shoulder and broke out of his embrace to take a few steps back. "Well, that's good to know," she said.

"I didn't mean it that way." Nico reached out for her, but she took another step back and crossed her arms.

"I guess if you don't need me, I can go back home. I've got a lot of homework to do."

With a sigh, Nico got up from the swing and walked over to her, putting his hands on her arms. "I'm sorry. I didn't mean to say that I don't need *you*. You're my girlfriend. My little honey bear. My..."

"Stop." Svenja's eyes glared at him, but her mouth twitched. She loosened her arms and wrapped them around his body. Then she stole another kiss. "I know you didn't mean it." In the darkness, her eyes were almost black as she stared deep into his eyes. "I'm glad you're done with your mother. She's a mess, and you don't deserve to be dragged down into it."

"No, I don't," he replied, almost in a trance, his lips far too close to hers. "But I would like to drag you down right now."

Svenja drew back and slapped his chest. "You're impossible tonight." She trailed her hand down to his stomach, coming precariously close to his hips, only to slip it into his hand instead. "Shall we go for a walk?"

"A walk that ends in your room?" Nico asked, bracing himself for another playful slap.

But Svenja only laughed huskily in a way that sent a tingle down his spine. "Well, my parents are out on a dinner date tonight."

The tingle became more intense. "Is that so?" Not only did it mean that they had the house to themselves, he wouldn't have to meet her father again. The looks he gave him made it clear he didn't approve of his daughter's choice, and he watched Nico closely while he was at their house, as if he was only dating Svenja to steal stuff from her parents.

Hand in hand, they started walking towards her home when Nico's phone buzzed. A text message from Jan lit up the screen: *The accident in the mine was caused by a monster. I'm going in. Are you guys game?*

Immediately, Nico's thoughts flew back to the afternoon they'd just spent with a séance. It had been one of the coolest things he'd done in his life. Until they'd learned of the accident. *A monster in the mine.* If it hurt him, would his healing powers save him?

He halted, pulling Svenja to a stop. "Uhm, hey, I've actually had something come up."

Her stare could burn holes into his shirt. "You've had something come up?"

"Yeah, a mon—" Svenja would laugh at him if he told her about the monster hunts. She wouldn't tolerate such nonsense. "*The* monster struck again. I need to get home to Rachel."

Svenja crossed her arms again. "She's an adult, or almost one. She can handle this by herself."

"She's my sister," Nico growled defensively. He had to actively remind himself that Rachel didn't *actually* need him.

"And I'm your girlfriend. You've been— Oh, you know what?" She threw her arms into the air. "Go! Go to your baby sister and your messy mum. I don't care."

Nico watched her stalk off, trying his hardest not to retaliate in a similar vein, since he'd just lied about his true reasons. Instead, he let her go. What she said was wrong. What he'd done was just as wrong. But surely, taking out a dangerous monster was the right thing to do when everything else was wrong.

Fabian

"So, I'm pretty sure that Zobel will ask us how the Great Depression of 1929 facilitated the collapse of the Weimarer Republic. So, let's examine all those factors," Samantha explained with the patience of an angel.

Still, Fabian felt a headache coming on. He would much rather eat snacks and put on a movie, but he'd promised Samantha that they'd study until ten. A lack of judgement for sure, because after the séance this afternoon, his mind was completely empty. "Was it because the parties didn't have enough money?"

Samantha glared at him, so his guess must've been spectacularly bad. Luckily, she knew him well enough to continue, regardless. "What effects did the Depression have on the people?"

"Well, they didn't have money." Fabian tried it with a smile this time.

"They actually had a lot of money. Everyone was practically a billionaire."

Fabian hit his forehead for his own stupidity as the class material came back to him. "Right, the inflation. Paying five million for a loaf of bread and withdrawing money in a wheelbarrow." Samantha smiled, which must mean he was finally on the right track. "They had a lot of money, but it was absolutely worthless, getting more and more ridiculous by the day."

"Right." Samantha straightened her back and nodded encouragingly at him. "Try to find some more appropriate words in the exam, but that's the gist of it. So, what else? Money became worthless..."

"And unemployment rose. Up to... was it thirty percent?" He vaguely remembered something about one in three.

"Yes! Thirty-point-eight, but I'm sure thirty is good enough. Now how does that feed into the political side? Think stability, frustration..."

Fabian's head began hurting again. He was okay with learning dates and events by heart, but those kinds of exams were a thing of the past. Now they had to write essays, answering one to three questions over the course of several hours. And sadly, none of those questions were a simple yes or no. He had to consider all the different factors, the background, the key players, and somehow keep them all straight while forming intelligent and informed theses and arguments.

Samantha realised his dismay and went back to sorting her study cards. "Alright, let's approach this from a different angle. Who was in charge in—" She never got any further because his mum knocked and put her head into the room.

"Hey, lovelies, your friends are here to join you. Do you need more snacks?" She nodded towards the half-empty bag of chips.

"Our friends?" Fabian blinked in confusion. They weren't expecting anyone else.

Just then, Nico and Jan entered the room. Jan took it upon himself to answer the question. "Some more snacks would be much appreciated, Caro. I haven't got around to eating dinner yet." He spoke with a familiarity that unnerved Fabian. Surely, his mother did not appreciate nicknames from random high schoolers.

But his mother lapped it all up. "Oh dear. Well, I'll put some mini pizzas into the oven and make sure you're properly fed for studying."

"Thanks!" The door closed again, and Jan sat down on the bed, pulling the bowl of snacks towards him. "Your mum is awesome, Fabian."

Samantha was as stunned as Fabian, looking back and forth between Nico and Jan. "You're here to study?"

"Ew, no." Jan flicked through the study cards and made a face. "Don't tell me we need to know all this shit by Monday."

Samantha grabbed the cards from him and sorted them with care. "If you want to pass." Then her face softened. "How's your dad?"

Jan's frown deepened. "Back to his old tricks." When everyone stared at him in confusion, he said, "Gaslighting everyone about monsters."

"What do you mean?" Fabian asked, grabbing a handful of chips.

"Well, his co-worker said there was a monster, and they heard voices. But my father was all like, no, monsters don't exist. He does it to me all the time." Jan turned to Samantha and sighed. "And before you judge me as a cold-hearted son, he's fine. Got a little knocked around but will most likely be released tomorrow."

"I'm glad to hear that," Samantha said with much more compassion than Jan could muster for his father.

Nico grabbed the bowl and helped himself, and between the three of them, they depleted the snacks in record time.

"So, Jan had this crazy idea. He's gonna get the keys to the mine from his father and let us in." Nico grinned. "And then we'll hunt this monster."

Fabian felt the blood drain from his face. "You want to hunt a monster? Tonight?"

"Of course tonight. Right now, the mine is closed," Jan explained. "Tomorrow, they'll start investigations and all that shit. It'll be impossible to enter. And also, tonight my dad won't miss his keys."

"This is crazy. Do you even know what kind of monster is in there? There was a collapse!" Surely, Jan couldn't be serious.

"A big and terrible monster," Jan said as if those words didn't alarm him at all. "That's what the miner said."

Samantha looked up from her phone. "Lucille's on board." She must've texted her right away.

"Yeah, Rachel's getting ready as well. She said she wants to find out if there are more ghosts," Nico announced.

"More ghosts?" Everything was moving too fast again. It was as if Fabian didn't have a say in it. Everyone just heard the word "monster" and decided the best course of action was to attract its attention. And now there would be ghosts as well. One ghost a day was more than enough in Fabian's opinion, but it looked like he was going to be overruled yet again.

Even Samantha had forgotten all about their study plans. Not that Fabian wanted to study. "Matt says he can be here in a minute."

"How can he be here in a minute?" Jan asked, squinting. "Does he live here?"

"No, he lives on the other side of town, next to the zoo," Fabian answered reflexively.

Samantha shrugged. "He probably has a date around here. Or, well, a sleepover." Her cheeks were slightly flushed.

Nico picked up on it and bumped her shoulder with his elbow. "A sleepover? How old are you? Twelve?"

"Fine." Samantha rolled her eyes. "He probably has a sex date around here. Better?"

"How crude," Jan teased her. "I wouldn't have expected such words from our Deputy Head Girl."

Exasperated, Samantha got up to her feet. "I'm gonna help your mum with the food."

As she stormed out of the room, Jan and Nico fist-bumped each other and giggled.

"Since when were you two best buddies?" Fabian said, eyes narrowing. He felt for his best friend, who was completely outnumbered by the testosterone in the room. Plus, he was still unhappy about the change of plans.

Nico shrugged. "We actually know each other from karate. And school, of course." By the way he kept glancing at the ground, that wasn't the whole truth. "So, are you in?"

"Am I... no!" Fabian made a show of grabbing Samantha's flashcards and flicking through them. "I need to prepare for the exam." His eyes saw the words, but his brain never registered them.

Jan pulled them out of his hands and threw them over his shoulder. "You've still got several days." The cards scattered on the ground, driving a spike of guilt into Fabian's gut. "Nico says that you're this powerful water mage who saved his sister from a demon. We need a guy like you."

"It wasn't a real demon," Fabian protested. "And I'm not powerful."

"You can shoot water out of your hands and flood an entire zoo hall," Nico reminded him. "I can only heal cuts and bruises. And Jan doesn't even have magic."

"Yet," Jan said. When they both stared at him, he shrugged. "It could rub off on me if I start hanging out with you."

Fabian snorted and got up to pick up Samantha's cards. "You should hope Samantha's knowledge rubs off on all of us, or we're going to fail politics." Had Nico just said he could heal cuts and bruises?

"Why do you care so much about that stupid exam?" Jan asked.

Before Fabian could tell him that it wasn't the exam he cared about as much as *not* fighting a monster in a collapsed mine, the door opened again, and Samantha returned with a plate full of mini pizzas and Matt in tow. "Careful, they're fresh out of the oven." Samantha handed the plate to Jan, then frowned at her still scattered cards. "Why are you throwing my cards around?"

Jan ignored her and called out to Matt instead. "Hope you don't mind us dragging you away from your... sleepover." He grinned wildly when he was only met with confusion.

"Yeah, Samantha was interested in a sleepover with you," Nico added, mirroring Jan's grin.

"You're what?" Matt asked Samantha, somehow managing to keep his question gentle instead of rude.

Samantha took a deep breath, clearly annoyed with the bunch of them. "I don't care about your sexual activities at all. Jan and Nico have just decided to act like fifteen-year-olds at the mere mention of sex."

"You were the one who started with the sleepover talk," Nico called her out and laughed again.

"Can you stop it?" Fabian had had enough. He'd spent years watching Samantha being ridiculed by the Elite Clique. She didn't need her friends to do the same. "Ganging up on her is not cool. Not at all."

Matt, who'd never so much as twitched with amusement, turned to Samantha with a deep frown. "I'm sorry they're acting like idiots. You said there was a monster?"

"Jan said there was a monster. Apparently, the miners saw something before everything collapsed." Faced with earnestness and true interest, Samantha quickly recovered. "Jan will get us the keys. I told Lucille to meet us there in half an hour. Which is probably cutting it a bit close because I need to pick up some stuff from home."

"Yeah, I'd better get changed into something more sensible if we're crawling into a mine," Matt agreed. Fabian hadn't even paid attention to what he was wearing. A white shirt and a well-fitting pair of jeans.

Nothing fancy, but he could see how Matt wouldn't want to get those dirty with coal dust. "I'll meet you in about half an hour at the mine, then."

"Sounds good." Samantha waved at the rest of them and left the room with Matt, leaving Fabian stunned.

Just like that, the whole affair was a done deal. He could either stay behind and tackle politics on his own, or join his friends in a sure-to-be dangerous expedition. With everyone going, Fabian didn't really see another choice.

Rachel

Earlier that night, Nico had told her about Jan's request. Under normal circumstances, Rachel wouldn't have bothered, but ever since they'd met the poltergeist, her curiosity had been piqued. There had been a kind of connection between her and the ghost. Some understanding. Perhaps because she felt like a ghost in her own home. The poltergeist had been angry and frustrated because no one had listened to him. Knowing full well how they felt, she wanted to be the one to listen, the one to see it through.

And so, she and the others met Jan outside the coal mine at the edge of town. While it was an active mine, it was one of the old ones that didn't allow big machinery and motorised transport inside. Still, Rachel knew that a maze would await them under the hill.

Jan, Matt, and Lucille were already there when the rest of them arrived. A ring of keys, stolen from his father, dangled from Jan's fingers. "There you are. Thought you'd leave us hanging."

"I wish," Fabian said and stepped closer. "We're not breaking in, are we?"

"It's not breaking in if you've got the keys."

Fabian pointed at a sign. "It says right there: 'No trespassing for unauthorised personnel. All visitors need to report to the office.'"

"Relax, dude!" Jan clicked his tongue. "Nobody's gonna find out. They don't even have security cameras. Budget cuts and all."

"But it's against the law!" Fabian protested.

At this point, Lucille stepped in. "Everyone, calm down. As far as I know, the mine belongs to the town. Since we are citizens of this town and pay taxes—well, our parents do—the mine also belongs to us. And just as you can't break into your own flat, we can't break into our own mine."

"I don't think it works that way," Samantha said.

Lucille clicked her tongue. "I know it doesn't. But the fact is that some kind of monster was responsible for the cave-in, and if that's the case, we can't let it roam free."

"Yeah, sure, let's challenge a monster that can collapse the mountain on top of us. Great idea," Fabian muttered.

And while he had a point, Rachel was also eager to get into the mine. "We owe it to the ghost."

"We owe... what?" Fabian looked at her in despair, but the rest of them got moving.

Jan opened the gate with his stolen keys. "Well, let's be as safe as we can. There are helmets and—" he checked out Lucille's shoes "—proper shoes down there. And hopefully, a better map."

A little later, they all entered the mine. Jan had found them some nice big flashlights to illuminate the tunnels. Up on this level, they were still wide enough for two or three of them to walk next to each other.

"This is so cool," Nico exclaimed, running his hand along the side. "I remember our school trip here, where it was all like 'don't touch anything'."

"Please don't touch anything," Fabian whined. Then he asked Jan, "So what does it mean, big and terrible?"

Leading the party, Jan shrugged. "I don't know. I assume it's some kind of monster that came after the men."

"Not helping!" Fabian stopped and turned around to the others. "Please, guys, this is madness."

Without a word, Nico and Matt put a hand each on his shoulder and pushed him along.

For a few moments, Rachel enjoyed the silence. They descended deeper, making frequent turns and walking through long dark tunnels. Cold seeped under their clothes as they made their way forward. Their lights flickered over wet surfaces, giving it a distinct sheen. Rachel thought it was beautiful. A cold draft caught her hair, whispering into her ears. She almost—

"How far do we have to go?" Lucille asked.

"Uhm, good question," Jan said, looking down at his map. "I'd love to answer it, but... I'm not quite sure I know where we are."

"I don't believe this," Fabian muttered. "First, we break into a mine, and then we get lost in it."

Jan folded the map in his hands. "It's not that big. We'll find our way out."

While everyone else panicked and started fighting over how to proceed, Rachel regarded the naked stone above them. The wind was stronger here, and it carried something with it.

"Can you feel this?" she asked, not really caring whether they understood.

Nico raised his head. "Feel what?"

"It's..." Voices. The wind carried voices. And suddenly, they were as clear as if someone had spoken next to her. "I know which way to go!"

Without discussing it with the others, she pushed past the group and followed the voices. Her friends' protests meant little because, for once, Rachel was absolutely sure of what to do.

The miner had said he'd picked up the voices, too. Rachel could feel their honesty. The voices couldn't lie. Not to her. These were souls without the protection of their bodies. The souls of miners buried in the mine many, many years ago.

"Where are we going?" someone asked behind her.

She'd run deeper, so deep, it was cold enough for their breath to show in the air. They were getting close now. But she also had to be careful. The ghosts were anxious here, and it showed in the flickering of their flashlights.

"Please, let's go back up," Fabian cried.

Rachel hated that she had to waste precious time to clue the others in. "The ghosts won't hurt us."

"We're following a bunch of ghosts?" Matt asked, casting around as if he could somehow detect them.

"Yes, and they're speaking to me. I can hear them clearly down here." They were telling her about the monster in the mine. The big, terrible monster they'd seen before the tunnel collapsed. "Your ghost is here, too, Jan."

Jan grimaced. "Cool. Send him my best."

"He can hear you." The ghosts saw and heard everything. They just couldn't talk to the others.

"Hi?" Jan said with a fake smile. Instantly, his light flickered, and his helmet dropped over his eyes. Annoyed, he pushed it up again. "Yeah, okay. He's here."

Rachel giggled. The ghost had obviously taken a liking to Jan. Probably because he was of miner blood or something silly like that.

"What do they want?" Matt asked.

"They want us to help them," Rachel said, sobering immediately. As delightful as the ghosts were, they had a serious request. "They all died down here. A little further ahead..."

Samantha directed the beam of her flashlight into the depths. "You mean over there?"

In front of them was a blockage. Someone had kept their wits about them enough to put a barricade up across the path. A little further behind, a pile of rocks covered the floor. That was where the ghosts had been leading them.

"Yes. That's it. This is where the disaster happened."

"Disaster... I bet there'll be another disaster any minute," Fabian whispered, but he sounded much more resigned than whiny.

Jan cracked his knuckles. "Alright. Let's find out what's so big and terrible." He climbed over the barrier and approached the pile of rocks.

Slowly, the others followed. Samantha, who was wearing a big bag over her shoulder, took out a glass vial containing some unknown liquid. Rachel was just about to ask her about it when the wind grew stronger and the voices boomed in her ears.

It's awakening! Run!

Deep from inside the tunnel, a low-pitched rumble rose. Gravel danced across the surface and fell from the ceiling. Jan had stopped, while Matt had drawn his sword, and Lucille had conjured her fireball.

"It's coming for us," Rachel finally said, her legs paralysed on the spot.

"Run!" Jan shouted, but it was too late.

In front of them, the pile of rocks was moving. No, it was rising. A few boulders rolled down to the sides, and then it came for them, so loud Rachel couldn't hear the ghosts anymore. Someone screamed. And someone else grabbed her by the arm, hauling her backwards.

"Lucille! Fire!" Samantha called over the noise. Then she threw her glass vial at the moving pile of rocks and crouched down in front of it. A second later, Lucille's fireball hit.

A massive explosion shook the tunnel. Rachel fell flat onto something soft, her ears ringing. A shower of gravel came down on them, pelting their skin. Dust filled the tunnel until the beams of their lights barely penetrated more than a metre. But there was silence behind them. Nothing moved.

Rachel realised that her soft cushion was Fabian. He coughed, then slowly pushed himself up. "You okay?" he asked. When she nodded, glad for the dust hiding her blush, he turned around. "Sam? Sam, where are you?"

They both rose from the ground. Jan and Nico moaned as they got to their feet, patting their clothes in a futile attempt to clean off the dust. Somehow, Matt had managed to shield Lucille, helping her up now. Fabian didn't waste another second on Rachel. He kept calling for Sam and rushed forward.

It didn't take him long to find her. She was covered with dust from head to toe and coughing, but she seemed alright. Fabian immediately confronted her. "What the hell was that? We could've died!"

"An explosive, inspired by our chemistry lessons," Samantha answered after clearing her throat. "I thought it could be useful."

"You know you could at least warn us before you throw things." Fabian may have been whining, but Rachel picked up on the concern in his voice. He always worried about Samantha, never her.

Her thoughts were quickly blown away when the voices returned. *It's not dead yet. It moved further down.*

"Well, I, for one, thought that was mega cool," Nico announced. He clapped Samantha's shoulder. "You're starting to surprise me, Kollmer." He kept walking, only to call out a little later, "Hey, check this out."

They all gathered around what was a big black hole in the ground. The smell coming out of it almost made Rachel retch. It was pungent, almost acidic, and rotten. Sulphur, most likely.

Matt stepped forward with his sword and poked at a leather-like piece stuck in the wall of the hole.

"Wait a minute!" Jan exclaimed. "Why do you suddenly have a sword? He didn't have a sword before, did he?"

"It's a magic sword," Samantha hushed him quickly.

Matt didn't seem to care about Jan's concerns. He raised the piece of leather to his flashlight and examined it closely. "There are scales on here. It's a piece of skin. It's probably corrosive, looking at how smooth those walls are."

"So, this isn't a hole," Fabian surmised carefully. "This is a tunnel dug by an animal?"

"If this was an animal, it's gigantic." Lucille stepped close to the hole, carefully peering inside.

"I suspect a wyrm," Matt said. "There are a few wyrm species that live inside the earth, and their skin is covered with poisonous slime. If we're unlucky, it can spit fire or acid."

"We're always unlucky," Fabian moaned.

Meanwhile, Rachel tried to listen to the ghosts. They were arguing with each other. One was worried about sending children any further, while the others called it their best chance. Then all went quiet, only to burst out with another warning.

"It's coming back!" Rachel shouted.

Not even a second later, the ground was rumbling again.

"Everyone, back to the upper level!" Matt called.

They turned around, but they'd barely started running when the gigantic wyrm broke through the ground in front of them. It was more than terrible. Only its head and a little of its body fit into the tunnel, and it opened its snout, exposing rows upon rows of needle-like, pointy teeth. Its scaly skin shimmered green, and from its snout, thick yellow saliva dripped on the ground. Where it hit the rock, a hiss cut through the air, and steam rose. Big yellow eyes glowed in the darkness.

Slowly, the group moved backwards when suddenly, Samantha cried out. Rachel looked over her shoulder just in time to see her stumble over the rim of the hole. Fabian grabbed hold of her arm, but his stance wasn't stable enough, and with a scream, both of them fell into the hole.

Rachel's heart skipped a beat, then she started running. "Fabian! Sam!"

"We're okay," Fabian's voice echoed from far below. "The tunnel makes a turn."

Rachel needed no more information. In an instant, she swung her legs over the rim and slid down the smooth cave walls. For a brief moment, she fell. Then her bum hit the ground, and her journey went more sideways than down. A little later, it stopped right next to Fabian and Samantha.

"Careful!" Samantha said, pushing her hands out. "There's glass everywhere."

Rachel shone her light down, wondering just how many vials Samantha had packed. Then she listened for more movement behind her. There were some shouts, but nobody came after them. The others were probably fighting the wyrm.

"I think I twisted my ankle," Fabian complained when he pulled himself up to lean against the tunnel wall. He grimaced in pain.

"Let me see." Rachel bent down to open his shoe. She'd brought a first-aid kit and knew enough to stabilise his foot.

While she was working, Samantha examined the tunnel. Her forehead was bleeding, as was her elbow, but they only looked like minor wounds. "We won't be able to climb back up here. The walls are too slippery."

"Does... does that mean...?" Fabian swallowed heavily, balancing on his other foot.

"It means we need to find another way. The wyrm came out ahead of us, so there must be another path." Samantha didn't sound particularly confident. "But my explosives all broke, so if..." She stopped talking and sifted through her bag instead.

Rachel knew exactly what she didn't want to say. The wyrm could come after them, and in that case, they had no way of defending themselves. None but Fabian's fickle powers.

Samantha was still examining the contents of her bag, wincing. "At least the salt didn't get wet. Here, hold this." She handed Fabian two big bags of salt.

"Uhm, were you planning to cook the wyrm?" he asked while carefully sliding his foot back into his shoe.

"No, I was thinking we might need to do another séance." Samantha took out the candles and handed them to Rachel. Then she carefully opened the strap of the soaked bag and put it down on the ground. "That's better. I don't want to blow us up by accident. Come here."

She steadied Fabian, and together they made their way down the tunnel, away from the black hole they'd fallen through.

The going was slow, thanks to the slippery surfaces and ever-winding path going up and down. If they'd hoped to quickly reach the other exit, their hopes were squashed a little later.

Rachel walked behind the two of them, replaying the scene of Samantha's fall in her mind. She wasn't disappointed that Fabian hadn't even hesitated to try to catch her. But everything that happened in this mine had made one thing clear: Samantha would always be the first thing on his mind. The one for whom he'd face every monster or go deep into dangerous mines, even though every fibre of his being screamed not to do it.

It was this quality of his, that despite all his complaining, Rachel loved so much. But it was time that she faced the truth. One day, Fabian might fall in love with someone other than Samantha, but it wouldn't be with her. She was invisible to him.

Just like the ghosts.

They came to a crossing of at least five tunnels and stopped. "What do we do now?" Fabian asked.

"We could try our luck," Samantha suggested, but her voice was shaking. The reality that they might be stuck down here forever seemed to set in. "The tunnels go round and round. I don't know which one leads to an exit."

"If this wyrm is as active as an earthworm, we're screwed," Fabian said, surprisingly calm. "This is worse than any maze. What if we were to go back and see if the others can rescue us? At least we're quasi-close to the surface there. Any of those tunnels, and we might get lost in the mountain and never find our way out."

It was a sound idea, but Rachel had a better one. She closed her eyes and, for the first time, reached out to the wind. "Ghosts! If you want us to help you, you need to help us first! Tell us which way to go!"

"Since when can you talk to ghosts?" Samantha asked.

"Since today," Rachel answered, finding nothing wrong with it. "Please," she whispered.

And there it was. A cold wind from the second tunnel on the right.

"Follow me," she said to the others, confidently taking the lead. It didn't matter that Fabian and Samantha had each other. Now she had the ghosts.

Lucille

"You know, now would be the perfect time to cut this wyrm into pieces," Jan told Matt.

Matt had his sword drawn, but he'd turned to stone, staring at the wyrm with wide eyes, his mouth half open. The blood had drained from his face.

"Matt!" Jan punched him in the arm. "MATT!"

Lucille knew exactly what was going on. "He's got a worm phobia, and this is one gigantic worm." If she was completely honest, she didn't know if her legs would carry her as she stared at this terrible beast. Compared to it, the insects and shadows they'd faced seemed like a piece of cake.

"Get him out of here!" Nico said, stepping in front of them and opening his arms wide. "There's a small ledge around the hole."

Was he going to sacrifice himself? For a moment, Lucille was so bewildered she didn't know what to do. With Samantha and Fabian falling, and Rachel jumping into the hole, she'd already had her fill of despair. She would not watch Nico get torn into pieces so they could have a head start.

"Jan, take Matt. He's got a worm phobia. Nico! Duck!" She calmed herself and summoned fire into her hand.

Jan stared for a moment as if she'd lost her mind, but then he grabbed Matt under the arm and dragged him towards the hole. Meanwhile, the wyrm shot forward, spewing acid.

"Nico!"

At the last second, Nico ducked, and Lucille hurled her fire at the wyrm. She didn't wait around to see what damage she'd done, but turned and ran after Jan and Matt. Matt had gathered enough of his senses to stumble along, his sword gone from sight for the moment. Nico had been right about the hole. There was a small ledge, just wide enough to scramble past.

Under normal circumstances, Lucille would never have dared it, being too afraid of falling in, but with the roaring wyrm behind her, she stepped onto the ledge without a second thought and was past the hole before she could even look down into it.

Nico was catching up with her. He was holding his arm, his face distorted in pain, but he didn't stop either. If her fireball had done any damage, it hadn't been enough to send the wyrm fleeing. It was still coming after them, screeching and roaring. Its massive body made the ground shake, rocks loosening from the ceiling.

Lucille screamed when a boulder missed her by a hair's width. Nico dragged her along, but she was quickly losing hope. There was nowhere to run to, only this long, endless tunnel leading deeper into the mine. Deeper into the wyrm's lair.

"Run!" she told Nico, while turning once more and closing her eyes. "Erit lux!"

Bright light flooded the adit, so bright she could even see through her closed eyes. The wyrm screamed unnaturally loud, and there was another rumble further down the tunnel.

"Lu!" Jan called to her from ahead.

She spun around, struggling to see anything. There was no sight of the boys. Panicked, she kept running when someone hissed at her from the side. They'd found an alcove, barely large enough to contain them all.

Lucille squeezed in with the boys and held her breath. The wyrm had resumed its pursuit. It was coming close quickly, banging its body left and right against the tunnel walls. The four of them cowered in despair. Jan was wheezing terribly. The monster moved past them, its large scales barely an arm's length away from Lucille. The rock from their hiding place began to melt before her eyes, hissing and steaming.

She bit down on a whimper, pushing as far as she could into Jan. The acid spread, but it didn't reach them. The wyrm slithered down the tunnel. It had missed their hiding spot. Further down, they could hear it rumble, eating its way into the soil. Then it was gone, and only the ragged sound of their breathing remained.

Lucille relaxed again, only now daring to check on the others. Jan pulled out an inhaler and quickly took two puffs before holding up his flashlight so they could see. His eyes dared Lucille not to comment on what she'd seen before checking on Nico. Matt was huddled in the smallest part of the alcove, rubbing his face in distress, while Nico and Jan examined his arm in the light. It had been hit by the acid, but the injury was healing in front of their eyes under a golden shimmer of light.

"Was that why you thought you could face him alone?" Lucille whispered.

Nico shrugged ruefully. "I figured I could hold it back a bit for you to escape."

"Talking about the escape," Jan started, turning to Matt. "What the hell was that, Ninja Boy?"

"I already told you! He can't stand worms," Lucille hissed. It was bad enough for Matt as it was.

Jan snorted. "Yeah, well. I can't stand this wyrm either. Doesn't mean I'll freeze on sight."

"Isn't that great for you?" Matt shot back at last. "Come on, let's check on the others."

They all made their way out of the alcove and trotted back. With the adrenaline level slowly sinking, Lucille began to work through what had happened. How stupid they'd been. Reckless. What were they thinking going in here? That their meagre magic powers would protect them from everything? From a monster like that? And now Samantha, Fabian, and Rachel were lost underground.

Nico reached the hole first, calling down to them, but only his own echo came out of it. "The-they're gone," he said, and she could hear the wave of despair threatening to overcome him.

"Shall we go after them?" Matt asked, having found his courage again.

"And faint there when that giant worm comes around the corner?" Jan mocked him.

Lucille massaged her temples. The last thing they needed now was a fight. "We need to get help. Real help," she decided. "Call the emergency services and get a rescue mission going." Their friends had been alive after their fall. And they still had to be.

"Can't we just go after them?" Matt asked.

"And get lost down there, too?" Lucille pushed her hands on her hips. "No, thank you. This adventure is over. We need to get professional help." Matt glared at her, as if he was thinking of declaring himself professional help. But it wasn't her who should make that decision. "What do you think, Nico?"

He was still sitting at the edge, clearly thinking of performing another reckless act of heroism, but he licked his lips and got up on his feet. "Lucille is right. Someone needs to go back and... We all need to go back and get help as fast as possible."

Lucille sighed in relief that they were all sticking together. Slowly, the group set their feet back the way they came.

"We're gonna be in so much trouble," Jan muttered.

From what Lucille had gathered at school and from the others, he was familiar with getting into trouble. But this was bigger. This would get them into national-television-kind-of trouble. Her father would be so disappointed.

None of them spoke on their way back. Twice Nico stopped and turned around, but decided against it. Lucille felt bad about practically abandoning the others as well. A part of her hoped that they'd managed to crawl out of the hole and were just a little ahead of them, but it wasn't a part she trusted much.

They reached an earlier crossing, where a bunch of rocks retrieved from the tunnel had been piled up on the side. From there, the way up was clearly marked. But before they got to the crossing, the rocks began to levitate and quickly assemble a wall.

"Oh no, don't you dare!" Jan raced ahead. The last stone sealed the wall as Jan threw himself against it. But no matter how much he punched or kicked, the stones wouldn't budge.

Matt and Nico also tried to break the wall, but to no avail. They were locked in.

"What just happened?" Lucille asked, unable to comprehend what her eyes had seen.

Jan kicked the wall again. "It's my poltergeist!"

"Can you please tell your poltergeist that this is *not* funny?" Her voice hitched. Nobody knew where she was. With the mine closed after the accident, it'd be ages until the stolen key would be found and their trespassing discovered. They *needed* to get up again.

"You heard her!" Jan shouted. "Open up!"

A voice rang from the right. "Jan?" The stones had left behind an empty wall. And a gaping hole. Through the hole, three figures appeared, one of them limping.

With a scream, Lucille ran to them. She first threw her arms around Samantha, then Rachel and Fabian. All three of them were there. Dusty and a little bloody, but on their feet. And now the tears were streaming down her face. "You're here!"

The others were also huddling around them. Nico wouldn't let go of his sister, squeezing her tight. Meanwhile, Matt procured a handkerchief for Samantha. "You're bleeding."

"I know." She dabbed her forehead. "What happened here?"

"My poltergeist has decided to keep us down here," Jan announced. He was punching the wall yet again.

Rachel freed herself from Nico's embrace and put her hands against the wall, listening to the air. "He wants us to kill the wyrm and make the mine safe again."

"Brilliant idea," Fabian laughed drily. "Easy peasy. Just give us a minute. Gosh, what a mess."

Lucille put her hand on his arm. "I'm sorry." After all, she'd helped convince him to go down here.

"And how are we supposed to do that?" Samantha asked. "All my explosive potions broke in the hole."

A couple of little stones hit Jan in the shoulder. "Hey!"

"He wants to help us," Rachel said.

"By stoning us before we starve?" Jan shouted. Another stone hit him in the forehead. "Stop that! Either do something useful or leave us alone!"

Suddenly, he keeled over, holding his stomach. Lucille jumped back when he started writhing on the floor in pain. "What's happening?"

"Jan?" Fabian lowered himself, reaching out for Jan.

As soon as it'd started, it stopped. Jan was down on all fours, panting. "What the hell?"

Rachel let go of the wall, looking more curious than terrified. "I think he wants to possess you."

Lucille had no idea how she could be so calm about all of this.

"Absolutely not." Jan crouched, still panting.

"But he needs you. He's too weak otherwise," Rachel insisted.

Jan pointed at the wall behind him. "He just closed off our only way back!"

"The stones aren't enough to kill the wyrm. He tried that!" Rachel declared, absolutely convinced of her words. "He wants to make sure that no more miners are hurt by this creature."

"Glad we aren't miners, then," Fabian muttered, and Lucille found herself nodding. The poltergeist obviously had no regard for their safety.

"But if he possesses Jan, he can help us?" Nico asked, taking his sister's side.

Rachel nodded. "Please. He's desperate."

Jan whimpered softly. He checked with each of them, then shrugged. "Fine. If he lets us out after that."

"I'm sure of it." Rachel sounded positively excited. "Samantha? You've got everything for a séance. That will help him gain control over Jan's body."

A curse split the air. Jan spat on the ground before looking up at them, visibly frazzled. "Yeah, great. That sounds reassuring."

"You're not going to faint, are you?" Matt asked, which settled the whole thing.

Jan glared at him. Then he got up to his feet and straightened his back, stepping into the middle of the tunnel. "Bring it on!"

For some reason, Samantha had all the ingredients for a séance with her. She drew a near-perfect pentagram around Jan and handed the candles to Lucille to light them.

"I hope this isn't a mistake," Lucille whispered as she called forth her fire.

"As long as the wyrm stays away," Matt said.

Fabian snorted softly. "I've got to say, I totally get your phobia regarding that creature."

Samantha took the candles from Lucille and handed them to the others, leaving Lucille out of the séance. "Ready?"

This time, Rachel led them in the chorus, while Lucille kept an eye on the dark hole and the tunnel. The last thing they needed was the wyrm finding them at this dead end.

As the calling went on, Jan's fingers started clawing. He hissed through his teeth and groaned. A force threw him onto the ground, and he writhed in pain again. The others stared at him in terror, but Rachel remained calm. "It's almost over." And sure enough, Jan's erratic movements stopped. He got up to his feet, though he leaned to the side as if drunk. "Now we can open the pentagram."

"No!" Matt called out before Fabian could lift his feet. "If we do that, we allow the ghost to take hold of him permanently."

"He won't do that," Rachel said, once more with utter confidence in the poltergeist's intentions. "He wants to make the mine safe again. Nothing more."

Matt shook his head. "But there's no guarantee. He might enjoy having a body of his own again. Without the pentagram, we have no power over him."

Lucille felt sick. She didn't know Jan very well. He didn't even call her by her full name, never asking permission to call her Lu. He was clearly the type of guy she'd normally avoid at all costs. One that would give Linda a heart attack if she brought him home. But even so, leaving him to this poltergeist, this unfamiliar entity that only cared about the mine and its workers and nothing else, was out of the question.

"I know where some explosives are hidden," Jan said with a voice that was both his and a lot deeper.

"Yeah, where?" Matt asked, clearly not impressed.

Jan smiled, and there was nothing comforting about it. "I can show you."

"Nice try."

Lucille took a deep breath. They'd already agreed to the possession. What was the point of it if they didn't let the ghost help? "We don't have a choice, Matt."

"But Jan—" Fabian said before a roar close to them shook the cave walls. "Show us!"

He and Rachel both broke the pentagram at the same time, much to Matt's dismay. Immediately, Jan lunged forward and sprinted down the corridor so fast the rest of them had trouble following.

The bad feeling in Lucille's stomach grew. Behind them, the wyrm was eating itself through the stone, and Jan's poltergeist had shown no regard for their safety. Now, he only seemed concerned with finding that old stash. What happened to them in the meantime was irrelevant.

Jan paused around the scattered pile of rocks they'd seen initially. "It's somewhere around here." He stretched out his arms, and the rocks moved again, exposing an old wooden door in the rock face. The lock had rotted away, which made opening it an easy exercise.

Just then, the wyrm reared its ugly head behind them. The floor shook again. Startled, Fabian raised his arms, and a stream of water hit the wyrm straight in the face. It was only a small distraction, but it lasted long enough for all of them to fit into the tight room behind the door.

Inside were several old boxes and a few digging tools last used at least half a century ago. Jan ripped open one of the boxes with bare hands, exposing yellow sticks of dynamite. He reached in to grab a bunch of them.

Matt grabbed his arm. "We need a plan first."

Jan glared at him. "I know what I'm doing, boy. This was my job!"

"Guys!" Lucille shouted. "I don't want to get in your way, but we have a small problem here. Or rather, a pretty big one. Big and terrible!"

The wyrm had found them. Its head was now turning towards them, its large snout opening.

"Water, now!" Samantha cried, giving Fabian a shove.

He managed to summon the water a second before the acid hit them. Lucille had turned away from the wyrm, but the liquid hit her back and splashed against her helmet.

Fabian's water had been just in time to dilute the acid enough for the protective gear they'd put on to do its job. Only a few drops made it past the fabric.

"We're all gonna die, right?" Fabian cried.

"Not on my watch!" Jan declared. He ripped his arm out of Matt's grip and pushed himself past them.

He was going to take on the wyrm on his own. "Are you crazy, Jan?!" Lucille called after him.

"This isn't Jan," Rachel said, though she was no longer calm and collected.

"But it's still Jan's body," Nico said.

Neither of them stopped him, though, and the warning didn't seem to mean anything to the poltergeist. Instead, Jan threw himself into the corridor and ran away from the wyrm, using rocks to lure it after himself.

"We don't have much time," Lucille said. "What's our plan?" Even with his poltergeist's powers, Lucille doubted that Jan would get far. He had nothing to light the fuses, either. Not like they had. "Shall we use the dynamite?"

"And blow ourselves up?" Fabian asked. "Even if we escape the explosion, the ceiling will collapse on us."

He had a point there. But what else were they supposed to do?

"Maybe I could—" Matt started. His breath was ragged, and there were beads of sweat on his forehead.

"Matt, it's enough for me if you don't lose your mind," Lucille assured him. "I don't think your sword will be much use against those scales."

"I've got an idea," Samantha said. "But we need to lure the wyrm to us for it to work." Fabian grimaced and shook his head but kept his mouth shut. "We've got the dynamite, but we've all seen how little it did to the wyrm when I used my potions. Its skin is just too thick." She licked her lips, then took a deep breath. "But if we get it to open its mouth... Lucille can light the sticks, and I can throw them in."

For a moment, they were all quiet. Then Nico said, "It's pure madness, but this might be our best shot." He stretched out his hands. "I've got some weird-ass healing powers. I'll do the throw."

"You'll what?" Rachel asked, but he waved her off.

Just then, Jan screamed in the distance. Nico grabbed the last bits of dynamite and ran out. The rest of them followed.

They didn't have to run far to find them. Somehow, the wyrm and Jan had switched places. Jan was in front of them, crumpled against a wall and moaning in pain. The wyrm opened its snout.

"We need to lure it to us!" Samantha shouted.

Promptly, Fabian's water beam hit it in the eye. "Take that, idiot!"

"Idiot?" Lucille asked, wondering what good petty insults would do against a wyrm.

"Watch out!"

The floor beneath them shook and stones fell from the ceiling. The wyrm was coming for them.

Fabian continued his water attack, growing more and more desperate. "Open! Your! Damn! Mouth!" The wyrm didn't care for his words, keeping its snout firmly shut for now.

"Please, ghosts, you need to help us," Rachel begged.

More stones shook free from the walls, but this time, they fell onto the wyrm. In pain, it screeched, finally opening its snout.

"Globus igneus!" Lucille shouted.

The green fire sprang alive in her hand. Nico jumped in, setting the fuses of his dynamite sticks on fire. Then he turned around and threw all four of them in quick succession into the wide-open snout.

A massive boom shook the cave. Lucille shrieked, throwing herself onto the ground. She landed on someone, and something landed on her, but she couldn't tell which way was up and which way was down anymore. There was dust and rocks, big and small. And something wet slinging itself around her neck.

For minutes, no one dared to move. But the dust settled, and judging by the groaning, they were still alive.

"Are you alright, kids?" Jan asked.

Lucille felt his hand grab hers and pull her out of the rubble. Everything hurt, but none of her bones seemed to be broken. The wet thing stuck to her neck looked like a piece of wyrm entrails. "Yuck!" The realisation made her shudder. She didn't want to know how bad her hair looked.

Then it occurred to her. If entrails were caught in their hair, the wyrm had to be dead. And truly, its remnants were lying in front of them, reduced to a giant dust-covered mass of scales, innards, blood, and poison. Samantha's plan had worked. They'd defeated the big and terrible monster of the mine.

It took them almost an hour to return to the surface with the injuries they had. Fabian was limping, and Nico was holding his arm, though his strange powers seemed to be already working their mysterious ways. Samantha's head wound had bled again, but the blood was now dried on her skin. Beautiful blue lights were illuminated around them, and Lucille imagined them whispering their thanks as they reached the exit.

"No worries," Rachel said to them. For their benefit, she explained, "They're free to go now."

"I'm so glad we were able to provide peace for a bunch of ghosts," Fabian said dryly.

Lucille giggled. "That's something, yes. But we also killed a massive wyrm, which had obviously been terrorising this mine for generations. There will be no more mining accidents from now on. At least, no supernatural ones."

"I'm sorry I was so useless," Matt said. He seemed to only now be coming to terms with the fact that he hadn't played a role in their victory over the wyrm.

Samantha put a hand on his arm. "Don't worry about it. We're a team. We look out for each other."

"That's right," Jan said loudly enough for his voice to echo in their ears. "Tomorrow, we'll attack the new lode!"

"Isn't it time for you to leave?" Matt asked, his eyes narrowing slightly.

Lucille had almost forgotten about the possession. Now she worried that the ghost wouldn't keep his promise.

But Jan deflated and lowered his head. "You're right. My time is over. You were a good crew, though. One of the best. Thank you."

And just like that, he collapsed into Matt's arms. Their flashlights flickered and rustled one more time before he departed. Jan was groaning.

"Are you okay, Jan?" Matt asked, helping him back up.

"Everything hurts." Jan shook his head. "What a trip! All of it!" He threw out his arms, turned around to face the mine, and laughed. "And you do that regularly?"

Fabian shuffled his feet. "We try not to. At least, I do."

Jan didn't really hear him. "This is awesome! I want to be part of your team, crew, whatever."

Fabian stared at him as if he'd gone mad. Then he turned around and hurried away. "I want my bed. Now."

"And I want to get this wyrm stuff out of my hair," Lucille announced, once again attempting to remove the slimy coating with her fingers.

"I mean it," Jan exclaimed. "I may not have any magic powers or enough brains to steal from our chemistry lab and do something useful with it, but I've got a black belt in karate, and I know a lot about occultism."

Samantha regarded him sideways. "If you promise not to tell anyone else. Especially not Cheryl."

"Ew, why would I do that?"

Nico slapped his back and put an arm around his shoulder. "Well then, welcome to the team."

"Yeah, man!" Jan clasped hands with him and grinned from ear to ear.

Lucille chuckled. It was hard not to in the face of such enthusiasm. "Fine, if you stop calling me Lu."

"Well, what's your real name?"

She groaned. He'd never even bothered to learn her name. "It's Lucille."

"Nah, still gonna call you Lu."

"Very well, Janni-boy," Lucille said through her teeth.

Jan grinned. At this rate, they were going to regret saying "yes" faster than they could imagine.

Jan

Thanks to the stupid poltergeist, Jan had a massive headache. Being possessed had been one of the weirdest experiences of his nineteen years, and he had been through a lot. Seeing his own body move in unfamiliar ways, hearing his tongue speak words he would never have thought of, and sensing a stranger inside himself had been a whole new level of weirdness.

In short, it had been awesome.

If only the poltergeist had taken better care of his body. Instead, Jan had a massive bruise on his back and several cuts and scrapes on his hands. Under normal circumstances, he would've used it as an excuse and stayed home for several days. However, Jan only skipped the first three periods—double Maths and Geography—and made his way to school in time for the big lunch break. There were things he needed to discuss with the others that couldn't wait.

The first person he spotted was Lu, her blonde hair soft and clean, as if it had never been dunked into wyrm innards. She was leaning against the wall in front of the school hall, talking to Alan Aster of all people. Judging by the way she was twirling a strand of her hair and smiling up at Mr Handsome, it appeared she was flirting with him.

Well, that would have to wait.

Jan swooped in and grabbed her arm, dragging her along with him. "We need to talk."

"What—" She turned her head back to Alan as she tried to keep pace in her impractical high heels. "Yes. I'll be there. I'll catch you later." Then she glared at Jan. "What are you doing?"

"Believe me, you don't want a date with him. He might be good-looking, but he's pretty dumb."

Lu had an amazing death stare. "Aren't you the one who's already failing Politics?"

Jan wanted to protest—the year had only just begun—but she was probably right. "Yeah, but Alan's boring."

"He didn't ask me on a date. He invited me to a party," Lu clarified as they made their way to the table where the other five had already claimed seats for their group.

"Oh, his parties are epic. When is it?"

Lu clicked her tongue. "Next weekend. Saturday." She greeted Samantha with a kiss on the cheek. "Hey, how was Physics?"

Further down the table, Fabian simply stuck up his middle finger, his head resting on his arms, while Rachel patted his back. Samantha shook her head, indicating that it was better not to ask for details.

"Uh, that bad?" Lu asked, taking a seat next to Samantha. "Well, I started reading my grandma's diaries, and you *need* to check them out too. I found a number of exercises that are supposed to help witches settle their minds and loosen their tongues." To illustrate, she swirled her tongue around in her mouth.

"I know a few uses for that!" Jan declared, dropping down onto a chair next to Matt. His comment earned him a smirk from the weirdo, endearing him a little to Jan.

Lu, however, grabbed Samantha's pen case and threw it at Jan. "Shut your filthy mouth!"

The throw was so poorly aimed Jan had to extend his hand to catch it and lob it back to Samantha.

"Where were you during Geography?" Matt asked.

Jan shrugged. "Sleeping. Did anything interesting happen?" Annoyingly, they shared both their majors and, therefore, most of the rest of their schedule.

"You missed your presentation, for starters."

Ah, shoot. "Was that today? Oh, well, it wasn't done, anyway." He hadn't even started on it. Jan began drumming his fingers on the table. "There's something interesting I need to tell you about yesterday."

Immediately, he had everyone's attention. "My poltergeist left me with a few nuggets of wisdom in my brain."

"Well, there's certainly enough space in there," Lu muttered.

Jan grimaced. "Charming! But no. Remember how he actually messed with us days before the accident?" When everyone nodded in agreement, Jan continued, "Turns out they've got a new manager at the mine. And that manager decided to open up an adit that was blocked up sixty years ago. That's where Polty died in the first accident. He was the shift leader. The survivors sealed the adit, ensuring it would never be opened again. Then this half-wit comes along and decides the profit is worth the risk, almost killing my dad in the process."

"Does that mean the poltergeist came to your father's house hoping to stop him from following through with the orders?" Rachel asked. Before Jan could answer, she nodded. "That makes sense. He was desperate."

"And for good reason," Jan said. "As we all know. So, anyway, I want to have a chat with the new manager, and by 'chat', I mean..." He smacked his fist into his other hand.

"He probably didn't know," Samantha said, regarding him with a bewildered look. "I mean, sure it reeks of greed, but that's pretty normal for managers, isn't it?"

Now, Jan was the one confused. "So, what's your point?"

"That it's not his fault that there was an enormous wyrm in his mine."

Jan shook his head. "I don't care about the wyrm. The adit was blocked for a reason. But he couldn't see past the end of his own... nose and had to open it. I just want to have some words with him."

Perhaps it was a remnant of the poltergeist in his mind, but Jan was convinced the shift leader would've been on board. That stupid manager was probably sitting around in his office making new risky plans about how he could dig up a new tunnel now that the profit stream of this one had dried up. His father and his men would live through this accident, but as much as he detested his old man, Jan didn't want to see him buried in the mine.

"I'm going whether you think it's a good idea or not," he declared.

Samantha and the others were packing up their stuff, following suit as most of the students around them did—a clear indication that it was about to ring for class. "Well, it's a particularly bad idea, so don't count on me," she said.

"Yeah, even if he was supernatural, I wouldn't go looking for trouble." As usual, Fabian was on her side. "I've got enough of that at school."

Rachel remained silent, and Matt simply clapped his shoulder. "Good luck."

"Listen!" Lu said, grabbing her own bag. "I'll come with you, but only to make sure you're not doing anything stupid."

Jan was too baffled to respond. She was the last person he would've expected to support him on this adventure. Then again, she clearly was someone who put adventure before rules and regulations, as she'd proven last night. So maybe he shouldn't be too surprised.

Finally, Nico got up as well. "I'm meeting up with Svenja after school." Despite going to meet his girlfriend, he seemed surprisingly glum. "Otherwise, I'd be game. Would love to see the look on that manager's face when you confront him."

Without Lu sweet-talking the secretary, they would've never even *seen* the manager. As it was, Lu proved herself immensely useful. "I got you in the door. Now remember, you need to—"

She probably had some excellent tips for him on how to deal with this type of man, but Jan had no interest in hearing them. He charged into the office, ready to give the office-squatter a piece of his mind.

His rant froze on his lips the moment his eyes met the cold stare of the man in a suit. Jan couldn't quite explain why he had such an effect on him. He normally had no trouble with authorities—well, a lot of trouble, according to their definition—but he'd never been cowed by their power before.

A sign in front of him declared the man to be Mr Malcolm, manager of Greenvalley Coal Mining Inc. He didn't seem like someone who had ever so much as held a pickaxe in his hand, let alone got dusty in a mine. Everything about him was sharp. His suit was impeccable and would've fit in just as well in a lawyer's office, or on a CEO of a bank. His black hair was precisely cut, with two lines above his ear as straight as a ruler. A short black beard ran around his mouth and up his sharp-edged jaw. And that stare—as if the two teenagers in front of him were nothing but two nasty cockroaches he had to exterminate.

"How may I help?" Mr Malcolm asked, and everything in his voice screamed, *Get out of my office before I forget myself.*

Jan swallowed. He tried to recall his carefully planned accusations, but his brain was completely empty.

Either Lu wasn't scared of anything or she'd dealt with men in suits her whole life, because she stepped forward with a soft smile on her face, her posture open and inviting. "We're sorry to bother you, Mr Malcolm. I'm sure you're a very busy man. My friend here is Jan Kerscher. He's the son of your employee Stefan Kerscher, who—"

"I don't know anyone with that name," the manager rudely interrupted.

"He's one of the shift leaders," Jan blurted out. What kind of manager didn't even know the names of his direct subordinates?

Lu gave him a warning glance. "Yes, um, he was one of the men injured in the accident."

"Ah, so he's one of the imbeciles," Mr Malcolm mused.

Jan clenched his fists, anger quickly rising within him. This smug guy in a suit, who'd never seen a mine from the inside, dared to belittle his father! A man who'd been working in this mine for more than thirty years! "He's the best!"

"The best in Greenvalley, maybe. Which isn't saying much." The man pursed his lips. Then he got up and sauntered around the table, forcing them both back until he could lean his backside against the edge. His hands rested on the table. "If you're here for money, take it up with his insurance. The mine won't be covering the accident, as it was clearly a human mistake. Your father was the shift leader?"

Jan's mouth fell open. He shut it, but it dropped open again. So much information had been thrown at him he couldn't process it all. Was his father at fault for the accident? Would his father's work insurance not cover anything? Had he just got his father into trouble? Gosh, he would never be able to live that down.

"What do you mean the insurance won't cover the workers?" Lu asked, still in her element. "This was a work accident and—" She was probably about to mention the wyrm, but now struggled to find her words. "Aren't you responsible for their health and safety?"

Mr Malcolm cocked his head. "I am responsible for turning this place into a gold mine, figuratively speaking. I can't do that if my workers insist on blowing themselves up. Or if a bunch of teenagers break into my premises at night to sniff around."

He pushed himself up and stepped closer to Lu. Jan commended her for not backing down. They were so busted, but Lu still managed to stare that manager down.

However, her confidence wavered when Mr Malcolm's eyes dropped to her chest, and he raised a hand to run a finger down her necklace. Lu shivered and hastily stepped back, clutching her necklace. "W-what—"

The creepy interaction helped wake Jan from his stupor. He stepped in, ready to get physical with this jerk. "Don't you dare touch—"

Mr Malcolm caught his wrists before he could even get close. His grip was so painful that Jan's knees almost gave way. The manager drew him close until he could look straight into his eyes. Mr Malcolm's eyes were of a deep brown, almost black, and so very cold.

"Get out!" he snarled.

He let go of Jan, sending him stumbling. If it weren't for Lu, Jan would've crashed into the wall.

She caught him and muttered, "Come on, Jan, let's go."

Together, they stumbled out of the office, not stopping until they were well clear of the mining offices. Only then did Jan allow himself to rub his wrists and take a shaking breath.

Lu shook herself as if she'd just been showered with wyrm entrails again. "What was that?"

"Are you okay?" Jan felt sorry for having dragged her into this. "Did he touch you?"

"Only my necklace," Lu said with a shake of her head. "Which is bad enough." When Jan frowned, she told him, "It's magical. I inherited it from my grandmother, who was a powerful witch."

"That's dope!" He shook his head. Now was not the time to marvel at all the magic that had suddenly entered his life. "I mean, so he wasn't a creep, only drawn to your magic?"

Lu scrunched up her nose. "No, he was definitely a creep. But," her voice dropped to a whisper, "I think he knew about the wyrm."

"He definitely knew about us." Jan kicked a pebble across the ground. "Damn it. I thought they didn't have security cameras. If this gets out, my father will tear me a new one."

"Well, *my* father will sue him into bankruptcy if he comes after me or my friends." Lu glared back at the mine. "If I tell him about this meeting, he'll be livid."

Jan regarded her with newfound respect. "Will you?"

Lu ran her finger across her necklace in a nervous gesture. "I'd probably have to explain where we went last night and..." She waved off the thought. "Promise me you'll stay away from that creep. If we don't go after him, he might leave us alone."

"Sounds good to me," Jan said instantly, but inside, his mind was churning. He hadn't got what he'd come here for. And after that meeting, his anger had only grown. Who did this suit-wearing creep think he was? Threatening them, going after his father, treating his workers as expendable resources?

Greedy. That's what he was. A greedy little bastard, and Jan was going to get his revenge one way or another. He just needed a different partner in crime than upstanding Lu.

Nico

Nico stared at the message on his phone while the bus drove through the city at its usual snail's pace.

Svenja: Hey Nico, can't come today. I've got so much to do. In fact, I don't think this is going to work with my big exams coming up and everything. Hope you don't hate me for it, but I'd rather concentrate on school for now. Sorry, S.

It wasn't hard to read between the lines, even if he tried. Of course, he could ask her and put it into words—*"Are you breaking up with me?"*—but the answer was already there, so what use was there in hurting himself even more?

The problem was that he couldn't really figure out why. Nico didn't believe for one second that it had to do with her schoolwork. Sure, this was her final year, but it was still six months until the big exams, and she was doing well in school without putting too much effort in. No, there was another reason, and he couldn't figure it out for the life of him.

Was it because of the time he moved their date for a monster hunt, claiming that Rachel had had a bad day and he needed to be there for her? Or was it her father who never really liked him all that well, always regarding him as if Nico was some kind of ghetto kid, the kind that didn't even exist in Greenvalley? Yeah, probably the latter.

Nico sighed, leaning his head against the seat. It was raining outside, just like it'd been raining while he waited in front of the cinema. Half an hour. That's when he asked Svenja where she was. Five minutes later, he'd received *that* reply. Oh well, it had been good while it lasted. He wasn't entirely sure his head had really been in the relationship in the end, either. Just too much had changed over the last few weeks. The monsters, all that magic popping up, plus his own powers. He might have been too preoccupied with all of that to make Svenja feel good.

The bus began rolling through the dark streets of the southern suburb. Not that Nico saw much of it, with his face reflecting clearer in the window than the houses behind it. He wondered if he'd miss Svenja. She'd been his first girlfriend, and he liked her a lot. Maybe he should've told her about the monsters. Then again, Svenja wasn't the type of girl who'd appreciate the supernatural world. Not like he did.

Nico couldn't wait for the next fight. He was itching to explore his powers, see how far he was able to push himself and still walk out unscathed. He already knew that cuts healed within minutes, same as acid spills. The poison of the konnurar insects had taken a few hours. But what happened if he broke a bone? Or cut a little deeper?

The thought of cutting into his own flesh made Nico shiver. That sounded so wrong. He shook his head and began rigorously deleting all texts and photos of him and Svenja.

The bus stopped around the corner of his house, and Nico got out. The rain had lessened to a drizzle. Nico would've preferred a good shower to fit his mood, but the sky wouldn't comply.

Their house seemed dark, apart from a faint light up in his sister's room. Nico smiled. He could always count on Rachel being home. After everything was said and done, his sister would be there for him.

"Where's Mum?" he asked once he'd dropped his wet jacket downstairs and entered her room, flopping down on her bed.

Rachel was sitting in front of the computer, scrolling through something. "At a party."

Nico snorted. "Why am I even asking? What are you doing there?" He got up again to take a look. Rachel's hand twitched, but she didn't hide her browser window. That wasn't her style.

Flights to Los Angeles. His sister was checking current prices.

"You're planning on visiting Dad?"

"Yes and no." Rachel took a deep breath. Her hands were folded in her lap when she turned around to him. "In less than a month, we'll both turn eighteen. That means we no longer have to stay with Mum.

And I was thinking of moving to the US instead. I talked to Dad about it, and he's on board. I can live with—"

"You're gonna leave me?" That was all Nico got from her uncharacteristically long-winded explanation. He stared at her, unable to grasp the revelation to its full extent. "When were you gonna tell me?"

Rachel sighed again, unable to meet his eyes. "Right now, apparently."

Nico snorted, shook his head, and snorted again. "I don't believe this." So, Rachel was going to leave him as well. Just like that. "Why?"

"Why should I stay?" Rachel said, her voice hitching slightly. "Mum has absolutely no interest in having any kind of relationship with us. Fabian will never look at me twice. It doesn't matter that Samantha has no romantic interest in him, she'll always be his number one. School isn't great. So, what else is there for me here that I can't find over there?"

"Me!" Nico blurted out. Surely, she must've thought about him at least once.

Rachel flinched as if he'd slapped her. Then her eyes softened. She put a hand on his cheek, but Nico turned his head, and her hand dropped into her lap again. "You're rarely around anymore," she whispered.

Nico sputtered. He opened his mouth to protest, but his mind was faster. It brought up all those times he'd spent with Svenja, making sure he was home as little as he could, and then the nights he'd met up with Jan. "I'm sorry."

"Don't be." Rachel shook her head. "It's only to be expected. We're both growing up. We won't be living together forever." She sounded so disgustingly mature.

"Yeah, especially not with you moving continents." Once again, the sarcasm overcame Nico. He didn't want to talk like this to his sister, but with Svenja's out-of-the-blue rejection and now *this,* he was unable to control his feelings. Not as Rachel always did. "What about our friends? Everyone's coming together. We're defending Greenvalley from monsters with our magic." He put his hand on her chair and leaned in, slowly clenching his fist. "Rachel. We've got magic." That had to count for something, didn't it?

Rachel only rolled her eyes and pushed his hand away. "My magic only happens in dreams. I'm practically useless in a fight."

"You weren't useless in the mine when you talked to ghosts."

"But there won't be ghosts all the time. They're not as common as people think they are."

Nico knew next to nothing about ghosts. It didn't matter to him either. He didn't want to lose his sister. Who else would care for him then? His alcoholic mother who forgot his name half the time? The father who was always a world away, occupied with his own life? Nico didn't have scheduled weekly video calls with him like Rachel did. Not for lack of interest from his father, but as a result of Nico's own choice a couple of years back. The clinical schedule and inability to choose when he wanted to talk to his father had been why he stopped those. He'd thought they'd still talk, just less forced, but the reality of different time zones meant they went months without chatting. And now his sister was going to leave as well, and he'd lose her too.

Rachel took his hands. "Come with me."

She said it as if it were easy to leave everything behind. To drop out of school when the year had only just begun. To leave their friends, this town, everything. Nico couldn't even imagine a different life. His early childhood in LA didn't count. And moving from a small town in rural Germany to a giant city in the States filled him with dread rather than excitement. To visit, yes. But to live there? With everything they heard on the news?

"Nope, you have to do this one without me if it's so important to you." He started backing away from her.

"Nico." Her voice hitched, but Nico chose to ignore it. She'd brought this onto herself after all.

"I'm gonna head out." He jerked his head towards the door. "If that's alright with you."

He knew it wasn't, but he couldn't resist the jab. He hadn't even been able to tell her about the break-up with Svenja. That meant Rachel still assumed he had a girlfriend here, and still, she'd asked him to leave his life behind to go with her. No, if Rachel wanted to run away from all her pain, that was her decision. He'd rather face his head-on.

And with that, Nico grabbed his still-wet jacket and headed back out into the night.

A few hours later, Nico was completely drunk. He'd been hanging out with Jan and his mates at the docks until late, not really caring about what he consumed as long as it took his mind off. Now he couldn't even remember what he was actually trying to take his mind off.

"So, are you in?" Jan asked.

He'd been explaining some convoluted plan that involved giving a prick some shit. Maybe even real shit. It could be burned, Nico remembered. "Yes. I'm down for anything."

"Awesome. Let's go!"

Jan helped him up, and they both staggered to the side because Nico had absolutely no sense of balance left. Laughing and coughing, Nico straightened himself. "Alright. Where to?"

"Back to the mine." Jan dragged him along.

At this time of night, the streets were empty. There was a night bus, but one look at the schedule told them they'd missed the bus by five minutes. And they weren't going to wait for an hour until the next one came.

So, instead, they walked through the streets, took some wrong turns, and fell over twice, but at last, they made it to the mine at the northern edge of the town. This time, Jan hadn't got the keys, so they had to climb the fence, which took them several tries and even more falls.

"What do you... what did you ha-have in mind?" Nico asked as they stumbled towards the dark office.

Nobody was around, just as there hadn't been the night before when they'd broken into the mine. The wyrm flashed through Nico's mind. How it'd opened its giant maw, acid dripping from its teeth. The few splashes had already healed, but he doubted that would be the case if he'd been bitten by a giant worm.

The thought made him giggle. A giant worm. They'd fought a freaking giant worm.

"Nico!" Jan hissed from further ahead. Somehow, he'd teleported to the building because Nico could've sworn he'd been right next to him just a minute ago. He was about to complain to Jan when he reached him, but his friend hushed him. "I think he's here."

"Who is?"

"The suit guy," Jan hissed. He pointed to the window at the back of the office complex. "It's three o'clock. What a weirdo."

Nico squinted. For the most part, the building was dark, but there was the faint glint of a light in the last room. Like the flicker of a flame. "Fire?"

Jan laughed. "Oh, Nico! What a brilliant idea. Well, if that jerk can't even stop working in the middle of the night, he deserves a little scare. Check the paper bin."

They ran to the garbage disposal area and raided the paper bin until they had enough to build a little pyre under the window of the office.

"He's gonna piss himself," Jan laughed, then took some time to light it up.

The earlier rain hadn't affected the paper in the garbage bin, and it caught fire quickly. Slapping each other's backs in glee, they ran back to the fence, this time clambering up a little faster. When they turned around, still laughing, the fire was in full force, burning through the thin material.

"There he is!" Jan pointed.

A shadow appeared at the window. From this distance, Nico couldn't tell, but he felt as if the man was looking straight at him despite the distance. All of a sudden, he felt terribly cold, and the laughter stuck in his throat.

Then the fire jumped over onto the building. Too late, Nico realised that the old office complex was mainly built from wood. It would burn down completely.

"Shit." Reason came back to him in a flash. What were they doing here? Arson? While a man was still in the building?

He wanted to get up to his feet, but at that moment, Jan's hand clawed into his arm. "What the hell is *that?*"

In front of them, the dark shadow of the man hadn't moved at all. Despite the roaring fire, he was still standing at the window, looking at them. Nico was sure of it. The guy saw them, knew them. Then two big, leathery wings spread on his back, bursting the window.

Nico lost control over his bladder when the man—*demon*—launched himself through the window and vanished. An unearthly roar shook the earth. Seconds later, the flames shot higher, engulfing the office building completely.

The mundane ringing of an alarm shook him out of his terror. Already, sirens could be heard in the distance.

"We need to leave!" He grabbed Jan, who still seemed stunned, and together, they ran deep into the forest, stumbling over sticks and stones until they collapsed near a different part of town.

Struggling for breath, Nico still had to get the words out. "Was that a demon?"

"Figures," was Jan's short answer. He was down on all fours, breathing heavily, only to convulse and throw up seconds later. Then he drew out an inhaler and took several puffs before his breathing calmed somewhat.

Nico fell into the pine needles. His head was throbbing from what he'd seen, and it still made no sense. "The new manager is a demon?"

"*Was* a demon," Jan said, wiping his mouth with the back of his hand. "He died, didn't he? The fire got him. Poof, and he was gone."

Nico wanted to believe that more than anything, so he nodded, but if he was true to himself, the flames hadn't seemed to bother the demon. He'd just... *vanished.*

"Do we tell the others?"

"About what?" Jan shook his head. "He's gone, Nico. That creep is gone. He can't hurt anyone anymore."

Even if the demon had fled, Nico had the feeling they would see him again. Especially because he'd seen *them*. And suddenly, Nico remembered exactly how cold the demon's gaze had been, even from a distance, and he wished he'd never left his home in the first place.

Part 4
Bites & Blood

Lucille

The first round of exams behind her, Lucille spent the afternoon with her grandmother's diaries. They were a wealth of information, not only because of the magic described within but also because they gave her insight into her grandmother's youth. Though there were only hints of Cecille's personal life, Lucille soaked them up like a sponge, feeling as though she was reconnecting with her grandmother.

Cecille had come from a long line of witches. They'd called themselves the Ilsenstein Witches. Every mother had whispered her secrets to her daughter, keeping alive a tradition spanning several centuries. Lucille knew that the de Cerques had a long family line—something her father was very proud of—but the Ilsenstein line surpassed her paternal ancestors by a long shot.

She also learned more about the history of witchcraft in the area. According to her grandmother's notes, there were up to twelve leading witches of the Harz Coven, who convened once a year in April at the Night of Walpurgis. There was the Quedlinburg Witch and the Wernigerode Witch, the witches of Harzgerode, Clausthal-Zellerfeld, Osterode, Blankenburg, and many more. And, of course, there was the Greenvalley Witch. Cecille's family had been Greenvalley Witches for over five centuries, but her grandmother had feared that it would pass her by.

"Mama is disappointed yet again. I've studied all night, know every shape and pattern, but when I hold the magic in my hand, it becomes as indiscernible as if I were to hold water. How does one weave the flow of water without it running through one's fingers? I can do spells, but

spells are nothing but tools. A real witch needs no tools. She's one with the magic around her."

"The magic around her" was what Samantha had referred to when she talked about the spring of magic. It was a power that was invisible to Lucille, just as it had been to her grandmother. As much as she sympathised with her grandmother, who had been only a year younger than her when she'd written those lines, Lucille knew that it had all worked out for Cecille. She may not have become the Greenvalley Witch like her mother or grandmother, but she'd been powerful enough to take on demons. And Lucille was determined that she would be just as powerful.

Her fingers itched to try out the plethora of spells Cecille had scribbled onto the sides of the pages, and the fervour made her necklace seem warmer. Her grandmother may not have been the Greenvalley Witch, but now there was a new de Cerque in town, and she would restore her family's destiny.

Lucille blinked. Where had that thought come from? She was nothing but a baby witch with only a handful of spells at her disposal. She still relied on her fireball and light spells for most of the fighting she'd done. And the pure magic, as it was called in the diaries, eluded her the same way it had eluded her grandmother.

"If only I could force that magic into its shapes, Mama would see me. She's already obsessed with Elda, though that girl has spent little to no time training her magic, while I... Oh, Mama, how can you choose her when I worked so hard for this? I was able to defeat that creature with my spells, but spells will never be enough. I need to weave the magic. I need to be powerful enough for you...

"I've been trying some spells lately. When I speak, the magic becomes more manageable. It does what I want. I only need to find the right words. And I think I've found them. This spell will grant me what doesn't come naturally: full control of the magic around me. Once spoken, the river will bend to my every word, and if that's not enough, nothing will ever be."

Lucille imagined how it would be if the magic was bound to her every word. If she could do anything she wanted. Her necklace burnt against her skin, as if begging her to try it out.

And why not? Her grandmother had developed this spell, a testament to how great she'd been even without that natural connection to the magic around her. And Lucille would be just as great. *Or greater.*

She sat upright in the middle of her room, legs crossed, and the diary in her lap. Would she be able to see the magic once the spell was spoken? Her grandmother always wrote in such reverence of it. It crossed Lucille's mind that it would be mightily unfair if she, as the only young witch in town, was unable to sense magic. No, she deserved to see it.

Grabbing the burning Enigma of Power she'd inherited from her grandmother, Lucille spoke the unfamiliar words, "Alae varyarith iyanna vee." Though she'd never heard those words before, her necklace guided her intonation, and the right pronunciation jumped to her mind without ever thinking about it.

As soon as Lucille had repeated it three times, a jolt ran through her body. She closed her eyes; her head dizzy for a moment. Something was opening deep inside her. It was like a hole, an emptiness that yearned to be filled. Only one thing could fill it: magic.

When Lucille opened her eyes again, she saw it. All around her, wispy strands of glitter floated through the room, like plumes of fog in the morning sun. Dazed by their beauty, Lucille ran her fingers through them. For the tiniest moment, she felt a silt-like texture, but it evaporated as quickly as she touched it.

Talk. That was the next step her grandmother had written down. *Talk, and the magic will follow the word.*

Lucille looked around, unsure of what to enchant in a hurry. Her eyes landed on an indoor plant by the window that had gathered a little more of the magic around it. Excited, she got up and put her hands on both sides of the pot. What was the spell Samantha had used? She didn't remember, but at the same time, it occurred to her that it didn't matter.

"Grow!" she said, and grow it did. First, the stems extended, then new ones sprouted, and on them dozens and dozens of leaves. Bigger and bigger the plant became until it covered half the window and most of her desk beneath it.

"Stop!" Lucille said, laughing with delight. This was better than anything she could've imagined. What a marvellous spell! "Bloom!"

She had no idea whether the plant had ever bloomed before, but it did so now, with big and beautiful flowers of a rich purple colour.

"I love it!" She clapped her hands and walked around her room to find objects to test her newfound powers with. There was no end to the magic inside her room. Quite the opposite. The more magic she did, the more came to her. An endless supply of magic for all her needs and wants. And oh, how she wanted all of it.

Just then, someone knocked at the door, and before Lucille was able to call out that it was open, her stepmother came in. Linda had barely set a foot into the room when she stopped, scrunching up her nose in distaste. "What is that?"

She was pointing at the rubber-like ruler in Lucille's hands. It had enough spring to catapult little balls of paper through the room. "This is one of those fancy new rulers they have at school." She bent it into a curve and watched it spring back into shape. "I like them."

Linda took a deep breath. "I don't see the use of making a ruler bendy if it doesn't stay in shape." The overgrown plant caught her eye next. "Oh dear, what is this doing in your room?"

"This," Lucille said pointedly, "is a school project. Biology."

"Wouldn't that be better placed in the glass house? It'll only attract vermin, never mind all the pollen." She waggled her hand in front of her nose, then focused on Lucille. "I was going to ask you something. What are your plans for the weekend?"

Alan's party was on Friday, and on Saturday, she had a date with her father. At last! But to her stepmother, she only said, "Why?"

"Well, because of the fashion show." Linda smiled exuberantly. "The council asked me to put on a little show down at the community centre. Normally, I wouldn't bother with such small events, but one might say you inspired me. I think it's a good charity event."

Lucille stared at her, trying to wrap her head around the fact that her attending public school could be seen as charity towards the local high school. "What does that have to do with me?"

"I want you to model my clothes," Linda said, grinning from ear to ear. "Since it's a charity event, I thought some of the girls here would like an opportunity they'll treasure for the rest of their lives. And of course, I want you as my main model. Imagine yourself in a wedding dress, drawing all the oohs and aahs of the crowd. What do you think?"

Lucille thought a lot. The condescension her stepmother handed out so casually was enough to make her dizzy. As if no one from Greenvalley would ever amount to anything or leave the town. And, of course, she didn't miss the notion that a charity event meant no money would be paid for real models. But the most baffling thing was that Linda seemed to think Lucille would enjoy such an opportunity.

"It's on Saturday, right?" she asked almost innocently. "That's when I have my date with Dad. So—"

"Oh, don't worry. I've already talked to Bastien. If he can fit it in, he'll be at the show, but we'll all go to the restaurant afterwards. I've already booked." Again, that awful smile. As if she hadn't just crushed Lucille's hopes and dreams in one fell swoop.

"That was *my* date." How did Linda not see how important it was for Lucille to spend quality time with her busy father? Linda had him to herself every night.

And now she was even laughing. "Lucille, darling. Your date, my date. We're a family."

"No, we're not. Dad and I are a family. You are always trying to get between us!" Lucille was so angry even the necklace around her neck flared up. "No! I do not want to be part of your fashion show! But more importantly, I don't want *you* to be part of our family. I want you to leave—go to Milan or Paris or wherever—and never come back!"

Linda swallowed heavily, her eyes glazed over in confusion, but then she backed away. "I need to pack my things."

"What?"

"And book a flight. To Milan. Or Paris. Or wherever. See you never." And as chipper as if she was going on another business trip, Linda bounced out of Lucille's room.

Now it was Lucille's turn to be confused. She followed her stepmother to the door and checked the corridor just in time to see Linda wishing Albert goodbye. The butler looked at Lucille in confusion.

Unable to answer his unspoken question, Lucille closed the door behind her and leaned against it. Her breath was coming faster. Her head was swimming. And then she saw all the things she had commanded into a different shape with her magic.

Magic! She'd used magic on her stepmother. She'd told her to leave, and now she was really leaving.

A giggle burst from her lips. Lucille covered her mouth with her hands, afraid that Albert would hear her, but she was unable to contain her joy. Her stepmother was finally gone! No more hogging of her father. No more dismissive comments about her new school or all the decisions Lucille dared to make about herself. She was gone. And now it was just Lucille and her father.

The sudden bliss made her sigh.

Finally, things were looking up, and it was all because of her grandmother's magic. Lucille touched her necklace, revelling in its heat. The gift her beloved grandmother had given her, with which she would turn things around at last.

She would have her date with her father. And many more. There was no way he could escape the magic.

The new spell Lucille had learnt from her grandmother was a revelation. She was able to do whatever her mind thought of, instead of trying to make things work with limited or complicated spells. There was no spell to command her Maths homework to do itself. But there was now!

"Now that is a spell I like," Fabian proclaimed and eagerly moved to copy it to his own folder. Both of them were sharing a free period in the hall.

Lucille smiled at him. "I thought you would." She looked around in the hall to find something else to put a spell on.

Perhaps she could lower the prices of the cafeteria—that would benefit all of them—but one look at the cafeteria owner made her reconsider. She didn't want to ruin his income. By the looks of his miserable face, it was all he had going for himself.

"Gosh, I hate those girls," Fabian muttered.

Lucille followed his gaze to the atrium, in which Cheryl and Ani were clearly making fun of something—or someone. "So, what's their deal?" she asked, leaning towards Fabian. "Why are they so mean... or rather, why are they picking on Sam?" Not that school bullies truly needed a reason.

"Fun fact: Ani and Sam were best friends during elementary school," Fabian explained. "We used to play with each other, and of course, Sam loved pretending to be a witch. And so did Ani."

Lucille didn't know what surprised her more: that Sam and Ani had been friends or that Ani had enjoyed the very thing she now made fun of.

"So, then in fifth grade, Cheryl comes into our class. And she's all... well, we were all barely ten years old, but Cheryl was already into fashion, music, and boys." Fabian rolled his eyes. "So grown up. And her and Ani just clicked. I'm not saying Cheryl stole her on purpose or anything, but she made sure everybody heard how childish it was of Sam to still believe in magic. Ani lapped it up like everybody else. And you know Sam. She's never backed down from her beliefs just to fit in."

"Good on her." Lucille said, observing Cheryl once more. She could easily see how it happened. One girl already well on her way to puberty, the other still more child than tween. "But that was seven years ago. Samantha has grown up."

"And she still believes in magic," Fabian pointed out. "Which makes sense since it's real."

Lucille found herself smiling. "Seems to me like Cheryl is in desperate need of some magic of her own." What should she do? Some sort of spectacle for sure. A wardrobe malfunction? An embarrassing fall in front of everyone?

No, Lucille wasn't *that* kind of girl, but literally the entire world was at her feet. With magic, there had to be something clever she could do to show Cheryl the error of her ways.

Just then, the first students were returning from their classes. She saw Samantha heading towards them, chatting with Cian. The two of them obviously enjoyed each other's company, laughing about something that had happened in Chemistry. Any moment, Cheryl would see them and ruin it. But not on Lucille's watch.

"Cian should ask Samantha to come to the party with him." As soon as Lucille had said it, she felt the magic taking hold. It was a warm sensation she instantly wanted more of.

Fabian, however, frowned. "That will never happen. And why Cian? She..."

He stopped when his gaze found Samantha and Cian. They, too, had paused, in front of the atrium, with Cian looking all cute at Samantha.

"Because he loves her," Lucille said, feeling entirely sure of it. She knew her way around boys. And a guy like him, who went out of his way to talk to a shunned girl like Samantha even after getting into trouble with his friends, was definitely interested. "Just wait." She barely even noticed the magic that flowed from her to Fabian.

A moment later, Cian and Samantha separated. Cian went into the atrium, and Samantha came to them, her face in shock. She slid into a seat next to Lucille and whispered, "You'll never believe what just happened."

"What?" Fabian asked, still frowning. "Did Cian—"

"He asked me out," Samantha blurted, then let go of a deep breath. "To the party, I mean. I'm going to Alan's party."

"Are you?" Fabian asked. "I wouldn't go there even if Cheryl invited me personally. It's a trick, right? He lures you to the party, and they'll get their laughs there."

"Gee, Fabian!" Lucille punched him in the arm. "Don't scare her. I bet Cian is genuine. Just look at him." She nodded at the atrium.

Cian must've informed Cheryl of his actions because she was clearly having a go at him. Her arms were flailing about, while her face was distorted by rage. Oh, yes, this spell had worked perfectly.

"I don't know," Samantha said, biting her lip. "Maybe Fabian's right."

"No, he's not!" Lucille pointed her finger at Samantha's face while holding Fabian back with her other hand. "Don't you dare say no to Cian." If a little bit of magic would help Samantha overcome her insecurities, she deserved that. "It will be lovely. We'll get ready together. I'll lend you a dress. And we'll have an amazing time with two boys who can't take their eyes off us."

She turned around to Fabian. "And you won't ruin that!"

Fabian raised his hands as the magic took hold of him. "I wasn't planning to..." He looked at Samantha and sighed. "Have fun, I guess."

Lucille nodded contentedly. "We will have so much fun. I guarantee it. Tomorrow night will be magical."

Samantha

Samantha thought about cancelling her date every five minutes. She'd never been to a party, not one like this—in the home of the most popular guy in their year. Nor had she had a date with someone other than Fabian. And Fabian had been all about comfort. This thing with Cian was as far out of her comfort zone as it could get.

But there was no backing out, not with Lucille around. Her friend had brought so much stuff over that it looked as if she was planning to move in with her. There were at least ten discarded dresses on the bed. Lucille had made her try them all until deciding on a simple green dress that accentuated Samantha's eyes—and unfortunately her breasts.

Samantha had the constant urge to cross her arms in front of her chest while Lucille was working on her hair. The same hair that was so hard to get under control, being thick and full of curls, became perfectly pliable in Lucille's hands. Within seconds, Lucille had draped it at the back of her head, leaving just enough length for her curls to tickle the nape of her neck.

"Did you use magic, or how did you get it so smooth?" Samantha looked at herself in the mirror, hardly recognising herself.

Lucille giggled. She was wearing a gorgeous gold-shimmering dress that looked like flowing water every time she moved. "Maybe. Okay, yes, I did." She grinned at Samantha through the mirror. "I found a spell that lets me manipulate magic however I want. One word and the magic happens. My grandmother developed it."

"Really?" Samantha had never heard of such a spell. It sounded too... *convenient.*

"Hush now. I'm gonna do your face." Lucille spun around and dragged a gigantic make-up box to the bed.

Samantha had never worn make-up other than a quick dash of mascara, but Lucille had the full program planned for her. "What if it's a joke?"

"He wouldn't dare," Lucille said, testing different make-up until she had found the right skin tone. "He likes you, Sam, whether you're prepared for it or not."

That didn't help quell the butterflies in her stomach at all. She'd broken up with Fabian because of Rachel's feelings—and because she had been looking for something more. That head-turning love you saw in movies and books, and which had been entirely missing from her relationship with Fabian. But now that she had a taste of it, she wasn't prepared for the experience.

When Lucille got ready to apply the make-up, it was too much. "I don't think I can do this."

"Sam, think of it as an evening with friends. It doesn't have to mean anything else."

Samantha felt a strange tingling. Lucille's words made so much sense. Too much sense, actually. "But we're not friends. I hardly know Cian."

"Then you'll get to know him." Lucille pushed her back down into her chair. "Now close your eyes."

For a few minutes, Samantha didn't dare to move. Lucille applied the make-up expertly, bringing out her natural bone structure and giving her eyes such a vivid uplift even Samantha was surprised by the intense green in them. Her mirror image was now truly unrecognisable.

When Lucille approached her lips, she pushed out her hand. "I hate lipstick. It makes me feel, like, forty years old."

"It's only lip gloss and not a bold colour," Lucille explained. "Really, don't you trust me? I know what I'm doing."

That much was true. While the make-up was unfamiliar, Samantha was unable to deny that her face, her hair, even her dress looked amazing. She appreciated Lucille's effort and was well aware that she couldn't exactly turn up in a T-shirt and leggings to a date with Cian or to Alan's party.

As if she'd summoned them with her thoughts, the doorbell rang.

Suddenly, Samantha was certain she had to cancel. Her butt was glued to the chair, and she wouldn't be able to get out of it without help. Help that Lucille happily supplied.

"Come on! They're here. And on time." She clicked her tongue and smiled. "I like that in a boy."

Samantha wished they would've been fashionably late or hadn't come at all. And it only got worse when her sister stormed into her room.

"Cian Funke and Alan Aster are in front of..." Her eyes roamed Samantha's new appearance. "Who are you, and what did you do to my sister?"

Lucille giggled. "She looks great, doesn't she?"

Meg only shrugged, of course. "You mean she looks like a girl, for once?"

Her backhanded compliment grounded Samantha and helped her find her way back to her usual self. She groaned and waved her outside. "You can go now."

But Meg wasn't even thinking of leaving. She crossed her arms, still seemingly fascinated by Samantha's looks. "Not until you tell me what's going on here."

Lucille hooked her arm under Samantha's and grinned. "Well, your sister has a date with Cian, and we're now going to Alan's party."

Meg's eyes grew large. "Can I come? I can get ready quickly."

"Absolutely not!" The last thing Samantha needed was babysitting her boy-crazy little sister. She would have to constantly look out for her and steer her away from the alcohol. "Go help Mum with dinner!"

Lucille laughed and used the distraction Meg had provided to drag Samantha out of her room. Meg was pouting, but Samantha was sure she'd get over it. On the way down the stairs, she tugged at her dress. The nervousness was back. The dress was so short she was sure everybody would be able to see under her skirt.

"It's long enough," Lucille whispered. Then she opened the door with a smile. "Hello, boys."

Alan looked bored, as if they'd left him waiting for an hour instead of five minutes, but Cian looked as nervous as Samantha was. "Hey." He smiled a little crooked.

"Finally," Alan moaned. He stepped closer to Lucille and kissed her cheek. "Can we go?" He didn't wait for her affirmation and pulled her away from the doorstep.

Cian was still looking at Samantha with an intensity that made her want to run back inside. But inside, Meg was watching. Even her mother had come to check who was taking her to her first party. Running was not an option. Nevertheless, Samantha avoided his gaze and tugged at her locks. At last, he smiled. "Who knew there was something so pretty hiding under the lab coat?"

Her cheeks flushed. That meant Lucille's beauty routine was working. Still, Samantha would've much rather preferred a crash course on how to flirt with boys instead. "Thank you."

He offered his arm like a gentleman. Samantha had no other choice than to take it, but her touch was tentative as he led her to his car. In front of her, Lucille was grinning, holding up one thumb, which gave her a little more confidence.

At the car, Cian jumped forward and opened the door for her. "So, I guess under your lab coat there's a gentleman." Samantha wanted to bite her tongue off after mangling that line, but Cian only grinned.

"All part of the date package." He got in the driver's seat.

Samantha caught Alan rolling his eyes, but he and Lucille got into the back and immediately started whispering and giggling.

"You should attend parties more often," Cian said, side-glancing at her as he started the car and rolled away from the curb.

The words reminded Samantha of her mother or Meg. *She was a teenager. She should be more social. Get out of the house and her own head more.* "You think so?"

Cian grinned. "Absolutely. Besides, if you did, we could go together more often."

Apparently, that was even too much for Alan. "Stop swooning like an idiot!" He accompanied his words with a kick against Cian's seat.

Lucille put a hand on Alan's arm. "Leave him." And within seconds, Alan was all into her again.

As the two started kissing in the backseat, Samantha turned towards the window, dying from the awkwardness in the car.

It was her first party. And all she wanted to know was how long she had to be there before she could leave.

Everyone was at the party, taking place all over the house and the garden. As expected, the entire Elite Clique was present, though Samantha and Cian had managed to evade them until now. Lucille was dancing with Alan, their bodies glued together. On the opposite side of the room, Samantha saw Matt with his arm around a boy, clearly flirting with Shayna.

Just then, the crowd hollered as Jan, Nico, and a group of unfamiliar guys entered the premises, carrying two boxes of beer. They put the boxes in a corner, quickly distributing the beers. Not that it was needed. Alcohol was everywhere. Some guests had brought their own, but Alan had provided plenty upfront, even splurging on a bottle of vodka.

The party was loud, rowdy, and people were getting drunker by the minute.

"Do you want to dance?" Cian asked, half-shouting into Samantha's ear.

The crowd hollered again as Alan had pulled Lucille close, and they started kissing on the dance floor. Cian's hand suddenly landed on Samantha's lower back as he grinned at his friend, and Samantha felt a surge of discomfort rising in her throat.

She shook her head. "I don't really enjoy dancing." Sure, she danced in her room when the music was good, but never in front of others.

Cian's eyes traveled down her body and then back up to her lips. "Do you want to go upstairs then? I can show you the house."

Samantha's throat tightened. She wasn't stupid. She knew where he was going with this, and she had absolutely no interest in making out at Alan's party, especially not with Cian. That much was clear to her now. His sudden aggressive pursuit was way too much, and she was convinced he only wanted her so he could go around and boast about hooking up with the class witch.

"No," she said somewhat confidently.

He sighed, looking almost desperate. "Then can I get you something to drink?"

"Yes!" Drinking was good. She could handle that.

"Beer?"

Samantha groaned internally. No, drinking wasn't good at all. "I don't really drink beer," she said diplomatically, hoping he would think she was boring and move on.

"We also have wine, or do you want something stronger?" he asked, glancing at the makeshift bar.

"Don't you have water?" Samantha was growing desperate. How could they be so out of sync? Then again, she had always felt out of sync with the rest of her class.

Cian frowned. "Water? Yeah, I think so. I mean, sure." Then he smiled again, as if eager to please. "I'll be back in a minute. Don't run away."

All she wanted to do was run away. Fabian and Rachel weren't here. They could've had a nice evening watching videos and eating chips. Instead, she was stuck on this uncomfortable date. And Lucille wasn't even around to help her as promised.

She pressed herself against the wall, hoping nobody would notice her and drag her into the drunken antics happening all over the place. Alan and Lucille were still kissing, now on the couch. They'd probably go upstairs at some point, if Matt didn't beat them to it.

Cian returned with a glass of water and a bottle of beer in his hand, but an unfamiliar girl with long brown hair stepped in his way, and they seemed to hit it off.

"Oh dear," a familiar voice said next to Samantha. Ani. "That was a short date with Cian."

Samantha sighed. Sometimes it baffled her that she'd ever been friends with Ani, but then again, Ani had changed so much, she was like a completely different person.

"I hope you didn't believe Cian was truly interested in you," Ani said with faked compassion. "He just needed someone to bring to the party, and well... he probably thought it would be fun to pick you."

It was clear to Samantha that Cian's idea of fun wasn't aligned with hers. She nodded vaguely. "Sure."

"Sammy!" Ani clicked her tongue. "You thought he really...? Oh gosh, just think about it. Tell me one good reason why Cian would suddenly be interested in you." When Samantha remained silent, Ani continued, "That's right. There isn't one. But hey, at least you got to attend a party for once in your life."

Samantha did her best to hold back the tears, but she was already so emotionally strained that they started to flow despite all her attempts. "Great." Her voice lacked any emotion, barely stable enough to utter the word.

"And now you can leave again," Ani said with a big smile, finally reverting to her true self. She wriggled her fingers in a mock-wave. "Bye."

Samantha pushed herself off the wall and ran away. She wanted to leave now more than anything, all the while berating herself for listening to Lucille and coming here in the first place.

Leaving wasn't easy. She had to push through the throng of people, and past Cian, who called after her. No, she certainly wouldn't turn back and face him. Not now when tears were streaming down her face, ruining Lucille's work.

She'd just managed to break through the main group when Cheryl stood in front of her. The queen of the Elite Clique had her hands down on her hips and looked absolutely furious. "What are you doing here?"

Samantha stumbled backwards, but there was nowhere to go. The other students were standing way too close, and now they turned around to be entertained by Cheryl's sure-to-be-epic takedown.

"Just because you now have a few friends who aren't losers doesn't mean you can come here." Cheryl was almost screaming.

Shayna stepped closer, putting a hand on Cheryl's arm. "Cian invited her," she said, sounding defensive.

Cheryl pushed her friend's hand away. "Yeah, and he's obviously lost his mind. You don't belong here, Samantha!" Her spit landed on Samantha's face. "Not at this party, and not anywhere near Cian."

"Hey!"

Samantha closed her eyes, praying this wasn't happening. Cian pushed through the crowd, taking her side. Ani was there too. Four out of seven of the Elite Idiots, and they had her cornered. This was quickly turning into her worst nightmare.

"Stop meddling with my relationships!" Cian exclaimed, his voice filled with anger. He put his hand on Samantha's shoulder as if she belonged to him. "Whether I have a crush on Samantha or not is my problem and mine alone."

"You don't have a crush on Samantha," Ani said, though doubt seeped into her voice.

"Oh, yes, I do!" Cian declared. "I love Samantha, and that won't change no matter what you think."

Everyone was stunned by his words, including Samantha. He *loved* her? It had to be a joke. Any moment now, he would admit to it and they'd all have a laugh.

But Cheryl had turned pale. She forced a fake laugh. "Cian, has Samantha bewitched you?" She scrunched up her nose as she regarded at Samantha. "Did you mix him one of your love potions?"

Samantha stared at her. Love potions. *What if...?* She looked around for Lucille, but the people were too close and she couldn't spot her friend and Alan, if they were still here. She turned back to Cheryl. "As if you would believe in that." Instantly, she regretted her words, but Cheryl had already seized upon them.

"Well, you'd certainly be desperate enough." Cheryl laughed again, this time more convincingly. "Little Sammy still believes in magic. And probably Santa too. Have you been a good girl this year, Sammy?"

Tears welled up in Samantha's eyes. Her throat and stomach ached. The laughter surrounding her felt like sharp blades cutting into her skin, and she wished the earth would open up underneath her and swallow her whole.

Instead, Cian faced her, and put his hands on her cheeks. "She's the best."

Samantha's eyes widened as he pressed his lips onto hers, forcefully thrusting his tongue into her mouth. Shock paralysed her entire body. She couldn't think, couldn't feel, and certainly couldn't push Cian away.

Suddenly, he was gone, stumbling backwards into the crowd. Matt was there, his shirt half unbuttoned, but his face filled with anger. Cheryl stifled a scream with her hand. Cian was helped to his feet by the crowd, who now started chanting, "Fight! Fight! Fight!"

The energy in the room turned tense. Fists were being pumped in the air, and then Cian went for Matt, pushing him into a group of drunken boys. Within seconds, there was a big fight.

Cheryl and her cronies shrieked, fists were thrown, and glass shattered. Samantha pushed her way through the crowd of people who either wanted to get away or join the fight. Someone hit her in the back of the head, sending stars dancing in her vision. When she regained her balance, she found herself leaning on the sofa. Someone fell over the armrest, narrowly missing her, and Samantha shirked away again.

Feeling disoriented and terrified, she stumbled through the crowd until she reached the door. Samantha flung it open and fled into the cold night. She only managed to get a few metres away from the house before the sobs erupted from her throat, and she had to cling to a tree as she cried. She couldn't believe Cian had kissed her, especially after a public declaration of love.

Part of her began connecting the dots, finding a reason for why Cian was so suddenly in love with her, why he'd even asked her out in the first place. But it didn't make the pain any less. If anything, knowing that Lucille's use of magic was probably behind it all made it worse. Cian had kissed her in front of everyone, without any regard for her or her feelings. And she probably couldn't even blame him.

"Sam?"

Oh no! Matt was coming after her. The last thing Samantha wanted was to talk to anyone, even a friend. She tried to walk away, but the heels Lucille had insisted she wear made her trip over her own feet.

Matt caught her before she hit the ground. "Where are you going?"

"Leave me, please!" She just wanted to go home.

Matt studied her face with concern. His eyes widened a little as if he had just noticed the tears and ruined make-up. Samantha tried to hold his gaze, but the longer he stayed silent, the harder it was to hold back her tears. Finally, a sob escaped her throat, and she clutched his shirt, hiding her face against at his chest.

Tentatively, Matt put an arm around her back and a hand on her head. "I swear, if Cian touches you again—"

"You'll beat him up?" she asked, crying anew. "He only kissed me. I just... it all happened so fast. Ani, Cheryl, Cian. The fight!"

"I know I shouldn't have pushed him," Matt admitted, sounding disgruntled. "But it looked to me like you didn't enjoy him kissing you. You seemed uncomfortable."

"True," Samantha whispered. She'd never felt so trapped in a kiss before.

Matt smiled sadly at her. "See, I can't stand that. Being this pushy with a girl—or anyone—kissing them without their consent? I hate that."

Samantha stared at him in surprise. He was a serial dater, always interested in someone, constantly on the prowl. Not the kind of guy she associated with respect and consent. "Wow. I didn't know you cared about that."

"If I can tell that the other person isn't interested, I won't pursue them," he said seriously.

Samantha couldn't help but be a little impressed. It wasn't often that a guy like him—or any guy at all—understood consent. "So, how often does that happen?" she teased him.

He chuckled. "Not very often, I admit." Smiling, he wiped away tears and mascara from her cheek with his thumb. "Did Lucille put you up to this? And put all that make-up on you?"

Feeling it smearing on her face, Samantha knew it was too much. It felt like a mask she wasn't wearing particularly well. "It looks horrible, doesn't it?"

"No!" Matt laughed and shook his head. "I mean, after all those tears, yes! But you're still very pretty." Samantha rolled her eyes but couldn't help smiling. "I just like you more without it. It suits you better."

Samantha stared at him, trying to process he'd just said. A guy like him, who only seemed interested in brief flings, appreciating natural beauty—or whatever she was—surprised her.

He was about to say something else when a scream pierced the night.

Matt and Samantha exchanged a look, then they both ran back towards the party.

Jan

This party was epic! Jan had no idea why it was happening, but there was a fight. The real deal, with crushed furniture, screaming girls, and fists thrown everywhere. It was awesome!

Jan and Nico had thrown themselves into the crowd, happy to punch whoever was closest and didn't duck out of the way fast enough. Someone wrapped their arms around Jan's hips and tried to bulldoze him onto the couch. Jan brought up a knee and got rid of his assailant in one quick throw. The guy landed in a standing lamp, which promptly folded and splintered as it crashed onto the windowsill.

"Stop it!" Next to him, Alan charged from the crowd, Lu behind him. His fists were clenched, and his face wasn't his usual brand of pretty, what with the snarl and blazing eyes.

Jan brought his own fists up, grinning wildly. "Want to join the fun, Aster?"

He didn't. "That was my mum's. You're ruining our house!"

"Oh, am I?" There were at least a dozen guys involved in the fight. "Is Daddy going to be angry?"

Alan let out a guttural scream and lunged at him. Jan easily side-stepped him, bumping into Nico as he did so, then grabbed Alan by the shoulder and landed his fist in his preppy face.

Oh, that felt good.

Blood spurted from Alan's nose, and his eyes widened in a daze. He stumbled backwards and fell over the couch, knocking his head against the wall. Jan grinned. Best day of his life!

"Everyone, stop fighting!" Lu screeched, her pretty face just as furious as Alan's had been.

To Jan's annoyance, everybody listened to her. Suddenly, the music could be heard again, no more fists smacking into flesh, and no more glasses being broken. The room was almost deadly quiet.

Lu knelt down next to Alan and tried to help him up, but he pushed her away. "Get away from me!"

Instead of at her date, Lu glared at Jan. "Really?"

"Come on, Lu, relax a little!" He was still grinning from ear to ear, hardly feeling the bruises he'd attained himself.

Lu wouldn't relax. Or calm down. Instead, she threw her hand in a pointed gesture towards the garden. "Get out! Both of you."

And though Jan had no intention of leaving the party, he walked out the door and into the garden, Nico on his heels.

Outside, the mood was a little lighter—boring one might say. Only about eight people stood out here. And the most exciting thing was two girls making out on a lawn chair. He couldn't even see drinks. Why had he listened to Lu?

"Is it over?" Robert asked from the questionable safety of a large flowerpot.

Jan sneered at him. "Yeah, no thanks to you."

Robert's eyes bulged as if he took the affront seriously. "I-I would have helped you, Jan, but—"

"Oh, shut up!" Jan waved him off. He couldn't think of a more annoying person at their school. For some reason, Robert thought himself his best friend or something, and it pissed Jan off. But he no longer felt like fighting, so a snarl had to suffice. The boy ran off immediately.

Jan turned around to Nico to complain, putting a hand on his shoulder, but his friend was preoccupied with marvelling at his own healing powers again. "I'm invincible," he said.

Jan snorted, wincing from the pain of his own injuries. "Yeah, right."

"Let's do something crazy!" Nico said, his dark eyes gleaming. "We could jump off the bridge into the Reese. Or you could beat me up. Come on, Jan. Let's do that."

"Alright." Jan certainly wasn't going to say no to someone begging him for a beating. And besides, Nico would heal. Any damage he did would be gone by the morning. His friend already looked better than anyone who'd been in the big scuffle, including Jan himself.

But the moment he raised his fist, a low growl almost made him shit his pants.

"Oh my god, what is that?" The girls jumped up from their chair, scuffling back. "Is it a dog?"

There was indeed some kind of dog on the other side of the fence. It was almost twice as big as any Jan had seen before, and there was a wildness to it that scared Jan even in his drunken state. Its fur was shaggy grey, but its eyes were bright yellow.

"I'll take you on," Nico declared, licking his lips. He held both of his hands in front of him, moving into a fighting stance.

Jan looked at him in bewilderment. This was definitely going too far. Surely, he—

The dog jumped over the fence, its claws digging into the pavement of the terrace, producing an ear-shattering screeching noise. The girls screamed, running inside. Someone threw a chair at it, but it broke on its back without bothering it.

"Nico, this—"

"Come here!" Nico shouted.

The dog ran at them, its snout opening with a snarl, sharp white teeth gleaming in the moonlight. And then it ran past them, jumping the fence again and running into the darkness.

"You're not getting away that easily." Nico jumped the fence as well, leaving Jan no choice but to follow him.

"Nico, wait!" He was fit, but his friend and that massive dog were quicker. And now his asthma was playing up again, the wheezing loud in his ears.

He normally didn't have an issue with it. It played up when he put too much stress on his body, but it wasn't life-threatening. Just bloody annoying. Jan dragged out his spray and took a few quick puffs to free up his lungs, losing precious seconds in his pursuit.

Soon they'd entered the forest. Though it was full moon, the forest was dark. Jan hardly saw where he ran, stumbling over sticks and stones, far from any human-made path. Only the sounds of Nico running in front of him led him through the forest.

He finally caught up to Nico when his friend stopped on one of the foresting roads, looking around frantically. "Did you get him?" he asked.

"No, he's gone." Nico was still moving, as if unable to stay still.

Jan used the break to catch his breath. They'd run so fast he'd even broken a sweat. "Let's go back."

"And let this monster escape?" Nico shook his head. "It's a monster, Jan. A big, giant wolf monster."

"A wolf?"

But before he got an answer, there was the sound of snapping wood ahead of them. Nico spun around and he was off again. Jan took a deep breath and followed him.

The area was now inclining quickly, and he had to be more careful where he placed his feet. There was still a lot of noise in front of him, and he didn't know whether he should be glad that he could still hear them or worried.

Nico wasn't giving up, so neither could he. Jan stumbled through the forest, narrowly avoiding a low-hanging branch. Blackberry vines tore at his pants, and something hit him in the face. Then his foot lost touch with the ground, and a second later, Jan was rolling down a slope, hitting a tree on his way down.

Pain numbed him for a second as he came to lie in the valley between two little mounds. Leaves plastered his arm and face, and he had to spit out a mouthful of dirt. Jan moaned. The shoulder he'd hit on a tree hurt with a vengeance, and his left ankle was burning. Pain shot through it when he tried to sit up.

And Nico was gone. There was only the wind in the trees.

That was until he heard a low growl from the undergrowth. Yellow eyes stared at him.

"Oh, no. Oh, f—!" Jan tried to crawl backwards, but pain shot through his ankle again, and he hissed.

At the same time, the dog—wolf—jumped, claws extended, snout snarling. Jan threw up his arms, trying to protect his face when something hit the wolf from the side and threw it into the bushes.

A glint of steel appeared in the darkness. A sword. Matt had found him, and he was taking on the wolf.

Jan watched in wonder as wolf and boy circled each other, eyes locked. The wolf snarled, drawing back its lips until even the back teeth were exposed. But Matt stayed absolutely calm, sword at the ready.

Then the wolf jumped, and Matt moved as well. The sword caught the moonlight a second before it separated the giant head from its body. It fell and rolled over the ground until it came to lie against Jan's thigh. The massive body collapsed a second later.

Jan didn't dare breathe. He stared at Matt and at the wolf, and at the head touching him.

Then he moved away with a shudder and got to his feet, bringing as much distance as possible between himself and the wolf body parts—and Matt—while he ignored the deep pain in his ankle. The man had just killed this beast with one fell swoop. Jan had always known there was something off about his "friend", but now he was sure beyond every doubt.

"How did you find us?"

"You realise how loud you've been?" Matt asked, sheathing his sword.

Jan was still panting. Had he been loud? The wolf had surprised him. But—He shook his head. There was something more important right now. "Nico. He was ahead of me. Probably still running through the woods." God, he hoped Nico was still running.

Matt frowned. "Well, I can't hear him. Do you know which direction he ran?"

Jan jerked his chin towards the left. "Should be this one."

"Then let's see if we can find him."

Limping, Jan followed Matt. As much as he distrusted his friend, he didn't dare stray from him. Sure, the wolf beast was dead, but who was to say it was the same one as before? There could be two—or more. And someone who dealt with them this quickly was good to keep close.

He was glad he didn't have to talk to Matt as they both called out for Nico. Now that he wasn't running, Jan got out his phone to light their path.

"He's definitely come through here." Matt said, kneeling on the ground and touching the leaves.

"What are you? Some kind of human hunter?" That would explain how he'd found Jan.

Matt snorted and got up again. "Sure. Do you see that hole in the blackberries? Someone stomped them all down."

Okay, Jan had to admit that was a pretty clear sign of a wild chase. Maybe Matt had found him the same way. Now that he was looking for it, he saw more of it. Nico and the wolf had left a trail of destruction behind them.

They followed it until they came to a clearing. There, Jan's heart skipped a beat. A piece of fabric was lying on the ground: jeans. And blood. So much blood.

"Nico?" Jan directed his beam of light in every direction, but he didn't see his friend anywhere. "Nico!"

Matt was kneeling by the blood again, looking a lot more disconcerted now. "He's not here."

"You think?" Jan blurted out. Matt's calm unnerved him even more. He was pulsing up and down on his heels despite the pain in his ankle, unable to stand still. "What do we do?"

"We follow the blood." Matt had his sword drawn again.

Jan whimpered. This had gone wrong. This had gone terribly wrong. Nico had wanted to test his healing powers, but not like this. Not by fighting off a rabid monster wolf.

They followed the trail of blood deeper into the forest, calling out for Nico, but never got a reply.

And then the trail stopped, and there was nothing around them. No wolf. No Nico. Nothing.

"What do we do now?" Jan whined. His thoughts tried to jump ahead, but he clamped down on them.

"I don't know," Matt said, a sliver of doubt finally creeping into his voice. "He vanished."

"Or he *was* vanished." Jan shivered and took his head. "It ate him, didn't it?"

Matt cocked his head and regarded the ground. "I don't think—"

"What do we tell Rachel?" Jan thought of her big brown eyes and her tiny frame. She would break when they brought her the news. Or... "She'll kill us."

Rachel

The sky was full of galaxies, while flowers bloomed beneath it. Rachel strolled through her dream meadow, looking for dreams. They were blooming around her, one by one. Some of them she knew—there was the rippling blue blossom of Fabian's dream—some of them were nightmares, their flowers wilting. Rachel didn't dare to touch them. She'd done that once and regretted it immediately. Though what the person had dreamed of had been nonsensical and something that didn't actually frighten her, the dreamer's fear had been so powerful she'd almost drowned in it.

Rachel liked the brightly coloured flowers the most: happy dreams that calmed her. Her favourites were those of happy families. Sometimes as nonsensical as the nightmares, but full of a warmth she only ever experienced in her dreams.

Today, a single black rose stood out from the others. Rachel didn't need to walk to it. She was simply there. Her fingers hovered around the flower as curiosity and fear battled inside of her. This flower felt different. It wasn't someone's dream but a vision. A very dark vision.

Her fingertip touched the flower. It grew, and a storm blew over the meadow, ripping black petals from the stem. An endless stream of darkness blocked out the stars, the meadow, and all the other dreams.

Rachel found herself in an unfamiliar forest, with trees so high they looked like they touched the sky. It was beautiful, but only for a moment. Then the light dimmed, and shadows crawled over the forest floor.

A snap of wood behind her.

Rachel spun around. Someone was coming closer, dragging his leg behind him. The shuffling noise was accompanied by a deep and terrible darkness that threatened everything she believed in. This was different. It was personal. It was Nico.

He stopped at the edge of the clearing to look at her. But it wasn't truly him. His eyes gleamed yellow. The way he snarled, drawing back his teeth until blood-red gums shone. He clenched his fingers, and his fingernails turned to claws.

Her breath catching in her throat, Rachel stepped back. She wished she'd never touched the black rose. She didn't want to know *this*. Didn't want to see where it led.

But Nico's transformation was unstoppable. He dropped onto four feet, fur sprouting from his face and on his back. His nose elongated, and the yellow of his eyes grew even more intense. Once he'd turned, he lunged at her, ripping his maw open so wide, he swallowed her whole.

Bathed in sweat, Rachel woke up. The dream had been so vivid she could still feel the wetness of the maw around her neck and Nico's teeth ripping at her skin. For a few moments, all she could hear was her own ragged breath and her heart pumping in her chest.

When the initial bout of fear had passed, Rachel pushed back her blanket and tiptoed to the bathroom. There, she washed her face and looked into the mirror. As usual, the dreams left no traces on her. No bite marks, no saliva.

What did it mean? Dreams weren't always literal—or were they? Rachel couldn't think of any reality in which Nico would attack or want to kill her. He had powers of healing, not destruction. No. There must be another explanation for this. Some metaphor for how his recent changes in lifestyle were devouring her own life, which was why she needed to get away from him. Or should she stay? Was it him who'd be devoured by all his anger and frustration if she left?

Rachel splashed some more water on her face, shaking her head. There was no use in over-analysing the vision. What happened in the dream would happen in reality, and no amount of foreboding would change that.

She turned the faucet off and dried her face, then went back out into the dark corridor. It must've been past midnight. Even her mother was sleeping. Rachel was about to go back to her dreamworld when she heard something. A groan and shuffling sounds.

Carefully, cautious not to make a sound, she walked over to Nico's room and put her ear against the door and heard him rummaging through something. Those weren't the sounds of someone sleeping and having a nightmare. He was definitely awake. Rachel bent down to the keyhole. She didn't normally spy on her brother, but the dream had left her anxious. Too anxious to just knock and walk in.

She couldn't see much through the keyhole. Nico was standing with his back to the door, one leg raised on his bed, his hands moving around it. Bandages!

The sight shocked Rachel so much she was through the door without ever knocking.

"Rachel!" Nico startled and turned around. He was indeed wrapping bandages around his leg, and they were already bleeding through. "What are you doing awake?"

"What are *you* doing?" She pointed at his leg, then noticed the swathes of blood-soaked tissues on the ground. "Nico, you need to go to the hospital!"

"No, no. I'm fine."

"You're *not* fine! You're bleeding heavily." She came closer. "Is that a bite wound?" It looked terrifying, as if whatever animal had done this had taken a whole chunk of flesh out of his leg. "Nico, please. This is no joke."

Nico pressed another tissue on the wound. "It's healing, Rachel. I'm gonna be fine in the morning. It looked much worse an hour ago. Help me clean this up, will you? Not that Mum would care."

Rachel crossed her arms. "You're trying to prove something to her, aren't you?"

"What do you mean?"

"You're playing with fire. Getting into trouble and pushing the boundaries to see when she'll notice you."

Nico sighed and bent down to examine his wound. The blood flow was indeed slowing, the wound closing. "She'll never notice. I bet when you move to the US, she'll come down two months later to tell me she hasn't seen you in a while."

Unfortunately, Rachel believed he was right. She expected as much from her mother. "But I see you."

He stared at her, unspoken words behind his eyes. Rachel could guess them only too well: you're not enough.

She decided to voice her fears. "How am I supposed to move away if you're acting out like this?"

"Well, don't!" Nico blurted out. "Just stay."

"Would that change anything?"

He paused a moment. Once again, he was drawn to the wound on his leg. It had closed now. But the skin wasn't smooth. Thick scars covered it instead. Nevertheless, Nico breathed out in relief. "You see that? I'm fine. I've got my healing powers. Nothing can hurt me."

Rachel didn't bother to protest. He didn't need to be told that he was, in fact, hurting badly. They both knew it, and they both had to deal with that pain in their own ways.

She turned away. "Goodnight, Nico."

He didn't even answer, eyes fixated on his wound. His power. His paper shield against all the pain.

Rachel knew what her dream had meant then. It was the pain that was devouring them both. Plus, he had most certainly been bitten by a werewolf.

Fabian

"I didn't see what happened in the back," Samantha told Lucille as she sorted through various candles.

The three of them had agreed to help Fabian's mother at the Magic Circle with restocking. Fabian could think of better ways to spend his Saturday, but of course, Samantha had jumped at the opportunity. As had Lucille. And now the two were talking about the stupid party they'd both gone to last night.

"Someone said there was a wolf or a big dog. Considering how drunk everyone was, it was probably a cat," Samantha said with an eye roll. "You didn't hear it at all?"

"I was... occupied," Lucille said. She lowered her eyes before grinning abashedly.

Samantha sighed. "Well, I'm glad you had fun."

Fabian perked up. That tone didn't sound like Samantha had had a lot of fun. He'd never said anything, but when he'd heard that she was going to the party with Cian, jealousy had reared its ugly head. Ever since Lucille had arrived—and he didn't blame her or anything—Samantha had been changing. First the whole magic thing, and now she attended parties with the Elite Clique.

"I saw the kiss online," Lucille admitted in a low voice that seemed more pitiful than excited.

"Kiss?" Fabian asked at the same time as Samantha asked, "It's online?"

Lucille got her phone out and opened a group chat Fabian had never seen before. She pressed play on a video and looked away.

In it, Samantha was caught with the Elite Clique. Cheryl was having yet another go at her, and whatever idiot had been filming it was zooming in on Samantha's tear-streaked face.

Fabian slid closer and put an arm around Samantha, quietly offering her support. She leaned into him with a worried face when Cian suddenly declared his undying love for her and went in for a kiss. A moment later, Matt appeared on the screen. He dragged Cian away from Samantha and pushed him into the crowd. As a fight ensued, the video tilted and then broke off.

"Everyone has seen that?" Samantha asked in a shaky voice. The view numbers on the video were well over a hundred.

"I can make the video disappear," Lucille offered.

"How?" Samantha asked, her voice caught between hope and devastation.

Lucille took her phone back. "With magic. I told you about it. Look." She straightened her back. "Make this video disappear from all devices and from the memory of all who have seen it."

"What did you just do?" Fabian asked, feeling a weird itch in his brain.

"I deleted the video," Lucille answered.

"Which video?" Samantha asked before Fabian could.

Lucille opened her mouth but didn't speak. Instead, she grabbed her necklace and laughed. "You don't remember seeing it?" As they both shook their heads, she laughed again. "Neither do I, but there was a video of you and Cian kissing."

"You kissed Cian?" Again, Fabian's head itched. He knew that already. Or didn't he? "What just happened?"

Lucille sighed with impatience. "Okay, there was a video of last night's kiss, which was shared with our school chat group—which you two should totally join, by the way. I used magic to delete it from all devices and people's memories, including yours and mine." She giggled. "I guess I need to be a bit more specific next time. Words!"

"No, I'm glad I don't remember that. It lives rent-free in my brain anyway," Samantha muttered.

While Fabian had no interest in seeing Samantha and Cian kiss on camera—or in real life—Lucille's magic use left him with a sour taste.

He let go of Samantha and complained, "You just meddled with our memories."

"How did you do it?" Samantha asked. Unfortunately, she sounded more curious than offended. "You didn't even use a spell."

"I told you. My grandmother invented this spell that allows me to bend the natural magic all around us to do my will. Look!" Lucille put down the box of candles. "All the candles will fly to their designated spot on the shelves." One by one, the candles rose into the air and travelled in one long line towards the shelf. There, they sorted themselves better than his mother could've ever done.

While Fabian had a funny feeling in his stomach, Samantha exclaimed, "That's incredible, Lucille! Impossible, I would say. I mean... it goes against everything I've learnt about magic."

"I found the spell in my grandmother's journal. She wrote that it helped a little, but I found it working a treat. Whatever I say, the magic moves to accommodate my words," Lucille explained proudly.

The funny feeling in Fabian's stomach intensified. "That's not how it's supposed to work, right? This is wrong. This is—"

Samantha turned around to him. "I know it shouldn't be, but it's working. So, how can it be wrong?"

"I don't know! Maybe because meddling with other people's memories or worse shouldn't be so easy." Anger exploded in his chest, saturating the fear in his stomach. In the back, the toilet flushed on its own. *That* magic was also too easy and powerful. "There need to be regulations! What's there to stop Lucille from destroying the world with a few chance words?"

"Oh, please!" Lucille rolled her eyes. "Stop being so dramatic. I have no intention of destroying the world."

Fabian crossed his arms, suddenly easily keeping his emotions in check. "It's wrong. This much power is wrong."

"You're just jealous because I have better control of my powers," Lucille said with a shake of her head and opened the next box.

"Do you?" Fabian spat. Again, he could hear water running.

"Guys, please." Samantha looked back and forth between them. "I... Lucille, I love this new power—it's amazing. But Fabian isn't completely wrong. And I think you need to be a little more careful." She took a deep breath. "You made Cian invite me, right?"

Lucille turned back. Her mouth opened in protest, but then she swallowed and nodded. "I only gave him a little push. He was interested in you before that, but when Alan invited me to the party, I thought it would be nice to go together. I also wanted to see Cheryl's face when she saw you with such nice arm candy."

"Well, she didn't take very well to it," Samantha said.

Her downcast eyes told Fabian that something had happened at the party, but for the life of him, he couldn't remember what it was. The frustration of it fuelled his anger. "And the kiss was your idea, too?"

"No!" Lucille shook her head. "That was all Cian."

Fabian wasn't ready to let go so easily. "How can you be sure? While we were at school, you said he loves Samantha. What if your awesome new power made him fall in love with her right at that second?"

Samantha stared at him, then Lucille.

Lucille clicked her tongue dismissively. "I only said that because he was interested. I didn't intend it as a spell."

"But are you sure you *didn't* put a spell on him?" Fabian didn't understand how she could be so careless. A power like that needed to be contained. Why couldn't she see that?

Samantha was fiddling with the tape on her empty candle box. "Can you turn him back to normal, just in case?"

Lucille nodded readily. "Yes, of course. Revert all magic spells on Cian Funke." She smiled. "That should do it. I still think he likes you, though."

Fabian held his breath. He knew the time would come when Samantha would move on. She'd told him she wasn't in love with him and never truly had been. Sooner or later, someone would sweep her off her feet, but he sure hoped it wouldn't be Cian Funke, of all people.

"Well, I don't," Samantha said. She took a deep breath afterwards, as if she was glad that was off his chest. "I mean, I enjoy spending time with him in Chemistry. He's fun, but going out with him... kissing him..." She shook her head. "It made me want to run the other way. And fast!"

Her admission was everything to Fabian. His anger was gone in a flash, and he happily pulled the next box closer. It was packed with all sorts of weird stuff he'd never seen in the shop. "What is that?" he asked, picking out a tough, knob-shaped thing that looked like a piece of coral but was darker and much heavier than any coral had a right to be.

Samantha's eyes lightened up. "That's a griffin's heart! They're very good for strengthening potions. Though grinding them is tough work. Those must be the ingredients for the back of the shop."

Fabian dropped the heart back in the box, feeling the sudden urge to wipe his hands. "These are ingredients? Shells?" He pulled up a piece of weirdly shaped wood. "Roots? And you drink that?"

Something else caught his eye: a beautiful blue feather as long as his lower arm. It didn't look like a normal bird's feather, with one central rachis and vanes to both sides. Instead, from the central rachis, several smaller ones sprouted, each of them a feather in a different hue of blue. Fabian ran his fingers over them, marvelling at the softness of the vanes. As if the wind was still caught in them.

"What kind of feather is that?" he asked Samantha, pulling it out of the box. The quill was long enough for his hand to fit around it naturally.

Samantha frowned. "I've never seen a feather like that. What kind of bird... or maybe it's a different species?"

"You mean like an angel?" Lucille asked, her eyes widened with awe.

The calming effect the feather had had on Fabian burst like a bubble. No, no. Angels didn't exist. Neither did any other sort of human-like species with wings. There couldn't be.

"Wait!" Samantha got out her phone and quickly scrolled through her photos. "What if it's *the* feather?"

"*The* feather?" That didn't sound good to Fabian.

Samantha landed on a scan of a book. On it were several sketches of a feather, but none of them looked like the blue feather. The closest one came was the one depicting five feathers sprouting from one quill.

Meanwhile, Samantha had zoomed in on the text. "The Feather of Shitaten. A wing feather of the mystical bird called Shitaten. This creature was part of the Old World and believed to be a symbol of hope. As such, its feather, gifted to Frey on his quest, is the Emblem of Hope. For there is no greater power than that given to us by hope. It keeps us going even in our darkest hour." She scrolled further down.

"Over the millennia, several feathers have thought to be the one plucked from Shitaten's wings. I have tracked down as many as I could find, but none of them were the right ones," she read on.

"Who's I?" Fabian asked.

"The Seer. They wrote the book," Samantha said in a tone as if he should know that. "They gathered every piece of information about the six Emblems of Power. Lucille's necklace is one of them, and so is Matt's sword, and now it looks like we've found the feather."

Fabian's insides turned cold. "No way! It doesn't look anything like those."

"Remember, they never found this emblem, so they don't know what it looked like. But listen to this." She zoomed in on another bit of text. "Its vanes are told to reflect the sky in all its many shades of blue. The feathers catch the wind and can turn it outward. Frey used it to defend his friends against arrows shot at them."

"Who's this Frey guy? He's already been mentioned twice." Fabian was growing more and more uneasy.

Samantha sighed. "I don't know. The previous owner of the feather, apparently. In some of the descriptions, the Seer mentions the people who the emblems were originally given to. Like in Lucille's case, it was given to a King called Morrigan in his hour of need. Anyway, it says here that one of the most remarkable powers of the feather is the ability to draw anything."

"Sounds more like Frey was able to draw anything," Fabian muttered. Drawing required skill, not magic.

"Let me try it!" Samantha stretched her hand out, but Fabian held it quickly out of her reach.

"No way! Didn't we all agree that we need to be careful with magic? Besides, you can't draw shit." It was one of the very few things Fabian was better at. Much better.

"Then you try it!" Samantha said. "We'll know whether it's Shitaten's feather."

"Because me drawing beautifully with a feather will prove anything." Fabian knew that his logic didn't make sense. If they wanted to prove the feather's identity, he would have to give it to Samantha. But he didn't want to do that. First, because he didn't want Samantha to be a great artist on top of everything else she was good at, but most importantly, he didn't want to prove this innocuous-looking feather to be an Emblem of Power. That would mean Nico's theory was right, and those horrible emblems were popping up around them, belonging to them.

"Nobody gets the feather," he declared. "I will dispose of it. Safely."

Samantha's eyes widened. "You can't dispose of it! Not if it is Shitaten's feather! And in any case, this is Caroline's delivery."

Fabian got up to his feet. "That's right. Mum ordered this. So, I'll take it home and ask her about it. I'm pretty sure she knows whether she ordered a magical feather or not."

"You're so stubborn!" Samantha said with a frustrated groan. "The feather isn't bad."

"That remains to be seen!" It didn't feel bad, but Fabian didn't trust magic. His own water power came and went as it pleased, and Lucille had just admitted to altering people's feelings with a simple sentence. No, there was entirely too much magic in his life already. There would not be a third Emblem of Power. "I'm going. You can just use magic to do the rest."

"Gladly!" Excitedly, Lucille spoke a few words and the rest of the boxes flew open, their contents soaring past Fabian to their designated spots. Quite a few of them hit him in the face or on the shoulder on their way.

He sighed. There certainly was such a thing as too much magic.

Fabian held onto the feather for the rest of the afternoon. Somehow, he didn't want to part from it. Not until he had made sure it was harmless.

At long last, his parents returned from their trip, bringing home takeaway from the Thai restaurant downtown. Fabian ignored the delicious smell of coconut and spices and dragged his mother aside. "Can I talk to you?"

She immediately looked concerned. "What is it? Did something happen at the shop?"

A lot of things had happened, but he doubted Lucille wanted his mother to know she'd restocked everything with a simple spell. "No, it's alright. We got everything done, including the ingredients you ordered for the back of the shop." He still wasn't over the griffin's heart.

"So, what do you want to talk about, then?" His mother continued to take off her coat and dropped her handbag on the counter.

"It's actually more like a question." Fabian pulled the feather from the back pocket of his jeans. "We couldn't figure out what kind of feather this was."

Caroline took the feather from him and turned it between her fingers. "Where's that from?"

Fabian felt his insides grow cold. "From your order. You know, the one with the griffin heart and shells and those weird little mushrooms."

Now, his mother frowned. "I never ordered this feather. Are you sure it was in the same box?"

He nodded, his desperation growing. "Yes. Does that mean your supplier just put it in there?"

"Possibly." She took out her phone and checked it with a frown. "There's no mention of it in the files. Do you want to have it?" She turned the feather between her fingers before handing it back to him. "I think it's just a very fancy feather."

"Right, just a normal feather from a normal bird." Somehow, Fabian was glad to have it back, as if something was missing if he didn't hold onto it.

His mother laughed. "Well, it doesn't look normal. It's probably fake or something. Come on! Set the table. Your dad says he's starving."

They had a perfectly normal dinner with no magic whatsoever. His parents told him about the trip, and Fabian glossed over what had happened at the shop. By the end of it, he'd almost forgotten about the feather.

"Do you want to watch the game?" his father asked, hopeful.

Sometimes, Fabian would do him a favour and watch a soccer game, but most of the time he opted out of the mind-numbing exercise to draw instead. Drawing was on his mind today as well. "No, I've got some homework to do."

"Suit yourself."

After tidying up the table, Fabian went upstairs to his room and sat down at his desk. He pushed his old drawings out of the way and pulled up a blank piece of paper. Did the feather need ink? He had a few bottles left over from an inking experiment, but he'd never drawn or written with a feather before. The tip of the quill didn't seem like it would soak up the ink easily. It wasn't pointed or appeared to be hollow like so many other feathers he knew.

Nevertheless, it lay perfectly in his hand, as if it had always belonged there. Fabian raised the feather and drew a few shapes in the air to test its movability. Simple blossoms as if he were drawing a cherry tree scene.

The feather had hardly finished the first shape when a real pink blossom fell into his lap.

"No way."

He tried it again, drawing several of them into the air, and sure enough, they rained onto him as if he was standing under a cherry tree.

One of the most remarkable powers of the feather is the ability to draw anything.

It didn't mean that the feather allowed anyone to draw like an artist. It actually allowed the artist to draw anything—to life!

Fabian drew a quick butterfly and watched it sprout from the tip of the feather. At first, its wings looked like paper, but then colour filled it in, and with the colour came life. The little butterfly flew around his room until it settled on the edge of his cupboard. Fabian got to his feet, the paper forgotten.

If he only swung the feather in meaningless strokes, nothing happened, but if he set his mind to it, intending an image, it came to life only a second later. Drawing into the air wasn't easy, especially with more complicated images, but the feather seemed to lead the stroke, and whatever he tried out turned real in his hand.

It only lasted for a bit, Fabian noted as he returned to his chair an hour later. The petals were gone. The butterfly, which had come down on his desk lamp, rose into the air and evaporated.

Short-lived, beautiful magic that didn't hurt anyone. Now *that* was magic he'd be down with.

Fabian grabbed his phone, ready to tell Samantha, when he remembered what she had said about the feather. How it was an Emblem of Power, and that it would be the third emblem that had found its way to Greenvalley. The necklace, the sword, and now the feather. There was no doubt in him that this was the real feather.

He stared at the beautiful shades of blue that caught the wind. An Emblem of Power. And all six of them would change the world.

Ice filled his intestines, and he stared at the feather. How could something so beautiful, so creative, be so powerful?

The Emblem of Hope.

Right now, Fabian hoped all of this was just a coincidence. Nothing meaningful. But the shimmering blue in his hands held a different story. It wanted to be used. It had to be used. Eventually, Fabian would have to give in.

Lucille

Wherever the magic had sent Linda, she hadn't come back. No more painfully awkward breakfasts for Lucille to suffer through, or incessant nagging about her outfits or the people she chose to 'acquaint herself with'. What Lucille hadn't realised was how empty it made her home. The fact that Linda was gone didn't mean she saw her father more often. If anything, she saw him less because Linda's constant nagging had at least called him to dinner from time to time. And with no one to shoo around the maids, there was no bustling in the rooms and corridors.

The only noise was the constant ringing of the house phone. Lucille was trying to put on her make-up for her dinner date with her father, practising her magic as she did so. But every time the phone rang, she had to start again. At last, she couldn't stand it anymore and barged down the corridor until she reached the foyer.

There, Albert was ending the call. "No, I don't know how to reach her. I'm sorry. Goodbye."

"Who keeps calling?" Lucille asked.

He carefully put down the phone. "People from the community centre and contractors Mrs de Cerque hired for her fashion show. It seems she has not appeared, and neither have the models." He frowned a little, as if he couldn't quite grasp why Mrs de Cerque was neither at the fashion show nor at home. "Should we be worried?"

Lucille quickly swallowed her guilty conscience. "I don't think so. She told me she's on a creative... journey or something. Probably to come up with a new collection. We're not supposed to contact her." The lie slipped so easily from her lips, but the words settled heavily in her stomach. Albert knew about magic. Samantha's grandma had said as much. If he caught wind of her spell, she'd be in trouble.

The phone rang again, and Albert picked up with the patience of an angel. "Villa de Cerque... I'm sorry to hear you can't reach Mrs de Cerque on her cellphone. Unfortunately, she is not at home... I don't know when she is expected back. She—"

"I want everyone to forget about Linda de Cerque and stop calling," Lucille said, and the magic rose through her necklace to follow her words.

"Goodbye," Albert said, frowning slightly. "What were you saying, Miss Lucille?"

She put on her best smile for him. "Nothing."

"Lucille, Albert!"

Her head whipped up towards the balustrade, while her heart did a little jump. There was her father, looking dapper in his dress shirt and ironed pants. "Can you tell..." He paused for a few seconds, and Lucille held her breath. "Actually, I was going to tell you"—he pointed at Lucille—"that I have to cancel dinner plans. An emergency meeting came up with a partner and—"

"No!"

Her father raised an eyebrow. "No?" He started fixing his right cuff. "I'm afraid I don't know what you mean."

Lucille felt the magic burn in her. The necklace urged her to use it. To set things right. "You are going to tell your partner that you already have plans, and then you will take me out for dinner as we planned and forget all about your stupid work."

Never in a million years would she have dared to talk to her father like that without the magic to back her up. Still, the words left her breathless. Her cheeks were flushed, and her skin was cold under the layer of heat.

Albert was staring at her, so scandalised he forgot to keep his appearance unaffected. But her father only frowned and raised a finger. "Can you give me a minute to tell my partner that I'm taking out my beautiful daughter tonight? I'll meet you down there in ten minutes." And then he even smiled and rushed off to his office.

Relief flooded Lucille so strongly her knees grew weak. How long had she waited for him to say these words, to put her first? Her heart beat faster, and she couldn't stop grinning. She turned around to Albert and let out a little squee. "We're going out for dinner. Tell Tobias to bring the car. I need to get ready!"

The butler looked as if he was about to say something, but Lucille was so excited she rushed back to her room and used her magic to finish her make-up and fix her hair. With another spell, she chose the perfect dress for her, the one her father would like best. No fretting needed.

Everything was working out perfectly.

The restaurant her father had reserved for the two of them lived off the typical Harzer rusticity. The tables and chairs were made of dark walnut, while the walls were panelled with reddish wood. Along the borders of the room and in the corners were artfully cut eaves and pictures of the beautiful landscape. Each tablecloth was hand-stitched with green pine cones and the red berries of mountain ash.

For such a rustic place, the menu was surprisingly modern. While there were staple items such as German dumplings and cuts of venison, wild boar, and hare, they also had some finer meals such as pork loin, fish, and round of beef with regionally sourced vegetables, and even vegan and gluten-free items.

Since it was the season, Lucille ordered a mushroom goulash that promised a wide variety of wild mushrooms as her main, and a ragout fin as an entrée. The latter was one of her favourite childhood dishes she remembered eating with her grandmother.

Her father ordered himself a wine and then looked askance at her. "You're old enough for wine, aren't you?"

Lucille laughed. "Yes, of course. I'm seventeen." She didn't even need her father's presence to have wine at a restaurant. But he didn't know any better. In his mind, she was still twelve or even younger.

"Seventeen already," her father said with a wistful smile that set everything right in Lucille. He ordered a fitting wine for them and even told the waiter that they were celebrating.

"What are we celebrating?"

Her father seemed to think about it but came up with an answer quickly. "Having you home, of course. I missed you, Lulu."

Lucille's cheeks grew pink. He hadn't called her by her childhood nickname for over ten years. "I love being home." To hear that he missed her was more than she could've ever dreamed of. And it was real. Not magic-induced like the date itself. Her father truly missed having her around, even if he didn't always show it.

The wine was brought a little later, and they toasted to her new school year in Greenvalley. Never once looking at his phone, he asked, "How are the classes?"

"Oh, they're going really well. I have some great teachers. I'm ahead in Latin, thanks to all the hours of vocabulary in Rosemary." How she'd hated that monotonous task. Necessary, yes, but oh so tedious. Latin spells were much more fun.

"I assume a school like Rosemary College has much bigger funds to hire only the best of the best," her father pointed out.

The argument was a little too close to Linda's reservations about Greenvalley High for Lucille's taste. She had no interest in discussing the inadequacy of her educational choices. "Well, there are a lot of things that they don't teach you at Rosemary."

"Such as?" her father asked, with mild curiosity in his eyes.

Lucille caught her breath. Did he know that his mother had been a witch? Had he grown up with that knowledge? Had he inherited any powers from her?

She was just about to confide in him when the door opened. In came Matt, laughing with a woman who was at least five, if not ten, years his senior.

"You've got to be kidding me," Lucille muttered. "Has he run out of schoolgirls?"

"Who are we talking about?" Her father turned and searched the room.

"Nothing," Lucille hurried to say, not wanting to discuss her failed attempt at a relationship with him over dinner. "It's only a friend of mine."

It was the wrong explanation. Her father's eyes widened with delight. "Wonderful. Introduce me to them. I want to know who my daughter spends time with."

Lucille bit back the comment that her friends had already come to visit several times while he'd been in the house. With his attention finally off work, her father was attempting to get up, looking to introduce himself.

"Sit down!" she commanded him, the necklace on her collarbone flaring up with comforting heat.

Her father sat back down and folded his napkin. "Were you saying something?"

From the corner of her eye, Lucille saw that Matt had noticed her. She smiled sweetly for his benefit and said, "Yes. I don't want you to introduce yourself to my friends. You're here with me. Focus on me." Again, with the direct words. Who would've thought it was so easy to make her wishes finally heard?

"Of course, darling. I want to know all about your life." He had settled into his chair again.

Just then, the food arrived. Lucille got her ragout fin, while her father had ordered a meat plate. Lucille took the lemon and squeezed its juice over the top of the cheese, then sprinkled a few drops of Worcestershire sauce over it. As a child, she'd always used the toasted triangles to scoop up the creamy goodness of meat, mushrooms, and cheese, but now she had better manners, using her spoon and taking the occasional bite of the bread. It was just as delicious as it had been back then, and it reminded her of her grandmother.

Her witch grandmother. Perhaps she should give her father a try. After all, she had her magic to back her up. If things went wrong, she'd just use another spell.

"Dad, there is something I've been meaning to ask you," she said between bites.

"What is it?"

"Did you know Grandmother was a witch?" Lucille didn't dare take another bite until she heard his answer.

Her father's face grew still, his hand, half-way to his mouth, sank down again. His eyes narrowed. "Who told you that?"

"Her good friend. Elda Kollmer. I'm friends with her granddaughter, Samantha."

"Never talk to her again!" her father said in a voice that could re-chill the white wine on the table.

"Who? Elda?"

"And her granddaughter."

Lucille stared at him. "What?"

Her father let out a heavy sigh. "I will not suffer this slander about my mother. She was an upstanding woman of society who had no interest in the arcane."

Lucille felt the need for her magic rise in her, as if her father were threatening to take it away from her. But he'd said arcane. Who called magic the arcane if they had no clue about it? "Are you lying to me? Tell me the truth." The magic slipped from her voice and entangled him even further.

Without missing a beat, her father said, "Yes. What your grandmother did was dangerous. It cost her her life, and I will not allow my daughter to suffer the same fate. I knew I should never have allowed you to come back here." He pushed his half-eaten plate to the side. "You will return to Rosemary College by Monday, even if I have to refurbish their library or build a pool for them."

There was such a thing as too much truth. "Stop!" Lucille grasped for the magic, which was already beckoning her. "Forget I ever asked you about magic or Grandmother."

Her father frowned a little. Had it failed to work? She hadn't paid any mind to the phrasing of her spell. What if he'd forgotten more than he should have? Her hands grew sweaty, and her heart was racing.

"Are you feeling unwell?" her father asked, reaching out a hand. "Is the food not agreeing with you?"

Lucille let out a breath of relief. He was back to being the attentive father he'd been a few minutes ago. "No, I'm fine, Dad. I... I just..."

She looked around, searching for an explanation. Just then, her phone pinged.

Matt: How much magic do you want to use on him?

Her gaze landed on Matt. For a moment, she'd been ready to believe that the woman he was entertaining tonight was his older sister. He had said he was the youngest of several siblings, after all. But judging by how far his tongue was down her throat, that possibility was out the window. Anger rose in her chest. How did *he* dare criticise her? The one who wouldn't recognise romantic feelings if they kicked him in the face?

Faintly, Lucille became aware that the rejection he'd delivered to her still hurt deep inside. She had wanted him. And if she couldn't have him, no one else should.

"I lied earlier," she told her father. "That guy over there is not a friend." Her eyes never left Matt, while her necklace burned with the desire to fulfil her every wish. "I mean, yes, he is part of my friend group, but I had a crush on him, and he... he's nothing but a man whore. A new date every night." Her voice grew sharper and sharper. "And what is he thinking, making out with an older woman like that? I want them to stop. She has somewhere to go and no interest in seeing that little boy again."

The snogging stopped almost immediately. Matt looked confused when the woman got up, shaking her head. Tidbits of their talk made their way to Lucille. The woman actually told Matt that he was nothing but a little boy playing with fire and that she had no interest in ever seeing him again. "Don't contact me," were her last words as she stomped out of the restaurant, leaving behind an increasingly confused Matt.

Then their eyes met, and Matt's eyes narrowed. Lucille hastily looked away, only to find her father looking at her with concern. "Do you want me to talk to him?"

No! That would be embarrassing. Without thinking, Lucille took hold of her magic again and said to him, "Forget what I just told you. Our food is coming."

The doors of the kitchen opened that very moment, and the server stepped out with their plates. There was a bit of shifting around since he hadn't tidied up their entrées yet, but at last, they had two new plates in front of them.

"This is a bit too bloody," her father said, gently poking the beef with the tip of his knife. It was practically raw. The server scratched his chin. "I have no idea how this could've hap—"

"It's fine!" Lucille commanded. "That steak is medium rare." She quickly sent more magic to follow the spell. "There was never any problem with it. You must've imagined it. This food looks delicious."

A little unsettled, the server took their entrée plates and returned to the kitchen. Lucille's father was in awe of what he saw on his plate. "I had no idea this restaurant was so good. Why aren't they more popular?"

Lucille felt exhausted. She scooped up a mushroom from her spectacular-looking dish and took a bite. It'd barely touched her mouth when she wanted to spit it out. Despite its looks, it hadn't actually seen the inside of a pan yet. Nor had it been properly cleaned yet.

With sand gnashing between her teeth, Lucille tried to swallow it quickly. This was no problem. She could fix this. But first a sip of wine.

As she was just about to reach for the glass, a hand wrapped around her upper arm and half-dragged her out of her chair. Matt. "We need to talk."

"Lulu?" her father asked with concern.

"It's fine. Don't worry!" she said, barely able to keep up with Matt.

And just like that, her father went back to eating as if nothing was wrong with the world. At least his meat was no longer raw.

Matt dragged her outside and towards the corner of the restaurant, so they would be out of the way of the patrons. He flew into a rage immediately. "What are you doing in there?" he shouted, wildly gesturing to the inside.

Lucille was a little preoccupied with the sand between her teeth. Wait. She had magic. It would all be fine. "I haven't eaten a sandy uncooked mushroom." There was a sudden pang in her stomach, and the sensation of sand vanished, leaving her breathless.

"I mean that!" Matt was pointing at her. "You're using magic left and right, with no regard for others. I told you that magic is dangerous!"

Annoyed, Lucille crossed her arms and rolled her eyes. "Yes, yes, it can get you killed. A big, bad demon will waltz in and rip my heart out if I use too much magic." She'd heard that complaint from her father's lips just minutes ago.

Matt narrowed his eyes suspiciously. "What?"

She opened her arms again, pushing forward. "I can handle it! The spell only does what I say."

"Well, then maybe you should shut your mouth."

Lucille gasped. "Did you really just say that? How about you shut your mouth?" The magic quelled inside of her, eager to fulfil her will.

But Matt only snorted. "You cannot run around and use magic as you please. You have no idea what you're messing with."

"And you do?" This was getting ridiculous. He didn't have any magic powers; she did! "Stop bothering me!" Again, the magic surged, and apparently hit a wall, because Matt didn't let up in the slightest. "Why is it not working?"

"Why can't you control my actions, memories, or feelings?" Now he was mocking her. But worse, his words flooded her with shame. Matt's voice softened. "What are you doing, Lucille? You've already put five, six, seven spells on your father before dessert."

The shame deepened. She hadn't realised how out of hand it'd gotten with her magic. "I'm just... I'm trying to fix things."

"Like you fixed my date?"

She rolled her eyes. "She was way too old for you."

"Oh, were you protecting me now?" The sarcasm was hard to miss.

"Why are you like this?" Lucille asked, her hurt feelings bubbling up again. "Why do you have to sleep with everyone?"

"There's nothing wrong with sex."

Lucille snorted. Pushing back her feelings, she raised her chin. "Well, there's nothing wrong with magic, either. You're addicted to sex; I'm addicted to magic. All is well."

"Really? Take Ada, for example." Apparently, that was his date's name. "You sent her away. What if you had wished for her to disappear? Where do you think she would've gone? And how do you propose we would've got her back?"

Lucille paled. While she'd done nothing like that to Ada, she had sent Linda away. Linda who everyone had been unable to reach and had forgotten about now. Where was she truly after Lucille had sent her to Milan, Paris, or wherever? The urge to use magic to fix it grew. She grabbed her necklace as if the touch would keep her from giving in. She *wanted* to do magic. She *needed* to.

Both their phones pinged at the same time, which could only mean one thing: a message in their group chat.

Samantha: There's a(nother?) werewolf on the loose. Meet at my grandma's place.

"A werewolf?" Lucille asked, swallowing hard.

At the same time, Matt asked, "Another?"

"What do you mean..." She shook her head. In a fight with a werewolf her magic would definitely be needed. And it would distract her from the havoc she may have caused with her other spells. "Let's go!"

"What about your father?" Matt asked, seeming half-ready to run as well.

Lucille looked through the window and watched him happily eating his venison steak. "He'll be alright. I told him not to worry."

Matt snorted, but he left it at that. They both turned away from the restaurant and began making their way to Elda's.

Rachel

"But why do we have to take on a werewolf?" Fabian complained. "We've already dealt with a giant wyrm and a disgusting insect dude. Can't someone else take on the werewolf?"

"Who else do you plan on sending?" Lucille asked him, fingering her necklace. "Do you want to send Samantha's granny out?"

They couldn't ask that of the old woman who'd opened her house to them after being woken up in the middle of the night, Rachel thought, but she didn't have the stomach to join their discussion. Instead, she shifted her gaze to Samantha and Matt, who were consulting one of the books about werewolves and discussing their findings.

"We have a full moon today," Samantha pointed out. "According to these books, werewolves only transform on the three nights around the full moon, which means once the werewolf gets through the night tomorrow, they'll be human for the rest of the month. We only need to secure them, make sure nobody gets hurt tonight and tomorrow night, and then we can figure out the rest next week when they're human again."

"Lycanthropes are monsters," Matt said. "They might have been humans once, but there's nothing human left in them after a few moons."

Rachel swallowed heavily. "Nothing human?"

Matt shook his head. "Sadly not. They take on their wolfish sides and are ruled by the beast. They're basically wolves in human skin. That's why they usually leave society to live in forests or deserted mountain areas. I guess the Harz suffices."

"Is that why you killed the one last night without any hesitation?" Samantha asked, then nibbled on her lip, fretting.

The first thing Matt had done when he arrived here was recount the werewolf he'd slain last night. The one that Nico and Jan had tried to hunt down. Just thinking about Matt's sword slicing through it made Rachel's stomach turn.

"I'm here," Jan announced loudly, stepping into the room. He staggered slightly, indicating that he had already had a couple of beers. "We're hunting another monster tonight? Whew. That's two in a row. No respect for a good party."

Even on her best days, Rachel could find nothing funny about Jan. Now, his subpar attempt at humour grated on her nerves. She watched him spin around to take in the situation. His eyes landed on her. "Looks like I'm not the last one." And with that, he threw himself on the couch and put his legs up as if he lived there.

Rachel's veins filled with ice. The casualness of his demeanour tore open the wound she'd been trying to hide ever since everyone had got together at Elda's place.

"Silver works best, but beheading also does the trick," Matt said, still entrenched in his strategy discussion.

"Can we not behead someone?" Fabian muttered.

"It won't do the trick tonight!" Rachel shouted, her nerves fraying at the edges.

Everyone turned to her, and she almost rolled her eyes. They always acted as if she'd never spoken up. "I know who it is, and he's plenty human, thank you very much." Tears were threatening to roll down her cheeks. Her eyes strained as she tried to keep them in. "It's Nico."

There was a collective gasp from the group. Jan shot back to a sitting position, knocking down a decorative bowl from the table.

"Why didn't you say so in the first place?" Samantha's eyes widened as she reflexively picked up the bowl.

"Nico is a werewolf?" Fabian asked at the same time.

Lucille chimed in as well. "Was he always a werewolf? I mean, he was okay last month, right?"

Rachel could only stare at her. As if she or Nico would've kept it a secret from everybody that he turned into a wolf three nights of the month and ran around biting people.

"He must've been bitten last night," Matt said in such a collected, confident voice that Rachel felt relief. "We couldn't find him at first, but after a while, he texted that he was safe at home. I should've followed it up."

"And beheaded him?" Rachel asked.

That Matt didn't immediately protest turned her stomach.

Samantha lowered her eyes and flicked through the book. Within seconds, she'd found a page and pointed at it victoriously. "I knew it! It says here that lycanthropy is an infection. Infections can be healed."

"No, they can't," Matt shot her down. "This one is incurable."

"How would you know?" Samantha asked, and Jan piped in, "Yeah, who made you the expert, Matt?"

Rachel wasn't sure what to make of their enthusiasm. At least Samantha was trying to help Nico, but Matt's words made her more and more queasy.

"I don't believe it's Nico," Fabian said, already grabbing his phone and calling, but to no avail. "He's probably busy with his girlfriend, or..."

"I've seen him change," Rachel whispered.

She shuddered just thinking about it. The whole day, Nico had been testy. She'd caught him staring at the raw meat in the fridge, and she knew it had barely seen the inside of a pan before he ate it. And once the sky had darkened, Nico had become restless and agitated, and then he'd been in pain. Terrible pain that had lasted for almost half an hour. And while he was writhing in pain, he'd changed just like he had in her dream.

He hadn't even completed the transformation before he'd tried to snap at her. By the time he'd been in full werewolf mode, only the steel door of their basement had held off his claws. Nico had, at last, escaped from the confinement of their home by jumping through a window, and ever since, Rachel had been following the Greenvalley news ticker for accounts of animal attacks.

"There must be a potion that can heal lycanthropy," Samantha insisted.

Matt was still shaking his head. "Believe me. Many have tried; no one has ever succeeded."

"What if there is one *you* haven't heard about?"

Matt took a deep breath, and Rachel saw his knuckles turning white, as if it took him great effort to remain calm. "So, you think you can find this potion?"

Rachel wanted her to say yes, but tears were filling Samantha's eyes. "I will try, at least." Her voice broke.

"Hey..." Matt reached out to Samantha, putting his hand on hers. "I know it's hard to accept..."

"Hard to accept?" Fabian asked loudly. "What's your solution? We go into the forest and murder one of our friends? Rachel's brother?"

Rachel could've kissed him.

"Yeah, dude," Jan chimed in. "We can't kill Nico. Seriously, what's wrong with you?"

"Nothing. I'm just being realistic."

Both Samantha and Fabian protested, and the discussion quickly turned into a shouting match. As the fight continued, the truth hit Rachel. Nico would have to die or live his life as a beast in human form. A gasp escaped her, shockingly loud. She clamped her mouth shut. And now the tears were falling.

Lucille put a hand on her shoulder, holding her necklace with the other hand. She hadn't said a word yet, but she also wasn't losing her mind, instead smiling confidently at her. "Guys!" she called out. "I've got a plan. Or rather, a solution."

The other four turned to her in confusion. Matt took one look and groaned. "You can't be serious!"

"Why not?" Lucille challenged him, but then she turned to Rachel. "I can turn him back into a human with my magic. I just have to say the right words."

"I doubt it's that easy," Samantha said, but she sounded much less sure.

"It's not!" Matt exploded. "You have no idea what is actually happening when you use your spells. Magic isn't wish fulfilment. It has rules and set properties. You might as well kill Nico with your spell."

Next to him, Jan scoffed. "And how is that different from cutting his head off?" He walked over to Lucille and planted his feet there. "I'm with Lu. I trust her a hundred times more than you."

"Her spells seem to work pretty well," Fabian said, though his voice was a lot more doubtful, and he immediately searched for Samantha. "Magic can do this, can't it?"

Perhaps Matt knew more about magic, though they still had no idea where he pulled all that knowledge from, but to Rachel and Fabian, Samantha was the expert. She was the one who read book upon book of theory.

Now she licked her lips, looking at Lucille apologetically. "It shouldn't. What you are doing is defying all laws I read about."

"You didn't read my grandmother's journals," Lucille answered. Then she softened her voice. "I promise I won't use my magic lightly, but this is an emergency. Nico needs us, and if my magic can help him—and it does whatever I want it to—it's worth a try. It certainly beats sword-slashing and potion-pampering."

Samantha winced and folded into the chair behind her. "Lucille's right. She's the most experienced with magic."

"One month of experience," Matt grumbled.

"What's your magic experience, Matt?" Lucille asked acidly.

"Yeah, if you're secretly a warlock, now's the time to tell us," Jan prompted, to which Matt only rolled his eyes.

Before it could turn into another shouting match, Fabian stepped between the groups, raising his arms. He would probably tell them that dealing with Nico tonight was too dangerous and how they should wait until the morning. But when he spoke it was, "It's Rachel's brother. She should decide how to proceed."

Stunned, Rachel felt all eyes falling on her. They weren't going to fight about this. But she was overwhelmed with the decision. The only thing Rachel knew for sure was that she wouldn't allow Matt to kill him. However, she didn't want Nico to kill anyone else, either.

Just then, her phone pinged with a notification: *Man in critical condition after animal attack on Barbarossaweg.*

Shakily, she closed her eyes for a minute. At least they had a lead now. "I trust you, Sam. If anyone can find a healing potion for the werewolf infection, it's you. But first, we need to catch Nico. And Lucille's spells will help us do that."

"So will a couple of silver chains," Matt muttered, but he no longer protested, and everyone else nodded their assent.

Rachel took a deep breath. "Then let's be quick, before he kills someone." As long as that man hadn't already succumbed to his injuries. She had no idea how to explain this all to Nico when morning broke.

Fabian

The werewolf had fled back into the forest. No! Nico had.

Fabian already had a headache just trying to wrap his head around the fact that one of his best friends had somehow turned into a werewolf. Everything was moving too fast for him. He wanted to sit down and discuss all their options, talk to someone who actually knew their stuff. Instead, they were running through the forest, led by a tracking spell Lucille had spoken, and guided by Matt's supernatural instincts.

Jan had a silver chain wrapped around his hand that had apparently once belonged to Samantha's long-dead grandfather: a real demon hunter. That would be a good person to ask for help, but unfortunately, he was dead, just like Lucille's grandmother who'd been this super-experienced witch. And all of that told Fabian that what they were doing was bloody dangerous, and sooner or later, they would all die.

But there was no turning back, not when his best friend was the one they were hunting, the one they had to somehow stop from going on a killing spree in his beast form and find a way to turn him back. Fabian was only glad that the father werewolf—or whatever they were called—was already dead. Then again, he'd been human, too, and that thought was impossible for Fabian to stomach, so he pushed it away.

Hunting demons, giant wyrms, or shadow creatures was one thing. They were monsters that had to be stopped, but most importantly, they weren't human. Nico was. And if things went terribly wrong tonight, one of them might have to push a silver dagger through their friend's heart.

Fabian shook his head. No, he couldn't allow that. Nico would live. They would catch him, and tomorrow they'd find a way to deal with this infection. Samantha would find a way, or Lucille would speak the right words. Nico would be fine. And so would they.

"We're getting close," Lucille announced, looking at her fiery arrow that was glowing so brightly they didn't need any light.

Watching the arrow, Fabian saw it slowly turning sideways. Nico was no longer far in front of them. They were so close the spell was picking up the slightest movements. And those movements brought him right into—

"Get down!" he shouted.

A rustling of leaves, then a gigantic wolf burst from the undergrowth, front paws stretched forward, claws glinting in the moonlight. Fabian jerked up his arms, and the water came to him, shooting towards Nico in a straight stream.

The werewolf's jump was diverted, and he landed a metre away from Rachel instead of on top of her. He was wet now, but it didn't seem to cool him down. Snarling, the wolf turned towards Rachel, exposing his monstrous teeth.

"It's me, Nico." Instead of running to safety, Rachel stretched out her hand and took a step closer. "I know that you're still in there. You—"

The wolf jumped. At the same time, Matt threw himself on Rachel. They both crashed down and rolled over the forest floor until they got caught in the undergrowth. Fabian's reaction was much slower, and his second attack did nothing but wet the floor. Instead, Jan had moved in and karate-kicked the wolf in the snout.

"Sorry, man," he said.

The werewolf didn't accept the apology. He lunged at Jan, who stumbled backwards and slipped on the wet ground. In a terrible moment, the wolf was on top of him, pinning Jan down with his paws and opening his maw wide. Hot spittle dropped onto Jan, whose eyes were opened wide.

"Nico, don't!" Rachel cried, while Lucille stretched out her hand and screamed, "Shield."

Fabian couldn't watch. The moment the werewolf's maw shot down at Jan, he turned his head away, bracing for the crunching and smacking noises that were bound to follow.

But the sounds never came. Instead, the werewolf suddenly flew past Fabian and crashed into a tree, a stream of darkness on his heels. Fabian blinked and followed the stream to its origin. Matt stood there, sword in one hand. His other hand was outstretched, palm showing. Rachel was clinging on to his sword arm, which explained why Matt had to use his other hand, but not how that blast of energy had erupted from it.

Not that there was any time to think about it. The werewolf howled, but he didn't seem hurt. His yellow eyes refocused on the group.

Shaken, Fabian raised his arms. He had no idea if he could call the water to him a third time. He was definitely emotional enough, but he was also exhausted from the previous blasts. Behind him, Jan got to his feet, groaning slightly.

"Let go, Rachel," Matt said, his voice sending shivers down Fabian's arms.

"Never!"

"I want—" Lucille started, but at that moment, the werewolf turned around and shot off into the dark. "Stop, Nico!" she bellowed.

Something burst in front of them. Two seconds later, a tree crashed into the forest floor with such force, the ground shook underneath them. Needles blew into Fabian's face along with a cloud of dirt. A high-pitched whine rose.

"Nico!" Rachel let go of Matt and ran after the wolf.

Matt cursed and took up the pursuit.

Meanwhile, Fabian's legs wouldn't move. The shock of the falling tree and what it might mean for Nico had blown into his legs. He felt as if he would crumple to the floor if he dared to take a step. But his eyes flitted to Lucille, who stood fixed on the spot just like him. Her mouth opened in a gasp.

"What did you do?" Fabian heard himself asking, and slowly, reality caught up with him. Lucille had cast another spell. But "Stop, Nico" hadn't forced the werewolf to stop; instead, the magic had risen to stop him. And now...

Another terrible whine.

"Should we follow them?" Jan asked, suddenly not so keen on continuing the hunt. His fall had drenched him in mud, and underneath the slashes of his jacket, Fabian thought he saw something wet glistening.

"Well, we can't leave Matt and Rachel alone," Fabian declared. The notion that his friends might be in danger gave him more confidence. What was he doing, standing here like an idiot? "And Nico might be in need of help."

At that, Lucille whimpered, but Jan took her arm almost gently and said, "Come on, Lu. I'm sure he's fine."

He didn't sound fine. The whining grew even pitchier.

Fabian's heart thumped heavily in his chest as they made their way towards the large break in the forest.

"Light?" Jan whispered to Lucille, but she only shook her head.

Instead, Fabian turned on his cellphone's flashlight and wished he hadn't in the same instance.

Blood stuck to the branches of the tree. The werewolf was caught between them, snapping wildly, then whining again. Lucille shuddered next to him and whimpered. Rachel had climbed onto the trunk, slowly inching towards Nico, while Matt used his weird black magic to break off the branches around Nico.

"Shouldn't we leave him there?" Jan asked.

Immediately, Rachel hissed at him. "And let him bleed to death?"

"Rachel—" Lucille started, but one glare from Rachel shut her up.

The werewolf snapped at Matt when he came too close, forcing Matt to jerk his hand back. "I can't get any closer to him."

"Nico," Rachel said, her voice now soft and sweet again. "We're just trying to help you."

The wolf growled, but when Matt moved closer, he snapped again. Matt shook his head. "This won't work. I have to get closer or risk hurting him even more."

As Lucille gasped, Jan drew her close, resting his hand on her back. "What else can we do? Maybe a spell—"

"I don't want to hear a single spell out of Lucille's mouth!" Rachel hissed again.

Her agitation translated to Nico, who growled deeper and tried to free himself from his predicament with a new burst of energy. Clawing at the branches that held him, he cracked a few, but also drove others deeper into his wounds. With a high-pitched whine, he crashed into the tree crown again.

Fabian's heart was thumping so hard his chest hurt. As if he could feel Nico's injuries, his breathing accelerated. With fumbling fingers, he patted his jacket and found the long hard rachis of the magical feather. Drawing. How could a drawing help them?

Again, Nico snapped at Matt as the latter tried to reach him again. His teeth. The snout.

"I've got an idea." With fumbling fingers, Fabian opened the zip of his jacket and seized the feather from the inside pocket. "Give me a second."

He was quite aware that they were all staring, but drawing was something that Fabian knew how to do. Even into the air in a dark forest. He took aim at Nico and drew a quick muzzle. A moment later, bands of leather snapped tight around the werewolf's snout. And while the beast hated it, he couldn't get rid of it.

"That's helpful," Matt acknowledged, already moving in. There were still the giant paws with their claws to account for, but Matt seemed to be able to handle those.

"It only holds about an hour, fifty minutes," Fabian informed him.

Matt nodded. "Jan, give me that chain."

Jan let go of Lucille and stepped closer with the silver chain. "What do you want to do?" He handed it over.

Matt took it, evaded a blow from the nearest paw, and wrapped the chain around Nico's scraggy neck. Then he locked it in and threw the other end to Jan. "Put that around the thickest tree you can reach."

Staring, Jan took a moment to answer, probably deciding whether he should actually do something Matt had said. Then the reality of the situation caught up with him and he snapped to attention. "Sure."

"What are you doing?" Rachel asked.

"The muzzle will keep him from hurting me while I free him, but we can't risk him running away again," Matt explained while he set to work.

"The silver will weaken him, but more importantly, he'll be chained to a tree."

Fabian quietly assisted him by drawing bonds around Nico's paws, allowing Matt to concentrate on the branches instead of the claws.

"How is he doing that?" Jan muttered behind Fabian to Lucille, but she was still in too much shock to reply.

Fabian grabbed his feather tighter. He hadn't yet told the others about its hidden powers. And he didn't quite feel like discussing it now. Instead, he drew a saw and set to help Matt the old-fashioned way, keeping a healthier distance from Nico.

"I want one, too," Rachel whispered to him, and he wordlessly gave her his before drawing a second one.

Together, they had Nico freed within a few minutes. The werewolf only collapsed, panting heavily. While Fabian kept his distance, Rachel hurried to her brother's side and dug her fingers into his fur. A second later, she, too, collapsed, though it was from relief, not exhaustion.

"His healing powers are kicking in."

"This quick?" Matt asked, doubt dripping from his words. "I'd say his healing powers got a substantial werewolf boost."

"Is that a thing?" Fabian asked.

Matt turned his head to him. "Werewolves heal much faster."

"So, does that mean you're a werewolf too?" Jan asked as he stepped closer. "Because I saw those claws ripping through your jacket when you saved Rachel and there's nothing." He poked at Matt's shoulder, where the jacket was indeed ripped.

"Jan," Matt said in a deadpan voice. "It's a full moon."

Jan looked up at the moon shining through the hole in the trees. "Right. You're not turned." But then he found his vigour again. "So, you can control this infection then?"

Matt groaned and turned away, testing the chain at the tree instead. "You shouldn't get too close to Nico," he told them, as if they'd already changed the topic. "Once Fabian's..."

"Drawings," Fabian offered helpfully and held his feather up. "Seems like Sam had it right, and it is another Emblem of Power."

Once again, Matt accepted the information with an ease Fabian envied him for. "Well, once they've vanished, he'll try to attack us. The chain should hold until morning, but we should keep watch just in case. And I guess so that someone's here when he transforms back."

"I'll be here," Rachel declared immediately. She ran her fingers through Nico's soft fur, then stepped away from him.

Fabian and Jan also went on a distance. "You want to stay the night in the forest?" Fabian asked. "It's gonna be cold and probably wet. We need shelter and blankets and ideally some hot tea to keep us warm if we're keeping watch."

Jan whistled through his teeth. "Since when were you a survival expert?"

Fabian felt his face blushing and mumbled, "Eight years of Junior Ranger program." His parents had signed him up when he was eight, and he'd enjoyed it until the only path to continue would've been to become a youth group leader himself. "Anyway. I would draw us some, but as I said, they only last about an hour."

"I could probably conjure what we need," Lucille offered in a meek voice. She'd been staying out of the action ever since the tree had fallen.

"Absolutely not!" Rachel hissed again. "I don't want you anywhere near either of us with your magic."

Even Fabian winced. "Rachel."

While she didn't snap at him, her eyes said it all. There would be no discussion about it. Then suddenly, tears sprang to her eyes. "She almost killed him."

"I'm sorry!" Lucille cried.

"Well, I hope you've learnt your lesson," Matt said with a snarl that indicated a previous spat.

Lucille swallowed heavily. "Then I'll go back to Elda and get what you need."

"No, Fabian knows best what we need," Rachel decided. Her unfamiliar firmness surprised Fabian. "He'll get the stuff. But you can go with him." She bit her lip. "Actually, I want to go too."

"And leave me alone with *him?*" Jan asked, pointing at Matt.

Matt growled, "I'm not a monster."

Jan snorted. "Yeah, right."

Fabian ignored both of them, focusing on Rachel instead. "You don't want to be here in the morning?"

Rachel shook her head. "I will be. But I need to see how Samantha is doing." She turned to stare at Nico, who was still recuperating from his injuries. "She can heal him. I'm sure of it."

Fabian's eyes wandered to Matt, and what he saw there didn't fill him with the same confidence. He had no doubt that Samantha was brilliant, but healing this infection was close to impossible. Even for her.

Samantha

Samantha was on her second pot of coffee, taking great care not to stain any of the many books that were open around her. She'd already scribbled down twelve pages of notes. Some of them she'd marked as important, then crossed them out when a new piece of information turned them into dead ends.

Her head felt like it was exploding from all the knowledge she'd been cramming into it, but she refused to give up. No matter how many times Samantha read that a witch had declared the healing impossible, she kept forging on. Anything could be healed. They just hadn't found out how yet.

"Are you still up, darling?" Her grandmother opened the door.

Samantha had barely registered the knock on the door, her mind focused on a particularly promising trial series with Aconite. The purple herb grew in damp forests and could be locally sourced. It was incredibly toxic, though with the right preparation, the toxins could be extracted. Most importantly, it was known among witches as wolfsbane. And for a good reason. Werewolves and other creatures kept a wide distance from places where it grew, which was one of the reasons her grandmother had planted them around her house many years ago.

There was truly no shortage of it, and according to the trial series, it at least had an effect on the werewolf affliction if given to the wolf as an infusion. According to the series, it suppressed transformation if drunk in high doses just before a full moon. The problem was: while it stopped the werewolves from changing for the time of intake, it slowly poisoned the bitten human. Within one or two years, all patients in the trial series had died.

Her grandmother shuffled closer as Samantha rubbed her eyes and reached for the cup of coffee again. Empty.

"How are you doing?" Elda asked, stroking her hair.

"I haven't found anything yet, but I'll keep looking." Something must've gone wrong with the clarification of the aconite. She grabbed a small green book about poisons. If she fixed that issue, she might have something working for Nico. Something that didn't kill him in the long run.

Her grandmother's hand halted on her shoulder, the grip intensifying slightly. "Samantha, nobody has ever—"

"Connected all the failed attempts and created something new out of it." There was something in the book about purifying aconite.

She found the page and skim-read it before closing it with annoyance. There was a way to draw the toxins out of the flowers, but it was the root that was the most toxic, rich in aconitine—and the most potent.

Elda let go of her and pulled up a chair. "There are other options."

"Such as?" Healing was obviously option number one, with killing being option number never.

"I know folks who would take him. They would take care that he doesn't hurt anyone."

Samantha wasn't sure she liked the sound of *"taking care"*. It sounded too much like what Matt had said. And there was something else. "Matt told us that werewolves become more and more beastlike, even during their human days."

Her grandmother sighed heavily. "And he's right about that. That's why these people are Nico's best chance. They'll also take care of him when he's... well, no longer able to keep up a human farce."

Vehemently, Samantha shook her head. "No! That can't be a solution." What would that do to Rachel to send her brother to some werewolf palliative care, where every time she came to visit, he'd be a little less human? Would Nico even agree to go while he still had his wits about?

"It would be the safest option," Elda said.

"But not his only one!" Samantha snapped. She immediately regretted snapping at her grandmother. But her brain refused to understand how her gentle grandmother could be as *"realistic"* as Matt had been. "I'm sorry, but Nico's still human. A breathing, feeling human!"

Elda nodded at that, her eyes full of pity. No, she wasn't like Matt. He'd been pragmatic, bordering on cold; her grandmother was all warmth and compassion. With all her experience, she just didn't believe in Samantha's success.

"I know exactly how you feel, darling. I knew a werewolf once." A little sigh escaped her, as if she'd been momentarily caught up in a memory. "She was a good friend of mine. We grew up together. After she was bitten, we tried for months. We sedated and chained her during nights of full moon. But she got loose more and more often and..." Her voice faltered. Samantha could imagine what happened when she got loose only too well.

"But the worst was how she changed in between the moons. She stopped talking, only answering in growls and snarls and whines. And once she bit me." Elda pushed back the sleeve of her blouse to reveal a faded bite mark on the aged skin of her wrist. It was clearly a human bite.

Suddenly, it was impossible for Samantha's lungs to fill with air. "Did you kill her?"

Her grandmother shook her head and let the sleeve fall again. "Eric did it. He was always the more pragmatic of the both of us."

Samantha hadn't known her demon-hunter grandfather. Her father never talked about him, and his grandmother had only ever passed on tiny tidbits. The only thing she knew was that in the thirty years since his death, Elda hadn't married anyone else. And she'd never got rid of his tools, though she'd kept most of them under wraps, until Samantha had brought Lucille to her.

If Nico lost the fight for his humanity, Matt wouldn't hesitate to kill him either. He would do it right now if he thought he'd get away with it. Because he knew, like her grandmother, that there was no cure for the infection.

Not yet. With new determination, Samantha turned to her open books. "I'll find something else."

"Of course you will," Elda answered with the comforting lie Samantha wanted to hear. "I'll boil you some more coffee."

Once more, she stroked Samantha's head, then grabbed the coffee pot and left. By the time the door closed, Samantha was already knee-deep in purification theory.

Jan

Fabian had been right; it was getting cold. Even with a sleeping bag and a blanket wrapped around his shoulders, Jan felt the cold creeping into his bones as he watched Nico.

The werewolf had given up the fight after an hour of clawing and biting at the chain that bound him to the tree. Now he lay with his head on his paws, watching them. Jan couldn't be sure, but he thought his yellow eyes looked at them with hatred.

Jan took out another cigarette and lit it up. He liked to pretend that the smoke he inhaled warmed him from the inside while his fingers froze. His mother hated that he smoked, especially with his asthma. But the cigarettes did their job and calmed him. He could almost imagine being on some cool hiking trip adventure. Fabian had brought a ton of snacks and fizzy drinks, plus the promised hot tea and coffee in thermos jugs. They'd built a makeshift shelter from the branches of Lucille's fallen tree and pine needles that managed to catch the drizzle that had started half an hour ago. It would've been a great bonding experience if not for the werewolf staring at them.

Or the creepy guy Jan had to share this trip with.

He gazed at Matt, who sat on the other side of the shelter, as far away from Jan as possible. He was matching the wolf's stares with one of his own, and Jan couldn't for the life of him decide who was the scarier of the two.

All things considered, he decided on Matt. The dude had killed a werewolf in one fell swoop with his magical sword last night. A werewolf who'd also been a human. Jan hadn't known it was a werewolf when it attacked him, but he wondered what he would see if he went back now to the valley where the wolf had died.

And then there was the black magic. No one could tell him that this was a normal talent. Sure, Matt had used it to save his life, but Jan had seen that blast. It'd knocked Nico right off of him and pushed him several metres away. All because Matt had raised a hand.

Screw this. He wasn't going to sit here and fret like some teenage girl with a crush.

Jan put out the cigarette stub and climbed out of his sleeping bag. He grabbed an unopened bar of chocolate on his way over, stepped over Fabian's legs, and plopped himself down on the ground next to Matt.

Matt gave him a sideway glance before shaking his head when Jan offered him the chocolate. "What do you want?"

"Talk," Jan answered in a similarly scruffy voice. There was no love lost between the two. Matt had made that much clear the first time they talked to each other.

Apart from sharing most of their classes, they were on the school's soccer team. Matt had nabbed the goalie position, and while Jan secretly thought it was because his ball-handling skills were woefully under-developed, his reflexes made him a fantastic goalie. The dream team, consisting of Alan and Cian, was no longer ruling the field, which was a source of glee for Jan. But when he'd tried to congratulate Matt on his skills, the other had brushed him off and pointed out that he already had enough friends.

That was before Jan had joined the group and found out that Matt wielded a bloody sword and shot black magic from his fingers in a pinch. And apparently healed faster than a werewolf. Jan's own wounds from Nico's claws had been patched up by Fabian, but they still burnt under their dressings.

"About what?" Matt asked.

What kind of monster is deadly afraid of worms? was the first question that came to Jan's mind. But he wasn't going to be that stupid. "You."

Matt rolled his eyes. "I'm not a monster."

This time the words slipped out of Jan before he could stop them. "Or so you say." When Matt's stare turned into a glare, he raised his hands and gave him a quick grin. "Fine, not a monster." The jury was still out on that, in his humble opinion. "You're still weird."

"How so?" Matt asked, perplexed.

There were a million reasons Jan could think of, even though he seemed to be the only one who cared. He went for the easiest one to try to get some information out of his mysterious friend. "Well, first up, you know an awful lot about the other monsters." Damn it. He'd said "other".

Matt only snorted. "I learnt a lot about them."

"Which school is teaching that?" Jan asked without missing a beat. "I wouldn't miss a single lesson." Which was more than could be said about his school.

"I had private teachers," Matt admitted, turning away to take up his staring contest with Nico again.

Look at that. A real tidbit of information here. Jan knew Matt's father was a teacher, but he doubted an elementary school teacher taught monster lore—and besides, Matt hadn't lived with him. "Your mother must be rich then."

Matt shrugged. "Maybe. She has a reputation."

What the hell was that supposed to mean? "She's famous, or what?"

"Not here."

So, she was famous in whatever place Matt had crawled out of. Jan regarded him anew. He certainly had the good looks of a celebrity child gifted with the genetics of two gorgeous parents—or at least one. He didn't remember Mr Traidous being breathtakingly handsome. The hazardous lifestyle with all the sleeping around would definitely fit a celebrity child, though Matt hadn't shown any kind of interest in trying out drugs, and Jan was convinced Matt would scoff at him if offered some.

Then again, all weird decisions aside, what kind of celebrity brought in private teachers in monster lore? "So, this private teacher taught you all this?"

Matt looked at him, and Jan was almost sure that he wouldn't answer. But he only sighed and started recounting, "He taught me about monsters, History, Magic Theory, Geography, Philosophy." For the last one, he rolled his eyes. "Oh, and fighting with a sword."

Now Jan was the one staring. He almost wanted to ask where he could sign up for that kind of education but caught himself. "No Maths or Physics?"

"He got other teachers for that." Matt sighed again. "Chay made sure I would never be bored. But I guess it wasn't for nothing. If I hadn't learnt all that, I'd be completely lost at Greenvalley High."

Jan could commiserate with that. He was constantly lost at Greenvalley High. "Oh, man, I figured life would be more relaxed with a private teacher. But that actually explains a few things."

"For example?" Matt asked, frowning at him.

"Why you're so obsessed with putting half of Greenvalley on its back." Jan grinned as he imagined Matt's escapades. "With such a strict education, you need to catch up."

Matt snorted and turned away again. "I actually... like sex. That's why I have it."

"But you're aware that you can have sex in a relationship? Like as much as you want?" Jan asked. As enticing as the idea of many sexual partners was, Jan considered himself a monogamist.

"That's boring," Matt said. "And not true."

Jan frowned at him. "What do you mean, not true?"

"I watched couples," Matt explained earnestly, as if he was discussing a school project. "The ones at school don't have sex all the time. First, they take ages to admit they're in love, and then all you see them do is cuddle and... do nothing." He shrugged. "Sure, some of them might have sex at home, but only there. And I'm pretty sure some don't, even there."

A million questions shot through Jan's mind. Where did Matt have his sex dates? Had he done it at school? And why did he talk about it as if the very idea of relationships baffled him?

"You know, some people like to wait to have sex," Jan said carefully.

"Why?"

Definitely baffled. Jan laughed softly. He couldn't believe it. This guy was so suave when it came to flirting and getting into everyone's pants, but had no clue about actual relationships. Even for a kid from divorced parents, it was a bit much. "Well, normal people don't jump into each other's beds on first eye contact. They like to get to know the other person and be... sure that sex is what they want."

"So, you *don't* want sex?" Matt asked.

Jan almost laughed again. "Of course, I do, but it's not just about me. If I like a girl, I want to make sure she enjoys it as well."

"My partners always enjoy themselves."

Talk about a boast! Jan had to take a deep breath. How had they even got here from monster lessons? Right, the tangent had been his fault. "For most people our age, it's the first relationship, and sex is kind of a big thing. At least, for the first time. People like to wait and share it with a special someone." Not that the girl he'd lost his virginity to had been particularly special after cheating on him three weeks later. "Wasn't it special for you?"

Matt shook his head, looking all introspective. "Not particularly, no."

"When was your first time?" Jan asked and beat himself up the next second because it wasn't actually any of his business.

Matt opened his mouth but thought better of it and closed it again.

Well, now Jan's curiosity was piqued. He'd lost his virginity at sixteen. That meant Matt... "Fourteen?" Matt didn't answer. Damn it! "Thirteen?" Now he was turning away from him and staring into the distance. "Twelve?" Jan asked, incredulous.

Abruptly, Matt turned back to him, his brows drawn together. "Why *do* you wait so long?"

Jan had no idea how to answer that. At twelve, he'd found most girls and their constant shrieking annoying. "Not everyone is born horny."

Matt snorted. "Yeah, right. So, you're okay without sex if you don't have a girlfriend, and if you had one, you'd still be happy to wait around. That explains why you're always on edge."

"I've got a hand, you know?" Jan snapped, then took another deep breath. "Yes, I'd be happy to wait around." Not too long, but he certainly wouldn't pressure a girl into something she wasn't ready for.

Matt shook his head as if he had real difficulty to grasp that concept. "You're weird. You'd prefer your hand even if you were in a relationship. And Fabian's just the same, even though Rachel would be all over him if he let her."

"Rachel would what?" Obviously, Fabian had woken from his slumber a while ago and listened in on their conversation. Now, Matt and Jan both turned to him with long looks. Fabian stared at them, elbows propping him up from the ground. "There's nothing between me and Rachel."

"Yeah, because you're ignoring her, cold-hearted man that you are," Jan said in a mocking tone.

Matt did the same. "You don't notice her mooning over you every day?"

Fabian grimaced. "What are you talking about? Either way, she is not all over me."

"As if you noticed the way *you're* still mooning over Samantha," Jan said. When Matt grinned at him, the same thought visible on his mind, he felt a connection for the first time. At least they'd both noticed what Fabian was too oblivious to see.

"I am not!" Fabian crossed his arms, furious with both of them. "That thing between us is over."

"She dumped him," Jan let Matt know.

Matt laughed. "That's what I thought."

"What's that supposed to mean?" Indignant, Fabian started freeing himself from his sleeping bag.

But Matt waved him off. "It doesn't matter. But hey, if Samantha is no longer interested in you and Rachel wants you, why don't you give it a shot?"

Fabian swallowed whatever he was about to say before. "Uhm, because I'm not super horny like you."

"Translation: because he's still super in love with Samantha," Jan offered helpfully.

"But she doesn't want him," Matt said, sounding baffled again. "Why chase someone who's not interested in you?"

Even in the darkness, Jan could see that Fabian's face was beet red. He almost felt sorry for him. Fabian snorted. "Because, unlike you, I can't just turn off my feelings and move on." This time, it wasn't a lie.

"I'm not turning off my feelings," Matt said, a little offended.

"He just doesn't have any," Jan joked, but then sobered quickly after noticing how differently that hit. "There is something off with you." He checked with Fabian. "Don't tell me you don't feel it too."

As Matt groaned, Fabian shook his head. "Why? Because he's not interested in relationships?"

"No, because, well, what was that black stuff you shot from your hands?" It was time to get it all out. No more lies.

"Black magic," Matt answered promptly.

"Ha! I knew it." Jan pointed at him while making sure Fabian had heard that. "Black magic. That's pretty hardcore. Evil and all."

Matt elbowed him. "Oh, shut up! You have no idea what you're talking about. It's the theory of colour magic. Black magic is the magic of destruction, just as white magic is the magic of construction—healing, so to speak. Neither is good nor evil. It's just magic."

"So, you're a witch?" Jan asked, trying his hardest not to get distracted by such cool concepts as coloured magic.

"No, I'm not anything other than me. I can fight with a sword and access destructive energy." Matt seemed to bite down on his tongue, as if to keep himself from adding more.

But Jan was convinced there was more. The lack of scratch wounds on Matt's perfect skin. "That's it. You're one of those fae things, right? Magical creatures, decidedly non-human."

"Jan," Fabian said in a warning tone. "What are you talking about? Matt is human. Have you forgotten that he's Mr Traidous' son?"

"A changeling! Gotcha!" Jan pointed his finger at Matt's nose a little too enthusiastically. "The real Matt is in some weird fairy realm, and you're his inhuman replacement."

Matt took his accusation in, then snorted. "You should try staying off the drugs. Just saying."

Jan knew he was right. Maybe not about the Wechselbalg, or the fae, or the witch, or anything yet, but there was something. "Well, then explain to me how a perfectly human being could just go and behead a werewolf, knowing that there is a human being inside there."

"Werewolves are not..." Matt's gaze drifted to Nico, who'd stood up, testing the limits of his chain again. "You mean yesterday's werewolf?" Jan nodded. "I'll show you your human."

He got out his smartphone and flicked through the apps until he could pull up the photos. The last few pictures showed something vaguely human on the forest floor, but it wasn't human. Not even close. The skin of the supposed werewolf—and Jan truly hoped there was only one beheaded creature in this wood—was almost leather-like and dark grey. Its limbs were a few joints too long.

Then the next picture showed the severed head. While it still looked somewhat human, the skin was far too taut over sharpened cheekbones. Its nose was longer, almost snout-like, and its teeth were definitely not human. "What the hell is that?"

"Hell is the keyword here. That creature has come straight out of Hell," Matt explained darkly.

"Why?" Fabian asked, his voice paper-thin. "Why would it come here?"

Matt put the phone away. "I believe it was placed here, just like the Konnurar. And didn't Elda say something powerful broke through her barrier? I think you should worry less about my inhumanity and more about the demon who sent this after you and Nico."

All the blood drained from Jan's face. After him and Nico. The demon in the mine's office, the one who'd vanished. They'd thought he'd died, but what if he hadn't? What if the werewolf bite hadn't been as random as Jan thought?

"Guys." His voice quivered slightly. "I think I need to tell you something."

Lucille

The walk back with Rachel and Fabian earlier had been pure torture for Lucille. Rachel hadn't said a single word, and neither had Fabian after picking up on the weird mood. Lucille wanted to talk about what had happened, but she didn't know where to start, and she was too afraid to say the wrong thing and accidentally cast a spell that would do even more damage.

At the same time, she was aching to use her power to set things right. She could force Rachel to forgive her and hated herself immediately for even considering that. All the little things she'd "fixed" with her magic came back to her. She'd altered the memory of everyone in her year, made her father forget his work and his wife—and probably the reason why he might still be sitting in that restaurant—and she'd made Linda disappear.

All of these had started with good intentions—well, apart from the Linda thing. That'd been petty and mean and half accidental. But she'd only made Cian invite Samantha because she'd felt sorry for her friend always being ostracised by the popular kids. And she'd made the video vanish that was so incredibly embarrassing for Samantha. And of course, her father... no, that had been selfish as well.

And while Lucille's thoughts circled in endless spirals, the three of them had arrived at Elda's home, Fabian had gathered everything he needed and more and set off again, and Rachel had vanished into the witch room, where Samantha was busy researching.

After a while of sitting alone in the living room, the door opened, and Samantha's grandmother entered. She put down a tray of cookies before sitting down next to Lucille. "How are you, darling? You look a bit glum."

How could she not after what had happened? The whole situation deserved all the glumness in the world. "Rachel's brother..."

"A terrible accident," Elda said with a nod. "I'm sorry this happened to you, and to him. I wish there was some hope I could offer, but..." She looked at the wall, behind which Samantha was doing her very best to save Nico's life. "There is no cure."

Lucille swallowed. Then she began fiddling with her necklace again, drawing strength from its heat. "What if there was a spell?" Gosh! What was wrong with her? How could she think of casting another spell after the near disaster she'd just caused? But if she was careful and laid out the exact words, perhaps talked them through with the others...

"There is no spell powerful enough to turn a werewolf back into a human." Elda sighed. "I mean, there are spells that have a temporary effect, but they only affect the body, not the spirit. He would still be a rabid wolf in human skin."

So, "turn Nico back into a human" wouldn't work. Her spell needed to cover the inner changes as well.

Lucille licked her lips. If she asked the others, she would only be met with outrage. Rachel was no longer speaking to her, and Matt would fly into a rage if she suggested it. She didn't trust Jan to add anything useful, and Fabian would run the other way if she tried. Not that he could help her. Samantha might be able to help, but she was already busy. And Lucille had kind of pissed her off when she called her talent "potion pampering".

When Lucille looked up, she noticed Elda's kind and compassionate eyes. Samantha's grandmother had been a witch all her life, she remembered. She'd been friends with her own grandmother, married to a demon hunter, and faced creatures far worse than they had. If anyone was able to help her, it was probably Elda. And there was a strange comfort in having an actual adult to confide in. Not like her father.

"Elda, can I ask you something?" Speaking was hard. Lucille had to think twice about each sentence to make sure she didn't accidentally cast a spell. Maybe she should ask her for a cab and drive home to cast the counter-spell to her infliction. But the very idea of losing this power sent shivers down her spine. No! She didn't want to give up her magic.

"Of course, my dear. What do you want to know?"

"Did my grandmother ever tell you about a spell she spoke to access... pure magic?" Lucille had obviously inherited the infliction from her grandmother because she'd never seen pure magic before her spell.

Elda folded her hands in her lap as she took a deep breath. "Cecille's mother was obsessed with it and disregarded her daughter's true talents. And for a while, Cecille tried to use her power to do what wasn't naturally given to her." She sighed. "You know, our friendship didn't have an easy start. Cecille came from a long line of witches and had all these expectations weighing on her shoulders. And then there I was. Practically new in town, a coal miner's daughter, who had a natural connection to the magic around her, doing things with ease that Cecille struggled with. And then her mother... She took me as her protégé and groomed me to become the next witch of Greenvalley. Obviously, your grandmother didn't take that particularly well."

Lucille sympathised with her grandmother—she was no stranger to expectations. While her family didn't know about the magic, she'd always felt the need to be the perfect daughter, to study hard, and to behave flawlessly in public. She still remembered her first birthday party after Linda had joined the family. Instead of inviting other children, Linda had dressed her in white and organised a lady's brunch. It had been exciting at first, but once the ladies had started chatting, she'd been nothing but a pretty doll in the corner for them to fawn over.

And all the time she'd been vying for her father's attention. What if Linda had had a child with him, and he'd showered them with all the attention she never got? It would have been a bitter pill to swallow, and she doubted she would've been a favourable older sister.

"But you became friends in the end?" she asked.

Elda nodded and smiled. "Yes, she eventually realised that not only did I care more about her than any praise from her mother, but also that her talents fit her perfectly just the way they were."

Lucille was reminded of Samantha and how she'd felt when Lucille had marched into her town and started throwing spells around that, after years of obsession, Samantha couldn't do. "It's like me and

Samantha. She has a talent with potions even though magic eludes her... I think." It would've almost been a spell, stunting whatever potential Samantha may still have.

"Perhaps. I personally believe she's just a late bloomer. Magic is weird. Look at Fabian. He's been an elemental mage since childhood. Then the fever came and he buried his talents completely, until you came along and exposed magic as real to him. It was always there."

"So, Samantha will develop magic powers of her own?" Lucille asked, barely digesting all the information. Fabian had suppressed his powers? That sounded like him.

"I was sixteen when I first saw the magic, but I've always had a connection to it, even if I didn't know it was around," Elda explained. "Samantha is the same. She senses it. It just hasn't happened for her yet. Do you really think potions are just like cooking and chemistry? They're not. There is so much magic that happens in the picking, the preparation, the actual potion-making. There's the recipe, and there's intuition, and Samantha has the latter. She just likes to be all logical about it, and maybe that's what's suppressing her true talents. She just needs to unlock the logic in magic."

While that was certainly something to talk to Samantha about, Lucille returned to her original question. "Well, I was reading my grandmother's journals. She developed a spell that allowed her to use her voice as a tool to access pure magic. I believe it made every word she said true."

"Oh, that one. She got into a lot of trouble with that." Elda laughed like one would over an old silliness. "She accidentally wished her mother to Hell."

Lucille gasped, her thoughts with Linda. "How did she get her back?"

"Oh, Martha had to fight her way through demons to a gate between worlds. She gave Cecille an earful when she returned. By then, even Cecille had realised how dangerous that spell is."

The blood drained from Lucille's face. Where exactly had she sent Linda? If it was Hell, then... It was a thought too terrible to behold. She shook her head. No, she hadn't sent her to Hell. She was in Milan or Paris. And even if she'd chosen wherever instead, it was some place that Linda could reach from this world.

"Is that the only danger of the spell? That you have to be extremely careful of what you say?"

Elda frowned. "No, it also drained her. When witches weave magic, it takes a lot of skill and concentration. The more complicated a spell, the more it drains us. If you only speak the words, it'd be easy. What's in a sentence? But the magic still takes from you. By the time Martha came back from Hell, Cecille was on all fours, her heart rate all over the place. She would've collapsed if not for me. And even I couldn't have helped her if she'd done another spell of such power."

Lucille froze in her seat. She'd been using the spell for five days now with no side effects that she'd noticed. "How long was the delay?" She started fiddling with her necklace again.

"Within the same day, for that particular spell. Though Cecille had used a lot of other magic as well before she sent her mother away." Elda leaned forward, regarding Lucille intently. "You haven't considered trying it, have you?"

Lucille's hands shot back into her lap. "No... I was just thinking about using it for Nico. If I could find the right words—"

"It might very well kill you."

Swallowing heavily, Lucille took a few breaths. Had she been lucky so far? Were the spells she'd spoken without thinking not as powerful as sending a woman to another world? The fallen tree didn't seem hard, though its results were devastating. But what about all the memory-altering spells? At least a hundred people had forgotten the video of Cian's and Samantha's kiss. And everyone had forgotten about Linda de Cerque. Those were thousands, perhaps even millions, of people. Her stepmother was a renowned designer, after all.

By all means, Lucille should be dead. Shuddering, she corrected that to she'd probably be dead once the delay kicked in. But it had been five days, and she felt nothing. Why was she feeling nothing?

The amulet. Its heat comforted her. That must be it. Samantha had said that the amulet enhanced her powers. It was an ancient Emblem of Power. Strong enough to change the world. Surely, that was why such a powerful memory spell had done nothing. Changing Nico might be in her power. The problem was, Lucille didn't know that. And despite all sympathy for him, she couldn't bring herself to try it. Not if Elda was so convinced it would've killed someone of her grandmother's calibre.

"I'm sorry, Lucille," Elda said, taking her hand. "I wish there was such an easy way to heal the boy, but the werewolf infection remains one of the nastiest curses. You might as well stop night from falling."

Lucille registered her comfort, but it did little to settle the unrest inside of her. With the amulet, small spells were safe. She could still fix some of the things she'd broken. Starting with Nico.

The moment Lucille stepped into the witch room, Rachel slunk out, muttering something about dreaming of Nico. The clock showed 2:14, definitely a good time for sleeping or dream wandering.

But Samantha didn't look like she'd go to bed anytime soon. The floor was covered with books, while she was building a complicated structure from glass bulbs, glass pipes, and burners that would have made any alchemist movie set proud.

"What is this?" Lucille asked.

"An attempt to separate the alkaloids from the rest of the aconite," Samantha answered. "I would love to use an HPLC for that, but unless we break into a well-stocked chemistry lab, I don't see that happening. So, old-school we go."

Apparently, progressive tiredness made Samantha hard to understand. "I have no idea what an HPLC is."

Samantha looked over her shoulder for the first time. "Do you want to know?"

Lucille quickly shook her head. She considered conjuring an HPLC for Samantha, but the thought of the magic building one out of thin air or stealing and transporting it from a faraway lab sounded too big a spell. There needed to be a simpler way to help. "Talk me through what you've got."

"Not much," Samantha said and sighed. "Lots of people tried a wolfsbane potion. Some work, but only temporarily. Like they can force a werewolf back into a human. Others slow the process or suppress the transformation, but the human still deteriorates. The most promising one is actually a simple concoction of aconite and catnip."

She pointed to a bunch of dried flowers and roots on the far side of the bench. "It's normally used to protect your house or yourself from werewolves. But there was a trial where it was injected into a werewolf. And it worked partially, but the subject was poisoned in the process. So, that's problem number one. Remove the poison." She fazed her glass contraption again, checking the various baubles and pipes.

Samantha turned to the cauldron, and Lucille noticed something cooking in there. Leaves, flowers, and other pieces were floating on a thick, purple-coloured liquid. Samantha moved the giant ladle counterclockwise for three rounds, and then half a round back. Immediately, the pieces on the surface broke into smaller parts, dissolving even further. "It's almost done."

"Wow." Lucille looked back at the glass contraption. "So, you use that to get rid of the poison?"

"The poison is in the alkaloids, or rather, the aconitine is the poison. Different components have different boiling points. So, when I heat the potion, it splits into different components. The ones with a lower boiling point turn to steam, which rises through the glass pipes until they're caught in the next trap. By consistently lowering the boiling point, you'll eventually separate all the components." Samantha pointed at a glass trap near the end of her contraption. "That should be the one where the aconitine lands."

Lucille's head was swimming with all the technical details. While she'd never been bad at Chemistry, it wasn't her favourite subject. Better than Physics, but she was glad to see the back of it next year. Still, it sounded marvellous. Separating chemical components with nothing but heat. "How long is it going to take?"

"A few hours." With a sigh, Samantha sat down in a chair. It lasted for all of five seconds before she jumped up again to check something in the books on the floor.

"I might be able to separate them quicker. Or accelerate the process," Lucille offered. That didn't sound like a life-threatening spell for her and the amulet.

Samantha frowned. "Rachel said—"

Lucille pushed her hands into her hip. "Yeah, what did Rachel say?" Maybe it was the lack of sleep and all the commotion, but she thought it was a bit rich of everyone to blame her. Matt had blasted Nico over a clearing into a tree and nobody gave him any flack. Or Jan for kicking Nico in the face and Fabian for his high-pressure water streams. "That Nico attacked us and then almost got away, but my spell made it possible for us to capture him?"

The emotions passing over Samantha's face made it clear she'd been told a different story by Rachel. "I wasn't there," she said at last, and Lucille could've kissed her for that diplomatic answer.

"Look, I get that Rachel is upset. I would be, too, if my brother turned into a werewolf, but we're all just trying to help. And I can help." She walked over to the table and put her hands on it. "You know my powers. Put me to help." And there it was: the spell her lips had been craving.

Samantha stared at her, her eyes slightly widening. Then she lowered her gaze and dropped to her knees next to a notepad. After a few moments spent scribbling around, she jumped up again and held a type of recipe in front of Lucille's face. "Tell me whether this will work."

It wasn't what Lucille had expected, and she had to take a couple of minutes to think through the words she would have to use. "Make this page glow if it contains a potent recipe for a potion that can truly cure the werewolf infection."

The magic left her tongue and wrapped around the page. No glow.

Samantha sighed. "Well, that saved me five hours at least. Okay. New idea." And back she went to the drawing board.

They spent the entire night this way. Samantha came up with new ideas, and Lucille tested them. With every spell, as tiny as it was, Lucille felt invigorated. The hours passed, and she felt more awake than she had all night. Yes, they hadn't found anything that would help Nico so far, but they'd cut so many corners that would've ended in frustration that Lucille could sense them getting closer to the one potion that would help. As time went on, Lucille refined her spell, asking the magic to show them at which step their potion would fail, helping Samantha to limit first her selection of ingredients and then the individual steps of the potion-making.

And at 7:42 in the morning, the fifty-eighth recipe glowed with a soft golden shimmer under Lucille's spell.

Their eyes met. Samantha's had dark shadows underneath, but they were gleaming with fervour, her black locks completely out of control, and a wild grin on her face. Lucille matched that grin, joy bubbling through her like a shaken Coke bottle.

"We found it!" Samantha laughed. "Now all we need is a werewolf." She looked down at the glowing page. "And I'd better get started on this."

With twenty-eight steps, the recipe was sure to take a few hours. Or more.

Lucille put a hand on Samantha's. "I'll help." With hands and magic: whatever was needed to save Nico's life.

Nico

Nico woke to the sound of forest birds chirping somewhere above his head. Sunlight filtered through the trees, hitting the soft ground beneath him. Dew covered his body from head to toe, and he was freezing.

It was the cold and a bone-deep pain that woke him. While the forest surroundings seemed no surprise to him when he first opened his eyes, they shocked him the moment his brain caught up with the information sent by his five senses.

What was he doing in the forest? Covered in blood, dirt, and dew—and naked by the feel of it. Panting, he sat up, only to find his head jerking against a heavy chain. The silver loop around his neck wasn't tight—he could easily lift it over his head—but the presence of it upset him even further.

"What the..." Nico looked around.

The chain was linked to a big tree. Another massive tree lay only a few metres next to him, and around its trunk a makeshift shelter had been erected. In it, the three slumped-over figures of Jan, Matt, and Fabian.

What had happened? Nico was under the impression he'd drunk too much and blacked out. He had no recollection beyond his chat with Rachel early in the night. Had he gone drinking with Jan? And Matt and Fabian? No, that didn't make sense.

Nor did lying around naked in the forest.

Steps were closing in, and the smell of freshly baked rolls of bread wafted through the forest.

"Nico!" Rachel came running, dropping to her knees in front of him. Her bag of baked goods fell on the ground, and she pulled him into such a tight embrace Nico gasped.

She was so nice and warm he never wanted to let go. His teeth started chattering, and he shuddered in her arms.

Rachel was the one to break the embrace. "Gosh, you must be freezing. Wait, I got you some clothes." She opened her backpack and rummaged through it, quickly producing some underwear, jogging pants, a shirt, and a warm sweater, plus his shoes and socks. Also, a towel, which she used to rub the dirt from him. "We'll get you to Elda and you can take a nice hot shower there."

In the meantime, the boys in the shelter were starting to wake up. Matt boxed Jan on the shoulder, frowning deeply. "You fell asleep during your watch?"

Jan shrugged and yawned wildly. "Relax, man. Nico's still here."

Nico looked from them to Rachel, still unable to grasp the situation. Why would it matter that he was still here? Was he supposed to keep watch? Or were they watching *him?*

"What is going on here?" he whispered to Rachel while pulling the shirt and sweater over his head. The warmth they provided made him feel better instantly.

Meanwhile, Rachel had produced a thermos jug of freshly made coffee. "Drink this."

"Not an answer." Still, Nico took the cup and drank from it. The hot liquid ran down his throat and into his stomach, spreading its heat all the way through his body.

Rachel opened the bag of bread rolls and offered it to Nico. "You must be starving."

Surprisingly, it was true. He was starving, as if he'd run a marathon on an empty stomach. Still, Nico pushed the bag away. "Tell me what happened!"

"You don't remember anything?" she asked, biting her lip.

Rachel never bit her lip! This was bad. Very bad. Nico shook his head slowly. How could he have forgotten an entire night?

"But you remember this?" Rachel pointed at his thigh. Yesterday he'd still been wearing the bandages, but today, they were gone. On his naked leg was a massive scar that looked as if it was several months old.

"Something bit me," he said. Though the details were fuzzy, he still remembered the big black wolf. "It healed."

Rachel's shoulders sank, and she sighed. "Only on the outside."

"What's that supposed to mean?"

Now she was looking for help from the other three. Matt stepped forward, then bent a knee to get down to their level. "You were bitten by a werewolf, Nico. He turned you. Last night, you transformed into a werewolf yourself. We had to find and contain you so you wouldn't hurt anyone el—anyone."

With each word, Nico's eyes grew wider while his heart sank. "Anyone else? I hurt someone?"

Rachel avoided his gaze, but Matt nodded, his face hardening. "He might survive. The news said critical condition, but I have no idea how we'd find out more."

"Well, there's no update on the news so far," Jan added, looking up from his phone. "I might be able to ask my mum, but she takes patients' privacy pretty seriously."

Nico pulled up his pants and jumped to his feet. Without socks and shoes, the cold seeped into his feet, destroying all the progress Rachel's warm coffee had made. "You're messing with me. This is a joke. A big joke, right? Right?!"

"Nico." There were tears in Rachel's eyes.

His sweet, soft-spoken sister wouldn't play a joke on him. The others, perhaps, but not her. His head began to spin. A werewolf bite. Someone in critical condition. Waking up naked in the forest. The blood. The chain. A silver chain.

Nico's legs gave way under him, and he landed back on his butt. "This can't be true." What was he going to do? "I..." He didn't like the idea of blacking out on a full moon and hurting people, no matter how cool being a werewolf sounded otherwise. "It can be managed, right? I can learn how to control it? How not to kill anyone?"

Matt took a deep breath that didn't hail anything good. "No, you can't. As I already told everyone else, you'll lose your humanity. You'll be just as dangerous in your human skin as you'll be as a wolf. There is no cure for it. No control."

"I swear if you talk Nico into taking his own life, I'll kill you myself," Jan growled.

"You want me to take my own life?" Nico's voice failed him. This was not cool at all. "Werewolves can't just... live?"

"No, they can't," Matt said without even hesitating. He said it with compassion, but also with a finality that robbed Nico of his breath.

Rachel put a hand on his wrist, leaning in. "But *you'll* live! Samantha is already working on a potion that will heal you. She promised me."

Next to her, Matt snorted and got up to his feet. "It's not gonna work. Generations of witches, alchemists, and sorcerers have tried their hands at this. I commend her for her enthusiasm, but she'll fail just like everyone else. Don't get his hopes up."

For a stunned minute, no one spoke. Nico's throat dried out. His heart was racing in his chest, while his brain was still playing catch-up.

"Remind me to never book you as a motivational speaker," Jan growled, first to speak.

Matt clicked his tongue in annoyance. "I'm well aware that this is all bad news, but pretending it isn't doesn't help anyone. If—"

"Let's take a walk, Matt," Fabian offered, already putting his hands on Matt's shoulders and turning him around. "No, really, let's go." The two of them wandered off.

"Man, he really has no tact," Jan said, shaking his head. "You know, he—"

"Please leave," Rachel interrupted him.

Her harsh tone startled Jan, but then he snapped to attention, quickly grabbed the remains of the shelter, and followed the others. Within five minutes, Nico and Rachel were alone.

Nico was still coming to terms with the truth of his infliction—with everything, really. "I... Can I have more coffee?" If he were completely honest, he preferred a strong drink, but he'd never get that from Rachel.

"Of course." She poured him another cup, while Nico put on his socks and shoes.

As he sat on the forest floor, fully dressed, with hot coffee and a fresh roll of bread in his hand, he could almost pretend this was normal. "So... a werewolf?"

"Mmm."

"And there's no cure?"

"Yet!" Again with that forceful tone. Rachel glared at him. "Matt's wrong. Samantha will find a potion that works. Maybe not today or tomorrow, but she won't rest until she's got it. We won't let you become a monster."

A monster. According to the news, he was already a monster. Nico thought of the person he had critically injured who might still be fighting for his life or had already died. Either way, his blood was on Nico's hands.

"What should I do?"

Rachel pulled him into another embrace, and he heard her sniffling next to his ear. But then she pulled herself together and said, "Well, right now, you will eat your bread roll and drink the coffee. And then we'll go to Elda, and you'll have a nice hot shower. Small steps, Nico." The last words she whispered. "One step in front of the other."

A few hours later, Nico knew all about his affliction. He'd taken a shower and eaten, but the cold was still inside of him. His eyes gazed into nothingness as he sat on Elda's couch. He hadn't found the strength to visit Samantha in the room next door, but Lucille had told him that they'd found a working potion. By tonight, they would know whether it truly worked. If he still turned, his life was over.

"So, it was vengeance for accidentally burning this demon's office?" Nico asked Jan, picking up a random thought from earlier. His head had been filled with so much information, he still hadn't been able to process everything.

"That's what Matt claims," Jan said. He seemed to bear some grudge against their handsome friend. "We saw that demon die."

No, we didn't, Nico thought. And it would certainly fit his idea of what a demon would do. Not a direct kill but ensure they all suffered as much as they could. "You didn't get bitten?" he asked Jan.

Guilt flickered across Jan's face, and he lowered his head. "It came back for me, but... Matt killed it before it could get to me." He rolled his eyes, seemingly annoyed at how he owed Matt his life for that.

"It came to the party... drew us away." Gosh, why had he followed a giant black wolf? Nico knew the answer. His budding healing powers had made him feel invincible. And when he was hunting monsters, he'd felt alive in a way neither Jan's alcohol nor drugs could do for him.

He'd been stupid, sure. But the price! The price was way too high.

Nico's throat tightened and he gulped heavily, his eyes stinging from unshed tears. Desperate for a distraction, he wondered what else he could ask, when the door opened and Matt entered the room.

He hadn't seen the blonde since this morning in the forest. Unlike everyone else, Matt had spent the last few hours helping Samantha. Now, he was carrying an empty bowl and a dagger. "Samantha needs your blood."

Nico's eyes bulged. Next to him, Rachel grabbed his hand, threading her fingers through his. Her skin felt cold to his touch. "Why?" she asked, her voice a breathless whisper.

Matt knelt in front of him, his dark brown eyes earnest. "Apparently, she's found something." Nico wasn't sure whether he was imagining it, but he thought he heard a hint of admiration in his voice. "She needs your blood to see if it works. You know, in case it does something we don't want it to do."

"Like kill me?" Nico asked. Immediately, he felt Rachel's grip intensifying. He didn't know why he wasn't more freaked out. Not that he wasn't freaking out. It was just simply too much to handle, too much to process, to add a mental breakdown on top of it.

"Yeah, she's trying not to do that," Matt said, still going strong with his no-nonsense approach.

Rachel readjusted her grip. "This is good." She even tried for a smile. "I told you Sam would do it."

"So, can she have your blood now?" Matt asked, raising the silver dagger in his hand.

Nico tore his hand from Rachel's. "Woah, you're taking my blood like that?"

"Syringes are out. Don't worry, I'll be quick." And before Nico could protest, Matt had grabbed his wrist and sliced his arm open.

The sudden pain jolted Nico fully awake. He wanted to draw his arm away, but Matt's grip might as well have been made of stone. All he could do was watch as the dark red blood gushed from his arm into the bowl. As deep as the wound was, the blood flow didn't hold for long. The bowl wasn't even a quarter full before smooth skin covered his arm. No sign of the cut remained.

Matt clicked his tongue. "I guess that has to suffice." He let go of Nico's arm.

Anger surged inside of Nico. "Has to suffice? You want more?" He rubbed his arm, though it wasn't even itching.

"I'll check with Samantha. But it looks like the werewolf healing powers gave your own a really good boost." Matt rose to his feet without another word and carried the bowl back next door.

Instead of his arm, Nico found himself rubbing his thigh. How big had that wound been? It'd been a gory mess in the forest, but somehow he'd managed to walk home, and by the time he'd arrived there, it hadn't looked too bad. And idiot that he was, he thought it was his awesome magic powers.

"I still think he's a werewolf himself," Jan muttered, glaring at the door after it closed behind Matt.

"Cut it out," Fabian said softly. He'd barely said a word all these hours.

Jan grumbled something unintelligible and sank deeper into the cushions of the armchair.

Nico resumed staring at the ground. The news that Matt had brought should've filled him with relief. Instead, he felt the delayed panic attack rolling in. Samantha had *something,* but she still wanted to test it on his blood to see if it truly worked. Matt had claimed there was no cure, and while there was a tiny possibility that Samantha had defied the odds and made the impossible possible, in a few hours, Nico would drink a highly experimental potion. The only way to save his life. If it didn't poison him in the process.

He ran his hands over his face and inhaled sharply. How had he got himself into such an inescapable situation? His breath hitched in his throat, and he blinked, bracing himself against the tears.

"Could you give us some space?" Rachel asked. Her hand came to rest on his back, providing a thin layer of comfort.

Fabian and Jan shuffled out of the room. The moment the door closed, Nico gasped. A sob burst from his lips, and the tears quickly wet his hands. Breathing was becoming harder by the minute. There just didn't seem to be enough air for him to breathe in.

"I don't want to die," he squeezed the admission out of his mouth, then threw his arms around Rachel and held her close, all the while sobbing into her shoulder.

Rachel stroked his back and hushed him. "You're not going to die, Nico. Samantha will heal you. And if... if she fails, then I'm not letting you die either. I'll take care of you. Somehow, we'll manage it."

"Take care of me?" Nico hadn't been spared any of the details. He knew what would happen if there was no cure. He would become a monster, a terrible, human-looking but definitely not human-acting monster. And he would hurt people, just like he had last night. And if Rachel was the one to take care of him, then she'd be the one he'd hurt first.

He would sink his teeth into her skin and tear through flesh, muscle, and bone. Blood would run down his snout, delicious warm blood.

Nico blinked and pushed himself away from Rachel. It was already starting. That hadn't been a human thought. For a flash of a moment, he'd fantasised about tearing his own sister apart. "You can't!"

Rachel shook her head. "Don't tell me that. I know you and I haven't been seeing eye to eye lately, and in fact..." She swallowed, blinking back tears of her own. "Part of why I wanted to leave was so I wouldn't have to see you going down the same spiral as Mum. I couldn't bear losing you, too. I *can't* bear losing you."

Nico's heart ached. How could he not have seen how much he'd already hurt her with his antics? They'd both suffered from the same negligence. Once, they'd sworn to each other to always be there for each other, and he'd taken that promise, ripped it apart, and trampled all over it.

Shaking, he put a hand on Rachel's cheek. "I don't want to drag you down. If I..." He had to take a deep breath before he could continue speaking. "If I remain a werewolf, I want you to get on that plane and be with Dad. Make your life in LA." Wolves couldn't cross oceans. She'd be safe there.

"Never." Her lips quivered as much as his.

Nico lowered his head to lay his forehead against hers. "You need to promise me."

"I can't." She took his hands and pulled them to her stomach. "You're my brother, my twin, my second half. I will not abandon you. Never. You remember that, don't you?"

He did now. And how could he ask her to go if he wouldn't do the same in her situation? "I'm sorry."

"Don't be." Rachel shook her head, creating a little distance between them, but only so she could look into his eyes. "This isn't on you."

Nico knew better, but he wouldn't tell her that. "So, about Mum..."

"Do you want her to know? Do you want her here?" Rachel asked.

He wanted his mum. But the probability of her not showing was far too high. The last thing he needed today was to find out that his mother literally didn't care whether he lived or died. "No. Not now. If it doesn't work... maybe." He would tell her eventually, if only to protect Rachel from any accusations. "But it will work, right?"

Rachel leaned into him, taking a shuddering breath. "It will."

There was a knock on the door, and Fabian put his head in. "Hey, I'm sorry to interrupt. You told us to get out, but Sam ran the tests." A hopeful smile slipped on his face. "It looks like we've got a cure."

Rachel took an earth-shattering breath. She even laughed. "See. I told you."

Nico wasn't that certain. It just seemed too good to be true. "So, what happens now?"

"Uhm, they want you to take it shortly before nightfall to see if it works. That way, if anything goes wrong, we'll notice it right away," Fabian explained. "Elda is preparing a magic circle outside to... well, to keep you from running off into the forest if it doesn't work."

Right, because then he'd start going after his friends again. Drink the potion and enjoy the side effects or turn into a werewolf and kill everyone. Nico knew which one he was going to choose.

"Let's do this."

Samantha

A magic circle of purple aconite flowers had appeared in front of the house. Her grandmother must've grown it all day to be perfectly round. If Nico turned into a werewolf, it would impede him.

Despite Lucille's truth-seeking spells, Samantha wasn't as confident as she would've liked to be in her potion. It had a lighter-violet colour, with swirls of gold flickering through the liquid. The most complicated potion she'd ever brewed. And an untested one.

The tests with Nico's blood had been encouraging. As soon as the potion had touched the blood samples, they had cleared, leaving behind perfectly human blood. It was working on paper. It was working in test tubes. But only time would tell if it would work on Nico.

The sun had already vanished behind the trees, though night hadn't quite fallen yet. Thirteen minutes, her clock told her. Thirteen minutes and she would know whether her almost twenty-four hours of potion-making had been worth anything.

The door opened behind her, and Nico and the others stepped out. Nico gave Rachel a long hug, whispering into her ear.

Meanwhile, Matt came to Samantha, a grim expression on his face. "It's almost time," he said, throwing a glance at Nico. "He must feel the draw of transformation."

"Let him say goodbye," she said gently. Not that she thought he needed to say goodbye. At least she hoped so.

"He needs to be in the magic circle," Matt grumbled.

When he'd come back from the forest, he'd slipped into her potion room under the guise of helping her. All he really wanted to do was rant about how blind the others were to the dangers surrounding Nico's transformation. Part of her understood where Matt was coming from, but Nico was their friend. It hit differently when the supposed monster was a friend.

Matt had listened, but Samantha doubted he'd accepted the explanation. Not judging by the frequent looks towards the sky. "Nico," he said when only six minutes remained.

Nico pulled himself away from Rachel and came over. Samantha saw him flinch as he saw the flowers. The wolf inside of him didn't like them. Instead of stepping in, he turned to Matt, and the two of them locked eyes. "I want you to promise me something, Matt," he said in a low voice that only Samantha and Matt could hear. "If this doesn't work and that circle isn't enough to hold me back," he took a deep breath, "I want you to make sure I won't hurt anybody." He swallowed. "I don't want to become a monster."

Matt didn't say anything dismissive, nor did he protest. He only nodded, his face even grimmer than before. "You've got my word."

"Good. Because I really... Thank you."

Samantha's throat tightened. She wasn't stupid. She knew what Nico had asked of Matt, the only one he could trust to follow through with such an enormous request. Still, it was a big thing to ask, and she had no idea how Matt would cope with it if he actually had to do it.

Nico turned to her. "Alright, let's see if you're really as brilliant as everyone says."

Samantha handed him the potion with a tortured grimace. "No promises."

"No complaints," Nico answered with a smile that didn't seem to fit such dire circumstances. Then he stepped into the magic circle, wincing visibly at the touch of the flowers.

Elda had come out as well, putting her hands on Samantha's shoulder, while Rachel had fled into Fabian's arms. "You did all you could," she whispered.

"Two minutes until sundown," Matt informed Nico.

Nico nodded. He took a deep breath, his eyes searching Rachel once more. Then he put the potion to his lips and drank it in one big gulp.

One minute. The waning moon already hung in the sky.

Inside the magic circle, Nico walked a few steps, increasingly reckless. He kept massaging his left thigh.

Nightfall.

Nico should be turning now. His face twitched, and he moaned. Matt drew his sword as quietly as possible, but Nico's features stayed the same. No fur, no elongation of nose and mouth, no growing of his teeth. He was in pain, grimacing and punching his leg now, but he wasn't transforming.

Just then, Samantha lowered her eyes to the thigh he kept digging his fingers into. A dark stain coloured his pants. A fast-extending dark stain.

"Nico!"

Panic filled her. Without thinking, she escaped her grandmother's hands and crossed into the magic circle.

"Sam!" Matt shouted, his voice echoing her panic.

She reached Nico the moment he staggered. His leg gave way under him, and he stumbled into her arms. Not prepared to hold him, they both went down. "It hurts," Nico panted. "Oh god, it hurts so much."

A fairy light sprung to life next to Samantha, her grandmother's magic. The spell provided just enough light for Samantha to see the blood seeping through Nico's pants. "It's your bite. It's his leg!" she shouted, pressing her hands against the wound.

When the potion had done its magic in Nico's body, it had reverted the werewolf's powers. Now the bite that had never truly healed opened again.

Within seconds, her fingers were slick with blood. Though they were shaking, she managed to open Nico's pants and drag them down enough to expose the bloody mess. The flesh was torn so deep Samantha saw the white of the bone gleaming in the fairy light. She whimpered and pressed her hands back on the wound.

"Someone call—"

Suddenly, Matt was there next to her, pushing his shirt into her hands. "Elda's already calling an ambulance."

Samantha took the shirt to cover a bigger area. "Hold on, Nico. We've got you."

Nico mumbled something, his eyelids fluttering.

Samantha wiped her forehead, not caring that she got blood on it. Her muscles were already screaming, but she wouldn't give in to them. This was her fault. This was her potion's doing. If not... She couldn't think about that now!

Instead, she pressed as hard as possible against the wound. The T-shirt was already soaked with blood. Matt had moved to Nico's head and cradled his face, holding eye contact with him. "Stay with us, Nico. Come on, you've got healing powers, too. You don't need that werewolf."

Someone handed Samantha fresh linen. Someone else spoke, but she didn't hear them. All she heard was the rush of her own blood in her ears and the sharp breaths in her lungs. If the wound showed any signs of healing, she didn't see them.

"Sam."

She kept pressing the linens into Nico's leg.

"Sam!"

Matt. She glanced at him, her own chest heaving with exhaustion. "I don't have a pulse."

The words made no sense. She had a pulse down here. The blood... no, it wasn't pulsing, it was just flowing from the wound. And Nico was lying there, his eyes closed.

"That can't be." She let go of the blood-soaked linens and slid over to Matt, pressing her finger against Nico's neck.

Nothing.

This couldn't be happening. He should be transformed. Or poisoned. Or healed. Not bleeding. Not dying.

Without further ado, Samantha moved to his chest, pressing her palms on top of each other and into Nico's ribcage. Her arms were already hurting from the previous exertion. Now they were burning like fire. She felt light-headed, the lack of sleep finally catching up to her. But she couldn't let it do that. Couldn't let Nico die.

Blood gushed out of his leg with every compression she did. "Someone needs to stop the blood flow," she shouted. "Why is nobody stopping it?" Her voice broke, drowning in tears.

She didn't understand why Matt just sat there, watching her with sorrow marring his face. Where was her grandmother? Where was Rachel?

A siren rang further down the forest road, and Samantha gasped for air. Help was coming. The blue and red light shone through the trees.

"Sam." Matt's voice was quiet. He put a hand on her arm. "The first responders are here."

She ignored him and kept pumping Nico's chest. If only her arms weren't hurting so much. And air. She needed more air. No, Nico needed air.

"Sam." Now, Matt's hands held both her arms. He was gripping her, pulling her away from Nico. "Let it go."

"No! Let me..."

"Sam!" Matt dragged her away, out of the magic circle.

The flowers were no longer there, purple petals scattered all over the ground, splattered with blood. So much blood. On her. On the ground. On Nico. Too much blood.

A first responder had taken her spot, but instead of compressions, he was only quickly checking on Nico. Why wasn't he helping him? Samantha tried to tear herself from Matt's grip, but he wouldn't let her. Instead, he pressed her against his naked chest, one arm around her back, the other hand braced against her head.

"You did all you could."

"I..." She wanted to tell him that there was more she could do. That she *needed* to do, but the finality in his voice finally cut through her daze. There was nothing more she could do. Nothing more anyone could do.

And with that thought, Samantha burst into tears.

Part 5

Magic & Demons

Rachel

Fabian: How are you today? the text read.

Always the same, first thing in the morning. Ever since Nico's death, Fabian checked in with her. It had been three days, but he wasn't giving up. He texted in the morning, texted from school, and called in the evenings.

Under normal circumstances, Rachel would've been over the moon, but how was she now? She couldn't tell. Nico was dead. And she... she felt nothing at all.

The moment Samantha had dashed into the magic circle and they'd both gone down, blood spreading through Samantha's fingers, Rachel had stopped feeling. She hadn't been able to move or speak. Everyone else had been in a flurry of activity: phone calls, linens, first aid. At one point, Fabian had wrapped his arms around her and held her.

And then Nico was dead. Just like that. Without another word. Without another look. The promise was broken, and she was alone.

No, not alone. Her friends were there for her. Fabian wasn't the only one checking in. Lucille had sent flowers, and Jan had sent her an awkward text to tell her that he would do whatever she needed from him. Rachel had no idea what she could need him for. But she thanked him, and she thanked Lucille, and she texted Fabian back that she was doing okay, all things considered. And when they talked, she even told him the truth.

The only calls she couldn't take were Samantha's. Samantha who'd given Nico the potion. Samantha who'd been covered in Nico's blood from head to toe after trying to save his life, while Rachel had just stood by.

Not that she blamed her. Not really, at least, but whenever Samantha's name flashed up on her phone, she was back in Elda's front yard, staring at Nico's bloodied corpse. Rachel was afraid that when she took that call, she'd start feeling again. That all the pain and grief would come crashing over her like two waves determined to drag her under.

She couldn't talk to Samantha. Not yet; at least, not until she knew she would survive it.

"I'm okay," she wrote back to Fabian. He would be getting ready for school now after feeding the chickens and his cute little cat.

The reply came within seconds despite it. "You don't have to be okay."

Rachel smiled. He didn't tell her that she wasn't okay. They both knew she wasn't. But he gave her permission to fall apart. If only she could allow herself to do that. "I know," she texted back.

Another ping. "Merle got into my colour pots. What a mess!" A couple of photos that must've happened last night were attached. They weren't of the mess but of a colourful, blotchy Merle looking awfully cute.

The pictures made Rachel laugh. As soon as the sound bubbled from her lips, she gasped. How could the first emotion she showed after Nico's death be amusement? Where were the tears? Where was... But she didn't want to cry. She wanted to look at silly cat pictures and... and not think about Nico's violent death.

"Maybe she's an artist too?" she wrote back.

The reply took a little time, but it came with another set of pictures: paper streaked with colour, the occasional paw shape between the blotches. "How much do you think they'll go for?"

For a couple of minutes, she texted back and forth with Fabian, planning Greenvalley's first-ever cat art show. Rachel laughed a little more, her chest expanding as fresh air filled her senses.

"Do you want to come over and appraise them in person today?" Fabian texted. "Or I could come and bring Merle with me. She'll probably scratch my eyes out for putting her in the box, but she does that anyway."

When Rachel smiled this time, she was filled with sadness. Could she handle meeting anyone in person? "Maybe."

"Let me know. Got to go."

"Give everyone my best." She hadn't been at school since.

When the phone was silent, the heaviness returned like a weighted blanket around her shoulders. At one point, she would have to go back to school, but how could she? How could she just keep on living her life when her brother was dead? Gone forever?

Just then, Rachel heard sounds from his room. Could that be...? She knew better than to hope he was alive. But what if he was a ghost? Nico would do that. He would keep his promise to never abandon each other—that was the deal.

Her heart thumping in her chest, Rachel walked into the room next door and stopped cold. "Mum?"

Her mother was standing in front of Nico's cupboard. She had one of his sweaters in front of her, sighed, and folded it into a box. A box!

"Are you out of your mind?"

Her mother turned to her in surprise. She hadn't heard her first question. "Rachel. You... Do you need something?"

"Do I need something? I need you to stop whatever you're doing there!" It wasn't the only box in the room. Her mother had managed to find four large moving boxes. And she was filling them with Nico's stuff.

Rachel strode into the room, grabbed the box from out of her mum's hands, and upended it. "You're already packing up what's left of him?"

Her mother only stared at her. She opened her mouth and closed it again. Rachel saw that her eyes were reddened, surrounded by dark shadows, but that was nothing unusual. Her mother always looked like that after a night spent with the wine bottle.

"You don't get to touch his things," Rachel told her as she knelt down and started gathering the clothes in her arms.

"Rachel—"

"He wouldn't want you to!"

Again, her mother stared. She swallowed a couple of times. "Okay. Whatever you say."

But Rachel wasn't finished yet. Suddenly, she had a lot to say, years of unsaid words. "Nico hated you. You never cared about him while he was still alive, so don't pretend you care now."

"Rachel, I—"

"And you don't care about me either. But that's fine because you're not exactly topping my list of people to care about either. In fact, you're at the very bottom." Each of the words she spoke cut through her chest like a knife. It was pain, but it was good pain. Freeing pain. "Yes, that means I hate you, too. And this," she pointed at the boxes, "proves it. What kind of mother packs up her child's life three days after his death?"

There was no reply. Her mother just kept staring, her eyes hollow from a lack of emotion. She might be hurting—a little—but Rachel was sure it was nothing that a bottle of wine couldn't fix. In fact, she suggested just that. "Why don't you go and drown whatever remorse you're feeling right now in alcohol?"

She would've said more, but at that point, the doorbell rang. Leaving her mother alone with her stupid boxes, Rachel went downstairs and opened the door. "What—?"

The word got stuck in her throat. A suitcase next to him, the visitor smiled at her. "Hey, Sweetie."

"Dad!" And as Rachel fell around his neck, all the feelings she'd suppressed came pouring out of her. Tears fell, quickly soaking his tweed jacket, and she blubbered on about Nico, and blood and death.

She was falling apart in the safety of her father's arms. The only place she truly wanted to be right now.

Samantha

The sun was sinking behind the tree line, the pale moon already in the sky. It was waning now, losing shape quickly. In a week, it would be gone, only to reappear. Samantha kept watching it for hours on end until her eyes hurt and she was tired enough to fall asleep the moment her head hit the pillow.

When the moon wasn't in the sky, she watched the trees. Occasionally, she would grab her phone and call Rachel, but she could only bear to hear it ring three times before she had to stop. Rachel wasn't speaking to her, and for good reason. She wouldn't speak to herself either. In fact, she hadn't really spoken to anyone.

Her grandmother had explained the situation to her parents, not mentioning the werewolf, her potion, or the fact she'd murdered one of her friends. They'd come immediately, showering her with worries, but what was she supposed to tell them? That she'd killed someone?

Life at her grandmother's was easy. Elda didn't encroach on her. She checked on her in the morning, in the early afternoon, and in the evening before she went to bed. Each time, she offered food, and Samantha took her up on most of the offers. The food sustained her, but it tasted like sand and ash.

Other than eating and watching the trees and the moon, Samantha did exactly nothing. No school, no homework, no reading, and certainly no potion-making.

The police assumed Nico's death was due to the same animal attack they'd had to deal with the prior day. Nico's victim had survived. Nico had not.

Her phone buzzed with a text from Fabian, and Samantha turned it face-down before reading half of it. Fabian wanted to talk and comfort her, but she couldn't bear that. She didn't need to be comforted. She should be tried for murder or manslaughter. Nico's death was her fault, and all those well-meaning attempts to comfort her felt like Band-Aids on flesh wounds.

The phone kept buzzing a couple of times, but she ignored them all. Finally, it stopped. She knew that Fabian was talking to Rachel—she'd read that in a text once—and that was exactly what he should be doing. Comfort the victim in this scenario, not the murderer.

When her grandmother knocked on the door, it was still a little until dinner. "Darling, Matt is here."

Matt? What was Matt doing here? Fabian, she understood, but Matt? With his pragmatism, he should be out enjoying life at school, finding a new date or a new monster to hunt. Maybe he'd been sent by the group to deliver a message or something. He'd be the only one who'd accept it with nothing but a shrug of his shoulders.

Unable to look at him, she heard him step into the room and pull a chair to the window where she was sitting. "Hey."

Red sunlight coloured the treetops, drenching them in blood. Shuddering, Samantha turned her eyes away and inadvertently settled on Matt.

He looked gorgeous as always. No sign of lack of sleep or a guilty conscience. Her mouth opened, but the answering "hey" never voiced itself.

"You haven't been at school," Matt stated. His eyes were searching her face. She had no idea what he found there, but he frowned in response. "You're not blaming yourself, are you?"

The corners of her mouth twitched in a sarcastic snarl. "It *is* my fault."

"No, it's not."

Samantha took a deep breath, half-rolling her eyes. So, he'd come to tell her how it wasn't her fault. That it was an accident. A cruel act of nature. A mishap. Matt opened his mouth, and she stopped him right there. "Before you start what is probably a really nice speech, the fact is that Nico would be alive if not for my potion. So, let's keep to the facts."

One side of his mouth lifted in amusement. What could possibly be amusing him about this situation? "Sticking to the facts, hmm? Okay, well, what you just said is not a fact. If you hadn't given Nico the potion, he would've turned into a werewolf. He would've escaped, and I would've killed him. Still dead."

His crudeness made her wince. "How can you be so casual about it?"

Matt sighed. To her surprise, he took her limp left hand into his. "Listen. I know I'm not very good at the emotional stuff. I get things done. I just don't see the point in fretting about things that can't be changed. On Sunday, you showed me the point."

"What?" Samantha was unable to follow him. Showed him the point in fretting?

Another deep breath. This wasn't as easy for him as Samantha had thought. "I thought that nothing could save Nico. I was taught that the werewolf curse was incurable. And if it had been up to me, I would've put Nico out of his misery. It would've been a shame, but it couldn't be changed. But you." He began drawing a line from her palm to her wrist. "You changed it. You refused to accept his fate, and you turned it around. You found the cure."

Samantha pulled her hand away and moaned. "I didn't cure him."

"Yes, you did." Matt didn't insist on taking her hand again, but he leaned forward and made it impossible for her to look away. "Nico died human. He didn't turn. His blood showed no abnormality. The werewolf curse had completely lifted. So, yes, you cured him."

"But he's still dead!" Samantha insisted, her eyes burning with the weight of the emotion she was keeping in.

Matt nodded. "And that's a fact. But here's another. The reason Nico is dead is that when you healed him, the wound held together by his werewolf powers turned human, just like the rest of him. He should've died Friday night when a giant wolf ripped his thigh apart. You didn't kill him; the werewolf did."

Samantha stared at him, unblinking. She hadn't wanted anyone's compassion, only the facts, and here was a fact she couldn't refute.

Only... "If we had waited, the wound might've healed naturally. In a few months, my potion would've cured and saved him."

"In a few months, Nico would've been living a miserable life locked up in a cell, scratching the walls each night until his fingers bled. Or he would've got out and killed someone. I know you can't see this now because on Sunday, Nico was healthy and sane, but that doesn't last. He was only a baby in werewolf terms. In a few months, there would've been nothing human to return to."

He took her hand again, grabbing it firmer. "You did something that generations of witches and alchemists have been unable to do. You created a werewolf cure in a single night. Can't you see how amazing that is?"

"How is that amazing?" Samantha cried, unable to hold back the tears any longer. "Whether I cured him or not is irrelevant. He's dead! Dead!"

With a swift movement, Matt was on the bench with her and had pulled her close. With one hand on her head, he stroked her back. "I know. I'm sorry."

He held her like he'd done the night Nico died. And somehow, it was okay. It wasn't gentle like Fabian's embrace would've been, and he didn't shower her with worried looks like her parents would. As sparse as his compassion seemed, it was the only amount Samantha could handle right now. She knew for certain that if she cried or told him all the dark details, he would keep holding her instead of falling apart himself. His stability allowed her to choose how much emotion she could handle.

"You saved him from becoming a monster," Matt whispered.

Samantha shuddered. She remembered how just before his death Nico had asked Matt to kill him if things went wrong. He hadn't wanted to live as a monster. "At least he would've lived," she cried. That would've been a good thing, wouldn't it?

"Sometimes life is worse than death."

New tears streamed down her cheeks and into Matt's shirt. The sobs shook her to the core, and she dug her fingers into his shirt. "It's not fair." How could it be fair that a seventeen-year-old boy just died one day? That within minutes, he went from young and healthy to dead?

Matt pressed her even closer, wrapped both his arms around her, and rested his chin on her head. "No, it's not fair. But the fact is, things like this happen. We go up against dangerous monsters and foes, and we won't win every time. We'll try our best, and we'll keep trying as long as there's still breath in our lungs. But we're not invincible, and we won't be able to save everyone."

"How...?" She pounded a hand against his chest, gasping for air. "How can you be so okay with it?"

That paused him. Once again, he searched her tear-streaked face, then ran a hand through her hair. "Because you showed me that whatever the odds, sometimes we make it. We still win. Even if all hope is lost."

Samantha drank the words from his lips, breathed them in, and anchored them in her brain. It wasn't a fact, but it was close enough.

Rachel

The funeral was on Friday morning. Apart from Rachel and her parents, only her friends and Svenja had come to the small cemetery southwest of town. In a few days, it would be her birthday. She would turn eighteen, but there would be no big party, not even a small one. How could she celebrate such a milestone when her twin brother would never turn eighteen?

The thought tightened her throat. So little time until she would be older than he'd ever be. She'd be an adult, while he would always stay a child.

It wasn't fair. None of this was. Last night, Jan had confided in her about the demon they'd both angered. But only Nico was dead, while Jan was fine. And as much as Rachel hated herself for it, that was the greatest injustice of all.

The reasonable part of her was well aware that it had been Nico's choice to hang out with a lout like Jan, to go drinking and smoking, and perhaps even try out drugs. But the unreasonable, emotional part blamed Jan for dragging her brother down to his level. However, as she saw him standing on the other side, eyes staring at the deep hole, she couldn't feel the same animosity. Yes, Jan was an idiot, but apparently, so had been Nico.

Rachel blamed her brother, too, even though he was dead. They'd always been together through all the heartbreak and family drama, and now they were not. But she also had to admit that they hadn't been for a while. Nico had chosen Jan to vent about their mother and everything else that bothered him. Such as that Svenja had broken up with him, something she'd only learnt when she took on the difficult job of informing her about his death. Nico had never even told her. For weeks, he'd been distancing himself from her, and now the bond between them had been severed.

But the person she really blamed wasn't present. Without their actions and their decisions, Nico would still be alive, possibly doing some other stupid thing, but he'd be alive. Her eyes searched for Samantha, accompanied by her grandmother. Rachel had heard from Fabian that the guilt was eating her alive, and that only added to Rachel's anger.

It was the demon she blamed. The demon she'd never even seen but who apparently thought Nico and Jan were annoying enough to retaliate against. If only they'd really burnt him, but even Jan admitted that it hadn't looked like it, and Matt had confirmed that demons were able to "jump through space", as he called it. The demon had been unharmed, and yet he'd found it necessary to not just go after the teenagers that had annoyed him but make sure they—or at least Nico—would die in the most traumatising way possible.

He'd begged Matt to kill him! Rachel felt the anger rise in her that her brother had been driven to the point where he would rather be dead than suffer the fate the demon had in store for him.

That was the person she was angry at. The only person who was truly to blame for Nico's death. And it grated on her that Nico was buried as the victim of a horrifying animal attack rather than the murder victim he was. And his murderer was still out there, potentially still in Greenvalley, where he was free to murder more children. And no one was even out looking for him.

Her father bumped her gently with his elbow, startling Rachel. Apparently, everyone was waiting for her to do something. She hadn't listened to the official's formal words; his speech was meaningless to her, just like all the others. Thankfully, her mother hadn't got up. She'd wanted to, but Rachel had made it very clear that she did *not* want her to speak about a son she'd never cared for. Instead, her father had done the job, though from the snippets she remembered from the speech, he barely knew the teenager Nico had become.

And now it was time to step up to the grave and say goodbye. Her father gently pointed to the plate of soil that stood ready for them. "Go ahead, Bug. Take all the time you need."

Time for what? To stare at a casket in the cold ground? Two handfuls of soil already covered the rich mahogany wood. Her father's and her mother's goodbyes.

Rachel dug her hand into the soil. It was slightly damp and stuck to her fingers. Once again, she looked at the casket as if she could see through the wood. But Nico wasn't there. His spirit had already moved on, not even leaving his ghost behind.

There were no words of goodbye in her mind. The grief was gone; only anger ruled. And it was that anger that came to her lips. "I will avenge you," she promised the dead wood quietly, then let her handful of soil rain down on it.

When the last crumb had fallen, Rachel stepped back, immediately pulled into an embrace by her father. Together, they stepped aside so the others could say their goodbyes. Once they were done, they gathered in little groups, talking quietly, or exchanging sorrowful looks.

The only one who had nobody around her was her mother. She stood there in the light drizzle and still stared at the hole, as if unable to grasp how one of her children had ended up in there. She probably only realised now how much she'd failed her child, Rachel thought unkindly.

Her mother had had a lot of chances, many more than she deserved, and she'd taken none of them. Other families might be brought together by such a tragedy, but for Rachel, her mother was another one who deserved nothing but blame. In her eyes, her mother's actions, or rather non-actions, had driven Nico into Jan's arms and from there to his ruin. So, the last thing Rachel considered doing was going over to comfort her.

Samantha was one of the last to step up to Nico's grave. Tears streamed down her face as she grabbed a handful of soil. Rachel knew what her words would be, even if she couldn't hear them: *I'm so sorry.*

Samantha turned away from the grave, still sobbing, and rubbed her eyes. When Fabian approached her and opened his arms, she quickly shook her head and stepped aside to stand next to Matt. The two of them didn't exchange so much as a look, but Matt's hand slipped into hers, and as she held Matt's hand, Samantha took a shuddering breath.

Rachel let go of her father. "I'll be back in a minute." Then she walked over to Samantha, whose eyes widened, clearly afraid that Rachel would guilt-trip her right there in front of Nico's grave.

She had no such intention. Instead, Rachel opened her arms and pulled Samantha into a hug before she could back away. Samantha stiffened in her embrace and gasped for air.

"You tried to save him, Sam," Rachel whispered. "I'm sorry I haven't thanked you yet."

"Thanked me?" Samantha's voice was brittle, on the very edge of breaking apart.

Rachel pulled back enough to look into her eyes. "Yes, thanked you. What you did for him was more than I could've asked for. Don't ever think I'm not grateful for what you did. Even if it didn't work in the end."

"But I..." Tears still shimmered in Samantha's eyes.

Rachel smiled at her sadly. "You tried. I won't forget that."

The tears spilled from Samantha's eyes, and she swallowed a sob a second before she pulled Rachel close and hugged her fiercely. "I'm so sorry, Rachel."

"Me too," Rachel answered. "Me too."

At home, she found her father packing. He'd been sleeping on the couch for the last few days, but now it seemed like he was done with that.

"You're flying back home?" Rachel asked, trying her hardest not to let her emotions slip into her voice.

Her father looked up, grief etched into his face. "Your mother doesn't want me here, and I... I need to be back at school. I've got a PhD candidate defending her thesis and—"

"It's alright." She didn't want to hear his excuses. She knew that he'd come spontaneously. His real trip had been planned for the next week for their birthdays.

For a moment, he stood there with his stuff forgotten in his hand. Then he blinked and drew a deep breath. "Look, Rachel. I remember we talked about you moving home... I mean to LA. If you want to, I'm happy to sort it all. I can get you into school. I've got a room for you, or two, if you want them. We can do this."

Behind him, her mother was staring at them from the kitchen pass-through. Rachel had never talked to her about it.

A week ago, she'd been happy to accept. Not because she wanted to leave her friends, but because she couldn't stand living with her mother anymore. It seemed a logical step. A new life, far away from all the heartbreak. Now more than ever.

She wasn't happy here. By right, Nico's death should cement that. No one would blame her for taking up her father's offer—apart from her mother, apparently.

But if she left, she would never get her revenge on that demon. Worse, he might kill one of her friends or all of them as they inevitably crossed his path again. Was she able to aid them with her dreams and ghosts? Probably not a lot, but Rachel would be damned if she didn't at least try.

"I can't," she told her father. "I'm needed here."

From the kitchen came a sigh of relief, and Rachel hated to think her mother believed she was the one who needed her. It couldn't be helped. If she stayed here, she would have to endure her mother. And who knew? Perhaps things would improve a little after that wake-up call her mother had received.

Her father smiled sadly but nodded. "I thought so. But if you ever want to come for a visit, I'm happy to have you anytime. I'll pay for the tickets and everything."

"I will," she said, then went over to hug him tight. "Thanks, Dad."

He stroked her hair and kissed her on the forehead. "Anytime, sweetie. Anytime. Oh!" He pulled away suddenly and dug something out of his bag. Two presents, wrapped in colourful paper.

Her father looked thoughtfully at them, as if he couldn't quite bear parting with them. "These were for your birthday."

Rachel understood. One of them was for her, the other for her brother.

He offered them both to her. "I don't know what to do with Nico's. Do you—"

She grabbed them. "I'll take it." Her brother might not be able to enjoy it, but she could have a little part of him with her. "Thank you."

"Come here, Sweetie," her father said, and pulled her into another hug.

Rachel wrapped her arms around him and sighed into his chest. She would miss having him around. The house would be much colder without both her father and brother.

Fabian

After returning from the funeral, Fabian spent an hour cleaning out the chicken enclosure, just so he could surround himself with their lively pecking. Merle was sneaking around the fence, always looking for a way in. When he'd finally finished, he had to use his foot to make sure the cat stayed outside where she belonged.

"If you're hungry, go to the kitchen." Despite his words, Fabian bent down and picked the cat up to scratch the back of her head.

Merle purred and allowed him to take her away from her prey. Together, they went back inside. The cat jumped off his arm before they'd even reached the kitchen, obviously not truly hungry. Fabian still went there anyway to wash his hands.

His mother was cutting vegetables and gave him a once-over. "You mucked out the chicken barn in your good shirt?"

Fabian lowered his eyes, noting the stains of sweat and dirt on the black shirt he'd worn for Nico's funeral. "Sorry."

His mother stopped her work and walked over to cup his cheek. "It's alright, darling. How are you feeling?"

It was a question he wasn't sure how to answer. How did one feel when their best friend died? Life continued, but now there was no Nico inside it. The seat next to him in Politics and German stayed empty, and there were no more infrequent messages with silly memes or random thoughts on his phone.

He shrugged. "I don't know."

His mother gave him a sympathetic nod. "It's hard. If you ever want to talk about it, you come to me, okay?"

Fabian nodded, his eyes gliding over the vegetables. "Can I have some crackers?" Dinner still looked an hour away.

With a snort, his mother opened the cupboard and pushed a box into his chest. "Knock yourself out."

"Thanks." He was just about to go upstairs to his room when he heard the doorbell. "I'll get it."

Merle was already at the door, meowing softly, and he picked her up again before opening the door. In front of it stood Samantha. She'd changed out of the dark blue dress she'd worn at the funeral into a more casual outfit, but her eyes and cheeks were still puffy and red. A helpless little smile slipped onto her lips. "Hey."

Fabian's heart went out to her, and he pulled her into a hug. "Hey!" He'd missed her so very much this last week. Her continued silence had hurt him on top of all the grief. He understood that she'd needed time to get over what had happened, but he'd wanted to be there for her, just like he'd been there for Rachel.

Finally, he let go of her. "Come in. I've got crackers." He lifted the box, drawing out a small chuckle.

A minute later, they were in his room, sitting on the bed. Samantha had Merle on her lap and held her a little closer than the cat normally preferred, but as usual, the animal was partial to Samantha and endured such treatment. She would've scratched Fabian's eyes out if he'd ever tried to do the same.

"How are you?" he asked, realising instantly that he'd just failed to answer that question for his mother.

"A little better," Samantha admitted. "I still feel like it was my fault, but both Matt and Rachel, and of course, my grandmother have said it wasn't, so I guess I need to start believing them."

Fabian remembered how she'd turned away from him at the funeral and sought solace in Matt's arms instead. He ignored the sting of that image and said, "Well, for what it's worth, I'm also convinced that you're not to blame."

Again, she smiled, though the sadness in her eyes remained. "Thank you." With a deep breath, she let go of Merle and pulled up her legs so she could turn to him. "I'm sorry I ignored you."

"That's fine," Fabian said, even though it hadn't been fine at all. "You needed space." But apparently not from Matt.

"Yeah." Another heavy sigh. "I didn't mean to. It was just too... too hard."

Fabian had no idea why it would be hard to seek comfort from one's best friend, but he just kept nodding. "Don't think about it. You're here now."

This time, her smile lit up her entire face. "I am. I figured I owed you an apology. And also, crackers!"

The little eye roll Samantha did to accompany the last word made Fabian laugh. He grabbed the box from the bedside table and opened it. His mother would complain about the crumbs, but Fabian figured if he just shook out his blanket, he'd be fine.

Together, they nibbled on the crackers and talked about unimportant things, like what she'd missed at school. Naturally, Nico's death had also made waves there. The entire class was down, and the teachers were more lenient than they'd ever been. Even Mr Harold had refrained from making his life miserable this week.

When the topic of homework had been exhausted, Samantha looked around the room. Her eyes came to rest on the blue feather lying on his desk. "I heard you used the feather to..." She couldn't end the sentence.

Neither could Fabian, but he got up and carried the feather over to her. "You were right. It is that bird's feather. Whatever his name was."

"Shitaten." Samantha looked at the feather but didn't reach out to touch it.

"Shitaten, right. Well, it's pretty powerful. I mean, the things only last for an hour, but they become real." The ability to turn drawings into life still amazed him.

Samantha nodded. "Have you tried controlling the wind with it?"

Fabian vaguely remembered there being a second power to it. He shook his head. "Water is bad enough." He truly didn't need another potentially devastating element to mess up his life.

He took a deep breath and pushed the feather towards Samantha. "If you still want the feather, it's yours." What he was about to tell her was not going to be well-received, but he had a week to think about it and was sure of it. "I'm done with magic."

Before she could protest, Fabian continued, "I mean it. We were in way over our heads. There are powers that... we can neither control nor fight, and..." He swallowed, his throat suddenly tight. "One death is enough." It should have never got that far in the first place.

To his surprise, Samantha nodded. "I'm with you." She put her hand on his, ignoring the feather. "No more magic."

"What?" he asked, caught by surprise. Embarrassed, Fabian cleared his throat. "No more magic?"

"You were right," Samantha said with a one-sided shrug. "The whole time, you were right. It is too dangerous. Meddling with magic, fighting monsters... it's not something a bunch of children should do. I should've never insisted on it."

"But..." She'd left him speechless.

"I love magic?" she asked, suddenly full of energy. "I don't even understand magic. I can't do magic and I never will. This dabbling in potions that I've done? Well, it just cost Nico his life."

This was wrong. Samantha hadn't dabbled in potions. She'd done the impossible. "You developed a working werewolf cure."

She held up a finger and waggled it. "No, I developed a potion that would turn a werewolf back into a human and reopen the wounds that would have otherwise healed."

So much for starting to believe it wasn't her fault. Fabian let go of the feather and turned his hand around so he could grab Samantha's. "You know that's rubbish, right?"

"It's not." She shook her head. "I checked it several times yesterday. The wounds only heal with werewolf powers. There is no natural healing process happening. It's magic. So, unless you have an amazingly competent healer on standby, my potion cures and kills them at the same time. It's useless."

Fabian wanted to protest, but he couldn't think of a good argument. He had no idea about werewolf lore or potion-making. He only knew that it wasn't her fault, but he couldn't deny that magic had killed Nico. "So, no more magic?"

Samantha pushed the feather away. "No more magic."

Samantha's promise should've filled him with relief, but Fabian found it hard to find any. On Monday, she came back to school—as did Rachel—and the entire day, she never mentioned magic once. There was no spell book in her bag, and no new artefact she'd picked up from the Magic Circle.

He knew he should be glad. His biggest wish had come true. No more magic meant no more monsters. And that meant nobody would get hurt or killed. But Samantha without magic was somehow wrong.

There was just something missing, like a spring in her step or a spark in her eyes. The new magic-less Samantha was all about school, her mind singularly focused on catching up on the week she'd missed and preparing for the exams that had been pushed out a *little* but not far enough for Fabian's liking.

When there was no more homework to do, she revised and started writing learning cards for the Abitur. The high school examinations wouldn't happen until the second semester of their next year of school, more than eighteen months away. If she continued like this, by then Samantha's pile of cards would be as high as the classrooms.

Fabian wasn't sure what to do. On one hand, he was glad he no longer had to worry about getting killed by some nightmare monster. On the other, just because he no longer wanted to deal with magic, it didn't mean the magic itself had left him. The water was still inside him. Contrary to Samantha, he would never be able to fully turn his back on his magic.

He could feel the water running through the pipes near the cafeteria or the bubbles rising in the water bottles of his fellow students. Sometimes, it reacted with his emotions. The flowers and vegetables around his home would've enjoyed the irrigation his grief had caused if it weren't already a cold and damp November.

Now that his emotions had settled a little, Fabian still found himself raising and lowering the water of his bottle, as if his powers were as bored as he was. He knew he should invest in his schoolwork as much as Samantha—or at least a little bit more than he currently did—but he couldn't motivate himself.

"Do you have your notes from the first week?" Samantha asked, scribbling on yet another flash card.

Fabian raised an eyebrow. "You want my notes?" Normally, he copied hers.

"There might be something in there that I missed."

"Yeah, right." He pulled his Physics folder out of his backpack and threw it to her.

She opened her mouth to protest, but then her eyes glided past him and widened. Fabian turned his head around to see Cian approaching them.

He didn't mind Fabian's frown and ignored him while pulling up a chair next to Samantha. "Hey, uhm... can we talk?" *Now* he looked at Fabian, and it was clear he wanted him gone.

No chance. Fabian turned his chair fully around and crossed his arms. "What do you want?"

Samantha threw him a worried glance. "I think it's okay. Remember that it was Lucille's..." She smiled vaguely at Cian. "Never mind. What did you want to talk about?"

Though Lucille's spell might have inspired Cian's sudden love for Samantha, it didn't explain why he would kiss her against her will. At least, in Fabian's opinion, it didn't.

Cian scratched his neck, a far-away picture from the usual confident jock. "Well, first off, I'm so sorry about the whole thing with Nico. I know you were friends and... The whole thing is pretty horrifying."

The animal attack didn't even come close to the truly horrifying truth.

"Yeah..." Samantha's voice lowered, a clear sign for Fabian that she wasn't really interested in talking about that. And for good reason. "I'm okay."

To Cian's credit, he accepted it with only a twitch of his mouth. "That's good to hear. Good to have you back, too."

"Why? So you can kiss her in front of everybody again?" Fabian muttered. Oh, damn it. Had he said that aloud?

Cian shot him a glance but quickly focused on Samantha again, once again scratching his neck. "About that. Uhm... I'm really sorry how it all escalated. I completely underestimated how much drama it would cause to invite you and... I didn't want to hurt you."

Samantha took some time to answer. "Okay." Apparently annoyed at her single-word answers, she clicked her tongue. "Well, let me just make this clear." She took a deep breath. "You and I won't work. We're better as—"

"Friends?" Cian asked, sounding almost hopeful.

"I wanted to say lab partners," Samantha admitted straight out. "But... Cheryl and Ani wouldn't be okay with that, either. Or Alan. He wasn't happy when you picked me up."

Cian groaned in annoyance. "He's not happy about a lot of things. Like Lucille acting as if they've never kissed, or Matt giving him a run for his money as the sexiest guy of the year." He sighed. "But you're probably right. We'll have to keep our friendship to the lab."

"Sounds amazing," Fabian muttered, and this time Samantha glared at him. He raised his hands and rolled his eyes. "Fine with me."

Cian chuckled, then extended his hand. "Alright. Friendly lab partners then."

To Fabian's annoyance, Samantha giggled and took Cian's hand. "To friendly lab partners."

"I'll give you the notes from last week," Cian promised as he got up again. He waved and went on his way again.

He was barely out of earshot when Fabian hissed, "Why are you so friendly with him? He made you uncomfortable and kissed you, embarrassing you."

Samantha turned back to him, taking a shuddering breath. "Because it's not his fault. Cian was a victim of Lucille's... spells. He was never in love with me, nor keen to prove it. But he's actually really nice. We have fun together in Chemistry. I like him. Just not *that* way."

Fabian sighed. "I'm sorry. I'm just so used to him being Alan's equally stupid sidekick."

That brought a smile to Samantha's lips. "Maybe he grew out of it. There's hope for the others yet."

"You can't say such things. It could spell the end of the world!" Fabian crossed his lower arms over his head and grinned. Her giggle was the best sound he'd heard in a week.

Before he'd even lowered his arms, Jan arrived, slammed his backpack on the table, and hunkered down next to him. "Look at this." He pushed a phone in front of them.

"Shouldn't you be in class?" Samantha asked. She and Fabian had a free period thanks to the lack of a sub for their sick teacher, but Jan should've been in Geography.

"You missed a whole week. I can't even get a few hours?" Impatiently, he tapped on the screen. "Animal attacks."

Next to Fabian, Samantha turned rigid. He didn't feel too well, either. "Animal attacks?" he whispered.

"Well, that's the official message, of course, but..." Jan swiped through the article. "That's a bit odd, isn't it? Three people were attacked last night. Two the night before. There's another werewolf."

"No, there isn't," Samantha said quietly. "It's almost new moon."

Jan frowned only for a short moment. "Didn't Matt say that older werewolves become just as bitey as humans?"

"And how would human bites appear like animal bites to the coroner?" Fabian asked. Despite his inclination, he'd begun to read parts of the article. Torn flesh, half-eaten corpses. No human body would be able to do that. "Maybe it's normal wolves. They're supposed to be back." It was one of the great successes that wolves were returning to Germany. Though it wouldn't be quite as celebrated if they turned out to be this aggressive towards humans.

This time, Jan's frown stayed in place. "Normal wolves? Aren't they a bit shy around human settlements? Only two of these were attacked in the forest. The other three were out on the streets." He faced Samantha. "It's something else, right? So, we need to check it out and stop it before more people get hurt."

Samantha's eyes were painfully empty as she stared at Jan. "I'm not going to check things out. Not anymore."

"So, what? We just let these *animals*"—Jan put air quotes around the last word—"roam free? Just wait for them to move on?"

"I'm not a witch," Samantha told him, her voice a little firmer. "I can't do anything about it."

"You have awesome explosive potions and whatnot!" Jan protested.

Fabian watched Samantha's face go rigid. "I've thrown all my potions away. I'm done with that. You need to look for someone else if you want to take on deadly monsters."

Jan whipped his head around to Fabian. "You're gonna come, right?"

"No." Fabian shook his head. "It's too dangerous." What could a bunch of teenagers do about such gory monsters?

Jan's mouth was hanging open. He looked from Fabian to Samantha and back again. "You're serious!" he said in an accusatory tone. "You're really gonna sit here and twiddle your thumbs while people are dying?"

"It's not our job to keep them safe!" Fabian hissed. "Look, it's horrible, but there's the police and..." Who else was there? "Other people. Why do *we* have to risk our lives? Do you want to see us all dead? Is one grave not enough?"

Next to him, Samantha whimpered. Teardrops stained the writing on her flashcards.

Fabian cursed himself for opening that wound again. "I'm sorry."

Jan's mouth was set, unimpressed. "*We* have to do it because *we*'re the only ones. Nobody else knows what's really happening. Only us."

"Not a good enough reason to keep risking our lives," Fabian said a little more gently.

Jan hit the table with his flat hand. "Right. Gotcha. I'll check it out alone then."

"That's how Nico got bitten," Samantha said, so quietly it barely carried. She stared at the table instead of at them. "And how you attracted that demon's ire in the first place. We've done enough messing around with magic, don't you think?" At the last word, she raised her head and stared at Jan.

He sank back into his chair, crossing his arms. "I don't like this."

Samantha returned to her flashcards, filed away the smudged one, and pulled up an empty one. But Fabian stared darkly at the table. If they were both right—and there was no good reason why they should keep exposing themselves to such dangers—why did it feel so wrong?

Lucille

"No, he's in. He just... he'll call you back later!" Lucille slammed down the phone and puffed out some air. Then she fixed it with a stare and whispered, "Don't call again." The magic flowed from her lips and settled around the phone. This particular contractor wouldn't bother them anymore.

"Lulu?" Her father put his head into her room, sporting a hideous outfit of white shorts and an equally white polo shirt with blue stripes and knee-high socks, again in white. But the worst offender was the white terry headband he wore. "Do you want to go play tennis?"

Lucille massaged her temples. Since the unfortunate date at the restaurant, her father had been obsessed with spending time with her. He was ignoring all his business calls and hadn't been in the office for days. At first, Lucille had liked the attention, and they'd made up for all the years they'd missed. It had been a welcome distraction from Nico's death. Her father took care of her, told her stories about her mum to help her sleep, and made sure she wanted for nothing.

But now she was exhausted. "You need to call your business partner back. I mean that guy. Hendriksen. Call Hendriksen back."

"Okay." Ordered around by yet another spell, her father took out his phone and called the contractor.

Things had been a mess ever since Nico's death. Lucille had meant to bring Linda back and return everything to order, but seeing someone she knew bleed out in front of her was something she couldn't deal with while also having her stepmother around. So, she left Linda wherever she was and surrounded herself with her father's attention instead. And magic.

So much magic. Lucille knew she needed to stop. Elda's warning was still ringing in her ears. The magic would consume her, and she couldn't deny it anymore. She woke up tired, so tired that she had to call in sick at school, but she couldn't stop. It was like eating ice cream after a nasty break-up or drinking alcohol to block out feelings. The magic made her feel better. It fixed problems.

And it caused so many more.

"No, the deal is off. Yes, I know it's short term, but I'm taking leave. I need to spend more time with my daughter," her father announced. "At the moment, indefinitely."

Lucille stared at him. "What did you just do?"

"I called off the building project. It would take too much time away." He smiled. "And I want to spend my time with you. Tennis?"

She had to take a very deep breath, forcing a wide smile on her face. "No. But do go play tennis by yourself."

He frowned a little, probably trying to figure out how to play tennis by himself, but then he shrugged and marched off, whistling happily.

Meanwhile, the amount of logic-defying magic made Lucille's head swim. She needed to stop. But before that, she needed to fix everything.

Her father couldn't just quit his job. Not only was their income on the line, there were contractors and employees to consider. The de Cerques would probably be fine, but Lucille wasn't so out of touch with the world that she didn't know how many other people relied on her father's work.

And on Linda's. Just this morning, she'd read in the Greenvalley Herald, the local newspaper, that the organisers at the city council were angry that the *Linda* fashion show had been cancelled on such short notice. There was no explanation as to why the designer had withdrawn her charity event, and the reporter had said some not so nice things about the de Cerque family. Obviously, the spell that had made everyone forget about Linda was starting to fail. It was too big to sustain indefinitely. Even so, people only remembered the brand and that it must have a designer, but not the actual person.

One step at a time, Lucille told herself, though the urge to just fix it all at once was overwhelming.

"Albert!" she called as she strode from her room. The butler appeared as faithful as always. He'd barely bowed before Lucille told him, "We are doing a charity event right here. Tomorrow night. I want you to alert the press and handle the invitations. I will take care of the set-up and the models and... everything else. Wait, no! I also need you to organise the caterer."

He bowed once more. "As you wish, Miss Lucille. I assume this will be a fashion show?"

"Yes. *Linda*, presented by me." Lucille frowned, unsure of where that had come from. She normally gave everything *Linda* a wide berth, but if she was doing this event, she wanted to be recognised for it. It would practically be all her work. "Hurry."

So many spells in a short time took their toll. As Albert hurried away, Lucille had to steady herself against the wall to keep upright when sudden dizziness made her head swim.

After a few minutes, the weakness passed, and Lucille continued her flurry of activity by checking the foyer. In her mind, she could already see the runway and the chairs. It would just need a little remodelling.

The fleeting thought of calling builders instead of using magic crossed her mind, but Lucille pushed it away. Builders took time and money. Why use them if she could do it better herself?

An entire pot of coffee had Lucille buzzing at the event. The foyer looked spectacular, with lifelike trees on both sides of a black runway. Fairy lights in the shapes of butterflies hung above them. All the seats near the runway were taken, but even more people milled behind them, enjoying delicious canapés and sparkling wine.

Her father was playing the gracious host, his face overflowing with pride. The *Linda* spring collection was arrayed behind closed doors. The photographers were at the ready. Everything was set. The only thing missing were the models. But Lucille had a plan for that as well.

She beamed at Rachel and Samantha who, along with the boys, had come to support her. "How do you feel about modelling?"

Rachel's scowl was instantly sobering, while Samantha's eyes widened. "Oh, no. I can't do that! I can't even walk in high heels."

"Don't worry, there's a spell for that," Lucille said, determined not to let such a small detail derail her plans.

"How many spells have you already cast?" Matt asked. As usual lately, he was glaring at her.

Lucille clicked her tongue in annoyance. "As many as I needed. Guys, this is important. My stepmum isn't here, and I need to save her reputation. And we're doing something good. All the proceeds are going to the children's wing at the hospital." She turned to Samantha, practically begging her. "It's for charity."

Samantha sighed heavily but hung her head. "Okay, I guess, if your stepmum is okay with it..."

"She had the idea first." Lucille swung around to Rachel. "I've got the perfect dress for you."

"No." Rachel's face hadn't changed one bit. "I will not model."

Magical words fell into her mouth, but Lucille forced herself to swallow them. She couldn't make Rachel do this after everything that had happened. Especially not in front of Matt. "Okay, but..." She pouted a little. "I can't just send Samantha up and down." Judging by the panicked look on her friend's face, she was about to lose the only model she had.

"You could ask my sister and little Meggy," Jan suggested. He was standing near the curtain and was peering outside. "They'd pee themselves for the chance. Or the Elite girls. They're dumb but pretty."

Lucille groaned. "Cheryl would never let me live this down. Or agree to it." But Jan was right. They would be the perfect models for her charity show. "Fine. Matt, can you ask them, while Jan gets his and Samantha's sister?"

"Me?" Matt asked in confusion.

"Yes, you. Aren't you a favourite with the girls?" Lucille snapped.

Matt took a deep breath, then shrugged. "Fine. At least you won't have to enchant them that way."

"You're a darling!" Lucille chirped sarcastically. Then she pulled Samantha's arm. "Let's get you into a dress."

Samantha was still looking unhappy, but she let herself be dragged towards the silver rail. "I can't pose or anything."

"You don't have to." Lucille faced the clothes. "Find the perfect dress for Samantha." A strand of magic freed itself from her and drifted through the air until it found a green dress that looked like giant banana leaves sewn together in a flattering hourglass shape. It would bring out Samantha's green eyes perfectly.

As Lucille held the dress to Samantha's body, her friend bit her lip. "Is Matt right? Did you use magic for all of this?"

"It's fine. I've got it under control. Come on, get dressed so I can fix your make-up." She hurried Samantha into the room next door for some privacy, then turned to see the Elite Clique girls as well as Meg and Anne approaching.

"Is it true? Can we walk the runway?" Meg asked, her eyes gleaming with delight.

Sometimes, Lucille wondered how two siblings could be so different. Not only was Meg blonde, whereas Samantha had black hair, she was also highly invested in fashion, parties, and celebrities, while her older sister barely acknowledged their existence. Today, that difference suited Lucille just fine. "Yes. Go and pick whatever you like."

It was as if she'd opened a candy jar. Meg dragged Anne, Jan's little sister, along, all the while squealing as only teenage girls could do.

Meanwhile, Lucille faced the four girls of the Elite Clique. The disdainful look on Cheryl's face made her already regret asking them. "How about you? Do you fancy a little modelling gig?"

"How much does it pay?" Cheryl asked, clicking her tongue as she gave Lucille the once-over.

Lucille had no idea why her outfit should be the cause of any disdain, but she forced herself to smile. "It's a charity event."

"You're paying the caterers."

"Do you want to cater instead?" Lucille snapped.

While Cheryl gasped, Shayna pushed herself to the front. "Well, if Cherry doesn't want to, I'm delighted to do it. It's not every day one can wear an original *Linda* dress and present it to the world."

"You mean Greenvalley," Cheryl muttered.

But Shayna only grinned. "Everyone starts out small. Can I just pick as well?"

Helplessly, Lucille offered the railing. "Sure."

"I'll do it," Cheryl announced suddenly. "But it'd better be me who presents the final dress."

Since Lucille hadn't even decided what the final dress would be, she only took a deep breath and nodded. "Go ahead. I'll put you on last."

She turned around and found herself face-to-face with Robert. For some reason, he was beaming at her. "I heard you were looking for models."

"And you—" Lucille massaged her temples in an effort of not to snap at him. "No. Thanks, but no." When he trotted off like a beaten dog, Lucille shook her head. "What's wrong with people?"

Her stepmother had never told her how stressful a fashion show could be, even with the help of magic. It had been too late to find a make-up artist or someone to fix the models' hair into a cohesive look, but she told herself that it would all be part of the charm of using inexperienced high school girls. Still, she couldn't stop herself from giving them a final touch-up before they went out on the runway.

"Your dress sits perfectly," Lucille said to Samantha, and the seams moved under her fingers until they sat snugly against Samantha's skin.

Samantha might have been reluctant to help her out, but Lucille thought she looked gorgeous with the green dress, and her black curls falling on her naked shoulders. "Don't be nervous," she added, and immediately, Samantha's face relaxed.

Half a minute later, Samantha walked onto the runway, strutting in heels as if she wore them regularly. Meanwhile, Lucille turned to

Shayna, who was wearing a black dress with red accents in a similar silhouette as Samantha's banana-leaf dress.

"That dress is a perfect fit. The red makes your personality glow," she said, then had to catch herself as the magic rushed through her, leaving her dizzy.

"Thank you." Shayna was already beaming, as if she'd never heard such a compliment before.

Next to her, Cheryl rolled her eyes. "Oh please, she's saying that to everyone." She made a distasteful noise at Lucille's reaction. "You must be very desperate to send those kids or someone like *Samantha* out there."

"She's doing a great job of it," Lucille snapped. She was too tired for this cattiness and had half a mind to send Cheryl to *wherever*.

"Are you saying I'm not doing a great job? If someone's bound to be a model, it's me," Cheryl declared, punching her hands into her hips where a flurry of white feathers rose, making her look like a puffy swan.

"Well, thank you," Shayna answered snidely.

Cheryl scoffed at her. "I wasn't talking about you. Go on, you need to go out and make your personality glow or something."

"You're impossible!" With an angry grunt, Shayna spun on her heels and marched to the runway.

She hadn't made it further than three steps before the red lines of her dress spontaneously caught fire. Lucille covered her mouth in shock. Everyone gasped, but Shayna only regarded the flames with mild interest, then strutted out on the runway as if the flames didn't bother her. A second later, raucous applause and awe could be heard from the crowd.

"Why is her dress burning?" Cheryl demanded, not worried in the slightest. "You gave me the wrong dress."

"I can make yours burn, too, if you want," Lucille snarled, and this time, Cheryl took a few steps backwards.

The magic wanted to follow through. It would be so easy. Lucille wouldn't even need her fireball. Just tell the magic to burn Cheryl and it would happen.

Whimpering, Lucille clamped down on her mouth, only to be assaulted by Matt. "What the hell are you doing?"

He and Fabian had hurried to the back. Fabian's fingers were twitching as he kept checking on Shayna, who was still presenting her burning dress to the adoring crowd. Meanwhile, Matt's fingers were digging into Lucille's arm as he pulled her aside.

"Are you trying to kill Shayna?" he asked.

"She seems to be fine!" Better make sure of that. "Shayna is fine. The dress is on fire, not her. And I only said that she was supposed to glow, not burn."

Matt bared his teeth in a snarl. "Stop using magic!"

Lucille ripped her arm out of his grasp. "Leave me alone." Once again, the magic pushed against Matt but didn't do anything. Robbed of that avenue, she turned away to welcome back Samantha. "You looked amazing, and you did so well. Thank you so much for helping."

"You were breathtakingly beautiful," Fabian said, his eyes shimmering a little as he regarded Samantha.

"Uhm, thanks," Samantha replied, her cheeks flushed. She checked with Matt, but he had crossed his arms and was glaring at all of them.

Rolling her eyes, Lucille decided to ignore him and started herding the models together. "As soon as Cheryl comes back, we're all going out."

Even though she was bone-deep tired, Lucille enjoyed the applause and the constant flashing from the cameras when she herself stepped onto the runway. She waved to the crowd and beamed more than any of her models. And there at the end stood her father, giving her a standing ovation. She'd pulled it off, a fashion show for Greenvalley to remember. Her father finally saw her.

Unfortunately, the bliss barely held as long as the runway did. As soon as they came off it, Cheryl had a go at her. "You promised that I could wear the final piece."

Her screeching voice made Lucille's head hurt. "You *wore* the final piece. You were the last one walking. Last, final. Get it?"

"I went last with the wrong dress," Cheryl complained, then shook her head. "Well, I guess there's a difference between a famous designer like Linda and a wannabe like you." She turned and pointed at Shayna taking off her dress, now no longer burning but still smouldering slightly. "That was the final piece."

"You picked the dress," Lucille pointed out, no longer caring whether she sounded catty or not. "You could've picked Shayna's."

Cheryl pursed her lips and narrowed her eyes. "And I would've if you'd told me that the black one had the wow effect. I thought white was the traditional showpiece." She tugged on the feathers, almost ripping them out. "Which dress, do you think, will be in the news tomorrow? Definitely not this cheap-ass one."

"Cheap-ass dress?" Lucille's own voice was nearing screeching territory. "That cheap-ass dress is worth a lot more than your trashy extensions."

"Girls, what are you doing?" Matt made the fatal mistake of trying to step in between them.

Both Cheryl and Lucille shouted at him. "Stay out of this!"

The power of her spell made Matt stumble backwards. A small victory at last.

But now, Shayna was coming over, dressed in her original outfit again. "He's right, though. You're squabbling like a bunch of seagulls over a piece of trash after we did an amazing show. Didn't you hear the crowd go wild?"

Cheryl whirled around. "For you, maybe. You had an exciting dress."

"So? Am I not allowed to have the better dress?" Shayna pushed her hands onto her hips. "God, Cherry, sometimes you're truly awful. Thank you for ruining what could've been a really cool event."

Lucille massaged her temples, glad that the heat was off her for the moment. She should've enjoyed the Elite Clique imploding, but she was too tired to find joy in that.

"I ruined this event? You were the one who had to take over. And, by the way, the whole thing was a big, fat mess. The designer isn't even here," Cheryl complained.

"A big, fat mess because I stole your spotlight?" Shayna asked, mimicking Cheryl's anger. "Oh, boohoo, the world is ending."

"Oh my gosh, there's a fire!" Samantha suddenly shouted.

Instantly, Cheryl lashed out at her. "Everyone knows the dress is burning, Sammy."

But Lucille looked past the fighting friends to where the *Linda* dresses were hanging. The entire railing had caught fire, and it was already licking at the wooden panels of the wall behind it.

In an instant, there was screaming. Anne and Meg fled the room, spreading the news. The four Elite Clique friends held each other, the fight between Shayna and Cheryl forgotten. Then the sprinkler turned on, spraying them all with water and eliciting new ear-piercing shrieks.

Fabian was the only one who managed to get his wits together. He pulled the water from the sprinkler and sent it out towards the source of the fire. As the water splashed past the group of girls, Shayna turned around, startled.

"You four can't see anything!" Lucille shouted. The magic slammed into her so heavily the world was spinning for a while. Her stomach felt as if someone had punched her or if she hadn't eaten in days.

There was now crying in the screams as the Elite Clique girls panicked about their sudden loss of eyesight. Lucille caught her breath and found Matt glaring at her. He was trying to calm them and slowly herd them towards the entrance.

"What is happening?" Ani squealed. "My eyes."

"It's the smoke!" Lucille said. "We can't see because—"

"Lucille, don't!" Matt bellowed.

"—the smoke is so thick."

Thick black smoke developed, quickly filling the room. It crept into their lungs and nestled there. Lucille started coughing, as did everyone around her. Fabian's water stopped as he bent over, gasping for air. There were tears and choked screams. Meanwhile, the empty feeling in Lucille's stomach intensified, and she doubled over. The entire room spun.

She needed to get out. Get everyone out. Stop the fire.

Instead, the world collapsed around her, and she lost consciousness.

Rachel

The fire had been quickly extinguished after the firefighters arrived. The mansion had suffered considerable damage, but nobody had been hurt and the smoke inhalation cases had been promptly dealt with. Instead of the dress on fire, the actual fire dominated the news. People demanded an explanation, but there was none.

Lucille had simply used too much magic.

And at last, she seemed to have realised the problem.

Even a short nap had done little to recover her. Rachel almost pitied her as she watched Lucille melting into Elda's couch, but she also felt a bit smug. Lucille's excessive magic use had almost killed Nico—not that it would've changed anything. And now it would've almost killed herself, Matt, Samantha, Fabian, and the four Elite Clique girls. Not to mention the severe damage to her own home.

Now, Little Miss Fashion was pale, her eyes reddened, and her face spoke of utter misery. "It's like an urge," she said, her voice fragile. "I can't control it." Lucille looked at Matt. "You say stop it, but the magic just wants to come out of me."

"It's like me and the drugs," Jan chimed in wisely.

"You want to stop taking drugs?" Fabian asked.

Jan shrugged. "Nah, not really. But Lu doesn't really want to stop using magic either, right?"

Lucille should've protested, but instead, her eyes widened, and her breathing quickened. "I-I don't want to hurt anyone. And I don't want to die either." No word about not wanting to do magic.

"Is there such a thing as magic rehab?" Fabian looked around, his gaze settling on Samantha.

Although Samantha was present, she didn't offer an opinion. She seemed to be there solely to hold Lucille's hand, neither condoning nor condemning the excessive magic use.

This was in stark contrast to Matt, who stood near the door with his arms crossed and a dark look on his face. "You only get addicted to magic if you think it solves all your problems."

Lucille moaned quietly. "That's easy for you to say. You're immune to it."

"Wait. You're immune to magic?" Jan's head whipped around. "Why are you immune to magic? What kind of creature is that?"

Matt rolled his eyes and took a deep breath. "None. It's just a specific talent, or rather non-talent, I was born with. And I'm not completely immune to it; I just have a higher tolerance for it. Happy?"

Jan narrowed his eyes, but he kept his mouth shut.

Once they'd all quieted down, Elda lowered her arms. Samantha's grandmother had been magically examining Lucille in ways that were invisible to Rachel. Something about strands of magic that showed the spells.

"The problem isn't you," she declared in a gentle voice. "The problem is your necklace."

Lucille clutched the beautiful necklace. "My grandmother's amulet?"

Elda nodded. "There are hundreds of spells tied to it. I can break them, but you will have to take it off for me to do it. That should take care of the fatigue, at least."

Lucille's eyes bulged. "Take it off? But it's mine."

"I didn't say I wanted to keep it. Just cleanse it, untangle the magic web you've accidentally woven..." Elda's voice faded, and her lips thinned. "You won't give it to me? Not even for a little?"

Curious, Rachel checked on Lucille. Her eyes were blazing, and red spots covered her cheeks. She was still clutching her necklace. "No one takes—"

Quick as lightning, Matt rushed forward, his shoulder bumping into Rachel, and clamped his hand over Lucille's mouth before she could finish the sentence. While the others were too stunned, Lucille fought back, throwing her arms up to remove Matt's hand, and then trying to hit him in the face when he wouldn't let go. Samantha tried to grab one of her arms to pin it down, while Matt did his best to dodge the wild flailing.

"Help!" Samantha called out.

Rachel stared at the scene, incapable of acting, but Fabian joined the fray and pinned down Lucille's other arm. Her shoulders kept jerking around, but she didn't stand a chance against all three of them.

"Is that really necessary?" Jan asked, sounding as if he was about to throw up.

"She speaks magic the moment she opens her mouth," Matt said, huffing as he helped Samantha with the left arm.

"It's a curse," Elda said. Her arms were half-raised, and Rachel wondered if she'd been planning to weave a spell to stop Lucille. "This is not a normal reaction."

"You don't say," Jan muttered, but the collective glares from the others made him shut up.

Elda stepped forward, her hand hovering over Lucille's necklace. Lucille struggled, and her arm broke free, hitting Samantha in the face before Matt could grab her wrist and hold onto to it.

"What's going on?" Fabian asked, sweat forming on his forehead.

"Someone has put a curse on this necklace. Lucille won't ever agree to take it off or stop using magic, even if it kills her." With a heavy sigh, Elda stepped back.

Guilt flooded Rachel as she realised that Lucille hadn't truly chosen to use her magic all this time. How long had it been going on? And had there been a time they could've stopped it before things got out of control?

"It was him, right?" Jan suddenly said, his face pale.

"Are you blaming me again?" Matt sounded exasperated. The strain of holding down Lucille and keeping her mouth shut was getting to him.

Jan's eyes jerked up from the necklace to Matt's face. "What? No! I meant the guy... the demon. The one that was behind the werewolf attack and the mine accident."

"Why would he attack Lucille?" Samantha asked, her gaze shifting between the struggling Lucille and Jan.

"Because she came with me." Jan looked dismayed. "I wanted to ask the new CEO why he'd pushed the miners to open up a sealed adit. Lucille and I talked to him, and then he got all creepy and touched her necklace. I thought he was a making a move on her, but instead he put a curse on her, right?"

"What kind of demon is this?" Elda asked Matt, for some reason.

He shrugged. "I have no i—Ow!" With a yelp, he let go of his hand and shook it. "She bit me."

"I want you all to—" Lucille's spell was broken off with a gurgling sound.

Water dripped from her mouth, while a panicked Fabian held out his hand. Lucille tried to gasp for breath, her eyes bulging, before she suddenly slumped and fell into Samantha's lap.

"Oh my god. Did I kill her? I didn't..." Fabian's eyes darted around the room. He breathed harder and harder with every passing second.

"Relax," Elda said. "I put her to sleep. It's easier that way." She nodded at Matt. "Can you remove the necklace?"

Fabian let out a massive sigh of relief, but Rachel could see that he was still deeply affected. He continued to stare at his fingers and huff.

Matt removed the necklace without any issues and handed it to Elda, who didn't touch it but took it from him on a cookie platter. "Greed," Matt sneered before wiping his hand.

"It was either that or gluttony." Elda sighed. "I will take care of this. Even a demon can't corrupt an Emblem of Power forever. As for Lucille, it's better if she sleeps off my spell. Then we'll see whether the curse has only been tied to the necklace or to her as well."

Once she left the room, a strange atmosphere settled over them. Samantha stroked Lucille's hair, her eyes shimmering. A purple bruise was already forming on her cheek. Matt seemed lost in thought, while Fabian still stared at his hands, struggling to keep himself together.

Rachel moved a little closer to Fabian and placed her hand on his arm. "It's okay."

Fabian whimpered as he looked up at her, but then nodded shakily.

Jan's phone chimed. "Oh, come on!" he swore after glancing at the screen. When everyone else looked at him, he explained, "Another animal attack."

Rachel shuddered. There it was again—the lie Nico had been buried under.

"That demon is messing with us," Jan continued to complain.

"Don't say that," Fabian pleaded. "I don't want to be target practice for some demon."

Matt snorted. "It's a little late for that. We need to look into it. It can't be a werewolf—"

"Because it's the new moon," Jan finished for him. "Samantha already said so. And she said to leave it be, but clearly this demon isn't."

Rachel noticed that, as proudly as Jan held his head, he was trembling. And why wouldn't he? Both Lucille and Nico had been targeted by the demon, while he'd got off without even a slap on the wrist. Until now. He must've been convinced that whatever *animal* was roaming the streets was after him.

"I don't want to leave these things. I want to make them stop," Jan declared. "Who's with me?"

"I'm coming," Matt said, but the reaction on Jan's face suggested that Matt wasn't the person he had hoped for. "Whatever this is, I want to know if it's connected to the demon that sent the other monsters and cursed Lucille's necklace. And if it is, I want to know what the hell his plan is."

Jan studied Matt once again before nodding sharply. "Alright. Anyone else?" *"Please"* hung like a breath in the air.

"Not me." Fabian shook his head. "I already told Samantha, and she agreed. We're done with magic and monsters and all that crap."

Rachel's hand slipped from his arm in shock. She couldn't have heard that correctly, could she?

"Well, that stuff isn't done with us." Jan pointed at Lucille.

"We need to stop before things get even worse. Nico's already dead. Lucille almost burnt down her house and looks half-dead herself. And... I can't deal with it anymore. I'm sorry."

Rachel stared at him, unblinking. He was *sorry?* "You've got to be kidding me."

She didn't realise she had spoken out aloud until everyone was looking at her.

Setting her jaw, Rachel stood up and faced Fabian. "You are done with magic?" The time for keeping her thoughts to herself was over.

Fabian seemed to shrink under her gaze. "It's too dangerous."

She scoffed at that, not bothering to dignify it with a response. Without saying another word, Rachel turned her attention to Samantha, who was still stroking Lucille's hair. "And you agree with him?" Her voice was ice cold.

Samantha glanced up briefly but quickly lowered her eyes. "It *is* dangerous. People are getting hurt."

Rachel knew Samantha was referring to Nico, but she couldn't accept it, especially *because* it happened to Nico. "My brother's murderer is running around in our hometown, killing at will, and you want to let him get away with it because it might be dangerous?"

"It's not that easy," Fabian protested.

"Yes! Yes, it is," Rachel snapped at him like she never had before. "I, for one, will not let him get away. I will not let him hurt anybody else. And if I die trying to stop him, at least I'll have done something!"

Jan pushed himself out of the armchair. "I'm not really keen on the 'die trying' part, but I'm with Rachel on this one."

Rachel continued to glare at Fabian and Samantha. Fabian had turned red, but he only shrank further. Clearly, he still had no intention of joining them. Samantha didn't even meet her eyes. "I don't even have any magic."

"Neither do I," Rachel snarled. "At least, not the kind that's useful in a fight. But you know what? I'm still going out there. Give me a weapon, and we'll see how good his magic is." Abruptly, Rachel turned on her heel and strode towards the hallway. "Let's go, boys. We've got a demon to kill."

Jan

Rachel had stayed true to her word and armed herself with a crossbow after Elda had recommended it. Now the shy girl from school carried a massive crossbow and an array of bolts, ready to take down these monsters. Jan approved.

"So, where do we start?" Matt asked.

"Kastanienweg. Most of the attacks have been in the forest, but the ones in town have always been near that street." Kastanienweg was one of the roads that bordered the forest, not too far from Elda's forest road. "Even if those animals aren't there, we should find traces of them."

The problem with this smaller group constellation was that it was full of awkward silences. Rachel was the opposite of talkative on a good day, and Jan doubted they had even the tiniest bit in common. And Matt still made him uneasy. He would've much preferred to do this with Fabian or Lu, but one was too chicken, and the other was not in any state to help.

They trudged down Kastanienweg, and Jan watched Matt search the area with all the expertise of a hunter. The blonde crouched over a trace, one hand on the ground, while his eyes roamed the darkness.

Jan stared at the footprint, cursing under his breath at how heavily it was imprinted in the grass. "Is that a dog?" He hoped it was just a dog. Animal traces were not something he was particularly proficient in.

"Werewolf?" Rachel asked, with a bolt lying on her crossbow.

"Hellhound," Matt said. Though there were a couple of other footprints to the side of the pavement, he straightened, brow heavily furrowed. "That's not good."

"And here I thought we'd get a good monster for a change." When nobody even smirked, Jan sighed. "What's a hellhound?"

Matt started walking towards the forest, forcing the others to follow him if they wanted any answers. "Large, massive, three heads, and pretty aggressive."

Jan shuddered. "So, like Cerberus?" No one could say he didn't know his mythology.

But Matt only frowned. "Think of it as a demon dog."

"That's what I... whatever." Muttering to himself, Jan followed him.

"Get your weapons ready." Matt drew his sword from thin air, squinting into the darkness of the woods.

Rachel cocked the crossbow and raised it to aim at the bushes. All Jan had was a pocket knife, and he suddenly felt silly for not picking up a crossbow as well, or something with a longer reach like Matt's sword.

The forest was eerily quiet, not a bird to be heard. A twig snapped. Jan threw his head around. Nothing.

"How...?"

Matt held up a hand, and Jan fell silent. Their eyes darted around as they held their breath. Just then, an unfamiliar smell reached them. It was pungent, like something rotten. A carcass?

"There," Rachel said, her crossbow pointing at the thicket.

Jan almost jumped when he saw a pair of red eyes staring back at them. Then a second pair, and then a third. *Three heads, one hound,* he told himself as he readjusted his grip around his knife.

"If you can, go for the heart. Otherwise, aim for the heads," Matt whispered from the corner of his mouth. At that moment, a fourth and fifth pair of eyes appeared. "Abort!" Matt hissed, but it was too late.

A snap accompanied the whirring sound of Rachel's crossbow bolt loosening. It struck something, and a second later, the thicket erupted.

Matt hadn't exaggerated when he said the hellhounds were massive. Even without considering the three heads, their black bodies were as big as a horse. Jan couldn't fathom how they had fit into that thicket.

Not that he cared, because the moment the three—not two!—hellhounds jumped from the bushes with their teeth bared, he turned around and ran. If Rachel had hit anything, it had only served to make them angrier.

The barking of the hellhounds shook the earth. The rotten stench intensified, and he realised that it was their breath, hot on his neck. In his mind, he could already feel their teeth sinking into his flesh, and he caught himself wondering why he should even try to run away.

His feet slowed. Then, Matt grabbed his arm and hauled him forwards just as one of the many heads snapped at Jan. The teeth grazed his free arm, and pain shot through his shoulder like fire.

Matt had forgone the sword and was dragging both him and Rachel along. Somewhere along the way, Rachel must've dropped her crossbow.

Jan glanced over his shoulder, immediately regretting it. Nine giant heads with an insane amount of sharp teeth and lolling red tongues snapped at their heels.

He ran into something hard. Disoriented, Jan felt as if he'd run face-first into a wall, but when he opened his eyes, he, Rachel, and Matt were sitting behind a wooden fence. A moment later, all three hellhounds slammed into the fence behind them. Wood creaked. The panels shuddered, but the fence held.

Slowly, the three of them backed away from the fence. Jan had no idea how they'd jumped the fence, but he was glad they had, even though the barrier didn't seem to hold for long.

"One I can deal with," Matt muttered, his face as pale as Jan's. "But three?"

"Five," Rachel said.

She had turned the other way, her eyes staring down the street. Jan's and Matt's eyes followed her gaze.

Two massive hellhounds stepped into the dead end, cutting off their only exit. Their eyes glowed as they growled, slobber dripping from their maws.

Jan freed himself from Matt's grip and backed against the fence, which shuddered behind him with infrequent impacts. His knees felt suddenly weak, and he sank to the ground just as Matt extended a hand towards him.

"Take my hand." He was already holding Rachel.

Jan had no idea how holding hands would make their imminent death any better. Instead, he crouched even deeper and held out his puny pocket knife.

"Jan!" Matt cursed and whirled around when claws scratched over the pavement.

His hand raised, he shot a stream of that black magic of his at the hellhounds. It hit one of the heads, but the hellhound it belonged to barely slowed. Its fangs exposed, it prepared to pounce. Jan raised his arms, forgetting all about the pocket knife. Rachel sprang back and fell while Matt stood there in front of them, both arms stretched out, shouting nonsense like, "Stop! Don't! Sit!"

Jan expected to see Matt mauled. He anticipated watching his friends die seconds before the teeth sank into his own flesh, tearing him apart. But there was nothing.

The hellhounds had gone completely quiet, both those behind the fence and the ones in front of them. They were sitting on their buttocks, bushy tails swinging happily as they looked straight at Matt.

"Couldn't you've done that earlier?" Jan asked, the words slipping from his mouth. He could barely comprehend what was happening.

"I don't even know what I did," Matt admitted, his breathing light, as if he didn't dare take in any more air. "I just... followed my intuition."

Rachel got back up, her hands scraped from the rough fall. "Your intuition just saved our lives. So, thanks." She regarded the two hellhounds that still towered over her, even though they were sitting. "What do we do now?"

Jan grabbed his pocket knife. "Well, we kill them, right? Before they start chasing us again." Not that he believed they would get very far.

"Kill them?" Matt asked, his eyes wide. "When they're this peaceful?"

"They won't always be peaceful!" Jan protested. Blood ran down his arm where the hellhound's teeth had grazed him. "Let's do it now while they're not eating us."

He stepped forward, but Matt pushed him back. Instead of drawing his sword, Matt approached the nearest hellhound and carefully extended his hand.

Jan was convinced Matt would lose his hand any minute. But the hellhound lowered its three heads, and the middle one gave Matt a quick sniff. Matt smiled and started scratching the giant head's ears.

Several times, Jan opened his mouth only to shut it again. All thoughts had fled his mind. Just a minute ago, he'd been sure he was going to die. Now, the two monsters sat in front of them like huge, oversized doggies. And Matt treated them as such.

"I'll bring them back into the forest," Matt promised, barely paying attention to Jan and Rachel. "Come on. Let's go."

Without hesitation, the two hellhounds followed him out of the street and away.

Jan blinked. The rotten stench was gone, which meant the three hellhounds behind the fence were also gone. He turned to Rachel, struggling to articulate his issues with the whole situation. "Did you see that?"

Rachel nodded. "Sure, I did. What does he mean by bringing them back to the forest?"

He let out a huge sigh of relief, glad that he wasn't the only one questioning it. "I have no clue. But let's get out of here before they decide Matt's cuddles aren't worth it."

There was no argument from Rachel. They'd barely escaped death, and Jan didn't trust Matt to keep them safe. In fact, he wasn't sure he trusted him at all. Only one thing was certain; they might've been able to take on one hellhound, but certainly not five. Or however many there truly were.

Rachel had decided that they would go to Samantha's house, which was closest to where they'd separated from Matt. Now they were sitting on the couch in the living room with cups of tea in front of them, while Samantha cleaned Jan's wound.

"It's not very deep. I don't think you need stitches," she said.

"Good. I'd hate to explain this to my mum," Jan replied. While his mum could probably stitch up his arm in her sleep, she would fuss over his "wild stories" and keep asking if he was on drugs.

"I'll go get our first aid kit."

As Samantha left the room, her sixteen-year-old sister came down the stairs, wearing AirPods in her ears and dancing to music only she could hear. Her blonde hair was tied in a messy bun, and she was only wearing what looked like pyjamas—a rose-coloured shirt and awfully small grey shorts.

Jan had known Meg for years, since she slept over at Anne's about once a week. He'd never paid her much attention. First, because she'd been nothing but a child, just like his own little sister, and second, because she and Anne were bloody annoying with their constant giggling and silly jokes. But then he'd seen her at Lu's fashion show.

While Anne had looked like she was playing dress-up in her *Linda* dress, Meg's performance had been like a bucket of Fabian's water dumped on his head. Not only had she brought the appropriate energy for a fashion show, she had looked absolutely stunning in her blue dress. She had grown into a full-blown teenager, both in attitude and body. A body that was emphasised even more by her tight pyjama set.

Another girl might have been embarrassed to be caught singing aloud, but not Meg.

She sauntered over and sneered at their cups. "Are you having a tea party? That's so cute."

"Meg," Rachel said in an icy voice.

Meg smirked. "You look horrible."

"Meg, scoot off!" Samantha barked as she returned with the first aid box. The harsh tone surprised Jan. She certainly didn't use that tone at school.

But Meg only shrugged and danced into the kitchen, her behind swinging in a way Jan couldn't ignore. He caught himself thinking that she wasn't actually that much younger than him.

A sudden pain brought him back to the present. His arm felt like it was on fire. "What are you doing?" he complained to Samantha.

"Making sure your wound doesn't get infected," Samantha said as she dabbed it with a clean tissue and some iodine. "Animal bites can be dangerous."

Jan winced as she continued.

"You're such a wuss." Meg had returned, holding a small bottle of Coke.

"I want to see you when your sister drowns you in iodine," Jan shot back.

Meg's mouth twitched. Instead of going back upstairs, she leaned against the wall and watched them.

Meanwhile, Samantha finished up the treatment. "You may not need stitches, but you should have a doctor check this just in case."

"Nah, it's fine."

Samantha lowered her voice. "You don't have to play the hero just because Meg is egging you on."

"What did you guys do?" Meg asked loudly.

"Nothing," Rachel replied.

Meg snorted. "Right. Jan bleeding all over our couch is nothing."

With a groan, Samantha started bandaging up Jan's arm. "Meg, I appreciate your concern for our couch, but do us a favour and go upstairs."

"You can't tell me what to do!" Meg screeched. "You're not my mum. This is my house too. I can be wherever I want."

Jan struggled to keep himself from laughing. "Can I?" he asked Samantha, who'd finished bandaging his arm.

She looked puzzled, so Jan got up and walked over to Meg, who watched him warily. He stopped in front of her, then bent his knees, picked her up by her hips, and threw her over his shoulder.

Cue high-pitched screaming and Meg's fists raining down his back. "Let go of me, you... you brute!"

With a smirk, Jan ignored the screams and carried her up the stairs. By the time they reached the second floor, Meg had given up and even pointed him to her room. It was like a mirror image of Anne's room. They obviously had the same taste in K-Pop boy bands and smelly candles they never burnt.

He dropped her onto her bed and checked out her music collection. While he was sure most of her music was on a streaming service, there were a few CDs and singles. "*Weird Dreams?*" he asked, picking up the only song he actually knew. It veered more into electronic music, which he preferred.

"Don't touch my stuff!" Meg sat up on her bed but made no move to stop him.

Jan put the CD back on her desk. Half-done math homework was covered by what looked like a mediocre attempt at fan art. "Not a big fan of school, huh?"

Meg snorted. "You're one to talk." She pursed her lips and looked him up and down. "Why are you suddenly hanging out with my sister? I thought you were cooler."

Mentally noting that Meg thought he was cool, Jan answered, "Your sister is pretty cool." After all, Samantha wasn't nearly as boring as he'd thought all these years. Anyone who fought monsters and brewed magic potions was pretty awesome in his book. "You wouldn't get it."

"You're not into her, are you?" The thought seemed to horrify Meg.

Jan almost laughed. "What? No, absolutely not. Not my type."

Meg relaxed. "Then, what is your type?" Instantly, she doused the question with some sarcasm. "Let me guess! A bunch of drugged-up streetwalkers."

This time, he couldn't help chuckling. "You got me. The dirtier, the better."

A little grin followed, almost too cute to behold. Gosh, when had Meg become so pretty?

Stretching out her toes playfully, Meg asked, "So, what bit you?"

"A dog."

"A dog," Meg repeated, not believing a single word. "Did you climb through backyards on your way here?"

"Pretty much."

She rolled her eyes and made a dismissive noise. "You know what I've always asked myself?" When Jan raised an eyebrow, she continued with a smug expression. "How did your parents manage to produce both you and Anne?"

Jan decided to play along, although comparisons to his sister were his least favourite subject. "I keep asking myself that, too. I mean, Anne is so boring."

Meg gasped. "No, she's not! Anne is the best. She's kind, diligent, always wants to help—"

"Yeah, yeah." He waved his hand, as if he could make the words go away like that. His mood had definitely taken a turn for the worse now. "My parents already sing enough of Anne's praises."

"You hate her, don't you?" Meg asked seriously.

Jan frowned. "Who says I hate her?" Surely Anne didn't believe that. Or did she? "She's my little sister. An annoying little know-it-all who butters up every parent or teacher she meets. But I don't hate her because of that." He would never admit it out loud, but he loved his little sister, even if they had nothing more in common than their stupid parents.

"You don't?" The doubt in Meg's voice pained Jan. He didn't want Anne to think he hated her. The only thing he detested was how everyone treated her, while he was the problem child—the one who had to repeat a year at school and constantly got into trouble.

But Jan didn't say any of that Meg. Instead, he snorted. "You should know better. Samantha hasn't drowned you, either, and you've got a bigger mouth than Anne."

Once again, Meg's mouth opened in outrage. She put her hands on her hips. "I just don't hold back like everyone else. If you have a problem with that—"

"I don't!" Jan grinned boldly. "I like you that way." And with that, he walked backwards out of the room.

Meg stared at him, speechless for once, but as soon as he closed the door, a pillow thumped against it from the inside.

Jan grinned. He was starting to really like that girl.

Samantha

While Jan took care of Meg, Samantha found herself alone in the room with Rachel. She hadn't forgotten Rachel's outburst earlier. The shame it had filled her with still turned her stomach. Rachel had lost her twin brother, and yet she kept on fighting. How could she be so selfish and not do the same?

"So, hellhounds?" Samantha asked, her voice annoyingly unstable.

Rachel regarded her with a long look. "I thought you were out."

Samantha shivered under her icy stare. She deserved every bit of this scorn, but her eyes filled with tears as she thought of how she'd already failed Rachel. "You came here," she pointed out.

"You lived closest."

"Rachel—"

"What?" Rachel lost her patience again. "If you're looking for forgiveness, I don't have any left to give. You want out? Fine! But you were the one who told us that we had to protect the town. That no one but us could do it."

Samantha swallowed heavily. Rachel may have forgiven her for her role in Nico's death, but it sounded an awful lot like she blamed her for ever getting him involved. "I'm sorry. I let the excitement get away from me. Everything I ever dreamed of was becoming real. There was real magic, and we fought monsters like my grandparents and..." How foolish had she been, thinking that hunting monsters was cool?

To her surprise, Rachel took her hands and squeezed them. "Then don't let this dream get away from you now."

"But it's a bloody nightmare!" Samantha's voice broke. Before her eyes, she saw Nico's blood seeping through her fingers.

Rachel scoffed, but there was a smile hiding in her eyes. "Dreams and nightmares often lie close together. Take it from someone who knows her way around them." She sobered up quickly, still holding Samantha's hands. "Sam, we were born for this life. Our powers. Our friendship. The resurgence in monsters. There is no one but us to fight them. If we don't, even more people will get hurt. People we love."

The words struck a chord with Samantha. She felt her tears running down her cheeks, but her eyes remained locked with Rachel's. "I don't want anyone to get hurt." But there was another issue. "I don't have any powers." She wasn't like Rachel, Fabian, and Lucille. Or Matt.

"Neither does Jan."

"He can fight." The guy had a black belt in karate and had survived several scuffles.

Rachel snorted again. "And so can you. I didn't see you back away from the wyrm. No, you threw an explosive potion at it. And when you were wrapped up in hellspider webs, surrounded by a million creatures that could have killed you, who told the rest of us to go on?"

Samantha smiled sheepishly. "Well, I don't see how useful that was."

"What about the anti-insect spray you developed? Do you think we would've lasted even a second in Terraria without you?" Rachel's lips curled, challenging her. When Samantha didn't give in immediately, she said, "Without you, we would've all been turned into puppets for the bogeyman. The entire town would've been lost. Do you really think you can just sit and watch this demon destroy us all?"

"Of course not!" As soon as she said it, Samantha realised the truth of her words. Rachel was right. If her friends or the town were in danger, she would do everything in her power to save them.

She let go of Rachel's hands and wiped her cheeks dry. "So. Hellhounds?"

Rachel's face split into a big smile. "Yes. Three-headed monsters out for blood. But you know the weirdest thing? When Matt called out to them to stop—like giving dog commands in a panic—they actually stopped."

Samantha's eyes widened. "They did?"

"Yes, and then he went and petted them like they were cute little doggies instead of five aggressive hellhounds."

Before Samantha could ask for more details, she heard footsteps on the stairs. Jan was returning with a smug smile on his face.

"Sorted the little shit out," he claimed. "What were you talking about?"

"The hellhounds," Samantha answered before Rachel could reveal their heart-to-heart conversation. "Rachel told me how they stopped when Matt ordered them to."

Jan grimaced, as he usually did when someone mentioned Matt. His made-up rivalry with Matt was getting on everyone's nerves. "He's probably half hellhound. That's why they like him."

"I highly doubt that," Samantha said, a soft smile slipping onto her lips as she tried to imagine Matt cosying up with a bunch of monsters. "So, you just left him with five aggressive hellhounds?"

"He seemed happy," Jan said. "Said he'd bring them back into the forest, and now they're probably frolicking under the trees and playing fetch with human bones."

Both Samantha and Rachel rolled their eyes. Jan just couldn't go a minute without proclaiming Matt to be some kind of monster.

Then Rachel said, "They *did* seem to like him. And he refused to kill them."

"That's weird." Samantha frowned. "He's usually more sensible." Had the whole thing with Nico changed his views? He'd told her that he saw things a little differently now. Because of her, Samantha thought, blushing.

Jan shook his head. "Told you. Half hellhound."

"Cut it out, Jan." Samantha glared at him for good measure. "He's obviously emotionally challenged, but he might like animals." She turned to Rachel. "I can go and check on him." She was too curious to not see this for herself.

Confused, Jan looked back and forth between the two girls. "Are you... does that mean you're in again?"

Swallowing, she nodded. "Yes. I... I may not be able to do much, but Rachel is right, and the hellhounds... Whether I like it or not, magic will always be a part of my life, and if there's something I can do to ensure people don't get hurt, then that's what has to be done."

"You could try talking Matt out of keeping a bunch of hellhounds as pets," Jan joked.

Samantha chuckled softly. "I'll try."

Walking through the forest at night all by herself was creepy on a normal day. Doing it while there was a pack of hellhounds on the loose made Samantha's heart beat twice as fast. With her phone used as a flashlight, she trod carefully along the paths. Matt had texted her to meet him near the Ilse-Cave.

The cave was only a three to four metres deep hole in the stone wall. In the darkness, it seemed a giant patch of black. The light from Samantha's phone reflected on the wet cave walls. She thought she saw a shadow, but it turned out to be just a crevice.

"Matt?"

No response.

When she heard a distant bark, Samantha froze. The hairs on her arms stood upright. Her feet froze to the ground. Her ears strained as she listened to the barking.

It wasn't coming any closer, and it didn't sound particularly vicious. But that didn't change the fact she knew it was the hellhounds. If she backed away now, she might be able to escape them.

Matt is with them, Samantha told herself. *They listen to him—or they've eaten him.*

Unable to move her feet, Samantha lowered her phone just enough to send him a new text.

There was no reply.

The longer she waited for an answer, the more her nerves shot through her brain. When the barking drew nearer, Samantha held her breath. Even so, the pungent stench of sulphur filled the air.

Stifling a gag, Samantha jumped into the cave and pressed her back against the rock. Water dripped into her hair and down her neck, but she didn't dare make a sound. Twigs snapped nearby now, and she could hear the hellhounds sniffing in the air. Her legs grew weak, and her heart beat so hard her chest hurt. Any minute, they would hear her heartbeat or smell her presence.

A dark shadow slunk past the cave. The beast was so big it blocked her line of sight, plunging her into complete darkness. Watching the muscles roll by her, not an arm's length away, almost made her lose control of her bladder.

"There you are."

Samantha jumped, bumped into the hellhound next to her, and threw herself forward again, straight into Matt's arms. He'd appeared suddenly on her other side. How, she didn't know, only that he was here now.

"Sit," Matt said—clearly to someone else and not her—and laughed. "It's alright. They're harmless."

Her breath came quick and hard, and it took her a few seconds to find the courage to turn around. There was the hellhound, sitting as still as the best-behaved dog, its three heads alert, tongues lolling.

Matt let go of her and stepped towards the beast. A wide grin split his face as he gave each of the three heads a cuddle. And the hellhound clearly enjoyed it. If it weren't for the fact that it smelled like it had taken a bath in a volcanic lake, it would've almost been cute.

"They're awesome, aren't they?" Matt looked so happy with them, a stark difference from his usual cool demeanour.

Samantha found herself chuckling. She never would've picked him for a big animal lover. Or was it a monster lover? "They are... big."

Even though the hellhounds behaved like oversized doggies, she couldn't pretend they didn't have three sets of very impressive teeth each.

"Yeah, but that means you can ride them." His eyes sparkled.

Samantha felt the blood drain from her face. "Riding?"

"Come here."

Before she could tell him to stop, Matt had grabbed her by the hips and lifted her onto the hellhound. Samantha twisted in his grip and grabbed Matt's shoulder in terror. The hellhound stood up, and she slid a few centimetres closer to its three heads. Matt let go of her before swinging up behind her. Wedged in between Matt and the hellhound, Samantha had nowhere to go.

"Please let me down," Samantha whimpered, her heart almost jumping out of her chest.

"Relax. I've got you." He slid his arm under hers and patted the middle head. "Take us home."

If Samantha had hoped the hellhounds would take her to her true home, she was sorely disappointed. Instead, the beast carried them deeper into the dark forest. The stench of sulphur became nearly unbearable. Her back was pressed against Matt's chest, and under her she could feel the great muscles moving up and down.

As they trudged through the forest, the other hellhounds joined them. Some came up barking in what Samantha fervently hoped was genuine joy to see them, while others fell into step silently. The one they were riding was the biggest, but the others weren't exactly tiny; the smallest of them was still as big as a cow.

"Where are we going?" Samantha asked once she had come to terms with the fact that she wasn't getting out of this anytime soon.

"It took me a while to figure it out, because they've been roaming so far, even going into the city, but their lair is out here. I think they're protecting something." As he spoke, Matt's breath was warm against her ear.

"Their litter?"

"No. It's just the five of them. I think... I'm pretty sure they're actually the demon's pets. And they're protecting something he wants to keep hidden."

His words set her nerves on fire. Suddenly, every breath she took was like needles in her chest. "We're going to the demon's lair?"

"He's not there," Matt reassured her. "He's abandoned them. That's why they were roaming into the city. They got hungry."

It didn't help. Samantha couldn't keep herself from whimpering. "Hungry?" There was not enough air in her lungs for full sentences.

"Yeah, but don't worry. I fed them. They're good, much more relaxed now. Not so aggressive."

Samantha didn't know whether to trust him on that. It seemed insane. How *did* he know so much about them? And why would the demon abandon them? Was he done with whatever he'd been doing in Greenvalley and had just left them behind? Or—and this was a much scarier thought—did he want them to be more aggressive?

The hellhounds stopped, and Matt slid off the back. He held up his hand to her. "You want to see what they're protecting?"

She couldn't deny her curiosity. This was important. If they figured out what had brought the demon to Greenvalley, they might be able to figure out how to get rid of him.

Matt still held her hand as he led her on a barely visible path through thorny thickets. When the bushes broke away, they stood in a clearing. The night sky above them was full of stars, even though there had been rain clouds only half an hour ago. But that wasn't the most magical part about the clearing. Not by far.

The whole clearing was magic. Samantha felt as if she'd stepped into another world. Surrounded by thorns, she had entered a lush paradise. Fern bushes covered most of the forest floor, and where they didn't, thick patches of moss grew. Hundreds of little white flowers bloomed in the moss, and little lights flickered around. At first, Samantha thought they were fireflies, but then she saw that they were little fairy-like creatures instead. Tiny bodies with huge butterfly, moth, or dragonfly wings flitted across the clearing, carrying little buckets with them, which they dipped into a green stream that had the appearance of water but wound its way from the ground into the air, before splitting into several thinner strands that flowed into the forest.

Samantha let go of Matt's hand and raised hers to touch the green band. For a moment, she thought she had it—her fingertips tingled—then it flowed around her fingers, opening and closing around her hand.

"It's beautiful, isn't it?" Matt's eyes were fixed on the fairies. "I wonder what they're doing."

Laughter bubbled up inside her. "Isn't it obvious? They're collecting drops of magic." Samantha had no idea how she knew, but the moment she'd touched the strand, it had been there. Magic. They were surrounded by wild magic.

Matt stared at her for a moment, then understanding dawned on him. "This is it. Greenvalley's spring of magic."

Samantha took a deep breath. The air here was cleaner than any she'd ever breathed before. Not a trace of the sulphur smell the hellhounds carried with them. It was the purest place in the world. A spring of magic. Greenvalley's most-guarded secret. "Yes."

Once more, she raised her hand to touch the magic Matt seemed unable to see. Flecks of green stuck to her fingertips, slowly dissolving until no trace was left. She couldn't explain why it made her so happy, but there was a quality to this pure, natural magic that spoke to her. A connection to the world she'd never felt before.

"Yes, this is Greenvalley's magic."

Rachel

"What does a demon want with a pool of magic?" Lucille asked when they'd all gathered the next day at Elda's. She was awake again, though she looked miserable. Rachel was just glad she couldn't detect any greedy envy in her question.

Matt shrugged. "Pretty much everything." He and Samantha had found the spring of magic that Greenvalley had built its whole legacy around. "I couldn't see it, but the power is tangible in that place. If the demon got his hands on it, he could do all sorts of things to this town."

"And those doggies protect it while he's away?" Jan asked, a deep frown creasing his forehead.

"Looks like it," Matt admitted.

Meanwhile, Fabian was still occupied with another issue. "The spring of magic is actually real?"

Samantha put a hand on his knee. "I've seen it. And my grandmother has been tending to it over the years. She never took me, but it's the source of all the magic around here. It is a literal source of magic."

Rachel tried to imagine it, but all she came up with was her dream meadow surrounded by trees. "Meaning?" The way Samantha's eyes were shining, she must have found her love for all things magic again.

"There are several in the world. Just like real rivers. Some call them node points, just as they call magical rivers ley lines, and stuff like that," Samantha explained. "But it's much more organic. Fluid. Like a river moving outside the laws of gravity. And all magic and, to an extent, life, is bound to them."

Fabian's mouth stood open. He blinked a couple of times. "Okay. That's—"

"Back to the problem at hand," Matt said, obviously deciding that this had to serve as an explanation.

"We need to kill the hellhounds?" Jan asked.

"No!" Matt clicked his tongue in annoyance. "The hellhounds are innocent. The demon put them there to guard the spring, then abandoned them. We need to find out what the demon wants with the magic."

"Yeah, but there is still the problem with the hellhounds."

"There is no problem with the hellhounds!" Matt barked.

Jan clenched his fists. "Yes, there is. For example, when they attack us when we try to check out this magical clearing."

"Actually, they didn't," Samantha said softly. "They listen to Matt, and as scary as they look—and probably are—they left me in peace."

That didn't sound like the hellhounds Rachel had met, but she trusted Samantha's verdict. Matt truly seemed to have them under control.

"So, we're letting them live in the forest?" Jan asked, regarding all of them helplessly. "How sure are we that their tearing-people-apart days are over?"

Matt's face darkened, and he crossed his arms. "A hundred percent."

"I wouldn't go that far." Samantha cocked her head. When Matt's expression turned upside-down as if she'd hurt him, she quickly amended, "What I mean is that it's only been a few hours. You might be able to control them, but what if you can't?"

Matt looked to the side. The whole thing was affecting him more than Nico's death had. Rachel was about to point that out when Matt turned back around again. "They need to leave Greenvalley. Agreed."

"Well, having them somewhere else isn't that much better," Lucille reminded him.

"I know. I wasn't talking about somewhere else. At least not in this world."

"This world?" Fabian asked, sinking a little deeper into the couch. "There is more than one world?"

Samantha's hand on his knee grabbed a little harder, but it was Matt who answered the question. "Well, yes. There is Hell, for example, which is where I intend to send them."

"There is Hell," Fabian's voice turned a little shrill. "Real Hell. Full of demons, I suppose."

"Yeeaah?" Matt seemed unsure of how to deal with Fabian's oncoming panic attack. "Since that's their home world, obviously."

Fabian was hyperventilating. Rachel's heart went out to him. While the confirmation of Hell was news to her too, she'd already assumed such a thing from the mere fact that their world didn't seem to be crawling with demons. If she were honest, though, an entire world of demons was as upsetting to think about as a forest full of hellhounds.

"Most demons aren't interested in Ashuan. Uhm... our world. That's the name they..." Matt waved it off. "Anyway. The hellhounds live in Hell, so we'll send them back there."

"And how do we do this?" Lucille asked. "I'm not using a spell." Her voice broke, and she blinked furiously.

Matt ignored it. "Well, option one is finding the gate to Hell that they originally came through, but that could be anywhere."

"There are gates to Hell," Fabian muttered, while Samantha patted his leg.

"Option two, we'll find someone who's proficient with banishing magic."

Fabian yelped. "I'm not even proficient in water magic."

"Well, that leaves option three. We open a gate to Hell."

Everyone stared. It was so quiet in the room that one could hear a pin drop.

"You can't be serious," Fabian whispered.

Matt shrugged, but he didn't seem as confident as before. "It would only be open for a bit. The gate opens, I tell the hellhounds to get through, and then we close it." With a lilt in his voice, he tried to make it sound more positive.

"Uhm..." Samantha started, biting her lip. "Purely hypothetically, could something come through from the other side while we do it?"

"Only if that something is close by and actually interested in coming." Despite Matt's casual tone, the anxiety in the room rose.

"That's not a no," Rachel pointed out quietly.

Matt spread his hands. "But it's not a yes either."

"Have you ever done that before?" Lucille asked.

"Of course he has!" Jan forcefully pointed at Matt. "Who do you think summoned the demon?"

Matt massaged the bridge of his nose while they all groaned at Jan's baseless accusations. "No, Lucille," Matt said at last, forcing a smile. "I haven't done it before." Then his face soured as he turned towards Jan. "And *no,* I didn't summon the demon either."

Jan only sneered. "That's what I would say if I were in your shoes."

"Jan, stop it!" Samantha shot up to her feet. "We are all in this together. Matt isn't some monster spying on us just because you don't like him. He saved my life. And yours! And I'm pretty sure that if he wanted to kill us, he would've done so two months ago."

Pretending to be unaffected, Matt pulled on his shirt. "I might reconsider that, though, if you keep annoying me."

Samantha took a deep breath, ignored Jan, and faced Matt. "How do we open a portal to Hell?"

"Well, it's actually pretty easy. You need a little blood and..."

"Blood?" Fabian asked.

Jan made a mute gesture by opening his eyes wide and nodding towards Matt. It was clear what he meant.

"As I said, it's just a little bit." Matt pointed at his palm, imitating a cut. "One small slash and..."

"I volunteer Matt for this blood sacrifice!" Jan announced loudly.

"I volunteer nobody," Fabian muttered.

Matt clenched his fists and approached Jan. "If you've got a problem—"

"Stop it!" Samantha jumped between the two, using her body to keep them at a distance.

"Oh, yeah, I've got a big problem with you!" Jan shouted over Samantha's head, shaking his fist.

Samantha pressed her hands against Matt's chest, but he ignored her to grab Jan's fist. "Then let's get it over with, once and for all."

"Boys!" Samantha cried, now wedged between them.

She had absolutely no chance. The two guys were snarling and throwing insults at each other that grew nastier with each exchange, while verging on the edge of a physical fight. Lucille cowered in her seat, covered her eyes, and started crying, while Fabian looked utterly helpless, still caught in his panic attack.

Rachel had had enough. A demon was treating Greenvalley as his own personal playground. He'd already taken her brother. He would not take her friends. And friends they were. All of them. Even though she wouldn't have believed to have anything in common with the likes of Jan, Lucille, or Matt.

She walked over to the table, where the big copy of the Seer's *Circle of Magic* book lay, raised it high, and slammed it back down on the table.

That got everybody's attention.

"Rachel?" Fabian asked, finally snapping out of his panic attack.

"This, right here." Rachel pointed at the book. "Nico was right."

"What are you talking about?" Jan asked as he took a step away from Matt.

Rachel opened the book and flicked through the pages until she came upon the page labelled "The Emblems of Power". "Matt's sword, Lucille's necklace, Fabian's feather, and my dreams, plus the other two." She pointed at Samantha and Jan. "Six Emblems of Power and six of us."

"Uhm, we actually have no idea where the flowers and the bracelet, or the dreamweb is," Samantha pointed out, then looked away dejectedly.

"It doesn't matter. I'm convinced they'll come to us." In her mind, she flashed back to the bus trip they'd taken back when everything had been so new and exciting. Nico's teeth had flashed in a grin as he'd proposed his theory. Everything pointed to him being right, apart from one thing. He wasn't one of the six bearers.

"That is a creepy thought," Fabian said, making her roll her eyes. "It's just a book, not some prophecy. Who wrote this book anyway?"

Matt stepped forward to look at the front. "The Seer," he said with a snort. "Of course."

"You know them?" Samantha asked.

"I-I've heard of him. He... he's pretty good," Matt admitted.

"Good as in...?" Rachel pointed to the book.

Matt nodded. "Oh, if he's made any predictions, they'll come true. It makes me wonder why he would deposit the book here."

"You think he deposited it at my grandma's?" Samantha asked.

"For certain. Ch... The Seer doesn't do anything without purpose. And he certainly doesn't write entire books and then lose track of them."

The entire room was quiet enough to hear a pin drop. Lucille was the first one to clear her throat. "What does this mean?"

No one stepped up to answer, so Rachel did. "I don't know, but I know what it means to me." She looked around the room. "It means that we're in this together. So, no more backing out," she pleaded Fabian. "And no more antagonising." Her pointed glare went to Jan, who lowered his head. "We were meant to meet each other." She was utterly convinced that the missing Emblems of Power would turn up sooner rather than later.

A tear ran down her cheek as she once again remembered that Nico wouldn't be part of it. "So, please, stop fighting and let's face this together as we're meant to."

Samantha slid an arm around her and nodded. "I may only be able to see magic and mix a few potions, but I'm in. I'm sorry I let my fear get the upper hand of me." She looked for help from Fabian. Was he still planning to sit on the sidelines? Or was he going to be the hero Rachel desperately wanted him to be?

Fabian raised his shoulders in a helpless shrug, but then he said, "I still think it's creepy that this book turned up here, but you've got one thing right. We're friends, and you know I could never abandon you, even if I pee myself."

Lucille stretched out her hand to clasp Fabian's and smiled at him. "You're not the only one who's afraid." She nodded at the rest of them. "I'm in. If you still want me."

"Well, it wasn't your fault the necklace got cursed, right?" Matt said. "And if it's cleaned again and you promise to exert some caution—"

"If *you* promise not to sneak away a hellhound to keep him as a pet," Jan interjected, but his jab lacked malice. He even smirked. "I guess a little blood is fine if it keeps our woods safe."

Rachel chuckled, then she promised, "That demon will lose a lot more blood."

"Alright!" Jan hooted. "Let's kick some demon ass... and evict a couple of lovely but dangerous hellhounds."

Jan

This time, all six of them went into the forest. Not that it made Jan feel much safer. Rachel's dreams wouldn't be much help, and neither would Samantha's ability to see magic. At least Rachel could shoot a crossbow, and Samantha somehow kept Matt's more psychopathic tendencies in check. Fabian was a hit or miss with his powers, and Lu wasn't even wearing her necklace, which was still being cleaned by Elda. They had tested whether she was still able to do spells. She was, but it was back to the limited spells she had learnt so far, and weaker versions of them on top.

The only one he could rely on in a fight was Matt, and his brain was addled by his strange love for the hellhounds. Rachel might be of the opinion that they belonged together, but Jan couldn't bring himself to trust Matt. There was a tingling, a premonition that Matt was keeping a secret from all of them. Something didn't add up. And perhaps Jan's suspicions were ridiculous and out of line, but he was used to people dismissing him. After all, his parents had always done that when he'd tried to tell them about his monster encounters as a child. The mistrust and constant dismissal had ruined his relationship with them. He should've just given up on the monsters, but he couldn't. And he wouldn't give up on his suspicions about Matt either. There was something wrong with him. Jan just couldn't prove it yet.

Lu rubbed her eyes tiredly. She was holding a light spell in her hand, but instead of the usual bright-as-daylight glare, it was little more than an orb-shaped lantern. It didn't bode well for when the hellhounds would eventually attack them.

They stopped at a junction of hiking paths, somewhere deep in the forest. Jan vaguely remembered it from school excursions. Other than that, he wasn't truly into going on walks in the national park. Not like Fabian, the Junior Scout.

"I think we should do it here," Matt told Samantha, as if the rest of them weren't even there. "While the gate will probably pop into existence at the spring, I'm afraid the magic would keep it open much longer than we want. Once we're ready, I'll get the hellhounds, and we can send them back."

A series of twigs snapped around them. Jan froze. All around them, red eyes glared at them from the darkness. The wind brought with it a cloud of rotten egg, making him gag, and then he saw *him*.

As silent as if he'd stepped into the forest this very moment, the demon stood on the path ahead of them, his yellow eyes burning through the night. It was the same guy Jan and Nico had angered, the one with the goatee and the meticulous suit. When the demon looked at them, Jan felt as if he was only watching him—and deciding how to kill him.

"Attack!" His voice was like a whip crack.

As one, the hellhounds sprang into motion. The friends jumped closer together. Jan pulled out his pocket knife, and Lu jumbled up the syllables of her defensive spell.

"Stop!" Matt shouted, arms outstretched.

To Jan's surprise, the hellhounds skidded to a stop. Some were snarling, others were whining and lowering their heads.

The demon was not impressed. He glowered at Matt. "Do you really think you're a match for me, kid?"

Matt drew his sword, but for once, he wasn't the uber-confident monster hunter. Jan saw his shoulders bunch a couple of times. Nevertheless, Matt said, "Let's see about that." Through his teeth, he hissed, "Run."

Fabian and Rachel took his advice immediately. Holding hands, they snuck past the hellhound behind them and quickly hurried away on the path.

Lu didn't act quite as cowardly—or sensibly. "But Matt..." Jan saw how frightened Lu was. This was the demon who'd wreaked havoc on her life, all with a simple touch. And still, she would battle him if Matt let her.

"Rip them apart!"

Samantha grabbed Lu's arm and dragged her with her. They didn't get further than a few steps before a hellhound snapped at them.

"Off! Sit! Down!" Matt's commands were like pistol fire, and again, the hellhounds complied, skittering to a stop in front of Matt.

Gasping, the girls slid past the hellhound to team up with Fabian and Rachel. Jan watched them huddle together before readjusting the grip on his pocket knife. He might not be Matt's biggest fan, but he wasn't going to leave him alone with five hellhounds and a kill-crazy demon. Let his parents explain away the bloody corpse of him this time!

"Go!" Matt hissed.

"I'm staying."

Matt barked out a laugh. "You won't get far with that little knife. Sit!"

While Jan had been determined to stand with Matt, a hellhound had edged closer. Now it whined under Matt's stare, and the idiot's gaze softened. He stretched out a hand, welcoming the hellhound and rubbing his head with one hand.

Jan was about to despair when Matt's eyes locked with his over the heads of the hellhound. The message was clear: *Get out of here while I keep him away from you.*

His resolve weakened. If Matt thought he could buy them some time, then his sacrifice shouldn't be in vain. Jan would meet up with the others, and they would come back for Matt with a plan.

He quickened his strides and was about to fall into a jog when the demon snarled. "Just you and me? Fine with me. But don't think I'll let the others run and tell." He bellowed at the hellhounds. "Leave this one for me! Rip apart the others."

The jog turned into a sprint when Jan heard the footfall of the hellhounds. While they adored Matt and wouldn't hurt him, they had no such qualms about the rest of them. The bloodthirsty barking reverberated through Jan's bones. He ran faster than he ever had, adrenaline rushing through his veins.

Behind him, Matt was still trying to command the hellhounds when his voice suddenly broke off, followed by a loud thud and the sound of something heavy rolling through the wet leaves. Hearing no scream, Jan hoped that meant Matt was alright.

Ahead of him, Fabian had helped Rachel and Lu onto the branches of a tree and was holding out a hand for Samantha, but a hellhound broke out of the thicket next to them and made for Samantha. Samantha shrieked and jumped to the side, but whether she escaped or not, Jan couldn't see.

He was being followed by two hellhounds, and they were nipping at his feet. He saw a large rock and began scrambling up on it. The surface was wet, and he bumped his knee before scraping his elbow in the process. Behind him, the claws of the hellhounds dragged across the stone. A terrible screeching noise tore the night apart.

Jan gasped for air as he balanced on the tip of the rock, way too close to the ground. The two hellhounds jumped at him, dug their claws in, and slid down again.

"Jan!" Samantha called. She'd managed to climb a tree not too far from him. The hellhound that had been following her had joined the others under the tree that held Fabian, Rachel, and Lu. The three of them slunk around the trunk, randomly throwing themselves against the wood.

A hellhound landed on the rock next to Jan, this time not going anywhere. His instincts kicked in, and he delivered a proper roundhouse kick to the hellhound. The impact threw the hellhound off the rock and into its companion.

But the momentum made Jan slip as well. He took the opportunity to jump off and landed on the soft forest floor, where he rolled his ankle in a small depression. Ignoring the pain, he jumped up and ran for Samantha's tree, practically throwing himself up. Samantha grabbed his upper arm, and together, they managed to pull him up just in time. A hellhound's teeth missed his shoe by only a few millimetres.

It was as if Jan had only now remembered how to breathe. Or rather, that he couldn't. He tried to draw air, but pitifully little made it into his tightening lungs. Stupid asthma attack. How was one supposed to fight monsters if their body didn't comply? Jan patted his jacket, then saw the inhaler lying on the ground. Dammit!

Samantha had climbed a little higher and regarded the hellhounds with worry. The beasts were drawing closer and closer. Sometimes, one of them would hit the tree with its front paws. The impact shook the tree so much that Jan felt like an apple on the cusp of falling. So long as the tree didn't break before then or he choked from his lungs seizing up.

Suddenly, Matt landed between the trees, leaving a scar in the leafy underground as he slid at least three metres over the ground. Jan winced just looking at it. It didn't surprise him that Matt remained lying on his back, groaning in pain.

The hellhounds had a new target now. One of them broke away from the tree and trotted over to him. As Matt lay there, it towered over him, lowering its three heads.

Above Jan, Samantha choked on a sob. He was unable to look away, trying his best to counter the asthma attack with the breathing techniques his mum had taught him long ago.

Matt didn't have a chance. He was hurt, and the hellhound had pinned him to the ground. His eyes had widened, and his breath had become ragged. Now the right head of the hellhound opened his mouth—and licked the scrapes on Matt's face.

When the hellhound raised his head again, tongue lolling happily, the wounds on Matt's face were gone.

"Did you have to soften them up?" The demon walked through the leaves as if he was on a Sunday stroll. "It'll take years to retrain their bite."

Matt got to his knees and used the hellhound to drag himself up further. "Perhaps they'd listen more to you if they liked you a little better." A second hellhound had come to Matt and pressed itself against his side.

The demon chuckled. "Liked me? These aren't pets, human bastard." He snorted at the affectionate display of his precious hellhounds. "Very well. Let's see if they like your friends as much as they adore you."

"I'll tell you later, but right now, we need to get out of here," he said, pushing her towards the door.

Just as Zax grabbed for the doorknob, the door swung open, and in came Professor Brian with one hand behind his back. He looked calm, but Zax caught a glimpse of something shiny sticking out to the Professor's side; he could only guess it to be some sort of weapon. Zax squinted and focused on the object in the Professor's hand. It was a knife handle.

"What's the rush? I thought you were here for detention," Professor Brian said in his thick German accent. He then nodded at his computer and, in his peculiar accent, continued, "By the way...you know, you shouldn't look at other peoples' computers without their permission." He clearly knew that Zax had seen the article by the fright in Zax's eyes and his haste to get out of the lab.

"What are you talking about?" Zax asked, trying to disguise his angst.

"There are cameras in the room, boy, and I have access to them," Professor Brian smirked. "Now, let's see what those cameras show, shall we?"

With the knife still behind his back, Professor Brian used his free hand to lift his cell phone out of his pocket and access his camera app. Zax glanced at Jaiden and saw the confusion on her face. Professor Brian, nor Jaiden, had any idea that he knew what was in the Professor's other hand.

"Well, well…" Professor Brian sneered. "The camera shows you reading something on my monitor. It appears that whatever you saw must have scared you, and you were running away." He looked up and into Zax's eyes. "So, what did you see that seemed to frighten you?" he asked with an arrogant look on his face. Zax knew, without a doubt, that Professor Brian knew *exactly* what he'd seen.

"Nothing," Zax said with a tinge of fear in his voice.

"I don't believe you," Professor Brian glared.

They all stood still for a moment as if they were in an old Western showdown. Then, out of nowhere, Professor Brian lunged at Zax with the knife. Zax raised his bare arms hoping to block the attack but thought how stupid he was to believe he actually could. He really didn't care if he was slashed, as long as Jaiden was safe. Right now, he was determined to protect her.

All at once, Zax realized he wasn't being cut into ribbons. He looked up and saw that Professor Brian's arms were being held by the same energy that he had been seeing everywhere. Jaiden and Professor Brian stared at him with astonishment. Zax was clearly confused; the stream of energy that held Professor Brian's arms led straight to Zax's hands.

Zax lowered his arms, and the energy dissipated. Professor Brian's arms dropped, and the knife fell to the floor. The three of them just stood

He raised his arms, palms pointing towards the two trees, and released two pulsing orbs of energy. The energy raced towards Jan. There was no escape. He pressed himself against the tree, bracing for impact.

The energy crashed into the tree. Wood splintered and gave way. Jan slid down, the bark ripping into his face. In pain, he let go, and slammed into the ground.

Though the impact drove the little air he had left from his lungs, he grabbed his inhaler and got up instantly, arms raised to defend himself against the hellhounds. Above him, Samantha hung from a cracked branch, the creaking noise not boding well. On the other side, Lu had fallen through the branches, while Rachel and Fabian had been lucky. They pressed against each other and the tree.

A growl made Jan whimper. The hellhound was coming for him.

Another blast of blinding energy raced past the corner of his eyes, and a heart-tearing howl arose. Matt had gone after one of the hellhounds at last. Sadly, not the one in front of Jan.

There was nowhere to run. He took a quick puff and exchanged the inhaler for his pocket knife. Then he held his other hand out, ready to grab the hellhound by one of his three necks while he used the knife. He doubted he'd ever make contact with the hellhound's skin before it ripped his arm off, but god dammit, he'd try.

Just as the hot, stinky breath hit him in the face, something snapped above him. A second later, Samantha and the remainder of a once thick and healthy branch landed squarely on the hellhound.

Jan dashed forward and plunged his pocket knife first into one throat, then into another. The third head snapped at Samantha, but Jan raised his knee and kicked the hellhound in the snout. The impact drove it back, and another kick cracked his skull. A few seconds later, the hellhound's legs folded.

"Thanks," Samantha whispered, her voice shaky. Her face was scratched by the branch, but other than that, she seemed fine.

Or not. When Jan helped her up, her foot gave way, and she gasped sharply. Jan put an arm around her and held her close as he quickly cast around to take in the situation. At least his lungs had expanded again.

Matt stood in front of Lu, his sword back in his hand. Three hellhounds approached them. When the first one took a jump, one fell swoop beheaded all three heads at once. The remaining creatures howled in despair, before they all came for Matt at once.

In that moment, a flood of water hit the hellhounds and pushed them several metres back. The two beasts whined, tucked their tails in, and ran into the darkness.

"Cowards."

Jan had almost forgotten about the demon, but his attention was now settling on Fabian. "Get down!" he hissed.

When Fabian didn't comply immediately, the demon suddenly sprouted wings. This close, Jan could see the veins in the thick leather. In an instant, he was in that tree, grabbed Fabian, and drove him into the ground.

Rachel screamed. Fabian tried to scramble away, but the demon hit him in the stomach, and Jan could hear how all the breath was knocked out of him. Gagging, Fabian cowered on the ground, unable to protect himself.

"No!" Sword raised high, Matt jumped at the demon.

But the monster was faster. He hurtled another ball of energy at Matt and threw him backwards. Then he kicked Fabian so hard the ginger flipped over at least four times.

"Fabian!" Samantha screamed.

She lunged forward to run to him, but Jan jerked her back. The deep growl of the remaining hellhound, the largest of them all, was suddenly at their side.

The demon went for Matt, his fingers closing around his neck. Matt gagged, his fingers digging into the hand that choked him. The hellhound bared his teeth. Jan and Samantha backed away until they hit the tree. Jan pushed himself in front of her, the hand with his pocket knife trembling.

Just then, a boom shook the forest. The hellhound jumped and dashed away.

Meanwhile, the demon had let go of Matt. He was crouching next to him, lightning crackling across his body.

Jan followed his line of sight to see a man standing on the path. He was about Matt's height and vaguely familiar to Jan, though he couldn't quite pin down where he knew the guy from. In his hand was a bronze gun with runes carved into every inch of the weapon. It pointed at the demon.

"Take your hands off my son!"

Matt's father. The elementary school teacher.

Before Jan could even begin to unwrap that revelation, a second shot loosened. It would've hit the demon, but the hell creature had vanished into thin air, just the way he'd done at the mine. He didn't reappear.

Mr Traidous lowered his gun, though he kept glancing into the forest. Only when he was satisfied that the demon wouldn't reappear did he come closer. By then, Matt had got back up on his feet, though he rubbed his bruised throat.

"How did you know we were here?" he asked.

"I didn't." Mr Traidous took a look at all of them. He transformed back into an unassuming teacher surprisingly quickly. "I've been following the demon's movements for the last few days. Unfortunately, I can't jump through space like he can, so it took me a while to get here. Are you guys okay?" He extended that question to all of them.

The six of them drew closer. Lu was limping, while Jan had to help Samantha hop over. Rachel had run to Fabian and assisted him with sitting up. Jan was glad to see his friend alive, with no obvious flesh wounds visible.

"That was amazing," Lu said.

Jan mirrored the awe on her face. "So cool. Where do we get a gun like that?" With a weapon as powerful as this one, their next encounter with a demon would be a breeze.

Mr Traidous sighed. He put the gun into the inner pocket of his jacket and said, "Nowhere. Such weapons aren't for children."

"I'm of age," Jan said. He truly wanted that weapon.

"Then get your gun license, and we'll talk about it." There was no way in hell that Jan would pass the qualifications. Matt's father studied them once more. "The demon will be back, as will his hellhounds. You need time to recover." He looked at Samantha. "Does your grandmother mind if we crash there?"

Samantha's eyes widened. "You know my... No, she wouldn't mind."

"Let's go, then. Matt, go help Rachel with Fabian," his father ordered. "Do you need help, Lucille?"

Lu shook her head. "I think I'm okay if we walk slow."

Mr Traidous glanced over his shoulder. "We'd better not be too slow."

As they filed into a long line to form the saddest march back home Jan had ever been part of, he was slowly putting the pieces together.

Matt's father knew about demons and hellhounds. And while he was an elementary school teacher by day, he was every bit as competent in the battle against the supernatural as his son. He even had a specialised anti-demon weapon. Suddenly, it wasn't so weird how knowledgeable and proficient, or even pragmatic, Matt was.

Jan assumed his mother was in the same business. He'd been raised that way, probably fighting monsters ever since he could hold that sword.

He'd finally solved the mystery around Matt, though why his friend didn't talk openly about it was still unclear. Maybe because, for the first time ever, he'd wanted to live a normal life. As a student, hanging out with friends, fooling around with even more. But there was no such thing as a normal life. Not in Greenvalley, and not for Matt.

Because, like his father, he was a demon hunter.

Fabian

Every step Fabian took was accompanied by pain, causing him to lean more heavily on Matt than he'd intended. On his other side, Rachel was deep in thought.

"How are you okay?" he asked Matt. "That demon threw you around like a rag doll."

"I'm just better at hiding it." Matt gave him a soft smile.

If that was true, he was one hell of an actor. Fabian didn't even try to attempt to hide his pain. It hurt way too much.

He glanced back over his shoulder, where his old elementary school teacher talked softly to Samantha. "So, your dad is a demon hunter?"

"Not really," Matt answered. "He told me he retired before I was born. But apparently, *his* father is."

"Apparently?"

"Never met him." Matt shrugged as much as Fabian's arm allowed. "They're not close. I didn't even know he kept some of his old stuff."

Fabian winced as a step drove another round of hot pain through his body. "Well, I'm glad he turned up when he did."

"Same."

"That demon was waiting for us."

Matt's face darkened. "Yeah."

Fabian watched him from the side. They'd set out to return the hellhounds to Hell. Now two of the beasts were dead, and the rest had fled. But most importantly, they'd turned on Matt. Or he'd been forced to turn on them.

"I'm sorry the plan didn't work."

"We'll have to try again," Matt said.

Fabian jerked his head around and immediately regretted the motion. "What?" Surely, this fight had proved that they were all in over their heads here.

"Well, right now, we have three hellhounds on the loose. If we can send them back, great, but if not, they need to be..." Matt's voice got lost in a mumble.

"Sorry," Fabian repeated softly.

Warm light flooded the path in front of them. They had arrived. Soon Fabian would be able to sit down and indulge in this pain. But first, he had to get past a surprising visitor.

"Meg? What are you doing here?"

Samantha's annoying little sister was standing at the door of the little cottage. She had her arms crossed and glowered at him. "I'm allowed to visit my grandma, am I not?" Her eyes roved across the sorry train of people in front of her. "Gosh, did you all roll down a hill?"

Reminded of rolling through the wet leaves, Fabian winced. "We fought off..." He couldn't tell Meg that. With her attitude, she would insist on joining them in the future, and as annoying as she was, he didn't want to get her hurt. She was like a sister to him, after all. "Rabid dogs."

"Your sister heroically saved my life by falling out of a tree," Jan boasted, grinning.

Meg burst into giggles. "Really? Oh my gosh, you're such a weird bunch." And then she did the most surprising thing ever. She took a step, grabbed Jan's hand, and said, "Come on, I'll get the first aid kit out."

Jan's eyes widened as she dragged him inside, but he didn't exactly protest.

Fabian searched for Samantha. As expected, she was as bewildered as him. Meg and Jan. That was certainly new.

The rest of them filed into the house and were welcomed by Elda. The older witch had already expected their return and prepared poultices and strengthening potions that came in the form of aromatic tea.

A couple of minutes later, Fabian was lying on the couch, the only acceptable kind of magic sinking into his muscles and easing the pain.

Rachel stayed at his side, constantly stroking his hand, if she wasn't jumping up to make him more comfortable. Gone was the bitter front she'd put on when she'd shamed him about being afraid of monsters.

"I'm so sorry I made us all go there," she whispered.

Fabian smiled at her. "Well, I wouldn't have let you go on your own."

Her eyes shimmered, and she quickly lowered her head. Fabian was reminded of what Jan and Matt had said the night they'd watched Nico. After the horrible day that had followed, he'd thought little about it, but her reaction brought it all back. How could he have ever been so blind?

On the other side of the room, Elda was caring for Samantha's swollen ankle. Lucille, Matt, and his father stood in one corner of the room and were discussing what had happened. As Lucille mentioned Matt's affection for the hellhounds, he let his head sink. If Fabian didn't know better, he would've thought Matt was about to cry. His father must've thought the same because he moved in and placed a hand on Matt's shoulder, gently letting him know he was there for him.

Jan and Meg were nowhere to be seen. It didn't take a genius to figure out what was going on there.

Elda finished up with Samantha's ankle. "You should be fine tomorrow." Then she picked up a bundle and walked over to the group of three to hand it to Lucille. "Here, darling. I've cleaned it from the demonic touch and put a protection spell on it. You should be fine to use it again."

Lucille unwrapped the bundle with trembling fingers and took out her necklace. "I still have to fix everything." Her voice choked on the words.

"Not everything," Elda said with a smile. "A lot of the more durable spells were still entangled with the amulet. I cut the magic free and sorted them. Transformations, memory spells, personality changes... all those kinds of spells are resolved. Things should be mostly back to normal, though damage has been done as a result of the magic that I couldn't fix so easily. But we'll look at that together."

Tears fell onto the necklace. "My grandmother would be so disappointed," Lucille cried.

Elda laughed. "Oh, no. She did the same thing and worse. We all mess up from time to time. Magic is a huge responsibility. To wield it, you need a lot of experience, but experience only comes from using it. And from making mistakes. You've learnt your lesson. And don't forget it was cursed with greed."

As Lucille put her necklace back on, Fabian pondered over the words. His own magic was unreliable at best. While he'd sent the hellhounds running today, his magic had failed him when he'd tried to defend Jan on that rock. Running away from his magic wasn't an option. The hellhound attacks of the last few days had shown that.

According to his mother, Fabian had repressed his talent for years, but he doubted he could do that again. Not that he wanted to. The sudden realisation surprised and scared him in equal amounts. But it was true. If his friends were in danger, he would use magic every time. And that meant learning how to control it better.

"I'm gonna take care of the hellhounds," Matt announced. His jaw set, he seemed to have come to a decision about their fate. "It's my fault the situation escalated as it did. I could've got rid of them when we first encountered them. So, I'm gonna do that now."

"Matt," Lucille put a hand on his shoulder. "Though I'm happy you changed your mind, what do we do if the demon comes back?"

"*We* won't do anything. I'll think of something." The lines of his jaw grew even sharper.

Samantha shook her head. "You're not going out there alone. We'll come with you."

"We will?" Fabian asked. He almost bit his tongue. Of course, he would go with Matt, especially if the others went too, but he would prefer if none of them went.

Rachel brushed his hand with a light touch. "Yes." Somehow, her unwavering belief in him made him want to be strong for her.

"We're a team," Lucille said, forcing a smile. "We're in this together, remember?"

For some reason, Matt seemed surprised, even touched by the declaration. He'd truly expected them to let him go out there alone.

His father crossed his arms, though. "You can't defeat that demon. My gun should've killed him, but it barely paralysed him. This particular one must be ancient. And powerful."

"I'm afraid we're not just dealing with a regular demon," Elda chimed in. "This is a demon of the House of Greed. Perhaps even a servant to the archdemon himself."

A chill ran down Fabian's spine. "Archdemon?"

He wasn't the only one shocked. Matt looked as if someone had slapped him across the face. "Why would an archdemon send their servants to Greenvalley?"

"The magic. At least that's what I think he's after." Elda nodded to herself. "It would be quite tempting, especially to a demon who can never have enough."

"Well, we can't—" Fabian started, but he never got around to saying that they couldn't possibly expect to face down someone that belonged to an archdemon's personal entourage.

"We should make a move while he's still incapacitated then," Matt said.

A normal father would've told Matt to forget it—that it was too dangerous—but Mr Traidous only nodded, deeply frowning. "I'll try to lure him away while you deal with the hellhounds. I can do a summoning." He definitely didn't teach them that in elementary school.

"And if he does turn up, Fabian will deal with him," Rachel of all people said.

Fabian stared at her, then laughed, which his bruised stomach complained about immediately. "That's a good one. Very good." What the hell was she talking about?

Rachel shook her head, no mirth on her face. "I mean it. You sent those hellhounds running, and suddenly you became his prime target."

"And that's a good thing?" Not in his book it was.

Now the others were chiming in. Lucille said, "It means he was afraid of you."

"Or not afraid, but he certainly thought you were a threat," Matt added.

"Ignoring Matt's battle experience, you're the most powerful of us," Samantha said.

Fabian was stunned. Never in a million years would he consider himself powerful. It was just a little water. Okay, a high-pressured jet stream of it when the magic actually came to him, but still. "We're talking an archdemon here. I didn't stand a chance once he was onto me."

For some reason, Rachel was grinning. "But this time, you've got the advantage."

"I do?"

She pointed at the windows. Long traces of water were running down the window. "It's started raining."

They didn't leave immediately. The rain was there to stay, and they desperately needed a break and some healing. Fabian dozed off on the couch after the second cup of tea, and when he woke, the world outside was grey instead of black, and his pain levels had been reduced to a colourful bruise.

It was a Friday morning, but none of them thought of school. Even Samantha agreed to let her mother call her in as sick. Fabian's own mother had asked a lot of uncomfortable questions, rightly assuming that there was a supernatural cause for his absence, but Fabian didn't want her to be a part of this and get hurt, so he held his tongue about the real reasons and feigned a sore tummy. That part, at least, was true.

Matt and his father returned in the morning, both clad for battle. At school, Mr Traidous had always looked a little like a desolate poet. Tall and lanky, with a beige coat and a dark turtleneck. Now he was wearing a long-sleeved black shirt, what looked like a bulletproof vest, and a belt with lots of pockets. His gun wasn't visible, but Fabian had no doubt that he'd brought it.

Matt, on the other hand, was wearing what looked like leather armour straight out of a fantasy movie. What would've looked costumey on anyone else, fit him like a glove, making him appear even more dashing.

"What's with the Lord of the Rings outfit?" Jan asked with a snort.

"It offers more protection and mobility than a pair of jeans and a T-shirt," Matt said drily, his look contrasting against Jan's casual attire.

Jan shrugged and pouted. "I can move just fine."

"Good," Matt said. "Are we ready to go?"

"I'll head off and draw out the demon," his father said. He put his hand on Matt's shoulder. "Be careful, okay?"

Matt seemed entirely unfazed by the looming doom, but he regaled his father with a curt, "You, too."

The rest of them had geared up with protective spells, courtesy of Samantha's grandmother, and weapons from her late-husband's stash. To Jan's dismay, there had been no gun, but he'd found himself a pretty set of long daggers.

Fabian was glad his powers meant he didn't have to pick a weapon. The whole thing was bad enough without him stabbing himself in the foot or fumbling around with a crossbow like the ones Rachel and Samantha carried.

Like him, Lucille was also relying on her powers, but she'd written a bunch of spells on the inside of her arm that she'd failed to cram into her brain last night. Doing magic the hard way had left dark circles under her eyes.

It was pouring when they left to march to the clearing. Fabian knew he should be happy about the advantage, but he was quickly overwhelmed with the wetness of his clothes and the constant water in his eyes. If only he could control the water in a way that wouldn't get him wet.

Once, he saw a group of birds huddling on a branch. Other than that, the forest was deserted. If only that could've been true of the hellhounds.

But the remaining three beasts were waiting for them in front of a series of thorny bushes, red eyes glowing, teeth bared, and snarling.

Matt raised a hand, and they came to a stop. "Calm!" he told the hellhounds. They whined and settled down, pushing their snouts between their paws. The creatures didn't like the rain any more than the humans did. Maybe even less.

"I know you're not used to wet coming from the sky," Matt said, as he crouched down. "It's not nice of your master to leave you out here when you're so miserable." He sighed and paused for a bit. Then he took a deep breath and started clearing away the leaves. "You don't like him very much, huh?"

Next to him, Samantha lowered herself to help him with the leaves, while she nervously kept glancing over her shoulder. She took a stick and began drawing a circle. "Like this?" she whispered.

Matt nodded at her. "Yeah. That's good." Once again, he addressed the hellhounds. "Let's return you to where you belong, okay?"

Samantha stepped away, and Matt stretched out his left hand towards Jan. Jan looked a bit apprehensive, but then he gripped his dagger tighter and put the tip on Matt's palm. There, he stopped. Fabian could see how he was trying to work himself up to draw blood and failed.

Instead, Matt folded his fingers around the dagger and sliced through his own hand. Fabian saw the bright red blood squeeze out from Matt's fist and turned his head away, nausea hitting his stomach.

Matt, however, didn't even flinch. He moved his fist over the centre of the circle and opened it. Blood dropped on the forest floor as he raised his voice. "Obre thorin a dûr lôrac e Hescaryn."

The words were unfamiliar to Fabian, and there was something sinister about them. Something that frightened him to the very core.

A small pool of blood congregated at Matt's feet, then shot outwards like the radial strings of a spider web. Matt stepped backwards, taking great care not to step on the outside circle, and watched the blood fill the line drawn by Samantha.

Fabian didn't have time to wonder how those few drops could've flown so far, much less filled the groove, because at the moment the blood met again in the circle, the air above it tore apart. There was no other way to describe it. A second earlier, Fabian had been unable to see anything, and suddenly there was something. A shimmer, like ripples in the air. It was visible and yet intangible.

"Did it work?" Lucille asked in a hushed whisper.

Instead of answering, Matt put first his hand and then his head in it, giving them all a fright when his head simply vanished. A second later, he pulled it out again. "Yep, that's Hell. Looks clear."

Fabian thought about whether he wanted to know what Hell looked like but decided he didn't need that kind of information. The hellhounds were more than enough Hell, in his opinion.

"How will you lure them through there?" Jan asked.

Matt frowned. "By asking." He stepped forward to kneel next to the circle. "Come here. That's the way home."

The hellhounds raised their many heads and sniffed in the air. They quickly came up to their feet, wagging their tails. As gruesome as they were, they were excited to go home. Just like normal dogs.

But before they'd come close to the circle, the demon appeared between them. "Halt!" His eyes were glowing, and he wiped blood from his chin. On his back, a pair of leathery wings were fully extended. They were partially ripped, but healing fast.

"Thought I'd find you here." He patted his clothes as if to shake off dust and smiled cruelly at Matt, who'd paled. "Hope you don't mind me being a bit late. I had to get rid of another caller."

Fabian's spine turned to ice. His stomach twisted into a painful knot. Mr Traidous was supposed to keep the demon's attention, to kill him if possible, but the demon was here. Mere minutes after Mr Traidous was supposed to engage him. And by the sounds of it, *had* engaged him.

"Matt," Lucille whispered, putting a hand on his shoulder.

Matt didn't shake it off. He kept staring straight ahead. From behind, Fabian could see his shoulders bunching. The sight made his own eyes burn with suppressed tears.

Then someone nudged him. "It's your turn," Rachel said.

For a moment, Fabian didn't understand what she meant, but then the memory came back to him. *He* was the next line of defence. The next one to face the demon and... probably die.

Trembling, he raised his arms to form a delta with his thumbs and index fingers. There was so much rain it should've been easy, but when he called the water, nothing came through.

The demon raised his head. "A gate to Hell?" He snarled. "You were going to send my hellhounds into the dûr lôrac? Naughty boy."

Matt finally moved and drew his sword. "Any time now, Fabian," he said through his teeth.

Fabian strained. His arms were shaking, and his breath was hitching in the chest. All the water around them and nothing was coming through his fingers.

The demon focused on him. "Is this little human supposed to stop me? Nice try." He lowered his voice to address the hellhounds. "Attack!"

The three creatures shot forward, now every inch the terrible nightmare beasts again.

Lucille hurled a fireball at them, but in the rain it hardly did more than singe some fur.

A bolt flew from Rachel's crossbow and hit one of the hellhounds in the eye. The hit head howled, but the rest of the hellhound jumped forward. Matt let go of his sword, ducked under the hellhound, and grabbed him just enough to hurl him through the gate next to him. Like Matt's head before, the hellhound vanished into the sliver in the air.

The second came to a halt in front of Matt and pushed one of his wet snouts into his hands. "I know," Matt mumbled, then the lines of his face hardened. "Attack your master!"

Instantly, the hellhound turned around and ran for the demon. The demon merely looked annoyed, raised his hand, and shot pure energy at the hellhound. It died with a heartbreaking whine.

"Ass!" Rage tore through Fabian. He would kill his own animals! Raindrops were altering their trajectory, pulling into his hands instead.

A powerful jet stream of water shot at the demon and hit him squarely in the chest. The impact caused him to stumble backwards, but then he dug his heels in and raised his hand, now glaring at Fabian.

Fabian adjusted his stream to hit the demon in the face. For a moment, he enjoyed the pressure under his fingers, but then it gave way as the demon vanished.

"Careful!" Samantha cried, just as Lucille shouted, "Proturgo."

Confused, Fabian turned around, only to see the demon reappearing to the side of him. A blast of energy raced towards Fabian, and all he could do was pull his arms up and try to protect his face.

The energy hit him, and his world exploded in pain. But it didn't last long. The feared impact was not much more than if he'd knocked his elbows against a table.

Confused, Fabian lowered his arms. There was Lucille, one hand on her necklace, the other outstretched towards him. She must've spoken a protective spell around him. The problem was, now the demon had targeted her.

In stepped Matt, sword raised. With a cry of anguish, he ran at the demon, only to skid to a stop when the last hellhound, the biggest of them all, jumped in front of the demon, ready to protect its master.

Matt stopped as the hellhound growled at him. The demon barely acknowledged the hound's sacrifice and only snarled, "Rip his throat out!"

The hellhound jumped forward. A bolt missed him by the breadth of a hair. And suddenly, Jan was at the demon's back, kicking and hitting him in the most impressive karate series Fabian had ever seen.

The demon barely seemed to register the impacts as he turned around. He brought his hand up just in time to catch Jan's foot and jerk him around to send the boy crashing to the ground. He was just about to kick him when a bolt hit him in the shoulder, sending him spiralling back.

Fabian saw Rachel on the opposite side, calmly reloading her crossbow. Inspired by her, he turned his water stream back at the demon's face.

"Stop! Sit!" Matt cried, but the hellhound threw his paws on Matt's shoulder and brought them both crashing down.

They only missed the gate to Hell because Samantha had stepped in at the very last second and dragged her foot through the bloody line. The gate fizzled out in an instant, and Matt and the hellhound landed at her feet.

"Proturgo! Proturgo!" Lucille screamed.

The spell didn't work. The hellhound's left mouth clamped its teeth around Matt's sword and ripped it from his grip. The right head bit into Matt's shoulder, while the middle one towered above him, spittle dripping from his feet.

The demon turned his face away from the water and raised one of his wings to block Fabian's attack. He saw Matt under the hellhound and sneered.

Jan flicked out his two daggers and ran at him, screaming his heart out. Meanwhile, Rachel let another bolt fly. Beleaguered from three sides, the demon simply vanished.

Rachel's bolt missed Jan's face by less than a centimetre, causing him to stumble back with a start. Fabian looked around frantically, searching for the demon, but he didn't reappear.

"Off!" Matt said, almost choking on the words.

The middle head of the hellhound was opened wide, its teeth hovering just over Matt's throat. Matt's eyes were wide, and his Adam's apple bopped nervously. Blood was streaming over his left shoulder, where the right head was still biting him.

But the hellhound had halted. Its six eyes softened, and instead of biting, it began licking Matt's wounds and face. Under the sudden care, Matt's injuries healed.

With his left hand, Matt stroked the middle head, tears in his eyes. As he did so, he gently pushed his right hand under the massive body. The tears ran down his cheeks. A second later, a stream of black magic tore through the hellhound, killing it instantly.

The hellhound collapsed to the side of him, and Matt raised his arms to press the heels of his hands against his eyes. He took a shuddering breath. As scary as the hellhounds had been, Fabian's heart broke right there with him.

Lucille raced to his side, tears streaming down her face and sobbing, and sank into the fallen leaves as Samantha stared down at them, her eyes wide with shock, face a little green. "Oh my gosh! Are you alright? My shield spell didn't work," Lucille wailed.

Slowly, Matt rose enough to sit. "It did work. Without it, the hound would've bitten right through the bone." He slowly moved his shoulder. "It's alright now."

"It was horrifying!" Lucille sniffled, then threw her arms around Matt. Samantha swallowed heavily.

He patted her hair and shot each of them a glance. "Are you all okay?"

"Yeah," Fabian answered, though he couldn't stop searching for the demon between the trees. "Is he really gone? He's probably gonna jump us from the side or something."

Jan clapped his shoulder with way too much enthusiasm. "Relax. Didn't you see how overwhelmed he was when we all hit him at once? That one's not coming back anytime soon."

Fabian wished he had the same faith in their ability to scare off powerful demons. He met Rachel's eyes and saw the same scepticism there. As she rolled her eyes, he chuckled. "Well, it seems like he's gone for now." That seemed to be as good as it would get in Greenvalley.

Around them, the two corpses of the hellhound dissolved and sank into the ground. The blood from the gate was also gone. All that remained were a flat circle and a few grooves where they'd slipped in the leaves. Rain was pouring down on them and Matt still sat on the ground, looking close to tears again, with Lucille wrapping her arm around him.

Fabian cleared his throat. "I don't know about the rest of you, but I think we all deserve a nice, warm shower, and hot chocolate." He knew it would hardly be enough to melt the terror out of his bones, but it was a start.

Samantha smiled at him, the colour returning to her face. "I'm sure my grandmother will be happy to provide."

Count on his best friend to echo his feelings. That's who she was and who she would always be for him: his best friend. Nothing could take away from that. Fabian finally got it. The deep level of comfort that existed between them was something precious, but it would never be the kind of love they were both searching for. Maybe it was time to look for love elsewhere.

He turned to Rachel and offered her his hand. "Let's go." As she shyly slipped her hand in his, Fabian smiled. "You're quite the shot."

"You think?" Rachel asked, barely daring to look up at him.

"I'd say so. It was impressive to watch."

When she smiled at him, it took a bit of the terror away from him.

Lucille

As it turned out, Matt's father had received a beating but ultimately survived his encounter with the demon. The demon had figured out that Mr Traidous was merely a distraction and came to hunt them down instead. Lucille was more than glad to hear from Matt's father. It was one less death to deal with.

In order to avoid even more casualties, Elda, Lucille, and Samantha trekked out to the spring of magic as soon as the rain had slowed to a drizzle. Elda led the way, with a plan to put a ban around the spring to keep the demon away from it. And she'd chosen Lucille and Samantha to help her.

Lucille tugged nervously on her necklace. She had yet to regain trust in its powers and her own. While Elda assured her that it had been the demon's curse, her heart believed differently. It had been as Matt said. She'd used her power to make her life easy, to ensure that everything went according to plan. The curse had pushed her further, but the decisions had been hers.

This wasn't what magic was about. As she watched Elda kneel between the pretty ferns and flowers, gently coaxing the strands of magic into a spell, Lucille realised how much she still had to learn about magic. It wasn't just spells and ideas, but a deep understanding of how the world worked, how it lived and breathed.

The magic itself was invisible to her when they stepped into the clearing, but once Elda started working with it, the strands became visible, just as they'd been when Lucille stood under her grandmother's spell. The magic Elda wove was so complex that it was impossible to fully understand. The pattern of the shield was awe-striking.

Lucille might never be able to create something this intricate, but she now understood how crucial it was for Greenvalley—and possibly their entire world—that the demon didn't succeed in stealing the magic. Removing it from this place would be like removing life. The leaves, still green despite winter approaching, would wither and turn to dust. The beautiful little fairies that flitted across the clearing would starve, and the world would be lesser for it.

"Do you see the strands?" Elda asked Samantha gently. "With a vision in mind, you can weave them into a spell. It takes finesse, and there are many patterns to work your way through, but eventually, you can do almost anything."

Lucille tried not to feel jealous. Like her grandmother, she would never touch it with her hands, only with the power of her voice. For a few days, she'd been able to do almost anything, and it had created more problems than it was worth. Perhaps she and her grandmother weren't meant for such an intimate relationship with magic. It didn't mean she would be any less, just different.

Elda's magic—and possibly Samantha's soon—was a slow and steady spell. Something like this ban required a perpetual web that couldn't be easily broken. It was intricate, but intricacy took time. Lucille's spell was quicker, as fast as the spoken word. They needed aim, intent, subtlety, and a great deal of training, but Lucille was ready to put in the work.

Maybe then she'd be skilled enough to confront demons, just as her grandmother had done.

"Come here, Lucille," Elda called, offering a hand.

Lucille stepped closer and knelt on her other side. Samantha was already holding Elda's left hand, eyes closed. Tentatively, Lucille took Elda's right hand. "Don't you need your hands to weave?"

Elda's smile was as warm as her own grandmother's had been. "The fingers are just an aid for visualisation. Magic starts in the mind. Some use words, and others use their imagination. Right now, we need your voice." She nodded at Samantha's free hand. "Take Sammy's hand, so we can close the circle. You'll be connected to the spell then. When you see it, say 'Amplificar'."

That was easy enough to remember. Lucille took a deep breath, then took Samantha's hand and gasped. The magic flowed through her, making her heart sing. Words formed on her lips, as if the magic itself had placed them there. Elda had never needed to tell her the spell. The pattern demanded it. Lucille would never fully understand the intricacies of magical weaving, but she didn't need to. All that was required was her voice.

With perfect enunciation, she said, "Amplificar!"

It was as if someone had pulled on a string. The loops in the pattern tightened until the dome shimmered like a green glass wall. No more holes. No weaknesses.

"This is the web we wove around Greenvalley, but because of its size, it was never as tight as this one," Elda explained before smiling at her. "You did well, my dear. The spring will be safe from the demon. He won't get a drop of magic."

As Lucille stood in front of her home, she thought that weaving a magical barrier around the source of all magic had been the easy part. Elda had said that most of her spells had been reversed, but the damage would still remain.

When Lucille had decided to move back home this year, she'd thought it would fix everything. Now she understood how deep the damage ran. The magic had helped her see it clearly. There was no easy fix. Her grandmother's death had changed her father for the worse. He knew about the arcane but had chosen to banish it from his life with as tight a web as they'd just woven. Lucille couldn't even blame him, knowing how he'd lost his mother. And he'd lost *her* mother as well. Another death, another grief dealt that led to suppressing everything else.

And in the process, he'd shut Lucille out. Understanding it didn't mean it hurt any less. Work had become his happy place when it should have been her place of connection.

Or even Linda, who—if she was honest—had nothing to do with her father's absence. For years, Lucille had harboured hatred towards the new woman at her father's side. It was the easiest way to cope with the deep sense of abandonment she'd felt. But now she realised what an impossible situation Linda had stumbled into. She had become surrogate mother, with no help whatsoever from the actual parent.

Had she got it terribly wrong? Sure. But Lucille refused to believe it was out of malice anymore. She'd deserved better, and so had Linda. Her stepmother certainly didn't deserve to be sent to "wherever".

Lucille took a deep breath. She'd faced a powerful demon. She could face the disaster she'd left in her wake.

Guilt overwhelmed her as she entered the foyer. Soot still stained the ceiling, and a group of workers were busy with the restoration.

"Welcome home, Miss Lucille," Albert greeted her, ready to take her jacket. "I assume you have been recuperating at Elda's?"

"Yes, I have." She handed him her jacket, her gaze still fixed on the black stains. "Is my father home?" She needed to make sure he remembered his wife before she started searching for Linda.

"Your father and Linda are in the dining room. I will instruct the maid to set a place for you."

Lucille barely registered his words. Her brain had stopped working after hearing "Linda". Ignoring how inappropriate it may seem, she rushed through the foyer, up the stairs, and burst into the dining room with its magnificent chandelier.

And there she was. Linda looked up from her plate, startled by Lucille's sudden appearance, and then smiled. "Hello, darling. I was wondering when I would get to see you. We're so glad you are able to join us. Aren't we, Bastien?"

Her father glanced up from the newspaper he was reading. "Yes, yes. It's lovely to have all of us back together again." The Sunday edition of the paper featured a familiar photo on its title page: Shayna in her burning dress.

Lucille's heart pounded heavily as she took her seat. Would Linda be mad about her disastrous attempt at a fashion show? She shook her head. Even if she was, at least she was back home.

To her surprise, Linda reached across the table and grasped her hand. "You won't believe this, but I completely forgot about the charity event. There I was, dining in Paris and meeting some colleagues to discuss a collaboration, when I was supposed to be here, putting on a show. Thank you so much for picking up the pieces and turning it into a success."

Lucille could hardly believe what she was hearing. "Success? There was a fire in our house."

Linda let go of her hand and waved the incident off. "It was quickly brought under control. What's truly on fire are my phone lines. Everyone wants to know how I pulled off the 'fire girl'. What's her name?"

"Shayna Richards, I think. She's a... classmate." One Lucille didn't particularly like, but at least she'd given Cheryl a hard time.

"You'll have to introduce me to her. Everyone's talking about her." Linda's eyes sparkled. "But more importantly, from now on, I want your input on all my fashion shows."

Surprised, Lucille struggled to form complete sentences. "Really?" A maid placed a plate and cutlery in front of her.

Linda beamed. "You bring a youthful touch that can only enhance my line. And you managed to pull off an entire fashion show by yourself. If that isn't talent, I don't know what is."

Lucille pressed her lips together, trying not to dwell on how much magic she'd used to make it work.

"Do you want to join me in the drawing room after dinner? I have so many ideas that I want to discuss with you." Linda grinned. "What do you think about a little collaboration?"

"Between you and me?" Lucille's cheeks flushed. This was a new concept. Until now, they'd always coexisted, with each interaction being awkward or even painful. Could they actually have something in common? Something to bond over after all these years? Lucille may have denied it if someone had asked, but fashion was important to her. And Linda's line was actually quite beautiful. But working with her? Spending time together?

Lucille smiled. "I would like that." She owed it to Linda to give it a try, at least.

Meanwhile, her father folded down the newspaper and stood up. "I still have a few calls to make, if you'll excuse me."

To Lucille's surprise, Linda rolled her eyes slightly. So, her stepmother was also annoyed by his workaholic attitude. Perhaps she felt as lonely in the house as Lucille often did.

Her father placed his hand on Lucille's shoulder and kissed her hair. "I can't wait to see what comes out of this collaboration."

The small gesture filled Lucille with warmth. Deserved or not, she loved her father dearly. At least he'd listened to their conversation. And, to be fair, he probably had a lot on his plate, considering how much time he'd spent with her, neglecting his work entirely.

Once the door closed behind him, Linda chuckled. "He'll never change." Then she let out a little squeal. "I can't wait to see what the two of us come up with."

Lucille grinned. "Me neither. But one thing is for sure: it will be magical."

Samantha

When Samantha returned from the forest, she was still buzzing. She had touched magic! Magic was real, more real than she could've ever imagined. When she'd held the strands for her grandmother to weave, she'd felt a deep connection to the world that was impossible to describe. Her human mind couldn't begin to comprehend the complexity of the magical rivers, but they seemed to touch everything that lived. She couldn't wait to experience it again.

As she walked down her street, her phone rang. "Hey, Fabi."

He mumbled something that was probably a complaint about his childhood nickname, then he asked, "How did it go?"

"All sealed." While Samantha had always known what her grandmother was theoretically capable of, seeing it in action was a completely different experience. "There's no getting through that one."

"Let's hope so," Fabian grumbled. "And hopefully that demon stops bothering us. I never want to face him again."

Samantha shuddered, remembering the terrifying fight. Matt had almost ended up in Hell, then got mauled by a hellhound, and barely survived. The rest of them hadn't fared much better. She still vividly remembered seeing the demon beat up Fabian as if he were nothing but a rag doll. For a moment, she'd thought she was losing him too. "How's your stomach?"

"Better." He took a shaky breath. "My mum freaked out a little. I think, despite her love for all things magic, she's not too thrilled about me fighting monsters and demons. We have that in common, I guess."

A smile graced Samantha's lips. "You don't want to fight them, but you do pretty well."

"Oh, please. I've never been more scared in my life. If we never come across another monster, I'll be happy."

"But you did so well! I meant it when I said you were the most powerful among us." In terms of raw power, only Matt could match him.

Fabian snorted. "Yeah, right. If it works." He sighed. "Look, I know I'm a coward—or how I would call it, the only normal person in this group." When Samantha laughed, he chuckled too. "But I understand that we're all in this together. So—" He took a deep breath. "I'm in. As long as everyone else is, I'll be there."

It was a huge step for him. Just two months ago, Fabian had vehemently believed that magic didn't exist. Samantha knew how much it had taken for him to come this far, but she had full faith that he would eventually grow comfortable with his powers.

"The monsters scare me too," she admitted. "But I guess I idolise Granny too much. Someone needs to protect Greenvalley, and it looks like it's our turn now."

"Yeah, hopefully not," Fabian said, though he didn't sound entirely convincing. "Alright, I've got to go eat dinner. See you tomorrow morning?"

"I'll wait for you at the bridge." From there, they would go to school together. "Then we can pick up Rachel." Samantha hadn't missed the sight of the two holding hands after the battle. "And don't forget to do your homework. Zobel won't accept 'a demon destroyed my essay' as an excuse."

With a groan, Fabian ended the call.

Samantha chuckled softly to herself. She was almost home now. There was the overgrown garden and the iron-wrought gate she knew so well. But as she reached it, she froze. Two dark figures were hugging near the entrance, out of view from the windows. And not just hugging, but kissing. She cleared her throat.

"Sam!" Her sister jumped away from Jan and tried to look innocent, but it wasn't a convincing attempt. "I thought you were staying at Granny's again?"

Jan was much less fazed. He raised a hand and grinned. "I guess I should get going."

"Probably a good idea," Samantha said, feeling a bit tense. As much as she appreciated Jan as part of their group, she wasn't sure if he would make a good boyfriend. But that was a discussion she was way too tired to have right now. "Good night, Jan."

Once he was gone, Meg hissed, "You didn't have to scare him away!"

"Better me than Dad." Samantha got out her keys.

"You're not going to tell him, right?" Meg's eyes widened.

Samantha shrugged. Their dad wasn't the type to believe there would never be a man good enough for his daughters. When she'd gotten together with Fabian, he'd been supportive. "Just stop sneaking around."

"Where's the fun in that?" With a teasing grin, Meg sauntered into the house first then made her way upstairs quickly, so that their parents only saw Samantha.

"Oh, you're back," her mother said, folding laundry over the backrest of the couch. "I didn't see you at all over the weekend."

"Sorry. We stayed at Granny's." She'd spent an awful lot of time there recently, enough to make her feel guilty. "I'll take a quick shower. Then we can talk or play a board game." It would be nice to have a normal Sunday night with her family.

Her mother smiled. "Sounds good."

Samantha followed Meg, but her sister had already closed her door. With a snort, Samantha walked past and into her own room. This new Jan situation could wait. She had something better to do.

Sitting down on her bed with her legs crossed, Samantha let go of the world. Her thoughts drifted away from her, and it didn't take long for the room to change. At first, the green threads of magic were barely visible, but the more she concentrated on them, the thicker they became. Eventually, a fine web of crisscrossing, flowing rivulets of magic moved around her room. Samantha dipped a finger into the nearest stream and marvelled at the tingling sensation.

Light, Samantha thought, trying to recall the pattern of a simple light spell, not too dissimilar to Lucille's. The pattern might have been easy, but working the magic was not. The threads slipped from her fingers until she stopped trying so hard and allowed the image in her mind to guide her. Magic didn't like to be forced, but it willingly followed when nudged in the right direction.

When the light bloomed in her hand, casting a green glow rather than a proper light, Samantha laughed.

After all these years, she had finally found her magic.

Rachel

Rachel dreaded going home, if one could even call it a home. Her father had returned to the US, and now she would be alone with her mother—a woman who hardly deserved to be called that. Since Nico's death, the house had become a strange place. It held her things and had a bed to sleep in, but it didn't feel like home. Perhaps it never had.

Now that she was eighteen, with her father's support, she might be able to rent a little flat instead. But Rachel doubted she would feel any different there. There was only one place she truly called her home. The one place where she felt at peace and longed to be. A place that didn't even exist, not really.

Bracing herself for another senseless party, Rachel entered the house and was met with silence. No loud music, no drunken phone calls, no male "friends" over. Instead, the floor was littered with used tissues and the usual bottles of wine.

Rachel tiptoed into the living room to find her mother passed out on the couch. Even in her sleep, she could see that her mother had cried, drank, and then cried some more. Despite all her misgivings, Rachel couldn't pretend she didn't know what hurt her so.

She sat down on the armrest near her mother's head and looked down at her. She took in the brightly coloured, short hair and the dark roots that should've been recoloured two weeks ago. There were wine stains on her mother's blouse, but more stains came from the tears she'd cried.

How many times had they found her passed out on the couch, battling her secret demons?

Rachel remembered how often Nico had picked up a blanket and covered their mother. It was something he'd started ages ago, because, for all her failings, he still loved her deeply.

She glanced around and found the blanket. If she held it close to her chest, she could pretend she was touching Nico. But he wasn't here. It was only her and her mum now.

With a sigh, Rachel spread the blanket over her mother, taking care to tuck it in under her chin. She left the rest of the living room as it was, but as she went upstairs, she felt a little more at home.

Her real home, however, was the dreamworld. The place where she was powerful and at ease. Where she controlled what happened to her and who she gave her time to. And tonight, she was going to fix something.

Rachel picked the black flower that held her mother's dream and dove into it.

The first step brought pain. Rachel looked down and saw the floor covered with broken pieces of glass. When she raised her head again, the light split on a jagged edge. The entire space was splintered, with sharp edges everywhere.

As she set her feet more carefully, Rachel peered into the pieces and caught glimpses of what must've been memories.

A glass of wine on the kitchen counter—the kitchen much fancier than theirs.

Her father on his wedding day—not so fancy, but so much younger than today and smiling.

Little Nico running into her mother's arms.

There were countless short moments. Many more happy moments than sad, as if the happy moments her mother had lost cut that much deeper. Was this how painful remembering their happy little family was for her?

Was this her life in literal pieces?

"Mum?"

Now that Rachel listened for it, she heard someone sobbing. Carefully, she searched her way through the splintered dream until she came across the brown-haired girl who was her dream mother.

The girl crouched over a pile of shards she was trying to put together. They didn't fit because they were all from different memories, and only splinters of them. Most of them showed parts of Nico at various ages, but some were pictures of Rachel, and even fewer of her father.

"They don't fit!" Annette wailed. "No matter how hard I try, it never fits."

The shards had cut into her hands, and blood was dripping into the memories like red wine. They stained Nico's smile and his warm brown eyes.

Rachel hugged herself. If she wasn't careful, she would add her own imagination to this nightmare, like images of her brother bleeding out under Samantha's desperate attempts to save him.

No. That wasn't how she wanted to remember him. Or how she wanted her mum to remember him.

"Mum?" She knelt before her, gently taking her mother's hands. It took a while for Annette to stop what she was doing and face Rachel. In her eyes, Rachel could see herself. "Come with me."

Slowly, they rose. Rachel led her mother like a little child. The shards crumbled under her feet, turning to glittering dust until they reached the door that would bring them away from here.

Rachel took one last look at her mother's shattered dream, committing it to memory. Then she pulled her through the gateway, into the meadow.

Instantly, Annette breathed easier. The lines of worry eased, and she appeared much younger. A young girl with long brown hair. Before she had children and before she had married a man she had hardly known. When her life had still been full of adventure and hope.

They sat down among the flowers, and Rachel let the peace of the meadow wash over them. The gentle dream wind tugged at her hair and whirled petals in the air. It played with Annette's brown locks, and she smiled at Rachel, full of warmth and love.

This was it. This was home.

Matt

The demon was gone. René was alive. Greenvalley was safe from "animal" attacks.

Matt should've been happy, content, and relieved, but he wasn't. Something was wrong, and he had no idea what it was.

After he'd made sure René was alive and well, he'd gone out. Sex always worked to relax him, but he had been just as agitated afterwards as he had been before. Even worse, it hadn't been enough. As if there was something more he needed.

It was drizzling again, so Matt decided to go straight home. He quickly checked if anyone could see him, then took the shortcut. René didn't like it when he jumped through space to get around Greenvalley, but it saved an unnecessarily long journey.

He arrived in the room he slept in, which proved to be a prudent choice since he could hear René talking to someone in the living room. A visitor.

Matt cast a glance around "his" room. It had been René's office before he'd turned up on his doorstep and asked if he could move in with him. That had been three months ago, but it already felt like a lifetime. Time moved faster in this place.

The room was shockingly bare. There was a bed and a desk, but the cupboard he was meant to set up was still in pieces, after all this time. René had claimed it would be easy if he followed the instructions, but Matt couldn't figure out how to do it, and he hadn't truly cared. The few clothes he'd brought with him did just as well on the floor as they would inside the wooden contraption.

The rest of the stuff belonged to René. It was carefully piled up along the other wall, giving him more space. Matt felt a little bad about infringing so much on his father after all these years, but it beat living on his own. As much as he hated to admit it, he needed his father to help him adjust to this place that was so different from home.

His ears perked up when he heard the visitor's voice. He knew that one. Knew it better than any other. In an instant, Matt was at the door, and burst into the living room.

The two men stared at him. René's left eye was swollen shut, and his chin showed a blue and green pattern that would probably get him in trouble at his school. The other man was younger, or rather, he looked younger, twenty-five at most. He had honey-blonde hair. His skin was pale, despite him spending most of his time travelling, and his eyes were an equally pale blue, like the colour of a winter sky, but his body had the muscular stature of a swordfighter. The best swordfighter Matt had ever met.

The smile that appeared on the visitor's face made Matt instantly feel better. "Chay."

Chay got up to his feet and took him in. "Looking good."

Matt snorted. He hadn't changed *that* much. And he was always looking good, courtesy of his mother. Not that it mattered. He was suddenly overcome with the desperate need to give Chay a hug, and only knowing how little his friend would appreciate it stopped him from doing so. Chay usually avoided skin contact at all costs, even from those he called friends.

"What are you doing here?" Matt asked, his voice still ravaged by emotion.

"I thought it was time to check in. How are you finding Ashuan?"

His answer made Matt snort again. If Chay thought it was time for something, then it was because he *was confident* it was the right time. There was a reason they called him "the Seer". He saw the future more clearly than anyone had ever done before him. One touch and Matt's whole life would pass in front of Chay's eyes. Since most lives ended eventually, it wasn't a pleasant experience for the Seer.

"Ashuan is—" His voice suddenly failed him. Such a simple question. Hey, how do you find Ashuan, the world you were born into? A few weeks earlier, Matt would've answered, "Interesting. Exciting. Different." Now, he couldn't put all those conflicting emotions into words.

"Overwhelming?" Chay asked gently. "It's a lot."

Matt's eyes stung again, as they had once before in the forest. When he'd been forced to kill the hellhound he'd bonded with.

"Hey, Matt," René called. He'd been watching their conversation quietly, not daring to interrupt until now. Matt wondered what had prompted him to do so. After all these weeks, he still struggled to fully understand his father.

René's smile, however, was so comforting. As if he understood better what Matt was going through than Matt did himself. "Come on. There's something I want to show you. He's sleeping now but have a look at him."

Confused, Matt walked deeper into the living room to where René was pointing. Next to the kitchen door, previously obscured by the table, was a small round bed, and in it was something even smaller. A little black nose trembled between the folds, reacting to a dream. Soft, golden fur made up most of the sleeping puppy.

"I can't get you a hellhound, but these are pretty cute as well."

Matt's heart was overflowing with emotion in a way he'd never experienced before. The last few weeks were finally taking their toll. "You got me a dog?"

"If you want him." René smiled at him before running a hand through Matt's hair. It was one of those strange gestures he sometimes did without thinking. At first, Matt had been confused, but now he'd come to like those touches. They meant something.

"Of course, I want him."

The little dog stirred, then opened his dark eyes.

"Hey, little sleepyhead." Matt crouched down and held a hand to the puppy's snout. As curiosity overcame the sleepiness, Matt found himself grinning. A moment later, the warm bundle of fur was settled in his arms.

Matt got up, unable to grasp how tiny the dog was. When he looked up, both René and Chay seemed amused. Matt's cheeks flushed a little, but he remembered his manners. "Thanks, René. He's the best."

As usual, calling René by his name added a touch of bitterness to his father's smile. "I'm glad you like him. I saw how hard you took the hellhounds' deaths."

Was that it? Was he taking it hard? They'd just been a bunch of hellhounds. There were hundreds of them in the dûr lôrac. Just like this ball of fluffiness was just a puppy, though he'd already eased some of the agitation in Matt's chest.

"Hellhounds?" Chay asked, arcing one eyebrow.

"Didn't see that coming, did you?" Matt teased and walked into his room. He was well aware that Chay didn't know every single thing about every single person, but he liked it when he knew something the Seer didn't. It happened far too little.

Chay was his best friend, his teacher, and more of a father to him than René had ever been. Not that it was René's fault. Matt's mother hadn't really left him a choice there. They just weren't very well acquainted. Whereas Chay had been there all his life.

Matt used to ask himself what he'd done to deserve the attention of the most famous seer, a man busy guiding whole nations to a better future. Now he had an inkling.

As soon as Chay had closed the door behind him, shutting René out of their conversation, Matt asked, "The Emblems of Power. You gave me that sword on purpose." Matt had assumed it'd been a graduation present after years of gruelling sword-fighting lessons, not a world-changing artifact.

Chay didn't deny it. "Of course. I usually do things with a purpose."

"Like leaving your book with Elda Kollmer?" Matt sat down on his bed and cuddled the little fur bundle to distract himself from the emotions behind the question.

Chay smiled. "Elda and I are old acquaintances. I knew it would eventually find its way into the right hands if I left it there."

Not *his* hands, Matt thought. Chay could've given him the book any time. "So, this whole 'Matt, go get to know Ashuan. You need to explore that side of your identity as well' had a deeper purpose as well?" Why was he even asking?

The smile vanished from Chay's lips, and he leaned against the desk. "*You* need to explore that side, but yes, I meant for the six of you to meet." He snorted. "Or rather, I saw you were going to meet. Fate was very clear about that. You know I can't change the future. Only see it. And prepare for it."

Matt's chest tightened. "So, what does it mean?"

"Everything." When Matt rolled his eyes, Chay laughed again. "Read the book. Or rather, let Elda's granddaughter read it. She's better with these things."

Elda's granddaughter. Samantha. She truly was better with the research side of things. Thinking of her brought back memories of magic in the forest, of the sadness in her eyes after Nico had died, and the stubbornness with which she'd tried to save his life.

And suddenly, the pain in his chest intensified, and his eyes felt wet. "What does it all mean?"

Chay raised his eyebrows. "What does what mean?"

The dam broke. Suddenly, the words came out hard and fast. He told Chay about their encounters with all these monsters, of the demon roaming Greenvalley, the hellhounds he had to kill, and Nico. "I've seen people die before. I've killed people. But this—I don't know what's wrong with me, why it hits me so hard. He was bitten by a werewolf. I was ready to kill him so he wouldn't become a danger. He even asked me to do it. But when he actually died, it... it hurt. Why does it hurt so much?"

He hugged the puppy closer, but even the tiny cold wet nose couldn't take the pain away.

Chay cocked his head. The gentle smile had reappeared. He didn't laugh at Matt's strange and confusing feelings. Instead, he offered compassion the way only he ever had.

"That's why you're here, Matt. To learn the answer to that question. It'll hurt a lot, but it's not just pain all around. The highs are as wonderful as the lows are devastating."

Always with the philosophical answers. "But why? Why do I suddenly feel so much?" Matt couldn't imagine his mother or siblings ever crying about some boy's death or caring whether their companions lived or died.

"Well." Chay folded his hands in his lap and took a deep breath as if steeling himself against a similar wave of emotion. "You and me, we got the magic. We got the healing powers, the strength, the incredibly long life. But as strong as our demon side may be, we're still half-human in the end."

A River of Magic

When the truth involves demons, murder, and magic, everybody gets hurt.

Fabian knows with magic comes pain. He already lost one friend to a demon attack. Now his best friend is falling apart in the bloody aftermath of what should have been a joyful celebration. With demons haunting the streets of Greenvalley, and dark secrets threatening to tear their group apart, Fabian wishes he'd never unlocked the water magic inside of him.

But he is no coward. Fabian might whine and moan, but when his friends are in danger, he knows he's got to step up. With an ancient prophecy set in motion, Fabian's ready to face his magic. Only to find it's gone.

A River of Magic is the second instalment of the action-packed urban fantasy series for fans of *Buffy*, *Charmed*, or the *Vampire Diaries*.

JANNA RUTH

A RIVER OF MAGIC

ASHUAN GREED BOOK 2

A Force of Nature

I've trusted nature spirits with my life, until the storm king decided I had to die.

Did you ever wonder what living on the streets of Berlin is like? My name is Rika and I've been homeless for eight years. It's not too bad, since I've got salamanders to warm me in winter and dryads to protect me from stragglers. People say I'm crazy, because to everyone else, those nature spirits are invisible. But they're real. Real and *dangerous*, as I learn when I accidentally cross the plans of the Erlking, an ancient and hate-filled spirit. Now he and his deadly storm are after me.
My only chance are the Spirit Seekers, an elite group of soldiers trained to battle nature's wrath. Since their precious commander is missing in action, they need me to be their eyes. Signing up with the Spirit Seekers is the opposite of run and hide, but they offer me protection and the tools to fight for my survival. All I have to do is betray my old spirit friends and try not to die.

Join Rika and the Spirit Seekers in this action-packed stormy urban fantasy adventure and start your supernatural trip to Europe today!

JANNA RUTH

A FORCE OF NATURE

SPIRIT SEEKER BOOK 1

Ghosts of the Catacombs

I'm a ghost whisperer, not a catacomb crawler. But when you live in Paris, sometimes you end up being both.

Hi, I'm Alix. During the day, I'm a history student at the time-honoured Sorbonne University. After class, I hang out with the ghosts of the revolution, the many undead misunderstood Parisian artists, and adventurous scientists that glow in the dark. None of them are alive, but they come to me to solve their problems with the living. When a recently deceased catacomb tour guide asks me to retrieve a mysterious personal item from the underground, things take a turn for the weird. Suddenly, I find myself in a city of ghosts, hunted by murderous cave crawlers, and stumbling across haunting secrets. If I'm not careful now, I might end up a ghost myself.

Urban Fantasy with a French twist. If you like cave-crawling adventures, hopeless romantics, and ghosts, you'll enjoy Ghosts of the Catacombs, the first book of the Parisian Ghosts series. Travel to Paris today to embark on your catacomb adventure.

JANNA RUTH
GHOSTS OF THE CATACOMBS
PARISIAN GHOSTS 1